ON H

Christmas
ON HIS RANCH

DIANA PALMER

Christmas
ON HIS RANCH

All rights reserved including the right of reproduction in whole or in part in any form. This edition is published by arrangement with Harlequin Books S.A.

This is a work of fiction. Names, characters, places, locations and incidents are purely fictional and bear no relationship to any real life individuals, living or dead, or to any actual places, business establishments, locations, events or incidents. Any resemblance is entirely coincidental.

This book is sold subject to the condition that it shall not, by way of trade or otherwise, be lent, resold, hired out or otherwise circulated without the prior consent of the publisher in any form of binding or cover other than that in which it is published and without a similar condition including this condition being imposed on the subsequent purchaser.

® and ™ are trademarks owned and used by the trademark owner and/or its licensee. Trademarks marked with ® are registered with the United Kingdom Patent Office and/or the Office for Harmonisation in the Internal Market and in other countries.

First Published in Great Britain 2016
By Mills & Boon, an imprint of HarperCollins*Publishers*
1 London Bridge Street, London, SE1 9GF

CHRISTMAS ON HIS RANCH © 2016 Harlequin Books S.A.

Maggie's Dad © 1995 Diana Palmer
Cattleman's Choice © 2014 Diana Palmer

ISBN: 978-0-263-92689-7

9-1116

Harlequin (UK) Limited's policy is to use papers that are natural, renewable and recyclable products and made from wood grown in sustainable forests. The logging and manufacturing processes conform to the legal environmental regulations of the country of origin.

Printed and bound in Spain
by CPI, Barcelona

MAGGIE'S DAD

DIANA PALMER

The prolific author of more than a hundred books, **Diana Palmer** got her start as a newspaper reporter. A multi–*New York Times* bestselling author and one of the top ten romance writers in America, she has a gift for telling the most sensual tales with charm and humour. Diana lives with her family in Cornelia, Georgia.

Visit her website at www.DianaPalmer.com

Prologue

Rain was peppering down on the roof of the small house where Antonia Hayes's parents lived. It was a cold rain, and Antonia thought absently that she was very glad it was summer, because by early autumn that soft rain would turn to sleet or snow. Bighorn, a small town in northwestern Wyoming, was not an easy town to leave once it was covered in ice. It was rural and despite having three thousand inhabitants, it was too small to offer the transportation choices of a larger town. There wasn't even an airport; only a bus station. The railroad ran through it, too, but the trains were spaced too far apart to do Antonia much good.

She was about to begin her sophomore year in college, at the University of Arizona in Tucson, and snow was fairly rare in that area in winter, except up in the mountains. The desert floor had light dustings, but not enough to inconvenience anyone. Besides, Antonia—having just finished her first year there—had been much too busy trying to pass her core courses and heal a broken heart to notice the weather. She did notice the summer heat now, though, she mused, and thanked God for air-conditioning.

The clock sounded and Antonia turned, her short, blond hair perky and her gray eyes full of sadness at having to leave. But fall semester started in less than a week, and she had to get back into her dorm room and set up some sort of schedule. The only comforting thing about going back was that George Rutherford's stepdaughter, Barrie Bell, was her dorm roommate, and they got along very well indeed.

"It's been lovely having you home for a whole week," her mother, Jessica, said warmly. "I do wish you could have stayed the whole summer...."

Her voice trailed off. She knew, as did Antonia and Ben, her husband, why Antonia couldn't stay in Bighorn very long. It was a source of great sadness to all of them, but they didn't discuss it. It still hurt too much, and the gossip hadn't quite died down even now, almost a year after the fact. George Rutherford's abrupt move to France a few months after Antonia's departure had quelled the remaining gossip.

Despite what had happened, George had remained a good, true friend to Antonia and her family. Her college education was his gift to her. She would pay him back every penny, but right now the money was a godsend. Her parents were well regarded in the community, but lacked the resources to swing her tuition. George had been determined to help, and his kindness had cost them both so much.

But George's son, Dawson, and his stepdaughter, Barrie, had rallied around Antonia, defending her against the talk.

It was comforting to know that the two people closest to George didn't believe he was Antonia's sugar daddy. And of course, it helped that Dawson and Powell Long were rivals for a strip of land that separated their respective Bighorn ranch holdings. George had lived on his Bighorn ranch until the scandal. Then he went back to the family home he shared with Dawson in Sheridan, hoping to stem the gossip. It hadn't happened. So he'd moved to France, leaving more bitterness between Dawson and Powell Long. There was no love lost there.

But even with George out of the country, and despite the support of friends and family, Sally Long had done so much damage to Antonia's reputation that she was sure she would never be able to come home again.

Her mind came back to the remark her mother had just made. "I took classes this summer," she murmured absently. "I'm really sorry, but I thought I'd better, and some of my new friends went, too. It was nice, although I do miss being home. I miss both of you."

Jessica hugged her warmly. "And we miss you."

"That damn fool Sally Long," Ben muttered as he also hugged his daughter. "Spreading lies so that she could take Powell away from you. And that damn fool Powell Long, believing them, marrying her, and that baby born just seven months later…!"

Antonia's face went pale, but she smiled gamely. "Now, Dad," she said gently. "It's all over," she added with what she hoped was a reassuring smile, "they're married and they have a daughter now. I hope he's happy."

"Happy! After the way he treated you?"

Antonia closed her eyes. The memories were still painful. Powell had been the center of her life. She'd never imagined she could feel a love so sweeping, so powerful. He'd never said he loved her, but she'd been so sure that he did. Looking back now, though, she knew that he'd never really loved her. He wanted her, of course, but he had always drawn back. *We'll wait for marriage,* he'd said.

And waiting had been a good thing, considering how it had all turned out.

At the time, Antonia had wanted him desperately, but she'd put him off. Even now, over a year later, she could still see his black eyes and dark hair and thin, wide mouth. That image lived in her heart despite the fact that he'd canceled their wedding the day before it was to take place. People who hadn't been notified in time were sitting in the church, waiting. She shuddered faintly, remembering her humiliation.

Ben was still muttering about Sally.

"That's enough, Ben." Jessica laid a hand on her husband's arm. "It's water under the bridge," she said firmly. Her voice was so tranquil that it was hard for Antonia to believe that the scandal had caused her mother to have heart problems. She'd done very well, and Antonia had done everything possible to avoid the subject so that her mother wouldn't be upset.

"I wouldn't say Powell was happy," Ben continued, unabashed. "He's never home, and we never see him out with Sally in public. In fact, we never see Sally much at all. If she's happy, she doesn't let it show." He studied his daughter's pale, rigid face. "She called here one day before Easter and asked for your address. Did she write to you?"

"She wrote me."

"Well?" he prompted, curious.

"I returned the letter without opening it," Antonia said tightly, even paler now. She looked down at her shoes. "It's ancient history."

"She might have wanted to apologize," Jessica ventured.

Antonia sighed. "Some things go beyond apologies," she said quietly. "I loved him, you know," she added with a faint smile. "But he never loved me. If he did, he didn't say so in all the time we went together. He believed everything Sally told him. He just told me what he thought of me, called off the wedding and walked away. I had to leave. It hurt too much to stay." She could picture in her mind that long, straight back, the rigid set of his dark head. The pain had been terrible. It still was.

"As if George was that sort of man," Jessica said wearily. "He's the kindest man in the world, and he adores you."

"Not the sort to play around with young girls," Ben agreed. "Idiots, people who could believe that about him. I know that's why he moved out of the country, to spare us any more gossip."

"Since he and I are both gone, there's not much to gossip about," Antonia said pointedly. She smiled. "I'm working hard on my grades. I want George to be proud of me."

"He will be. And we already are," Jessica said warmly.

"Well, it serves Powell Long right that he ended up with that selfish little madam," Ben persisted irritably. "He thinks he's going to get rich by building up that cattle ranch, but he's just a dreamer," Ben scoffed. "His father was a gambler, and his mother was a doormat. Imagine him thinking he's got enough sense to make money with cattle!"

"He does seem to be making strides," his wife said gently. "He just bought a late-model truck, and they say a string of ranches up in Montana have given him a contract to supply them with seed bulls. You remember, Ben, when his big purebred Angus bull was in the paper, it won some national award."

"One bull doesn't make an empire," Ben scoffed.

Antonia felt the words all the way to her heart. Powell had told her his dreams, and they'd planned that ranch together, discussed having the best Angus bulls in the territory...

"Could we not...talk about him, please?" Antonia asked finally. She forced a smile. "It still stings a little."

"Of course it does. We're sorry," Jessica said, her voice soft now. "Can you come home for Christmas?"

"I'll try. I really will."

She had one small suitcase. She carried it out to the car and hugged her mother one last time before she climbed in beside her father for the short ride to the bus depot downtown.

It was morning, but still sweltering hot. She got out of the car and picked up her suitcase as she waited on the sidewalk for her father to get her ticket from the office inside the little grocery store. There was a line. She'd just turned her attention back to the street when her eyes froze on an approaching pedestrian; a cold, quiet ghost from the past.

He was just as lean and dark as she remembered him. The suit was better than the ones he'd worn when they were dating, and he looked thinner. But it was the same Powell Long.

She'd lost everything to him except her pride. She still had it, and she forced her gray eyes up to his as he walked down the sidewalk with that slow, elegant stride that was particularly his own. She wouldn't let him see how badly his distrust had hurt her, even now.

His expression gave away nothing that he was feeling. He paused when he reached her, glancing at the suitcase.

"Well, well," he drawled, watching her face. "I heard you were here. The chicken came home to roost, did she?"

"I'm not here to stay," she replied coolly. "I've been to visit my parents. I'm on my way to Arizona, back to college."

"By bus?" he taunted. "Couldn't your sugar daddy afford a plane ticket? Or did he leave you high and dry when he hightailed it to France?"

She kicked him right in the shin. It wasn't premeditated, and he looked as shocked as she did when he bent to rub the painful spot where her shoe had landed.

"I wish I'd been wearing steel-toed combat boots like one of the girls in my dorm," she said hotly. "And if you ever so much as speak to me again, Powell Long, I'll break your leg the next time!"

She brushed past him and went into the depot.

Her father had just paid for the ticket when his attention was captured by the scene outside the depot. He started outside, but Antonia pushed him back into the building.

"We can wait for the bus in here, Dad," she said, her face still red and hot with anger.

He glanced past her to where Powell had straightened to send a speaking look toward the depot.

"Well, he seems to have learned to control that hot temper, at least. A year ago, he'd have been in here, right through the window," Ben Hayes remarked coldly. "I hope you crippled him."

She managed a wan smile. "No such luck. You can't wound something that ornery."

Powell had started back down the street, his back stiff with outrage.

"I hope Sally asks him how he hurt his leg," Antonia said under her breath.

"Here, girl, the bus is coming." He shepherded her outside, grateful that the ticket agent hadn't been paying attention and that none of the other passengers seemed interested in the byplay out the window. All they needed was some more gossip.

Antonia hugged her father before she climbed aboard. She wanted to look down the street, to see if Powell was limping. But even though the windows were dark, she wouldn't risk having him catch her watching him. She closed her eyes as the bus pulled away from the depot and spent the rest of the journey trying to forget the pain of seeing Powell Long again.

Chapter 1

"That's very good, Martin, but you've left out something, haven't you?" Antonia prompted gently. She smiled, too, because Martin was very shy even for a nine-year-old and she didn't want to embarrass him in front of her other fourth graders. "The secret weapon the Greeks used in battle…a military formation?"

"Secret weapon," he murmured to himself. Then his dark eyes lit up and he grinned. "The phalanx!" he said at once.

"Yes," she replied. "Very good!"

He beamed, glancing smugly at his worst enemy in the second row over, who was hoping Martin would miss the question and looked very depressed indeed that he hadn't.

Antonia glanced at her watch. It was almost time to dismiss class for the day, and the week.

Odd, she thought, how loose that watch was on her wrist.

"It's time to start putting things away," she told her students. "Jack, will you erase the board for me, please? And, Mary, please close the windows."

They rushed to obey, because they liked Miss Hayes. Mary glanced at her with a smile. Miss Hayes smiled back. She wasn't as pretty as Miss Bell down the hall, and she dressed in a very backward sort of way, always wearing suits or pantsuits, not miniskirts and frilly blouses. She had pretty long blond hair, though, when she took it out of that awful bun, and her gray eyes were like the December sky. It would be Christmas soon, and in a week they could all go home for the holidays. Mary wondered what Miss Hayes would do. She never went anywhere exciting for holidays. She never talked about her family, either. Maybe she didn't have one.

The bell rang and Antonia smiled and waved as her students marched out to waiting buses and cars. She tidied her desk with steady hands and wondered if her father would come for Christmas this year. It was very lonely for both of them since her mother's death last year. It had been hard, coping with the loss. It had been harder having to go home for the funeral. He was there. He, and his daughter. Antonia shivered just remembering the look on his dark, hard face. Powell hadn't softened even then, even when her mother was being buried. He still hated Antonia after nine years. She'd barely glanced at the sullen, dark-haired little girl by his side. The child was like a knife through her heart, a reminder that Powell had been sleeping with Sally even while he and Antonia were engaged to be married; because the little girl had been born only seven months after Powell married Sally. Antonia had glanced at them once, only once, to meet Powell's hateful stare. She hadn't looked toward the pew where they sat again.

Incredible how he could hate Antonia after marriage and a child, when everyone must have told him the truth ten times over in the years between. He was rich now. He had money and power and a fine home. His wife had died only three years after their wedding, and he hadn't remarried. Antonia imagined it was because he missed Sally so much. She didn't. She hated even the memory of her one-time best friend. Sally had cost her everything she loved, even her home, and she'd done it with deliberate lies. Of course, Powell had believed the lies. That was what had hurt most.

Antonia was over it now. It had been nine years. It hardly hurt at all, in fact, to remember him.

She blinked as someone knocked at the door, interrupting her train of thought. It was Barrie,

her good friend and the Miss Bell of the miniskirt who taught math, grinning at her. Barrie
was gorgeous. She was slender and had beautiful
long legs. Her hair was almost black, like a wavy
curtain down her back. She had green eyes with
mischief in them, and a ready smile.

"You could stay with me at Christmas," Barrie
invited merrily, her green eyes twinkling.

"In Sheridan?" she asked idly, because that
was where Barrie's stepfather's home was, where
George Rutherford and her stepbrother Dawson
Rutherford, and Barrie and her late mother had
lived before she left home and began teaching
with Antonia in Tucson.

"No," Barrie said tightly. "Not ever there. In
my apartment here in Tucson," she added, forcing a smile to her face. "I have four boyfriends.
We can split them, two each. We'll have a merry
whirl!"

Antonia only smiled. "I'm twenty-seven, too
old for merry whirls, and my father will probably
come here for Christmas. But thanks anyway."

"Honestly, Annie, you're not old, even if you
do dress like someone's maiden aunt!" she said
explosively. "Look at you!" she added, sweeping
her hand toward the gray suit and white blouse
that was indicative of the kind of clothes Antonia favored. "And your hair in that infernal bun…
you look like a holdover from the Victorians! You
need to loose that glorious blond hair and put

on a miniskirt and some makeup and look for a man before you get too old! And you need to eat! You're so thin that you're beginning to look like skin and bones."

Antonia knew that. She'd lost ten pounds in the past month or so and she'd finally gotten worried enough to make an appointment with her doctor. It was probably nothing, she thought, but it wouldn't hurt to check. Her iron might be low. She said as much to Barrie.

"That's true. You've had a hard year, what with losing your mother and then that awful scare with the student who brought his dad's pistol to school and held everybody at bay for an hour last month."

"Teaching is becoming the world's most dangerous profession," Antonia agreed. She smiled sadly at Barrie. "Perhaps if we advertised it that way, we'd attract more brave souls to boost our numbers."

"That's an idea," came the dry agreement. "Want adventure? Try teaching! I can see the slogan now—"

"I'm going home," Antonia interrupted her.

"Ah, well, I suppose I will, too. I have a date tonight."

"Who is it this time?"

"Bob. He's nice and we get along well. But sometimes I think I'm not cut out for a conventional sort of man. I need a wild-eyed artist or a composer or a drag racer."

Antonia chuckled. "I hope you find one."

"If I did, he'd probably have two wives hidden in another country or something. I do have the worst luck with men."

"It's your liberated image," Antonia said in a conspiratorial tone. "You're devil-may-care and outrageous. You scare off the most secure bachelors."

"Bunkum. If they were secure enough, they'd rush to my door," Barrie informed her. "I'm sure there's a man like that somewhere, just waiting for me."

"I'm sure there is, too," her friend said kindly, and didn't for a minute let on that she thought there was already one waiting in Sheridan.

Beneath Barrie's outrageous persona, there was a sad and rather lonely woman. Barrie wasn't at all what she seemed. Barrie basically was afraid of men—especially her stepbrother, Dawson. He was George's blood son. Dear George, the elderly man who'd been another unfortunate victim of Sally Long's lies. The tales hadn't fazed Dawson, though, who not only knew better, but who was one of the coldest and most intimidating men Antonia had ever met where women were concerned. Barrie never mentioned Dawson, never talked about him. And if his name was mentioned, she changed the subject. It was common knowledge that they didn't get along. But secretly, Antonia thought there was something in their past, something that Barrie didn't talk about.

She never had, and now that poor George was dead and Dawson had inherited his estate, there was a bigger rift between them because a large interest in the cattle empire that Dawson inherited had been willed to Barrie.

"I've got to phone Dad and see what his plans are," Antonia murmured, dragging herself back from her memories.

"If he can't come down here, will you go home for Christmas?"

She shook her head. "I don't go home."

"Why not?" She grimaced. "Oh. Yes. I forget from time to time, because you never talk about him. I'm sorry. But it's been nine years. Surely he couldn't hold a grudge for that long? After all, he's the one who called off the wedding and married your best friend less than a month later. And she caused the scandal in the first place!"

"Yes, I know," Antonia replied.

"She must have loved him a lot to take such a risk. But he did eventually find out the truth," she added, tugging absently on a strand of her long, wavy black hair.

Antonia sighed. "Did he? I suppose someone told him, eventually. I don't imagine he believed it, though. Powell likes to see me as a villain."

"He loved you…"

"He wanted me," Antonia said bitterly. "At least that's what he said. I had no illusions about why he was marrying me. My father's name carried some weight in town, even though we were not rich. Powell needed the respectability. The love was all on my side. As it worked out, he got rich and had one child and a wife who was besotted with him. But from what I heard, he didn't love her either. Poor Sally," she added on a cold laugh, "all that plotting and lying, and when she got what she wanted, she was miserable."

"Good enough for her," Barrie said curtly. "She ruined your reputation and your parents'."

"And your stepfather's," she added, sadly. "He was very fond of my mother once."

Barrie smiled gently. "He was very fond of her up until the end. It was a blessing that he liked your father, and that they were friends. He was a good loser when she married your father. But he still cared for her, and that's why he did so much to help you."

"Right down to paying for my college education. That was the thing that led to all the trouble. Powell didn't like George at all. His father lost a lot of land to George—in fact, Dawson is still at odds with Powell over that land, even today, you know. He may live in Sheridan, but his ranch covers hundreds of acres right up against Powell's ranch, and I understand from Dad that he gives him fits at any opportunity."

"Dawson has never forgotten or forgiven the lies that Sally told about George," came the quiet reply. "He spoke to Sally, you know. He cornered her in town and gave her hell, with Powell standing right beside her."

"You never told me that," Antonia said on a quick breath.

"I didn't know how to," Barrie replied. "It hurts you just to have Powell's name mentioned."

"I suppose Powell stood up for her," she said, fishing.

"Even Powell is careful about how he deals with Dawson," Barrie reminded her. "Besides, what could he say? Sally told a lie and she was caught, red-handed. Too late to do you any good, they were already married by then."

"You mean, Powell's known the truth for nine years?" Antonia asked, aghast.

"I didn't say he believed Dawson," the other woman replied gently, averting her eyes.

"Oh. Yes. Well." Antonia fought for composure. How ridiculous, to think Powell would have accepted the word of his enemy. He and Dawson never had gotten along. She said it aloud even as she thought it.

"Is it likely that they would? My stepfather beat Old Man Long out of everything he owned in a poker game when they were both young men. The feud has gone on from there. Dawson's land borders Powell's, and they're both bent on empire building. If a tract comes up for sale, you can bet both men will be standing on the Realtor's doorstep trying to get first dibs on it. In fact, that's what they're butting heads about right now, that strip of land that separates their ranches that the widow Holton owns."

"They own the world between them," Antonia said pointedly.

"And they only want what joins theirs." Barrie chuckled. "Ah, well, it's no concern of ours. Not now. The less I see of my stepbrother, the happier I am."

Antonia, who'd only once seen the two of them together, had to agree. When Dawson was anywhere nearby, Barrie became another person, withdrawn and tense and almost comically clumsy.

"Well, if you change your mind about the holidays, my door is open," Barrie reminded her.

Antonia smiled warmly. "I'll remember. If Dad can't come down for the holidays, you could come home with me," she added.

Barrie shivered. "No, thanks! Bighorn is too close to Dawson for my taste."

"Dawson lives in Sheridan."

"Not all the time. Occasionally he stays at the ranch in Bighorn. He spends more and more time there these days." Her face went taut. "They say the widow Holton is the big attraction. Her husband had lots of land, and she hasn't decided who she'll sell it to."

A widow with land. Barrie had mentioned that Powell was also in competition with Dawson for the land. Or was it the widow? He was a widower, too, and a long-standing one. The thought made her sad.

"You need to eat more," Barrie remarked, concerned by her friend's appearance. "You're getting so thin, Annie, although it does give you a more fragile appearance. You have lovely bone structure. High cheekbones and good skin."

"I inherited the high cheekbones from a Cheyenne grandmother," she said, remembering sadly that Powell had called her Cheyenne as a nickname—actually meant as a corruption of "shy Ann," which she had been when they first started dating.

"Good blood," Barrie mused. "My ancestry is black Irish—from the Spanish armada that was blown off course to the coast of Ireland. Legend has it that one of my ancestors was a Spanish nobleman, who ended up married to a stepsister of an Irish lord."

"What a story."

"Isn't it, though? I must pursue historical fiction one day—in between stuffing mathematical formulae into the heads of innocents." She glanced at her watch. "Heavens, I'll be late for my date with Bob! Gotta run. See you Monday!"

"Have fun."

"I always have fun. I wish you did, once in a while." She waved from the door, leaving behind a faint scent of perfume.

Antonia loaded her attaché case with papers to grade and her lesson plan for the following week, which badly needed updating. When her desk was cleared, she sent a last look around the classroom and went out the door.

Her small apartment overlooked "A" mountain in Tucson, so-called because of the giant letter *A* that was painted at its peak and was repainted year after year by University of Arizona students. The city was flat and only a small scattering of tall buildings located downtown made it seem like a city at all. It was widespread, sprawling, sandy and hot. Nothing like Bighorn, Wyoming, where Antonia's family had lived for three generations.

She remembered going back for her mother's funeral less than a year ago. Townspeople had come by the house to bring food for every meal, and to pay their respects. Antonia's mother had been well-loved in the community. Friends sent cartloads of the flowers she'd loved so much.

The day of the funeral had dawned bright and sunny, making silver lights in the light snow covering, and Antonia thought how her mother had loved spring. She wouldn't see another one now.

Her heart, always fragile, had finally given out. At least, it had been a quick death. She'd died at the stove, in the very act of putting a cake into the oven.

The service was brief but poignant, and afterward Antonia and her father had gone home. The house was empty. Dawson Rutherford had stopped to offer George's sympathy, because George had been desperately ill, far too ill to fly across the ocean from France for the funeral. In fact, George had died less than two weeks later.

Dawson had volunteered to drive Barrie out to the airport to catch her plane back to Arizona, because Barrie had come to the funeral, of course. Antonia had noted even in her grief how it affected Barrie just to have to ride that short distance with her stepbrother.

Later, Antonia's father had gone to the bank and Antonia had been halfheartedly sorting her mother's unneeded clothes and putting them away when Mrs. Harper, who lived next door and was helping with the household chores, announced that Powell Long was at the door and wished to speak with her.

Having just suffered the three worst days of her life, she was in no condition to face him now.

"Tell Mr. Long that we have nothing to say to each other," Antonia had replied with cold pride.

"Guess he knows how it feels to lose somebody, since he lost Sally a few years back," Mrs.

Harper reminded her, and then watched to see how the news would be received.

Antonia had known about Sally's death. She hadn't sent flowers or a card because it had happened only three years after Antonia had fled Bighorn, and the bitterness had still been eating at her.

"I'm sure he understands grief," was all Antonia said, and waited without saying another word until Mrs. Harper got the message and left.

She was back five minutes later with a card. "Said to give you this," she murmured, handing the business card to Antonia, "and said you should call him if you needed any sort of help."

Help. She took the card and, without even looking at it, deliberately tore it into eight equal parts. She handed them back to Mrs. Harper and turned again to her clothes sorting.

Mrs. Harper looked at the pieces of paper in her hand. "Enough said," she murmured, and left.

It was the last contact Antonia had had with Powell Long since her mother's death. She knew that he'd built up his purebred Angus ranch and made a success of it. But she didn't ask for personal information about him after that, despite the fact that he remained a bachelor. The past, as far as she was concerned, was truly dead. Now, she wondered vaguely why Powell had come to see her that day. Guilt, perhaps? Or something more? She'd never know.

* * *

She found a message on her answering machine and played it. Her father, as she'd feared, was suffering his usual bout of winter bronchitis and his doctor wouldn't let him go on an airplane for fear of what it would do to his sick lungs. And he didn't feel at all like a bus or train trip, so Antonia would have to come home for Christmas, he said, or they'd each have to spend it alone.

She sat down heavily on the floral couch she'd purchased at a local furniture store and sighed. She didn't want to go home. If she could have found a reasonable excuse, she wouldn't have, either. But it would be impossible to leave her father sick and alone on the holidays. With resolution, she picked up the telephone and booked a seat on the next commuter flight to Billings, where the nearest airport to Bighorn was located.

Because Wyoming was so sparsely populated, it was lacking in airports. Powell Long, now wealthy and able to afford all the advantages, had an airstrip on his ranch. But there was nowhere in Bighorn that a commercial aircraft, even a commuter one, could land. She knew that Barrie's stepbrother had a Learjet and that he had a landing strip near Bighorn on his own ranch, but she would never have presumed on Barrie's good nature to ask for that sort of favor. Besides, she admitted to herself, she was as intimidated by Dawson Rutherford as Barrie was. He, like Powell, was high-powered and aggressively masculine. Antonia felt much safer seated on an impersonal commuter plane.

She rented a car at the airport in Billings and, with the easy acceptance of long distances on the road from her time in Arizona, she set out for Bighorn.

The countryside was lovely. There were scattered patches of snow, something she hadn't thought about until it was too late and she'd already rented the car. There was snow on the ground in Billings, quite a lot of it, and although the roads were mostly clear, she was afraid of icy patches. She'd get out, somehow, she told herself. But she did wish that she'd had the forethought to ask her father about the local weather when she'd phoned to say she was leaving Tucson on an early-morning flight. But he was hoarse and she hadn't wanted to stress his voice too much. He knew when she was due to arrive, though, and if she was too long overdue, she was certain that he'd send someone to meet her.

She gazed lovingly at the snow-covered mountains, thinking of how she'd missed this country that was home to her, home to generations of her family. There was so much of her history locked into these sweeping mountain ranges and valleys, where lodgepole pines stood like sentinels over shallow, wide blue streams. The forests were green and majestic, looking much as they must have when mountain men plied their trade here. Arizona had her own forests, too, and mountains. But Wyoming was another world. It was home.

The going got rough the closer to home she went. It was just outside Bighorn that her car slipped on a wide patch of ice and almost went into a ditch. She knew all too well that if she had, there would have been no way she could get the vehicle out, because the slope was too deep.

With a prayer of thanks, she made it into the small town of Bighorn, past the Methodist Church and the post office and the meat locker building to her father's big Victorian house on a wide street off the main thoroughfare. She parked in the driveway under a huge cottonwood tree. How wonderful to be home for Christmas!

There was a decorated tree in the window, all aglow with the lights and ornaments that had been painstakingly purchased over a period of years. She looked at one, a crystal deer, and re-membered painfully that Powell had given it to her the Christmas they'd become engaged. She'd thought of smashing it after his desertion, but she couldn't bring herself to do it. The tiny thing was so beautiful, so fragile; like their destroyed rela-tionship. So long ago.

Her father came to the door in a bathrobe and pajamas, sniffling.

He hugged her warmly. "I'm so glad you came,

girl," he said hoarsely, and coughed a little. "I'm much better, but the damn doctor wouldn't let me fly!"

"And rightly so," she replied. "You don't need pneumonia!"

He grinned at her. "I reckon not. Can you stay until New Year's?"

She shook her head. "I'm sorry. I have to go back the day after Christmas." She didn't mention her upcoming doctor's appointment. There was no need to worry him.

"Well, you'll be here for a week, anyway. We won't get to go out much, I'm afraid, but we can keep each other company, can't we?"

"Yes, we can."

"Dawson said he might come by one evening," he added surprisingly. "He's just back from Europe, some convention or other he said he couldn't miss."

"At least he never believed the gossip about George and me," she said wistfully.

"Why, he knew his father too well," he replied simply.

"George was a wonderful man. No wonder you and he were friends for so long."

"I miss him. I miss your mother, too, God rest her soul. She was the most important person in my life, next to you."

"You're the most important person in mine," she agreed, smiling. "It's good to be home!"

"Still enjoy teaching?"

"More than ever," she told him warmly.

"There's some good schools here," he remarked. "They're always short of teachers. And two of them are expecting babies any day. They'll have problems getting supply teachers in for that short little period." He eyed her. "You wouldn't consider…?"

"I like Tucson," she said firmly.

"The hell you do," he muttered. "It's Powell, isn't it? Damn fool, listening to that scatterbrained woman in the first place! Well, he paid for it. She made his life hell."

"Would you like some coffee?" she asked, changing the subject.

"Oh, I suppose so. And some soup. There's some canned that Mrs. Harper made for me."

"Does she still live next door?"

"She does," he murmured with a wicked smile, "and she's a widow herself. No need to ask why she brought the soup, is there?"

"I like Mrs. Harper," she said with a grin. "She and Mother were good friends, and she's like family already. Just in case you wondered what I thought," she added.

"It's only been a year, girl," he said, and his eyes were sad.

"Mother loved you too much to want you to go through life alone," she said. "She wouldn't want you to grieve forever."

He shrugged. "I'll grieve as long as I please."

"Suit yourself. I'll change clothes and then I'll see about the soup and coffee."

"How's Barrie?" her father asked when Antonia came out of her bedroom dressed in jeans and a white sweatshirt with golden sequined bells and red ribbon on it.

"She's just fine. Spunky as ever."

"Why didn't you bring her with you?"

"Because she's juggling four boyfriends," she said, chuckling as she went about warming soup.

"Dawson won't wait forever."

She glanced at him. "Is that what you think, too? She won't talk about him."

"He won't talk about her, either."

"What's this rumor about him and the widow Holton?"

He sat down in a chair at the table with a painful breath. "The widow Holton is redheaded and vivacious and a man-killer," he said. "She's after Dawson. And Powell Long. And any other man with money and a passable face."

"I see."

"You don't remember her, do you? Came here before you went off to college, but she and her husband traveled a lot. She was some sort of actress. She's been home more since he died."

"What does she do?"

"For a living, you mean?" He chuckled and had

to fight back a cough. "She's living on her inheritance. Doesn't have to do anything, lucky girl."

"I wouldn't want to do nothing," Antonia remarked thoughtfully. "I like teaching. It's more than just a job."

"Some women aren't made for purposeful employment."

"I guess not."

She finished heating the soup and poured the coffee she'd made. They ate in silence.

"I wish your mother was here," he said.

She smiled sadly. "So do I."

"Well, we'll make the most of what we have and thank God for it."

She nodded. "We have more than some people do."

He smiled, seeing her mother's face in her own. "And a lot more than most," he added. "I'm glad you came home for Christmas."

"So am I. Eat your soup." She poured him some more, and thought that she was going to make this Christmas as happy for him as she could.

Chapter 2

Dawson Rutherford was tall, lean and drop-dead gorgeous with blond, wavy hair and eyes that seemed to pierce skin. Even if he hadn't been so handsome, his physical presence was more than enough to make him attractive, added to a deep voice that had the smoothness of velvet, even in anger. But he was as icy a man as she'd ever known, especially with women. At his father's funeral, she'd actually seen him back away from a beautiful woman to avoid being touched. Odd, that, when she knew for a fact that he'd been quite a rounder with women in his checkered past.

If Antonia hadn't given her heart to Powell Long so many years before, she wouldn't have minded setting her cap at Dawson, intimidating though he was. But he was plainly meant for another type of woman altogether. Barrie, perhaps.

It was Christmas Eve, and he'd stopped by with a pipe for her father. Antonia walked him out a few minutes later.

"Shame on you," she muttered, pausing on the porch.

Dawson's green eyes twinkled. "He'll get over the bronchitis. Besides, you know he won't quit smoking, whether or not I give him a new pipe. You've tried and I've tried for years to break him. The best we can do is make him smoke it out-doors."

"I know that," she agreed, and smiled. "Well, it was a nice gesture."

"Want to see what he gave me?" he asked, and produced a smooth silver lighter with inlaid turquoise.

"I didn't know you smoked," she observed.

"I don't."

Her eyes widened.

"I did, just briefly, smoke cigars." He corrected himself. "I gave it up months ago. He doesn't know, so don't tell him."

"I won't. But good for you!" she said approvingly.

He shrugged. "I don't know any smokers who don't want to quit." His eyes narrowed, and he watched her without blinking. "Except one, maybe."

She knew he was talking about Powell, who always had smoked cigars, and presumably still did. Her face began to close up. "Don't say it."

"I won't. You look tortured."

"It was nine years ago."

"Somebody should have shot him for the way he treated you," he replied. "I've never liked him, but that didn't win him any points with me. I loved my father. It was a low thing, for Sally to make him out a foolish old man with a lust for young girls."

"She wanted Powell."

His eyes narrowed. "She got him. But he made her pay for it, let me tell you. She took to alcohol because he left her alone so much, and from all accounts, he hated their daughter."

"But why?" Antonia asked, shocked. "Powell loved children, surely…!"

"Sally trapped him with the child," he replied. "Except for that, he'd have left her. Don't you think he knew what a stupid thing he'd done? He knew the truth, almost from the day he married Sally."

"But he stayed with her."

"He had to. He was trying to build a ranch out of nothing, and this is a small town. How would it look for a man to walk out on a pregnant woman, or on his own newborn daughter?" He pursed his lips. "He hates you, you know," he added surprisingly. "He hates you for not making him listen, for running. He blames his misery on you."

"He's your worst enemy, so how do you know so much?" she retorted.

"I have spies." He sighed. "He can't admit that the worst mistake was his own, that he wouldn't believe Sally capable of such underhanded lies. It wasn't until he married her that he realized how she'd conned him." He shrugged. "She wasn't a bad woman, really. She was in love and she couldn't bear losing him, even to you. Love does crazy things to people."

"She destroyed my reputation, and your father's, and made it impossible for me to live here," Antonia said without pity. "She was my enemy, and he still is. Don't think I'm harboring any tender feelings for him. I'd cut his throat given the slightest opportunity."

His eyebrows levered up. Antonia was a gentle soul herself for the most part, despite an occasional outburst of temper and a keen wit that surprised people. She hadn't ever seemed vindictive, but she harbored a long-standing grudge against her former best friend, Sally. He couldn't really blame her.

He fingered the lighter her father had given him. "How's Barrie?" he asked with deliberate carelessness.

"Fending off suitors," she said with a grin, her soft gray eyes twinkling. "She was juggling four of them when I left."

He laughed coldly. "Why doesn't that surprise me? One man was never enough for her, even when she was a teenager."

She was curious about his antagonism toward Barrie. It seemed out of place. "Why do you hate her so?" she asked bluntly.

He looked surprised. "I don't...hate her," he said. "I'm disappointed at the way she behaves, that's all."

"She isn't promiscuous," she said, defending her colleague. "She may act that way, but it's only an act. Don't you know that?"

He looked at the lighter, frowning slightly. "Maybe I know more than you think," he said curtly. His eyes came up. "Maybe you're the one wearing blinders."

"Maybe you're seeing what you want to see," she replied gently.

He pocketed the lighter with a curt gesture. "I'd better go. I've got a deal cooking. I don't want the client to get cold feet."

"Thanks for coming to see Dad. You cheered him up."

"He's my friend." He smiled. "So are you, even when you stick your nose in where you shouldn't."

"Barrie's my friend."

"Well, she's not mine," he said flatly. "Merry Christmas, Annie."

"You, too," she replied with a warm smile. He was kind, in his way. She liked him, but she felt sorry for Barrie. He was a heartbreaker. And unless she missed her guess, Barrie was in love with him. His feelings were much less readable.

After he left, she went back to join her father in the kitchen, where he was fixing hot chocolate in a double boiler. He glanced over his shoulder.

"Did he leave?"

"Yes. Can I help?"

He shook his head. He poured hot chocolate into two mugs and nodded for her to take one while he put the boiler in water to soak.

"He gave me a pipe," he told her when they were seated at the small kitchen table, sipping the hot liquid. He grinned. "Didn't have the heart to tell him that I've finally given it up."

"Dad!" She reached across and patted his hand. "Oh, that's great news!"

He chuckled. "Figured you'd like it. Maybe I won't have so much trouble with my lungs from now on."

"Speaking of lungs," she said, "you gave Dawson a lighter. Guess what he's just given up, and didn't have the heart to tell you?"

He burst out laughing. "Well, maybe he can use it to light fires under his beef cattle when he throws barbecues out on the Rutherford spread."

"What a good idea! I'll suggest it to him the next time we see him."

"I wouldn't hold my breath," he replied. "He travels a lot these days. I hardly ever see him."

He lifted his eyes to hers. "Powell came by last week."

Her heart fluttered, but her face was very composed. "Did he? Why?"

"Heard I was sick and came to check on me. Wanted to know where you were."

Her frozen expression grew darker. "Did he?"

"I told him you didn't know about the bronchitis and that he should mind his own business."

"I see."

He sipped hot chocolate and put the mug down with a thud. "Had his daughter with him. Quiet, sullen little thing. She never moved a muscle the whole time, just sat and glared. She's her mother all over."

Antonia was dying inside. She stared into her hot chocolate. That woman's child, here, in her home! She could hardly bear the thought. It was like a violation to have Powell come here with that child.

"You're upset," he said ruefully. "I guessed you would be, but I thought you'd better know. He said he'd be back to check on me after Christmas. Wouldn't want him to just show up without my telling you he was expected sooner or later. Not that I invited him," he added curtly. "Surprised me, too, that he'd come to see about me. Of course, he was fond of your mother. It hurt him that the scandal upset her so much and caused her to have that first heart attack. Anyway, he's taken it upon himself to be my guardian angel. Even sent the doctor when I first got sick, conspired with Mrs. Harper next door to look after me." He sounded disgusted, but he smiled, too.

"That was nice of him," she said, although Powell's actions surprised her. "But thanks for warning me." She forced a smile to her lips. "I'll arrange to do something in the kitchen if he turns up."

"It's been nine years," he reminded her.

"And you think I should have forgotten." She nodded. "You forgive people, Dad. I used to, before all this. Perhaps I should be more charitable, but I can't be. He and Sally made my life hell." She stopped, dragging in a long breath.

"No other suitors, in all that time," he remarked. "No social life, no dating. Girl, you're going to die an old maid, with no kids of your own, no husband, no real security."

"I enjoy my own company," she said lightly. "And I don't want a child." That was a lie, but only a partial one. The children she had wanted were Powell's, no one else's.

Christmas Day passed uneventfully, except for the meager gifts she and her father exchanged and their shared memories of her late mother to keep them company.

The next day, she was packed and dressed for travel in a rose knit suit, her hair carefully coiffed, her long legs in hose and low-heeled shoes on her feet. Her burgundy velvet, full-length coat was slung over one arm, its dark lining gleaming in the overhead light, as she put her suitcase down and went to find her father to say goodbye.

Voices from the living room caught her attention and she moved in that direction. But at the doorway, she froze in place, and in time. That deep, gravelly voice was as familiar as her own, despite the many years since she'd last heard it. And then a tall, lean man turned, and cast narrow black eyes on her face. Powell!

She lifted her face slowly, not allowing a hint of emotion to show either in her posture or her eyes. She simply looked at him, reconciling this man in his thirties with the man who'd wanted to marry her. The memories were unfavorable, because he was definitely showing his age, in the new lines beside his mouth and eyes, in the silver that showed at his temples.

He was doing his share of looking, too. The girl he'd jilted was no longer visible in this quiet, conservatively dressed woman with her hair in a bun. She looked schoolmarmish, and he was surprised that the sight of her was still like a knife through the heart, after all these years. He'd been curious about her. He'd wanted to see her again, God knew why. Maybe because she refused to see him at her mother's funeral. Now here she was, and he wasn't sure he was glad. The sight of her touched something sensitive that he'd buried inside himself.

Antonia was the first to look away. The intensity of his gaze had left her shaking inside, but that reaction was quickly hidden. It would never do to show any weakness to him. "Sorry," she told her father. "I didn't realize you had company. If you'll come and see me off, I'll be on my way."

Her father looked uncomfortable. "Powell came by to see how I was doing."

"You're leaving so soon?" Powell asked, addressing her directly for the first time in so many long years.

"I have to report back to work earlier than the students," she said, pleased that her voice was steady and cool.

"Oh, yes. You teach, don't you?"

She couldn't quite meet his eyes. Her gaze fell somewhere between his aggressive chin and his thin but sensuous mouth, below that straight, arrogant nose and the high cheekbones of his lean face. He wasn't handsome, but five minutes after they met him, most women were enchanted with him. He had an intangible something, authority perhaps, in the sureness of his movements, even in the way he held his head. He was overwhelming.

"I teach," she agreed. Her eyes hadn't quite met his. She turned to her father. "Dad?"

He excused himself and came forward to hug

her. "Be careful. Phone when you get there, to let me know that you made it all right, will you? It's been snowing again."

"I'll be fine. I have a phone in the car, if I get stuck."

"You're driving to Arizona, in this weather?" Powell interrupted.

"I've been driving in this weather most of my adult life," she informed him.

"You were terrified of slick roads when you were in your teens," he recalled solemnly.

She smiled coldly at him. "I'm not a teenager now."

The way she looked at him spoke volumes about her feelings. He didn't avert his gaze, but his eyes were dark and quiet, full of secrets and seething accusation.

"Sally left a letter for you," he said unexpectedly. "I never got around to posting it. Over the years, I'd forgotten about it."

Her chest rose in a quick, angry breath. It reminded her of the letter that Sally had sent soon after Antonia had left town, the one she'd returned unopened. "Another one?" she asked in a frozen tone. "Well, I want nothing from your late wife, not even a letter."

He bristled. "She was your friend once," he reminded her curtly.

"She was my enemy." She corrected him. "She ruined my reputation and all but killed my mother! Do you really believe I'd want any reminder of what she did?"

He didn't seem to move for a minute. His face hardened. "She did nothing to hurt you deliberately," he said tersely.

"Really? Will her good intentions bring back George Rutherford or my mother?" she demanded hotly, because George himself had died so soon after her mother had. "Will it erase all the gossip?"

He turned away and bent his head to light a cigar, apparently unconcerned. Antonia fought for control. Her hands were icy cold as she picked up her suitcase and winced at her father's worried expression.

"I'll phone you, Dad. Please take care of yourself," she added.

"You're upset," he said distractedly. "Wait a bit…"

"I won't… I can't…" Her voice choked on the words and she averted her eyes from the long back of the man who was turned away from her. "Bye, Dad!"

She was out the door in a flash, and within two minutes she'd loaded her cases into the trunk and opened the door. But before she could get in, Powell was towering over her.

"Get a grip on yourself," he said curtly, forcing her to look at him. "You won't do your father any favors by landing in a ditch in the middle of nowhere!"

She shivered at the nearness of him and deliberately backed away, her gray eyes wide, accusing.

"You look so fragile," he said, as if the words were torn from him. "Don't you eat?"

"I eat enough." She steadied herself on the door. "Goodbye."

His big hand settled beside hers on the top of the door. "Why was Dawson Rutherford here a couple of nights ago?"

The question was totally unexpected. "Is that your business?" she asked coldly.

He smiled mockingly. "It could be. Rutherford's father ruined mine, or didn't you remember? I don't intend to let his son ruin me."

"My father and George Rutherford were friends."

"And you and George were lovers."

She didn't say a word. She only looked at him. "You know the truth," she said wearily. "You just don't want to believe it."

"George paid your way through college," he reminded her.

"Yes, he did," she agreed, smiling. "And I rewarded him by graduating with honors, second in my graduating class. He was a philanthropist and the best friend my family ever had. I miss him."

"He was a rich old man with designs on you, whether you'll admit it or not!"

She searched his deep-set black eyes. They never smiled. He was a hard man, and the passing years had only added to his sarcastic, harsh demeanor. He'd grown up dirt poor, looked down on in the community because of his parents. He'd struggled to get where he was, and she knew how difficult it had been. But his hard life had warped his perception of people. He looked for the worst, always. She'd known that, somehow, even when they were first engaged. And now, he was the sum of all the tragedies of his life. She'd loved him so much, she'd tried to make up to him for the love he'd never had, the life his circumstances had denied him. But even while he was courting her, he'd loved Sally most. He'd told Antonia so, when he broke their engagement and called her a streetwalker with a price tag....

"You're staring," he said irritably, ramming his hands into the pockets of his dark slacks.

"I was remembering the way you used to be, Powell," she said simply. "You haven't changed. You're still the loner who never trusted anyone, who always expected people to do their worst."

"I believed in you," he replied solemnly.

She smiled. "No, you didn't. If you had, you wouldn't have swallowed Sally's lies without—"

"Damn you!"

He had her by both shoulders, his cigar suddenly lying in the snow at their feet. He practically shook her, and she winced, because she was willow thin and he had the grip of a horseman, developed after long years of back-breaking ranch work long before he ever made any money at it.

She looked up into blazing eyes and wondered dimly why she wasn't afraid of him. He looked intimidating with his black eyes flashing and his straight black hair falling down over his thick eyebrows.

"Sally didn't lie!" he reiterated. "That's the hell of it, Antonia! She was gentle and kind and she never lied to me. She cried when you had to leave town over what happened. She cried for weeks and weeks, because she hadn't wanted to tell me what she knew about you and George! She couldn't bear to see you two-timing me!"

She pulled away from him with a strength she didn't know she had. "She deserved to cry!" she said through her teeth.

He called her a name that made her flush. She only smiled.

"Sticks and stones, Powell," she said in a steady, if husky, tone. "But if you say that again, you'll get the same thing I gave you the summer after I started college."

He remembered very well the feel of her shoe on his shin. Even through his anger, he had to stifle a mental smile at the memory. Antonia had always had spirit. But he remembered other things, too; like her refusal to talk to him after her mother's death, when he'd offered help. Sally had been long dead by then, but Antonia wouldn't let him close enough to see if she still felt anything for him. She wouldn't even now, and it caused him to lose his temper when he'd never meant to. She wouldn't let go of the past. She wouldn't give him a chance to find out if there was anything left of what they'd felt for each other. She didn't care.

The knowledge infuriated him.

"Now, if you're quite through insulting me, I have to go home," she added firmly.

"I could have helped, when your mother died," he said curtly. "You wouldn't even see me!"

He sounded as if her refusal to speak to him had hurt. What a joke that would be. She didn't look at him again. "I had nothing to say to you, and Dad and I didn't want your help. One way or another, you had enough help from us to build your fortune."

He scowled. "What the hell do you mean by that?"

She did look up, then, with a mocking little smile. "Have you forgotten already? Now if you'll excuse me…?"

He didn't move. His big fists clenched by his sides as she just walked around him to get into the car.

She started it, put it into Reverse, and pointedly didn't look at him again, not even when she was driving off down the street toward the main highway. And if her hands shook, he couldn't see them.

He stood watching, his boots absorbing the freezing cold of the snow around them, snowflakes touching the wide brim of his creamy Stetson. He had no idea what she'd meant with that last crack. It made him furious that he couldn't even get her to talk to him. Nine years. He'd smoldered for nine years with seething outrage and anger, and he couldn't get the chance to air it. He wanted a knock-down, drag-out argument with her, he wanted to get everything in the open. He wanted…second chances.

"Do you want some hot chocolate?" Ben Hayes called from the front door.

Powell didn't answer him for a minute. "No," he said in a subdued tone. "Thanks, but I'll pass."

Ben pulled his housecoat closer around him. "You can damn her until you die," he remarked quietly. "But it won't change one thing."

Powell turned and faced him with an expression that wasn't easily read. "Sally didn't lie," he said stubbornly. "I don't care what anyone says about it. Innocent people don't run, and they both did!"

Ben studied the tormented eyes in that lean face for a long moment. "You have to keep believing that, don't you?" he asked coldly. "Because if you don't, you've got nothing at all to show for the past nine years. The hatred you've saved up for Antonia is all that's left of your life!"

Powell didn't say another word. He strode angrily back to his four-wheel-drive vehicle and climbed in under the wheel.

Diana Palmer

Chapter 3

Antonia made it back to Tucson without a hitch, although there had been one or two places along the snow-covered roads that gave her real problems. She was shaken, but it never affected her driving. Powell Long had destroyed enough of her life. She wasn't going to give him possession of one more minute of it, not even through hatred.

She kept busy for the remainder of her vacation and spent New Year's Eve by herself, with only a brief telephone call to her father for company. They didn't mention Powell.

Barrie stopped by on New Year's Day, wearing jeans and a sweatshirt and trying not to look interested in Dawson's visit to Antonia's father's house. It was always the same, though. Whenever Antonia went to Wyoming, Barrie would wait patiently until her friend said something about

Dawson. Then she pretended that she wasn't interested and changed the subject.

But this time, she didn't. She searched Antonia's eyes. "Does he...look well?" she asked.

"He's fine," Antonia replied honestly. "He's quit smoking, so that's good news."

"Did he mention the widow?"

Antonia smiled sympathetically and shook her head. "He doesn't have much to do with women, Barrie. In fact, Dad says they call him 'the iceman' around Bighorn. They're still looking for a woman who can thaw him out."

"Dawson?" Barrie burst out. "But he's always had women hanging on him...!"

"Not these days. Apparently all he's interested in is making money."

Barrie looked shocked. "Since when?"

"I don't know. For the past few years at least," Antonia replied, frowning. "He's your stepbrother. You'd know more about that than I would. Wouldn't you?"

Barrie averted her eyes. "I don't see him. I don't go home."

"Yes, I know, but you must hear about him...."

"Only from you," the other woman said stiffly. "I don't...we don't have any mutual friends."

"Doesn't he ever come to see you?"

Barrie went pale. "He wouldn't." She bit off the words and forced a smile to her face. "We're poison to each other, didn't you know?"

She looked at her watch. "I'm going to a dance. Want to come?"

Antonia shook her head. "Not me. I'm too tired. I'll see you back at work."

"Sure. You look worse than you did when you left. Did you see Powell?"

Antonia flinched.

"Sorry," came the instant reply. "Listen, don't tell me anything about Dawson even if I beg, and I swear I won't mention Powell again, okay? I'm really sorry. I suppose we both have wounds too raw to expose. See you!"

Barrie left, and Antonia quickly found something to do, so that she wouldn't have to think any more about Powell.

But, oh, it was hard. He'd literally jilted her the day before the wedding. The invitations had been sent out, the church booked, the minister ready to officiate at the ceremony. Antonia had a dress from Neiman Marcus, a heavenly creation that George had helped her buy—which had become part of the fiasco when she admitted it to Powell. And then, out of the blue, Sally had dropped her bombshell. She'd told Powell that George Rutherford was Antonia's sugar daddy and he was paying for her body. Everyone in Bighorn knew it. They probably did, Sally had worked hard enough spreading the rumor. The gossip alone was enough to send Powell crazy. He'd turned on Antonia in a rage and canceled the wedding.

She didn't like remembering the things he'd said to her.

Some of the guests didn't get notified in time and came to the church, expecting a wedding. Antonia had had to face them and tell them the sad news. She had been publicly humiliated, and then there was the scandal that involved poor George. He'd had to move back to Sheridan, to the headquarters ranch of the Rutherford chain. It had been a shame, because the Rutherford Big-horn Ranch had been his favorite. He'd escaped a lot of the censure and spared Antonia some of it, especially when he exiled himself to France. But Antonia and her father and mother got the whole measure of local outrage. Denial did no good, because how could she defend herself against knowing glances and haughty treatment? The gossip had hurt her mother most, leaving her virtually isolated from most of the people who knew her. She'd had a mild heart attack from the treatment of her only child as a social outcast. Ironically that had seemed to bring some people to their senses, and the pressure had been eased a bit. But Antonia had left town very quickly, to spare her mother any more torment, taking her broken heart with her.

Perhaps if Powell had thought it through, if the wedding hadn't been so near, the ending might have been different. He'd always been quick-tempered and impulsive. He hated being talked about. Antonia knew that at least three people had talked to him about the rumors, and one of them was the very minister who was to marry them. Later, Antonia had discovered that they were all friends of Sally and her family.

To be fair to Powell, he'd had more than his share of public scandal. His father had been a hopeless gambler who lost everything his mother slaved at housekeeping jobs to provide. In the end he'd killed himself when he incurred a debt he knew he'd never be able to repay. Powell had watched his mother be torn apart by the gossip, and eventually her heart wore out and she simply didn't wake up one morning.

Antonia had comforted Powell. She'd gone to the funeral home with him and held his hand all through the ordeal of giving up the mother he'd loved. Perhaps grief had challenged his reason, because although he'd hidden it well, the loss had destroyed something in him. He'd never quite recovered from it, and Sally had been behind the scenes, offering even more comfort when Antonia wasn't around. Susceptible to her soft voice, perhaps he'd listened when he shouldn't have. But in the end, he'd believed Sally, and he'd married her. He'd never said he loved Antonia, and it had been just after they'd become engaged that Powell had managed several loans, on the strength of her father's excellent references, to get the property he'd inherited out of hock. He was just beginning to make it pay when he'd called off the wedding.

The pain was like a knife. She'd loved Powell more than her own life. She'd been devastated by his defection. The only consolation she'd had was that she'd put him off physically until after the wedding. Perhaps that had hurt him most, thinking that she was sleeping with poor old George when she wouldn't go to bed with him. Who knew? She couldn't go back and do things differently. She could only go forward. But the future looked much more bleak than the past.

She went back to work in the new year, apparently rested and unworried. But the doctor's appointment was still looming at the end of her first week after she started teaching.

She didn't expect them to find anything. She was run-down and tired all the time, and she'd lost a lot of weight. Probably she needed vitamins or iron tablets or something. When the doctor ordered a blood test, a complete blood count, she went along to the lab and sat patiently while they worked her in and took blood for testing. Then she went home with no particular intuition about what was about to happen.

It was early Monday morning when she had a call at work from the doctor's office. They asked her to come in immediately.

She was too frightened to ask why. She left her

class to the sympathetic vice principal and went right over to Dr. Claridge's office.

They didn't make her wait, either. She was hustled right in, no appointment, no nothing.

He got up when she entered his office and shook hands. "Sit down, Antonia. I've got the lab results from your blood test. We have to make some quick decisions."

"Quick...?" Her heart was beating wildly. She could barely breathe. She was aware of her cold hands gripping her purse like a life raft. "What sort of decisions?"

He leaned forward, his forearms on his legs. "Antonia, we've known each other for several years. This isn't an easy thing to tell someone." He grimaced. "My dear, you've got leukemia."

She stared at him without comprehension. Leukemia. Wasn't that cancer? Wasn't it...fatal?

Her breath suspended in midair. "I'm...going to die?" she asked in a hoarse whisper.

"No," he replied. "Your condition is treatable. You can undergo a program of chemotherapy and radiation, which will probably keep it in remission for some years."

Remission. Probably. Radiation. Chemotherapy. Her aunt had died of cancer when Antonia was a little girl. She remembered with terror the therapy's effects on her aunt. Headaches, nausea...

She stood up. "I can't think."

Dr. Claridge stood up, too. He took her hands

in his. "Antonia, it isn't necessarily a death sentence. We can start treatment right away. We can buy time for you."

She swallowed, closing her eyes. She'd been worried about her argument with Powell, about the anguish of the past, about Sally's cruelty and her own torment. And now she was going to die, and what did any of that matter?

She was going to die!

"I want…to think about it," she said huskily.

"Of course you do. But don't take too long, Antonia," he said gently. "All right?"

She managed to nod. She thanked him, followed the nurse out to reception, paid her bill, smiled at the girl and walked out. She didn't remember doing any of it. She drove back to her apartment, closed the door and collapsed right there on the floor in tears.

Leukemia. She had a deadly disease. She'd expected a future, and now, instead, there was going to be an ending. There would be no more Christmases with her father. She wouldn't marry and have children. It was all…over.

When the first of the shock passed, and she'd exhausted herself crying, she got up and made herself a cup of coffee. It was a mundane, ordinary thing to do. But now, even such a simple act had a poignancy. How many more cups would she have time to drink in what was left of her life?

She smiled at her own self-pity. That wasn't

going to do her any good. She had to decide what to do. Did she want to prolong the agony, as her aunt had, until every penny of her medical insurance ran out, until she bankrupted herself and her father, put herself and him through the long drawn-out treatments when she might still lose the battle? What quality of life would she have if she suffered as her aunt had?

She had to think not what was best for her, but what was best for her father. She wasn't going to rush into treatment until she was certain that she had a chance of surviving. If she was only going to be able to keep it at bay for a few painful months, then she had some difficult decisions to make. If only she could think clearly! She was too shocked to be rational. She needed time. She needed peace.

Suddenly, she wanted to go home. She wanted to be with her father, at her home. She'd spent her life running away. Now, when things were so dire, it was time to face the past, to reconcile herself with it, and with the community that had unjustly judged her. There would be time left for that, to tie up all the loose ends, to come to grips with her own past.

Her old family doctor, Dr. Harris, was still in Bighorn. She'd get Dr. Claridge to send him her medical files and she'd go from there. Perhaps Dr. Harris might have some different ideas about how she could face the ordeal. If nothing could be done, then at least she could spend her remaining time with the only family she had left.

Once the decision was made, she acted on it at once. She turned in her resignation and told Barrie that her father needed her at home.

"You didn't say that when you first came back," Barrie said suspiciously.

"Because I was thinking about it," she lied. She smiled. "Barrie, he's so alone. And it's time I went back and faced my dragons. I've been running too long already."

"But what will you do?" Barrie asked.

"I'll get a job as a relief teacher. Dad said that two of the elementary school teachers were expecting and they didn't know what they'd do for replacements. Bighorn isn't exactly Tucson, you know. It's not that easy to get teachers who are willing to live at the end of the world."

Barrie sighed. "You really have thought this out."

"Yes. I'll miss you. But maybe you'll come back one day," she added. "And fight your own dragons."

Barrie shivered. "Mine are too big to fight," she said with an enigmatic smile. "But I'll root for you. What can I help you do?"

"Pack," came the immediate reply.

As fate would have it, when she contacted her old school system in Bighorn, one of the pregnant teachers had just had to go into the hospi-

tal with toxemia and they needed a replacement
desperately for a fourth-grade class. It was just
what Antonia wanted, and she accepted grate-
fully. Best of all, there had been no discussion of
the reason she'd left town in the first place. Some
people would remember, but she had old friends
there, too, friends who wouldn't hold grudges.
Powell would be there. She refused to even en-
tertain the idea that he had any place in her reasons for wanting to go home.

She arrived in Bighorn with mixed emotions.
It made her feel wonderful to see her father's
delighted expression when he was told she was
coming back there to live permanently. But she
felt guilty, too, because he couldn't know the real
reason for her return.

"We'll have plenty of time to visit, now," she
said. "Arizona was too hot to suit me, anyway,"
she added mischievously.

"Well, if you like snow, you've certainly come
home at a good time," he replied, grinning at the
five feet or so that lay in drifts in the front yard.

Antonia spent the weekend unpacking and
then went along to work the following Monday.
She liked the principal, a young woman with
very innovative ideas about education. She remembered two of her fellow teachers, who had
been classmates of hers in high school, and nei-

ther of them seemed to have any misgivings about her return.

She liked her class, too. She spent the first day getting to know the children's names. But one of them hit her right in the heart. Maggie Long. It could have been a coincidence. But when she called the girl's name and a sullen face with blue eyes and short black hair looked up at her, she knew right away who it was. That was Sally's face, except for the glare. The glare was Powell all over again.

She lifted her chin and stared at the child. She passed over her and went on down the line until she reached Julie Ames. She smiled at Julie, who smiled back sweetly. She remembered Danny Ames from school, too, and his redheaded daughter was just like him. She'd have known Danny's little girl anywhere.

She pulled out her predecessor's lesson plan and looked over it before she took the spelling book and began making assignments.

"One other thing I'd like you to do for Friday is write a one-page essay about yourselves," she added with a smile. "So that I can learn something about you, since I've come in the middle of the year instead of the first."

Julie raised her hand. "Miss Hayes, Mrs. Donalds always assigned one of us to be class monitor when she was out of the room. Whoever she picked got to do it for a week, and then someone else did. Are you going to do that, too?"

"I think that's a good idea, Julie. You can be our monitor for this week," she added pleasantly.

"Thanks, Miss Hayes!" Julie said enthusiastically.

Behind her, Maggie Long glared even more. The child acted as if she hated Antonia, and for a minute, Antonia wondered if she knew about the past. But, then, how could she? She was being fanciful.

She dismissed the class at quitting time. It had been nice to have her mind occupied, not to have to think about herself. But with the end of the day came the terror again. And she still hadn't talked to Dr. Harris.

She made an appointment to see him when she got home, smiling at her father as she told him glibly that it was only because she needed some vitamins.

Dr. Harris, however, was worried when she told him Dr. Claridge's diagnosis.

"You shouldn't wait," he said flatly. "It's always best to catch these things early. Come here, Antonia."

He examined her neck with skilled hands, his eyes on the wall behind her. "Swollen lymph nodes, all right. You've lost weight?" he asked as he took her pulse.

"Yes. I've been working rather hard," she said lamely.

"Sore throat?"

She hesitated and then nodded.

He let out a long sigh. "I'll have him fax me your medical records," he said. "There's a specialist in Sheridan who's done oncology," he added. "But you should go back to Tucson, Antonia."

"Tell me what to expect," she said instead.

He was reluctant, but when she insisted, he drew in a deep breath and told her.

She sat back in her chair, pale and restless.

"You can fight it," he persisted. "You can hold it at bay."

"For how long?"

"Some people have been in remission for twenty-five years."

She narrowed her eyes as she gazed at him. "But you don't really believe I'll have twenty-five years."

His jaw firmed. "Antonia, medical research is progressing at a good pace. There's always, always, the possibility that a cure will be discovered...."

She held up a hand. "I don't want to have to decide today," she said wearily. "I just need... a little time," she added with a pleading smile. "Just a little time."

He looked as if he were biting his tongue to keep from arguing with her. "All right. A little time," he said emphatically. "I'll look after you. Perhaps when you've considered the options, you'll go ahead with the treatment, and I'll do everything I can. But, Antonia," he added as he stood up to show her out, "there aren't too many miracles in this business where cancer is concerned. If you're going to fight, don't wait too long."

"I won't."

She shook hands and left the office. She felt more at peace with herself now than she could ever remember feeling. Somehow in the course of accepting the diagnosis, she'd accepted something much more. She was stronger now. She could face whatever she had to. She was so glad she'd come home. Fate had dealt her some severe blows, but being home helped her to withstand the worst of them. She had to believe that fate would be kinder to her now that she was home.

But if fate had kind reasons for bringing her back to Bighorn, Maggie Long wasn't one of them. The girl was unruly, troublesome and refused to do her schoolwork at all.

By the end of the week, Antonia kept her after class and showed her the zero she'd earned for her nonattempt at the spelling test. There was another one looming, because Maggie hadn't done one word of the essay Antonia had assigned the class to write.

"If you want to repeat the fourth grade, Maggie, this is a good start," she said coolly. "If you won't do your schoolwork, you won't pass."

"Mrs. Donalds wasn't mean like you," the girl said snappily. "She never made us write stupid essays, and if there was a test, she always helped me study for it."

"I have thirty-five students in this class," Antonia heard herself saying. "Presumably you were placed in this grade because you were capable of doing the work."

"I could do it if I wanted to," Maggie said. "I just don't want to. And you can't make me, either!"

"I can fail you," came the terse, uncompromising reply. "And I will, if you keep this up. You have one last chance to escape a second zero for the essay you haven't done. You can do it over the weekend and turn it in Monday."

"My daddy's coming home today," she said haughtily. "I'm going to tell him that you're mean to me, and he'll come and cuss you out, you just wait and see!"

"What will he see, Maggie?" she asked flatly. "What does it say about you if you won't do your work?"

"I'm not lazy!"

"Then do your assignment."

"Julie didn't do all of her test, and you didn't give her a zero!"

"Julie doesn't work as fast as some of the other students. I take that into account," Antonia explained.

"You like Julie," she accused. "That's why you never act mean to her! I'll bet you wouldn't give her a zero if she didn't do her homework!"

"This has nothing to do with your ability to do your work," Antonia interrupted. "And I'm not going to argue with you. Either do your homework or don't do it. Now run along."

Maggie gave her a furious glare. She jerked up her books and stomped out of the room, turning at the door. "You wait until I tell my daddy! He'll get you fired!"

Antonia lifted an eyebrow. "It will take more than your father to do that, Maggie."

The girl jerked open the door. "I hate you! I wish you'd never come here!" she yelled.

She ran down the hallway and Antonia sat back and caught her breath. The child was a holy terror. She was a little surprised that she was so unlike her mother in that one way. Sally, for all her lying, had been sweet in the fourth grade, an amiable child, not a horror like Maggie.

Sally. The name hurt. Just the name. Antonia had come home to exorcise her ghosts and she wasn't doing a very good job of it. Maggie was making her life miserable. Perhaps Powell would interfere, at least enough to get his daughter to do her homework. She hated that it had come to this, but she hadn't anticipated the emotions Maggie's presence in her class had unleashed. She was sorry that she couldn't like the child. She wondered if anyone did. She seemed little more than a sullen, resentful brat.

Powell probably adored the child and gave her everything she wanted. But she did ride the bus to and from school and more often than not, she showed up for class in torn jeans and stained sweatshirts. Was that deliberate, and didn't her father notice that some of her things weren't clean? Surely he had a housekeeper or someone to take care of such things.

She knew that Maggie had been staying with Julie this week, because Julie had told her so. The little redheaded Ames girl was the sweetest child Antonia had ever known, and she adored her. She really was the image of her father, who'd been in Antonia's group of friends in school here in Bighorn. She'd told Julie that, and the child had been a minor celebrity for a day. It gave her something to be proud of, that her father and her teacher had been friends.

Maggie hadn't liked that. She'd given Julie the cold shoulder yesterday and they weren't speaking today. Antonia wondered at their friendship, because Julie was outgoing and generous, compassionate and kind...all the things Maggie wasn't. Probably the child saw qualities in Julie that she didn't have and liked her for them. But what in the world did Julie see in Maggie?

Chapter 4

Powell Long came home from his cattle-buying trip worn out from the long hours on the plane and the hectic pace of visiting three ranches in three states in less than a week. He could have purchased his stud cattle after watching a video, and he sometimes did if he knew the seller, but he was looking over new territory for his stock additions, and he wanted to inspect the cattle in person before he made the acquisition. It was a good thing he had, because one of the ranches had forwarded a video that must have been of someone else's cattle. When he toured the ranch, he found the stock were underfed, and some were lacking even the basic requirements for good breeding bulls.

Still, it had been a profitable trip. He'd saved several thousand dollars on seed bulls simply by going to visit the ranchers in person. Now he was home again and he didn't want to be. His house, like his life, was full of painful memories. Here was where Sally had lived, where her daughter still lived. He couldn't look at Maggie without seeing her mother. He bought the child expensive toys, whatever her heart desired. But he couldn't give her love. He didn't think he had it in him to love the product of such a painful marriage. Sally had cost him the thing he'd loved most in all the world. She'd cost him Antonia.

Maggie was sitting alone in the living room with a book. She looked up when he entered the room with eyes that avoided his almost at once.

"Did you bring me something?" she asked dully. He always did. It was just one more way of making her feel that she was important to him, but she knew better. He didn't even know what she liked, or he wouldn't bring her silly stuffed toys and dolls. She liked to read, but he hadn't noticed. She also liked nature films and natural history. He never brought her those sort of things. He didn't even know who she was.

"I brought you a new Barbie," he said. "It's in my suitcase."

"Thanks," she said.

Never a smile. Never laughter. She was a little old woman in a child's body, and looking at her made him feel guilty.

"Where's Mrs. Bates?" he asked uncomfortably.

"In the kitchen cooking," she said.

"How's school?"

She closed the book. "We got a new teacher last week. She doesn't like me," she said. "She's mean to me."

His eyebrows lifted. "Why?"

She shrugged, her thin shoulders rising and falling restlessly. "I don't know. She likes everybody else. She glares at me all the time. She gave me a zero on my test, and she's going to give me another zero on my homework. She says I'm going to fail fourth grade."

He was shocked. Maggie had always made good grades. One thing she did seem to have was a keen intelligence, even if her perpetual frown and introverted nature made her enemies. She had no close friends, except for Julie. He'd left Maggie with Julie's family, in fact, last week. They were always willing to keep her while he was out of town.

He glowered at her. "Why are you here instead of at Julie's house?" he demanded suddenly.

"I told them you were coming home and I wanted to be here, because you always bring me something," she said.

"Oh."

She didn't add that Julie's friendship with the detestable Miss Hayes had caused friction, or that they'd had a terrible argument just this morning, precipitating Maggie's return home. Fortunately

Mrs. Bates was working in the house, so that it was possible for her to be here.

"The new teacher likes Julie," she said sullenly. "But she hates me. She says I'm lazy and stupid."

"She says what?"

That was the first time her father had ever reacted in such a way, as if it really mattered to him that someone didn't like her. She looked at him fully, seeing that angry flash of his black eyes that always meant trouble for somebody. Her father intimidated her. But, then, he intimidated everyone. He didn't like most people any more than she did. He was introverted himself, and he had a bad temper and a sarcastic manner when people irritated him. Over the years Maggie had discovered that she could threaten people with her father, and it always worked.

Locally he was a legend. Most of her teachers had bent over backward to avoid confrontations with him. Maggie learned quickly that she didn't have to study very hard to make good grades. Not that she wasn't bright; she simply didn't try, because she didn't need to. She smiled. Wouldn't it be nice, she thought, if she could use him against Miss Hayes?

"She says I'm lazy and stupid," she repeated.

"What's this teacher's name?" he asked coldly.

"Miss Hayes."

He was very still. "Antonia Hayes?" he asked curtly.

"I don't know her first name. She came on account of Mrs. Donalds quit," she said. "Mrs. Donalds was my friend. I miss her."

"When did Miss Hayes get here?" he asked, surprised that he'd heard nothing about her returning to Bighorn. Of course, he'd been out of town for a week, too.

"I told you—last week. They said she used to live here." She studied his hard face. It looked dangerous. "Did she, Daddy?"

"Yes," he said with icy contempt. "Yes, she used to live here. Well, we'll see how Miss Hayes handles herself with another adult," he added.

He went to the telephone and picked it up and dialed the principal of the Bighorn Elementary School.

Mrs. Jameson was surprised to hear Powell Long on the other end of the phone. She'd never known him to interfere in school matters before, even when Maggie was up to her teeth in trouble with another student.

"I want to know why you permit an educator to tell a child that she's lazy and stupid," he demanded.

There was a long pause. "I beg your pardon?" the principal asked, shocked.

"Maggie said that Miss Hayes told her she was lazy and stupid," he said shortly. "I want that teacher talked to, and talked to hard. I don't want to have to come up there myself. Is that clear?"

Mrs. Jameson knew Powell Long. She was intimidated enough to agree that she'd speak to Antonia on Monday.

And she did. Reluctantly.

"I had a call from Maggie Long's father Friday afternoon after you left," Mrs. Jameson told Antonia, who was sitting rigidly in front of her in her office. "I don't believe for a minute that you'd deliberately make insulting remarks to that child. Heaven knows, every teacher in this school except Mrs. Donalds has had trouble with her, although Mr. Long has never interfered. It's puzzling that he would intervene, and that Maggie would say such things about you."

"I haven't called her stupid," Antonia said evenly. "I have told her that if she refuses to do her homework and write down the answers on tests, she will be given a failing grade. I've never made a policy of giving undeserved marks, or playing favorites."

"I'm sure you haven't," Mrs. Jameson replied. "Your record in Tucson is spotless. I even spoke to your principal there, who was devastated to have lost you. He speaks very highly of your intelligence and your competence."

"I'm glad. But I don't know what to do about Maggie," she continued. "She doesn't like me. I'm sorry about that, but I don't know what I can do to change her attitude. If she could only be helpful like her friend Julie," she added. "Julie is a first-rate little student."

"Everyone loves Julie," the principal agreed. She folded her hands on her desk. "I have to ask you this, Antonia. Is it possible that unconsciously you might be taking out old hurts on Maggie? I know that you were engaged to her father once.... It's a small town," she added apologetically when Antonia stiffened, "and one does hear gossip. I also know that Maggie's mother broke you up and spread some pretty terrible lies about you in the community."

"There are people who still don't think they were lies," Antonia replied tersely. "My mother eventually died because of the pressure and censure the community put on her because of them."

"I'm sorry. I didn't know that."

"She had a bad heart. I left town, to keep the talk to a minimum, but she never got over it." Her head lifted, and she forced a weak smile. "I was innocent of everything I had been accused of, but I paid the price anyway."

Mrs. Jameson looked torn. "I shouldn't have brought it up."

"Yes, you should," Antonia replied. "You had the right to know if I was deliberately persecuting a student. I despised Sally for what she did to me, and I have no more love for Maggie's father

than for his late wife. But I hope I'm not such a
bad person that I'd try to make a child suffer for
something she didn't do."

"Nor do I believe you would, consciously,"
Mrs. Jameson replied. "It's a touchy situation,
though. Mr. Long has enormous influence in the
community. He's quite wealthy and his temper is
legendary in these parts. He has no compunction
about making scenes in public, and he threatened
to come up here himself if this situation isn't re-
solved." She laughed a little unsteadily. "Miss
Hayes, I'm forty-five years old. I've worked hard
all my life to achieve my present status. It would
be very difficult for me to find another job if I lost
this one, and I have an invalid husband to support and a son in college. I plead with you not to
put my job in jeopardy."

"I never would do that," Antonia promised.
"I'd quit before I'd see an innocent person hurt by
my actions. But Mr. Long is very wrong about the
way his daughter is being treated. In fact, she's
causing the problems. She refuses to do her work
and she knows that I can't force her to."

"She certainly does. She'll go to her father,
and he'll light fires under members of the school
board. I believe at least one of them owes him
money, in fact, and the other three are afraid of
him." She cleared her throat. "I'll tell you flat that
I'm afraid of him, myself."

"No freedom of speech in these parts, I gather?"

"If your freedom impinges on his prejudices, no, there isn't," Mrs. Jameson agreed. "He's something of a tyrant in his way. We certainly can't fault him for being concerned about his child, though."

"No," Antonia agreed. She sighed. Her own circumstances were tenuous, to say the least. She had her own problems and fear gnawed at her all the time. She wasn't afraid of Powell Long, though. She was more afraid of what lay ahead for her.

"You will try...about Maggie?" Mrs. Jameson added.

Antonia smiled. "Certainly I will. But may I come to you if the problem doesn't resolve itself and ask for help?"

"If there's any to give, you may." She grimaced. "I have my own doubts about Maggie's cooperation. And we both have a lot to lose if her father isn't happy."

"Do you want me to pass her anyway?" Antonia asked. "To give her grades she hasn't earned, because her father might be upset if she fails?"

Mrs. Jameson flushed. "I can't tell you to do that, Miss Hayes. We're supposed to educate children, not pass them through favoritism."

"I know that," Antonia said.

"But you wondered if I did," came the dry reply. "Yes, I do. But I'm job scared. When you're my age, Miss Hayes," she added gently, "I can guarantee that you will be, too."

Antonia's eyes were steady and sad. She knew that she might never have the problem; she might not live long enough to have it. She thanked Mrs. Jameson and went back to her classroom, morose and dejected.

Maggie watched her as she sat down at her desk and instructed the class to proceed with their English lesson. She didn't look very happy. Her father must have shaken them up, Maggie thought victoriously. Well, she wasn't going to do that homework or do those tests. And when she failed, her father would come storming up here, because he never doubted his little girl's word. He'd have Miss Hayes on the run in no time. Then maybe Mrs. Donalds would have her baby and come back, and everything would be all right again. She glared at Julie, who just ignored her. She was sick of Julie, kissing up to Miss Hayes. Julie was a real sap. Maggie wasn't sure who she disliked more—Julie or Miss Hayes.

There was one nice touch, and that was that Miss Hayes coolly told her that she had until Friday to turn in her essay and the other homework that Antonia had assigned the class.

The next four days went by, and Antonia asked for homework papers to be turned in that she'd assigned at the beginning of the week. Maggie didn't turn hers in.

"You'll get a zero if you don't have all of it by this afternoon, including the essay you owe me," Antonia told her, dreading the confrontation she knew was coming, despite all her hopes. She'd done her best to treat Maggie just like the other students, but the girl challenged her at every turn.

"No, I won't," Maggie said with a surly smile. "If you give me a zero, I'll tell my daddy, and he'll come up here."

Antonia studied the sullen little face. "And you think that frightens me?"

"Everybody's scared of my dad," she returned proudly.

"Well, I'm not," Antonia said coldly. "Your father can come up here if he likes and I'll tell him the same thing I've told you. If you don't do the work, you don't pass. And there's nothing he can do about it."

"Oh, really?"

Antonia nodded. "Oh, really. And if you don't turn in your homework by the time the final bell sounds, you'll find out."

"So will you," Maggie replied.

Antonia refused to argue with the child. But when the end of class came and Maggie didn't turn the homework in, she put a zero neatly next to the child's name.

"Take this paper home, please," she told the child, handing her a note with her grade on it.

Maggie took it. She smiled. And she didn't say a word as she went out the door. Miss Hayes didn't know that her daddy was picking her up today. But she was about to find out.

Antonia had chores to finish before she could go home. She didn't doubt that Powell would be along. But she wasn't going to back down. She had nothing to lose now. Even her job wasn't that important if it meant being blackmailed by a nine-year-old.

Sure enough, it was only minutes since class was dismissed and she was clearing her desk when she heard footsteps coming down the hall. Only a handful of teachers would still be in the building, but those particular steps were heavy and forceful, and she knew who they belonged to.

She turned as the door opened and a familiar tall figure came into the room with eyes as dark as death.

He didn't remove his hat, or exchange greetings. In his expensive suit and boots and Stetson, he looked very prosperous. But her eyes were seeing a younger man, a ragged and lonely young man who never fit in anywhere, who dreamed of not being poor. Sometimes she remembered that young man and loved him with a passion that even in dreams was overpowering.

"I've been expecting you," she said, putting the past away in the back drawers of her mind. "She did get a zero, and she deserved it. I gave her all week to produce her homework, and she didn't."

"Oh, hell, you don't have to pretend noble motives. I know why you're picking on the kid. Well, lay off Maggie," he said shortly. "You're here to teach, not to take out old grudges on my daughter."

She was sitting at her desk. She folded her hands together on its worn surface and simply stared at him, unblinking. "Your daughter is going to fail this grade," she said composedly. "She won't participate in class discussions, she won't do any homework, and she refuses to even attempt answers on pop tests. I'm frankly amazed that she's managed to get this far in school at all." She smiled coldly. "I understand from the principal, who is also intimidated by you, that you have the influence to get anyone fired who doesn't pass her."

His face went rigid. "I don't need to use any influence! She's a smart child."

She opened her desk drawer, took out Maggie's last test paper and slid it across the desk to him. "Really?" she asked.

He moved into the classroom, to the desk. His lean, dark hand shot down to retrieve the paper. He looked at it with narrow, deep-set eyes, black eyes that were suddenly piercing on Antonia's face.

"She didn't write anything on this," he said.

She nodded, taking it back. "She sat with her arms folded, giving me a haughty smile the whole time, and she didn't move a muscle for the full thirty minutes."

"She hasn't acted that way before."

"I wouldn't know. I'm new here."

He stared at her angrily. "And you don't like her."

She searched his cold eyes. "You really think I came all the way back to Wyoming to take out old resentments on Sally's daughter?" she asked, and hated the guilt she felt when she asked the question. She knew she wasn't being fair to Maggie, but the very sight of the child was like torture.

"Sally's and mine," he reminded her, as if he knew how it hurt her to remember.

She felt sick to her stomach. "Excuse me. Sally's and yours," she replied obligingly.

He nodded slowly. "Yes, that's what really bothers you, isn't it?" he said, almost to himself. "It's because she looks just like Sally."

"She's her image," she agreed flatly.

"And you still hate her, after all this time."

Her hands clenched together. She didn't drop her gaze. "We were talking about your daughter."

"Maggie."

"Yes."

"You can't even bring yourself to say her name, can you?" He perched himself on the edge of her desk. "I thought teachers were supposed to be impartial, to teach regardless of personal feelings toward their students."

"We are."

"You aren't doing it," he continued. He smiled, but it wasn't the sort of smile that comforted. "Let me tell you something, Antonia. You came home. But this is my town. I own half of it, and I know everybody on the school board. If you want to stay here, and teach here, you'd better be damn sure that you maintain an impartial attitude toward all the students."

"Especially toward your daughter?" she asked.

He nodded. "I see you understand."

"I won't treat her unfairly, but I won't play favorites, either," she said icily. "She's going to receive no grades that she doesn't earn in my classroom. If you want to get me fired, go ahead."

"Oh, hell, I don't want your job," he said abruptly. "It doesn't matter to me if you stay here with your father. I don't even care why you suddenly came back. But I won't have my daughter persecuted for something that she didn't do! She has nothing to do with the past."

"Nothing?" Her eyes glittered up into his. "Sally was pregnant with that child when you married her, and she was born seven months later," she said huskily, and the pain was a living, breathing thing. Even the threat of leukemia wasn't that bad. "You were sleeping with Sally while you were swearing eternal devotion to me!"

Antonia didn't have to be a math major to arrive at the difference. He'd married Sally less than a month after he broke up with Antonia, and Maggie was born seven months later. Which meant that Sally was pregnant when they married.

He took a slow, steady breath, but his eyes, his face, were terrible to see. He stared down at her as if he'd like to throw something.

Antonia averted her gaze to the desk, where her hands were so tightly clasped now that the knuckles were white. She relaxed them, so that he wouldn't notice how tense she was.

"I shouldn't have said that," she said after a minute. "I had no right. Your marriage was your own business, and so is your daughter. I won't be unkind to her. But I will expect her to do the same work I assign to the other students, and if she doesn't, she'll be graded accordingly."

He stood up and shoved his hands into his pockets. The eyes that met hers were unreadable. "Maggie's paid a higher price than you know already," he said enigmatically. "I won't let you hurt her."

"I'm not in the habit of taking out my personal feelings on children, whatever you think of me."

"You're twenty-seven now," he said, surprising her. "Yet you're still unmarried. You have no children of your own."

She smiled evenly. "Yes. I had a lucky escape."

"And no inclination to find someone else? Make a life for yourself?"

"I have a life," she said, and the fear came up into her mouth as she realized that she might not have it for much longer.

"Do you?" he asked. "Your father will die one day. Then you'll be alone."

Her eyes, full of fear, fell to the desk again. "I've been alone for a long time," she said quietly. "It's something…one learns to live with."

He didn't speak. After a minute, she heard his voice, as if from a distance. "Why did you come back?"

"For my father."

"He's getting better day by day. He didn't need you."

She looked up, searching his face, seeing the young man she'd loved in his dark eyes, his sensuous mouth. "Maybe I needed someone," she said. She winced and dropped her eyes.

He laughed. It had an odd sound. "Just don't turn your attention toward me, Antonia. You may need someone. I don't. Least of all you."

Before she could say a word, he'd gone out the door, as quietly as he'd come in.

Maggie was waiting at the door when he walked in. He'd taken her home before he had his talk with Antonia.

"Did you see her? Did you tell her off?" she

asked excitedly. "I knew you'd show her who's boss!"

His eyes narrowed. She hadn't shown that much enthusiasm for anything in years. "What about that homework?"

She shrugged. "It was stupid stuff. She wanted us to write an essay about ourselves and do math problems and make up sentences to go with spelling words."

He scowled. "You mean, you didn't do it—any of it?"

"You told her I didn't have to, didn't you?" she countered.

He tossed his hat onto the side table in the hall and his eyes flashed at her. "Did you do any of the homework?"

"Well…no," she muttered. "It was stupid, I told you."

"Damn it! You lied!"

She backed up. She didn't like the way he was looking at her. He frightened her when he looked that way. He made her feel guilty. She didn't lie as a rule, but this was different. Miss Hayes was hurting her, so didn't she have the right to hurt back?

"You'll do that homework, do you hear me?" he demanded. "And the next time you have a test, you won't sit through it with your arms folded. Is that clear?"

She compressed her lips. "Yes, Daddy."

"My God." He bit off the words, staring at her furiously. "You're just like your mother, aren't you? Well, this is going to stop right now. No more lies—ever!"

"But, Daddy, I don't lie…!"

He didn't listen. He just turned and walked away. Maggie stared after him with tears burning her eyes, her small fists clenched at her sides. Just like her mother. That's what Mrs. Bates said when she misbehaved. She knew that her father hadn't cared about her mother. Her mother had cried because of it, when she drank so much. She'd said that she told a lie and Powell had hated her for it. Did this mean that he hated Maggie, too?

She followed him out into the hall. "Daddy!" she cried.

"What?"

He turned, glaring at her.

"She doesn't like me!"

"Have you tried cooperating with her?" he replied coldly.

She shrugged, averting her eyes so that he wouldn't see the tears and the pain in them. She was used to hiding her hurts in this cold house. She went up the staircase to her room without saying anything else.

He watched her walk away with a sense of hopelessness. His daughter had used him to get back at her teacher, and he'd let her. He'd gone flaming over to the school and made all sorts of accusations and charges, and Antonia had been the innocent party. He was furious at having been so gullible. It was because he didn't really know the child, he imagined. He spent as little time with her as possible, because she was a walking, talking reminder of his failed marriage.

Next time, he promised himself, he'd get his facts straight before he started attacking teachers. But he wasn't sorry about what he'd said to Antonia. Let her stew on those charges. Maybe it would intimidate her enough that she wouldn't deliberately hurt Maggie. He knew how she felt about Sally, he couldn't help but know. Her resentments were painfully visible in her thin face.

He wondered why she'd come back to haunt him. He'd almost pushed her to the back of his mind over the years. Almost. He'd gone to see her father finally to get news of her, because the loneliness he felt was eating into him like acid. He'd wondered, for one insane moment, if there was any chance that they might recapture the magic they'd had together when she was eighteen.

But she'd quickly disabused him of any such fancies. Her attitude was cold and hard and uncaring. She seemed to have frozen over in the years she'd been away.

How could he blame her? All of Antonia's misfortunes could be laid at his door, because he was distrustful of people, because he'd jumped to conclusions, because he hadn't believed in Antonia's basic innocence and decency. One impulsive decision had cost him everything he held dear. He wondered sometimes how he could have been so stupid.

Like today when he'd let Maggie stampede him into attacking Antonia for something she hadn't done. It was just like old times. Sally's daughter was already a master manipulator, at age nine. And it seemed that he was just as impulsive and dim as he'd ever been. He hadn't really changed at all. He was just richer.

Meanwhile, there was Antonia's reappearance and her disturbing thinness and paleness. She looked unwell. He wondered absently if she'd had some bout with disease. Perhaps that was why she'd come home, and not because of her father at all. But, wouldn't a warm climate be the prescription for most illnesses that caused problems? Surely no doctor sent her into northern Wyoming in winter.

He had no answers for those questions, and it would do him well to stop asking them, he thought irritably. It was getting him nowhere. The past was dead. He had to let it go, before it destroyed his life all over again.

Chapter 5

Antonia didn't move for a long time after Powell left the classroom. She stared blindly at her clasped hands. Of course she knew that he didn't want her. Had she been unconsciously hoping for something different? And even if she had, she realized, there was no future at all in that sort of thinking.

She got up, cleared her desk, picked up her things and went home. She didn't have time to sit and groan, even silently. She had to use her time wisely. She had a decision to make.

While she cooked supper for her father and herself, she thought about everything she'd wanted to do that she'd never made time for. She hadn't traveled, which had been a very early dream. She hadn't been involved in church or community, she hadn't planned past the next day except to make up lesson plans for her classes. She'd more or less drifted along, assuming that she had forever. And now the line was drawn and she was close to walking across it.

Her deepest regret was losing Powell. Looking back, she wondered what might have happened if she'd challenged Sally, if she'd dared Powell to prove that she'd been two-timing him with her mother's old suitor. She'd only been eighteen, very much in love and trusting and full of dreams. It would have served her better to have been suspicious and hard-hearted, at least where Sally was concerned. She'd never believed that her best friend would stab her in the back. How silly of her not to realize that strongest friends make the best enemies; they always know where the weaknesses are hidden.

Antonia's weakness had been her own certainty that Powell loved her as much as she loved him, that nothing could separate them. She hadn't counted on Sally's ability as an actress.

Powell had never said that he loved Antonia. How strange, she thought, that she hadn't realized that until they'd gone their separate ways. Powell had been ardent, hungry for her, but never out of control. No wonder, she thought bitterly, since he'd obviously been sleeping with Sally the whole time. Why should he have been wild for any women when he was having one on the side?

He'd asked Antonia to marry him. Her par-

ents had been respected in the community, something his own parents hadn't been. He'd enjoyed
being connected to Antonia's parents and enjoyed
the overflow of their acceptance by local people in the church and community. He'd spent as
much time with them as he had with Antonia.
And when he talked about building up his little
cattle ranch that he'd inherited from his father, it
had been her own father who'd advised him and
opened doors for him so that he could get loans,
financing. On the strength of his father's weakness for gambling, nobody would have loaned
Powell the price of a theater ticket. But Antonia's
father was a different proposition; he was an honest man with no visible vices.

Antonia had harbored no suspicions that an
ambitious man might take advantage of an un-
tried girl in his quest for wealth. Now, from her
vantage point of many years, she could look back
and see the calculation that had led to Powell's
proposal of marriage. He hadn't wanted Antonia
with any deathless passion. He'd wanted her father's influence. With it, he'd built a pitiful little
fifty-acre ranch into a multimillion-dollar enter-
prise of purebred cattle and land. Perhaps breaking the engagement was all part of his master
plan, too. Once he'd had what he wanted from
the engagement, he could marry the woman he
really loved—Sally.

It wouldn't have surprised Antonia to discover

that Sally had worked hand in glove with Powell to help him achieve his goals. The only odd thing was that he hadn't been happy with Sally, from all accounts, nor she with him.

She wondered why she hadn't considered that angle all those years ago. Probably the heartbreak of her circumstances had blinded her to any deeper motives. Now it seemed futile and unreal. Powell was ancient history. She had to let go of the past. Somehow, she had to forgive and forget. It would be a pity to carry the hatred and resentment to her grave.

Grave. She stared into the pan that contained the stir-fry she was making for supper. She'd never thought about where she wanted to rest for eternity. She had insurance, still in effect, although it wasn't much. And she'd always thought that she'd rest beside her mother in the small Methodist church cemetery. Now she had to get those details finalized, just in case the treatment wasn't successful—if she decided to have it—and without her father knowing. He wasn't going to be told until the last possible minute.

She finished preparing supper and called her father to the table, careful to talk about mundane things and pretend to be happy at being home again.

But he wasn't fooled. His keen eyes probed her face. "Something's upset you. What is it?"

She grimaced. "Maggie Long," she said, side-stepping the real issue.

"I see. Just like her father when he was a kid, I hear," he added. "Little hellion, isn't she?"

"Only to me," Antonia mused. "She liked Mrs. Donalds."

"No wonder," he replied, finishing his coffee. "Mrs. Donalds was one of Sally's younger cousins. So Maggie was related to her. She petted the kid, gave her special favors, did everything but give her answers to tests. She was teacher's pet. First time any teacher treated her that way, so I guess it went to her head."

"How do you know?"

"It's a small town, girl," he reminded her with a chuckle. "I know everything." He stared at her levelly. "Even that Powell came to see you at school this afternoon. Gave you hell about the kid, didn't he?"

She shifted in her chair. "I won't give her special favors," she muttered. "I don't care if he does get me fired."

"He'll have a hard time doing that," her father said easily. "I have friends on the school board, too."

"Perhaps they could switch the girl to another class," she wondered aloud.

"It would cause gossip," Ben Hayes said. "There's been enough of that already. You just stick to your guns and don't give in. She'll come around eventually."

"I wouldn't bet on it," she said heavily. She ran a hand over her blond hair. "I'm tired," she added with a wan smile. "Do you mind if I go to bed early?"

"Of course not." He looked worried. "I thought you went to see the doctor. Didn't he give you something to perk you up?"

"He said I need vitamins," she lied glibly. "I bought some, but they haven't had time to take effect. I need to eat more, too, he said."

He was still scowling. "Well, if you don't start getting better soon, you'd better go back and let him do some tests. It isn't natural for a woman your age to be so tired all the time."

Her heart skipped. Of course it wasn't, but she didn't want him to suspect that she was so ill.

"I'll do that," she assured him. She got up and collected the plates. "I'll just do these few dishes and then I'll leave you to your television."

"Oh, I hate that stuff," he said. "I'd much rather read in the evenings. I only keep the thing on for the noise."

She laughed. "I do the same thing in Tucson," she confessed. "It's company, anyway."

"Yes, but I'd much rather have you here," he confessed. "I'm glad you came home, Antonia. It's not so lonely now."

She had a twinge of conscience at the pleasure

he betrayed. He'd lost her mother and now he was going to lose her. How would he cope, with no relatives left in the world? Her mother had been an only child, and her father's one sister had died of cancer years ago. Antonia bit her lip. He was in danger of losing his only child, and she was too cowardly to tell him.

He patted her on the shoulder. "Don't you do too much in here. Get an early night. Leave those if you want, and I'll wash them later."

"I don't mind," she protested, grinning. "I'll see you in the morning, then."

"Don't wake me up when you leave," he called over his shoulder. "I'm sleeping late."

"Lucky devil," she called back.

He only laughed, leaving her to the dishes.

She finished them and went to bed. But she didn't sleep. She lay awake, seeing Maggie Long's surly expression and hating eyes, and Powell's unwelcoming scrutiny. They'd both love to see her back in Arizona, and it looked as if they were going to do their combined best to make her life hell if she stayed here. She'd be walking on eggshells for the rest of the school year with Maggie, and if she failed the child for not doing her homework, Powell would be standing in her classroom every day to complain.

She rolled over with a sigh. Things had been so uncomplicated when she was eighteen, she thought wistfully. She'd been in love and looking forward to marriage and children. Her eyes closed on a wave of pain. Maggie would have been her child, her daughter. She'd have had blond hair and gray eyes, perhaps, like Antonia. And if she'd been Antonia's child, she'd have been loved and wanted and cared for. She wouldn't have a surly expression and eyes that hated.

Powell had said something about Maggie... what was it? That Maggie had paid a higher price than any of them. What had he meant? Surely he cared for the child. He certainly fought hard enough when he felt she was attacked.

Well, it wasn't her problem, she decided finally. And she wasn't going to let it turn into her problem. She still hadn't decided what to do about her other problem.

Julie was the brightest spot in Antonia's days. The little girl was always cheerful, helpful, doing whatever she could to smooth Antonia's path and make it easy for her to teach the class. She remembered where Mrs. Donalds had kept things, she knew what material had been covered and she was always eager to do anything she was asked.

Maggie on the other hand was resentful and ice-cold. She did nothing voluntarily. She was still refusing to turn in her homework. Talking to her did no good. She just glared back.

"I'll give you one more chance to make up this work," Antonia told her at the end of her second week teaching the class. "If you don't turn it in Monday, you'll get another zero."

Maggie smiled haughtily. "And my daddy will cuss you out again. I'll tell him you slapped me, too."

Antonia's gray eyes glittered at the child. "You would, wouldn't you?" she asked coldly. "I don't doubt that you can lie, Maggie. Well, go ahead. See how much damage you can do."

Maggie's reaction was unexpected. Tears filled her blue eyes and she shivered.

She whirled and ran out of the classroom, leaving Antonia deflated and feeling badly for the child. She clenched her hands on the desk to keep them from shaking. How could she have been so hateful and cold?

She cleaned up the classroom, waiting for Powell to storm in and give her hell. But he didn't show up. She went home and spent a nerve-rackingly quiet weekend with her father, waiting for an explosion that didn't come.

The biggest surprise arrived Monday morning, when Maggie shoved a crumpled, stained piece of paper on the desk and walked back to her seat without looking at Antonia. It was messy, but it was the missing homework. Not only that, it was done correctly.

Antonia didn't say a word. It was a small victory, of sorts. She wouldn't admit to herself that she was pleased. But the paper got an A.

* * *

Julie began to sit with her at recess, and shared cupcakes and other tidbits that her mother had sent to school with her.

"Mom says you're doing a really nice job on me, Miss Hayes," Julie said. "Dad remembers you from school, did you know? He said you were a sweet girl, and that you were shy. Were you, really?"

Antonia laughed. "I'm afraid so. I remember your father, too. He was the class clown."

"Dad? Really?"

"Really. Don't tell him I told you, though, okay?" she teased, smiling at the child.

From a short distance away, Maggie glared toward them. She was, as usual, alone. She didn't get along with the other children. The girls hated her, and the boys made fun of her skinny legs that were always bruised and cut from her tomboyish antics at the ranch. There was one special boy, Jake Weldon. Maggie pretended not to notice him. He was one of the boys who made fun of her, and it hurt really bad. She was alone most of the time these days, because Julie spent her time with the teacher instead of Maggie.

Miss Hayes liked Julie. Everyone knew it, too. Julie had been Maggie's best friend, but now she seemed to be Miss Hayes's. Maggie hated both of them. She hadn't told her father what Miss Hayes had said about her homework. She wanted her teacher to know that she wasn't bad like her mother. She knew what her mother had done, because she'd heard them talking about it once. She remembered her mother crying and accusing him of not loving her, and him saying that she'd ruined his life, she and her premature baby. There had been something else, something about him being drunk and out of his mind or Maggie wouldn't have been born at all.

It hadn't made sense then. But when she was older, she'd heard him say the same thing to the housekeeper, that Maggie had been born prematurely.

After that, she'd stopped listening. That was when she knew her father didn't love her. That was when she'd stopped trying to make him notice her by being good.

Her daddy knew Miss Hayes. She heard him tell the housekeeper that Antonia had come to Bighorn to make his life miserable and that he didn't want her here. If she'd been able to talk to Miss Hayes, she'd have told her that her father hated both of them, and that it made them sort of related.

She wondered if her dad hadn't wanted to marry her mother, and why he had. Maybe it had something to do with why her daddy hated her. People had said that Sally didn't love her little child, that Maggie was just the rope she'd used to tie up Powell Long with. Maybe they were right,

because her mother never spent any time doing
things with her. She never liked Maggie, either.

She slid down against the tree into the dirt,
getting her jeans filthy. Mrs. Bates, the housekeeper, would rage and fuss about that, and she
didn't care. Mrs. Bates had thrown away most of
her clothes, complaining that they were too dirty
to come clean. She hadn't told her dad. When she
ran out of clothes, maybe somebody would notice.

She wished Mrs. Bates liked her. Julie did,
when she wasn't fawning over teachers to make
them give her special privileges. She liked Julie,
she did, but Julie was a kiss-up. Sometimes she
wondered why she let Julie be her friend at all.
She didn't need any friends. She could make it
all by herself. She'd show them all that she was
somebody special. She'd make them love her one
day. She sighed and closed her eyes. Oh, if only
she knew Julie's secret; if only she knew how to
make people like her.

"There's Maggie," Julie commented, grimacing as she glanced toward her friend. "Nobody
likes her except me," she confided to Miss Hayes.
"She beats up the boys and she can bat and catch
better than any of them, so they don't like her.
And the girls think she's too rough to play with.
I sort of feel sorry for her. She says her daddy
doesn't like her. He's always going away somewhere. She stays with us when he's gone, only
she doesn't want to this week because—" She

stopped, as if she was afraid she'd already said too much.

"Because?" Antonia prompted curiously.

"Oh, nothing," Julie said. She couldn't tell Miss Hayes that she'd fought with Maggie over their new teacher. "Anyway, Maggie mostly stays with us if her dad's away longer than overnight."

Involuntarily, Antonia glanced toward the child and found her watching them with those cold, sullen eyes. The memories came flooding back—Sally jealous of Antonia's pretty face, jealous of Antonia's grades, jealous of Antonia having any other girlfriends, jealous…of her with Powell.

She shivered faintly and looked away from the child. God forgive her, it was just too much. She wondered if she could possibly get Maggie transferred to another class. If she couldn't then there was no other option. The only teaching job available was the one she had. She couldn't wait for another opening. Her eyes closed. She was running out of time. Why, she asked herself, why was she wasting it like this? She'd told herself she was coming home to cope with her memories, but they were too much for her. She couldn't fight the past. She couldn't even manage to get through the present. She had to consider how she would face the future.

"Miss Hayes?"

Her eyes opened. Julie was looking worried. "Are you all right?" the little girl asked, concerned.

"I'm tired, that's all," Antonia said, smiling. "We'd better go in now."

She called the class and led them back into the building.

Maggie was worse than ever for the rest of the day. She talked back, refused to do a chore assigned to her, ignored Antonia when she was called on in class. And at the end of the day, she waited until everyone else left and came back into the room, to stand glaring at Antonia from the doorway.

"My dad says he wishes you'd go away and never come back," she said loudly. "He says you make his life miserable, and that he can't stand the sight of you! He says you make him sick!"

Antonia's face flushed and she looked stunned.

Maggie turned and ran out the door. Her father had said something like that, to himself, and it made her feel much better that she'd told Miss Hayes about it. That had made her look sick, all right! And it wasn't a lie. Well, not a real lie. It was just something to make her feel as bad as Maggie had felt when Miss Hayes looked at her on the playground and shuddered. She knew the teacher didn't like her. She didn't care. She didn't like Miss Hayes, either.

* * *

Maggie was smug the next day. She didn't have any more parting shots for Antonia, and she did her work in class. But she refused to do her homework, again, and dared Antonia to give her a zero. She even dared her to send a note home to her father.

Antonia wanted to call her bluff, but she was feeling sicker by the day and it was increasingly hard for her to get up in the mornings and go to work at all. The illness was progressing much more quickly than she'd foreseen. And Maggie was making her life hell.

For the rest of the week, Antonia thought about the possibility of getting Maggie moved out of her class. Surely she could approach the principal in confidence.

And that was what she did, after school.

Mrs. Jameson smiled ruefully when Antonia sat down beside her desk and hesitated.

"You're here about Maggie Long again," she said at once.

Antonia's eyes widened. "Why…yes."

"I was expecting you," the older woman said with resignation. "Mrs. Donalds got along quite well with her, but she's the only teacher in the past few years who hasn't had trouble with Maggie. She's a rebel, you see. Her father travels a good deal. Maggie is left with Julie's family." She grimaced. "We heard that he was thinking of marrying again, but once that rumor started, Maggie ran away from home. She, uh, isn't keen on the widow Holton."

Antonia was wondering if anyone was keen about the widow Holton, from what she'd already heard from Barrie. It was a surprise to hear that Powell had considered marrying the woman—if it was true and not just gossip.

The principal sighed, her attention returning to the task at hand. "You want Maggie moved, I suppose. I wish I could oblige you, but we only have one fourth-grade class, because this is such a small school, and you're teaching it." She lifted her hands helplessly. "There it is. I'm really sorry. Perhaps if you spoke with her father?"

"I already have," Antonia replied calmly.

"And he said...?"

"That if I pushed him, he'd do his best to have me removed from my position here," she said bluntly.

The older woman pursed her lips. "Well, as we've already discussed, he wouldn't have to work that hard to do it. It's a rather ticklish situation. I'm sorry I can't be more optimistic."

Antonia leaned back in her seat with a long sigh. "I shouldn't have come back to Bighorn," she said, almost to herself. "I don't know why I did."

"Perhaps you were looking for something."

"Something that no longer exists," Antonia replied absently. "A lost part of my life that I won't find here."

"You are going to stay, aren't you?" Mrs. Jameson asked. "After this school term, I mean. Your students say wonderful things about you. Especially Julie Ames," she added with a grin.

"I went to school with her father," Antonia confessed. "To this school, as a matter of fact. She's just like her dad."

"I've met him, and she is a lot like him. What a pity all our students can't be as energetic and enthusiastic as our Julie."

"Yes, indeed."

"Well, I'll give you all the moral support I can," Mrs. Jameson continued. "We do have a very good school counselor. We've sent Maggie to her several times, but she won't say a word. We've had the counselor talk to Mr. Long, but he won't say a word, either. It's a difficult situation."

"Perhaps it will work itself out," Antonia replied.

"Do think about staying on," the older woman said seriously.

Antonia couldn't promise that. She forced a smile. "I'll certainly think about it," she agreed.

But once out of the principal's office, she was more depressed than ever. Maggie hated her, and obviously would not cooperate. It was only a matter of time before she had to give Maggie a failing grade for her noneffort, and Powell would either come back for some more heated words or get her fired. She didn't know if she could bear another verbal tug-of-war with him, especially after the last one. And as for getting fired, she wondered if that really mattered anymore. At the rate her health was failing, it wasn't going to matter for much longer, anyway.

She wandered back to her schoolroom and found Powell sitting on the edge of her desk, looking prosperous in a dark gray suit and a red tie, with a gray Stetson and hand-tooled leather boots that complemented his suit. He was wearing the same signet ring on his little finger that he'd worn when they were engaged, a script letter L. The ring was very simple, 10K gold and not very expensive. His mother had given it to him when he graduated from high school, and Antonia knew how hard the woman had had to work to pay for it. The Rolex watch on his left wrist was something he'd earned for himself. The Longs had never had enough money at any time in their lives to pay for a watch like that. She wondered if Powell ever thought back to those hard days of his youth.

He heard her step and turned his head to watch her enter the classroom. In her tailored beige dress, with her blond hair in a bun, she looked thinner than ever and very dignified.

"How you've changed," he remarked involuntarily.

"I was thinking the same thing about you," she said wearily. She sat down behind the desk, because just the walk to the office had made her tired. She looked up at him with the fatigue in her face. "I really need to go home. I know why you're here. She can't be moved to another class, because there isn't one. The only alternative is for me to leave...."

"That isn't why I came," he said, surprised.

"No?"

He picked up a paper clip from the desk and looked at it intently. "I thought you might have something to eat with me," he said. "We could talk about Maggie."

She was nauseated and trying not to let it overwhelm her. She barely heard him. "What?"

"I said, let's get together tonight," he repeated, frowning. "You look green. Put your head down."

She turned sideways and lowered her head to the hands resting on her knees, sucking in air. She felt nauseous more and more these days, and faint. She didn't know how much longer she was going to be mobile. The thought frightened her. She would have to make arrangements to get on with the therapy, while there was still time. It was one thing to say that dying didn't matter, but it was quite another when the prospect of it was staring her in the face.

"You're damn thin." He bit off the words. "Have you seen a doctor?"

"If one more person asks me that...!" She

erupted. She took another breath and lifted her head, fighting the dizziness as she pushed back a wisp of hair from her eyes. "Yes, I've seen a doctor. I'm just run-down. It's been a hard year."

"Yes, I know," he said absently, watching her.

She met his concerned eyes. If she'd been less feeble, she might have wondered at the expression in them. As it was, she was too tired to care.

"Maggie's been giving everyone fits," he said unexpectedly. "I know you're having trouble with her. I thought if we put our heads together, we might come up with some answers."

"I thought my opinion didn't matter," she replied dully.

He averted his gaze. "I've had a lot on my mind," he said noncommittally. "Of course your opinion matters. We need to talk."

She wanted to ask what good he thought it would do to talk, when he'd told his daughter that he was sick of Miss Hayes and wanted her out of town because she was making his life miserable. She wasn't going to mention that. It would be like tattling. But it hurt more than anything else had in recent days.

"Well?" he persisted impatiently.

"Very well. What time shall I meet you, and where?"

The question seemed to surprise him. "I'll pick you up at your home, of course," he said. "About six."

She really should refuse. She looked into his

dark eyes and knew that she couldn't. One last date, she was thinking sadly. She could have one last date with him before the ordeal began....

She managed a smile. "All right."

He watched her sort out the papers on her desk and put them away methodically. His eyes were on her hands, on the unusual thinness of them. She looked unwell. Her mother's death surely had affected her, but this seemed much more than worry. She was all but skeletal.

"I'll see you at six," she said when she'd put up the classroom and walked out into the hall with him.

He looked down at her, noting her frailty, her slenderness. He still towered over her, as he had years before. She was twenty-seven, but his eyes saw a vivacious, loving girl of eighteen. What had happened to change her whole personality so drastically? She was an old soul in a young body. Had he caused all that?

She glanced up at him curiously. "Was there something else?"

He shrugged. "Maggie showed me an A on her homework paper."

"I didn't give her the grade," she replied. "She earned it. It was good work."

He stuck his hands into his pockets. "She has a bright mind, when she wants to use it." His eyes narrowed. "I said some harsh things the last time I was here. Now's as good a time as any to apologize. I was out of line." He couldn't go further and admit that Maggie had lied to him. He was still raw, as Antonia surely was, about Sally's lies. It was too much to admit that his daughter was a liar as well.

"Most parents who care about their children would have challenged a zero," she said noncommittally.

"I haven't been much of a parent," he said abruptly. "I'll see you at six."

She watched him with sad eyes as he walked away, the sight of his long back reminding her poignantly of the day he'd ended their engagement.

He paused at the door, sensing her eyes, and he turned unexpectedly to stare at her. It was so quick that she didn't have time to disguise her grief. He actually winced, because he knew that she'd looked like that nine years ago. He hadn't looked back, so he hadn't known.

She drew in a steadying breath and composed her features. She didn't say anything. There was nothing to say that he hadn't already read in her face.

He started to speak, but apparently he couldn't find the words, either.

"At six," she repeated.

He nodded, and this time he went through the doorway.

Chapter 6

Antonia went through every dress she had in her closet before she settled on a nice but simple black crepe dress with short sleeves and a modest neckline. It reached just below her knees and although it had once fit her very nicely, it now hung on her. She had nothing that looked the right size. But it was cold and she could wear a coat over it, the one good leather one she'd bought last season on sale. It would cover the dress and perhaps when she was seated, it wouldn't look so big on her. She paired the dress with a thin black leather belt, gold stud earrings and a small gold cross that her mother had given her when she graduated from high school. She wore no other jewelry, except for the serviceable watch on her wrist. She saw the engagement ring that Powell had bought for her, a very modest little diamond in a thin gold setting. She'd sent it back to him, but he'd refused to accept it from her father. It had found its way back to her, and she kept it here in her jewelry box, the only keepsake she had except for the small cross she always wore.

She picked the ring up and looked at it with sad gray eyes. How different her life, and Powell's, might have been if he hadn't jumped to conclusions and she hadn't run away.

She put the ring back into the box, into the past, where it belonged, and closed it up. This would be the last time she'd go out with Powell. He only wanted to talk about Maggie. If he was serious about the widow Holton, of whom she'd heard so much, then this would certainly not be an occasion he'd want to repeat. And even if he asked, Antonia knew that she would have to refuse a second evening out with him. Her heart was still all too vulnerable. But for tonight, she took special care with her makeup and left her blond hair long around her shoulders. Even thin, she looked good. She hoped Powell would think so.

She sat in the living room with her curious but silent father, waiting for the clock to chime six. He had ten minutes left to make it on time. Powell had been very punctual in the old days. She wondered if he still was.

"Nervous?" her father asked gently.

She smiled and nodded. "I don't know why he

wanted to take me out to talk about Maggie. We could have talked here, or at school."

He smoothed a hand over his boot, crossed over his other leg. "Maybe he's trying to make things up with you."

"I doubt that," she replied. "I hear he's been spending time with the widow Holton...."

"So has Dawson. But love isn't the reason. They both want her south pasture. It borders on both of theirs."

"Oh. Everybody says she's very pretty."

"So she is. But Dawson won't have anything to do with women in a romantic way, and Powell is playing her along."

"I heard that he was talking marriage."

"Did you?" He frowned. "Well...that's surprising."

"Mrs. Jameson said his daughter ran away when she thought he was going to marry Mrs. Holton."

Her father shook his head. "I'm not surprised. That child doesn't get along with anyone. She'll end up in jail one day if he doesn't keep a better eye on her."

She traced a pattern in the black crepe purse that matched her dress. "I haven't been quite fair to her," she confessed. "She's so much like Sally." She grimaced. "She must miss her."

"I doubt it. Her mother left her with any available babysitter and stayed on the road until the drinking started taking its toll on her. She never was much of a driver. That's probably why she went into the river."

Into the river. Antonia remembered hearing about the accident on the news. Powell had been rich enough that Sally's tragic death made head-lines. She'd felt sorry for him, but she hadn't gone to the funeral. There was no point. She and Sally had been enemies for so long. For so long.

The sound of a car in the driveway interrupted her musings. She got up and reached the door just as Powell knocked.

She felt embarrassed when she saw how he was dressed. He was wearing jeans and a flannel shirt with a heavy denim jacket and old boots. If she was surprised, so was he. She looked very elegant in that black dress and the dark leather coat she wore with it.

His face drew in sharply at the sight of her, because even in her depleted condition, she took his breath away.

"I'm running late." She improvised to explain the way she was dressed. "I've just now come back from town," she lied, redfaced. "I'll hurry and change and be ready in a jiffy. Dad can talk to you while I get ready. I'm sorry…!"

She dashed back into the bedroom and closed the door. She could have died of shame. So much for her dreams of the sort of date they'd once shared. He was dressed for a cup of coffee and a sandwich at a fast-food joint, and here she was rigged out for a restaurant. She should have asked him where they were going in the first place, and not tried to second-guess him!

She quickly changed into jeans and a sweat-shirt and put her hair up in its usual bun. At least the jeans fit her better than the dress, she thought dryly.

Powell stared after her and grimaced. "I had an emergency on the ranch with a calving heifer," he murmured. "I didn't realize she'd be dressed up, so I didn't think about changing...."

"Don't make it worse," her father said curtly. "Spare her pride and go along with what she said."

He sighed heavily. "I never do the right thing, say the right thing." His dark eyes were narrow and sad. "She's the one who was hurt the most, and I just keep right on adding to the pain."

Ben Hayes was surprised at the remark, but he had no love for Powell Long. He couldn't forget the torment the man had caused his daughter, nor what Antonia had said about Powell using his influence to open financial doors for him. All Powell's pretended concern for his health hadn't changed what he thought of the man. And tonight his contempt knew no bounds. He hated seeing Antonia embarrassed like that.

"Don't keep her out long," Ben said coldly. "She isn't well."

Powell's eyes cut around to meet the older man's. "What's wrong with her?" he asked.

"Her mother's barely been dead a year," he reminded him. "Antonia misses her a lot."

"She's lost weight, hasn't she?" he asked Ben.

Ben shifted in the chair. "She'll pick back up, now that she's home." He glared at Powell. "Don't hurt her again, boy," he said evenly. "If you want to talk to her about your daughter, fine. But don't expect anything. She's still raw about the past, and I don't blame her. You were wrong and you wouldn't listen. But she's the one who had to leave town."

Powell's jaw went taut. He stared at the older man with eyes that glittered, and he didn't reply.

It was a tense silence that Antonia walked back into. Her father looked angry, and Powell looked...odd.

"I'm ready," she said, sliding into her leather coat.

Powell nodded. "We'll go to Ted's Truck Stop. It's open all night and he serves good coffee, if that suits you."

She read an insult into the remark, and flushed. "I told you I was dressed up because I'd just come back from town," she began. "Ted's suits me fine."

He was stunned by the way she emphasized

that, until he realized what he'd said. He turned on his heel and opened the front door for her. "Let's go," he said.

She told her father goodbye and went through the door. Powell closed it behind them, shutting them in the cold, snowy night. A metallic gold Mercedes-Benz was sitting in the driveway, not the four-wheel-drive vehicle he usually drove. Although it had chains to get through snow and ice, it was a luxury car and a far cry from the battered old pickup truck Powell had driven when they'd been engaged.

Flakes of snow fell heavily on the windshield as he drove the mile down the highway to Ted's, which was a bar and grill, just outside the Bighorn city limits. Ted's sold beer and wine and good food, but Antonia had never been inside the place before. It wasn't considered a socially respectable place, and she wondered if Powell had a reason for taking her there. Perhaps he was trying to emphasize the fact that this wasn't a routine date. It was to be a business discussion, but he didn't want to take her anyplace where they might be recognized. So if that was the case, maybe he really was serious about the widow Holton after all. It made her sad, even though she knew she had no future with him, or with anyone.

"You're quiet," he remarked as he pulled up in the almost deserted parking lot. It was early for

Ted's sort of trade, although a couple of tractor trailers were sitting apart in the lot.

"I suppose so," she replied.

He felt the unease about her, the muted sadness. He felt guilty about bringing her here. She'd dressed up for him, and he'd slapped her down unintentionally. He hadn't even considered that she might think of this as a date. She was as sensitive now as she had been at eighteen.

He went around the car to open her door, but she was already out of it and standing in the snow when he got there. She joined him at the fender and walked toward the bar. Her sneakers were getting wet and the snow was deep enough that it leaked in past her socks, but it didn't matter. She was so miserable already that cold feet just seemed to go with her general mood.

Powell noticed, though, and his lips compressed. It was already a bust of an evening, and it was his own damn fault.

They sat down in a booth and the waitress, a big brunette named Darla, smiled and handed them a menu.

"Just coffee for me," Antonia said with a quiet smile.

Powell's eyes flashed. "I brought you here for a meal," he reminded her firmly.

She evaded his angry eyes. "I'll have a bowl of chili, then. And coffee."

He ordered steak and salad and coffee and

handed the menu back to the waitress. He couldn't remember a time when he'd felt as helpless, or as ashamed.

"You need more than that," he said softly.

The tone of his voice brought back too many memories. They'd gone out to eat very rarely in the old days, in his old Ford pickup truck with the torn seat and broken dash. A hamburger had been a treat, but it was being together that had made their dates perfect. They'd wolf down their food and then drive out to the pasture near Powell's house. He'd shut off the engine and turn to her, and she'd go into his arms like a homing pigeon.

She could still taste those hot, deep, passionate kisses they'd shared so hungrily. It was amazing that he'd had the restraint to keep their dates innocent. She'd rushed headlong into desire with no self-preservation at all, wanting him so much that nothing else had mattered. But he'd put on the brakes, every time. That hadn't bothered her at the time. She'd thought it meant that he respected her enough to wait for the wedding ceremony. But after he'd called off the wedding and married Sally, and Maggie was born seven months later, his restraint had made a terrible sort of sense. He hadn't really wanted Antonia. He'd wanted her father's influence. She'd been too much in love to realize it.

"I said, you need to eat more than that," he repeated.

She looked up into his dark eyes with the

memories slicing through her. She swallowed. "I haven't felt too good today," she said evasively. "I'm not really hungry."

He saw the shadows under her eyes and knew that lack of sleep had certainly added to her depleted health.

"I wanted to talk to you about Maggie," he said suddenly, because it bothered him to be with Antonia and remember their old relationship. "I know she's given you problems. I hope we can work out something."

"There's nothing to work out," Antonia said. "She's done her homework. I think she'll adjust to me eventually."

"She had a lot to say about you last night," he continued, as if she hadn't spoken. "She said that you threatened to hit her."

She looked him right in the eye. "Did she?"

He waited, but she didn't offer any defense. "And she said that you told her that you hated her and that you didn't want her in your class, because she reminded you too much of her mother."

Her eyes didn't fall. It wasn't the truth, but there was enough truth in it to twist. Maggie certainly was perceptive, she thought ruefully. And Powell sat there with his convictions so plain on his lean face that he might as well have shouted them.

She knew then why he'd invited her here, to this bar. He was showing her that he thought too little of her to take her to a decent place. He was putting her down in a cold, subtle way, while he raked her over the coals of his anger for upsetting his little girl.

She managed a smile. "Does the city cab run out this far?" she asked in a tone that was tight enough to sound choked. "Then I won't even have to ask you to take me home." She started to get up, but he rose, too, and blocked her way out of the booth.

"Here it is." The waitress interrupted them, bringing steaming black coffee in two mugs. "Sorry I took so long. Is anything wrong?" she added when Powell didn't move.

"No," he said after a minute, his eyes daring Antonia to move as he sat back down. "Nothing at all. But we'll just have the coffee, if it isn't too late to change the order."

"It's all right, I'll take care of it," the waitress said quickly. She'd seen the glint of tears in Antonia's eyes, and she recognized a kindling argument when she saw one starting. She put down the cream pitcher and wrote out the check. If she was any judge of angry women, there would barely be time for them to drink their one cup each before the explosion.

She thanked them, put down the check and got out of the line of fire.

"Don't cry," Powell said through his teeth as he stared at Antonia's white face. "Don't!"

She took a steadying breath and put both hands

around the coffee cup. She stared at it instead of him, but her hands trembled.

He closed his eyes, fighting memories and prejudices and gossip and pain. He'd forgotten nothing. Forgiven nothing. Seeing her alone like this brought it all back.

She was fighting memories of her own. She lifted the coffee to her lips and burned them trying to drink it.

"Go ahead," he invited coldly. "Tell me she's lying."

"I wouldn't tell you the time of day," she said in a voice like warmed-over death. "I never learn. You said we'd discuss the problem, but this isn't a discussion, it's an inquisition. I'll tell you flat-out—I've already asked Mrs. Jameson to move Maggie out of my class. She can't do that, and the only option I have left is to quit my job and go back to Arizona."

He stared at her without speaking. He hadn't expected that.

She met his startled eyes. "Do you think she's a little angel?" she asked. "She's rebellious, haughty and she lies better than her mother ever did."

"Damn you!"

The whip of his voice made her sick inside. She reached for her purse and this time she got up. She pushed past him, and ran out into the snow with tears streaming down her face. She'd walk back to town, she would…!

Her foot slipped on a patch of ice, and she went down hard. She felt the snow on her hot face and lifted it, to the cooling moisture of fresh snow-flakes, just as a pair of steely hands jerked her back to her feet and propelled her toward the car.

She didn't react as he unlocked the door and put her inside. She didn't look at him or say a word, even when he fastened her shoulder har-ness and sat glaring at her before he finally started the car and headed it back toward town.

When they arrived at her father's house, she reached for the catch that would unfasten the har-ness, but his hand was there, waiting.

"Why can't you admit the truth?" he de-manded. "Why do you keep lying about your re-lationship with George Rutherford? He bought your wedding dress, he paid your college tuition. The whole damn town knew you were sleeping with him, but you've convinced everyone from your father to George's own son that it was per-fectly innocent! Well, you never convinced me and you never will!"

"I know that," she said without looking at him. "Let me go, Powell."

His hand only tightened. "You slept with him!" he accused through his teeth. "I would have died for you…!"

"You were sleeping with my best friend!" she

accused hotly. "You got her pregnant while you were engaged to me! Do you think I give a damn about your opinion or your feelings? You weren't jealous of George! You never even loved me! You got engaged to me so that my father's influence could get you a loan that you needed to save your family ranch!"

The accusation startled him so much that he didn't have the presence of mind to retaliate. He stared at her in the dim light from the front porch as if she'd gone mad.

"Sally's people didn't have that kind of clout," she continued, tears of anger and pain running down her cheeks like tiny silver rivers. "But mine did. You used me! The only decent thing you did was to keep from seducing me totally, but then, you didn't need to go that far, because you were already sleeping with Sally!"

He couldn't believe what he was hearing. It was the first time in his life that he'd been at a loss for words, but he was literally speechless.

"And you can accuse me of lying?" she demanded in a choked tone. "Sally lied. But you wanted to believe her because it got you out of our engagement the day before the wedding. And you still believe her, because you can't admit that I was only a means to an end for your ambition. It isn't a broken heart you're nursing, it's broken pride because you couldn't get anywhere without a woman's family name to get you a loan!"

He took a short breath. "I got that loan on my own collateral," he said angrily.

"You got it on my father's name," she countered. "Mr. Sims, the bank president, said so. He even laughed about it, about how you were already making use of your future father-in-law to help you mend your family fortunes!"

He hadn't known that. He'd put the land up for security and he'd always assumed that it had been enough. He should have realized that his father's reputation as a gambler would have made him a dangerous risk as a borrower.

"Antonia," he began hesitantly, reaching out a hand.

She slapped it away immediately. "Don't you touch me," she said hotly. "I've had the Longs to hell and back! You can take this for gospel—if your daughter doesn't study, she won't pass. And if that costs me my job, I don't care!"

She jerked open the door and got out, only to find Powell there waiting for her, dark-eyed and glowering.

"I'm not going to let you take out any sort of vengeance on Maggie," he said shortly. "And if you don't stop giving her hell because of grudges against her mother, you'll be out of a job, I promise you."

"Do your worst," she invited with soft venom, her gray eyes flashing at him. "You can't hurt me more than you already have. Very soon now, I'll be beyond the reach of any vengeance you like to pursue!"

"Think so?" With a lightning-quick movement, he jerked her against his lean, hard body and bent to her mouth.

The kiss was painful, and not just physically. He kissed her without tenderness, with nothing more than a need to punish. His tongue insinuated itself past her lips in a cold, calculating parody of sex, while his hands twisted her body against his lean hips.

She stiffened, trying to fight, but she was too weak to force him to let go. She opened her eyes and looked at him, stared at him, until he thought she'd had enough. Just at the last, he relented. His mouth became soft and slow and sensuous, teasing, testing. His hands slid up to her waist and he nibbled at her lower lip with something like tenderness. But she refused him even the semblance of response. She stood like a statue in his grasp, her eyes open, wet with tears, her mouth rigid.

When his eyes opened again, he looked oddly guilty. Her mouth was swollen and her face was very pale.

He winced. "I shouldn't have done that," he said curtly.

She laughed coldly. "No, it wasn't necessary," she agreed. "I'd already gotten the message. You held me in such contempt that you didn't even change out of your working clothes. You took me to a bar.…" She pulled away from him, a little shakily. "You couldn't have made your opinion of me any plainer."

He pushed his hat back on his head. "I didn't mean it to turn out like this," he said angrily.

"Didn't you?" She stared up at him with eyes that hated him and loved him, with eyes that would soon lose the ability to see him at all. She took a breath and it ended on a sob.

"Oh, God, don't," he groaned. He pulled her into his arms, but this time without passion, without anger. He held her against his heart with hands that protected, cherished, and she felt his lips in her hair, at her temple. "I'm sorry. I'm sorry, Annie." He bit off the words.

It was the first time he'd used the nickname he'd called her when she was eighteen. The sound of his deep voice calmed her. She let him hold her. It would be the last time. She closed her eyes and it was as if it was yesterday—she was a girl in love, and he was the beginning of her world.

"It was…so long ago," she whispered brokenly.

"A lifetime," he replied in a hushed tone. His arms cradled her and she felt his cheek move tenderly against her blond hair. "Why didn't I wait?" he whispered almost to himself, and his eyes closed. "Another day, just one more day…"

"We can't have the past back," she said. His arms were warm against the cold, and strong, comforting. She savored the glory of them around her for one last time. No matter how he felt about her, she would have this memory to take down into the dark with her.

She fought tears. Once, he would have done anything for her. Or she'd thought that he would. It was cruel to think that he had only used her as a means to an end.

"You're skin and bones," he said after a minute.

"I've had a hard year."

He nuzzled his cheek against her temple. "They've all been hard years, one way or another." He sighed heavily. "I'm sorry about tonight. God, I'm sorry!"

"It doesn't matter. Maybe we needed to clear the air."

"I'm not sure we cleared anything." He drew back and looked down at her sad face. He touched her swollen mouth tenderly, and he looked repentant. "In the old days, I never hurt you deliberately," he said quietly. "I've changed, haven't I, Annie?"

"We've both changed. We've grown older."

"But not wiser, in my case. I'm still leading with my chin." He pushed a few wisps of blond hair away from her mouth. "Why did you come home? Was it because of me?"

She couldn't tell him that. "My father hasn't been well," she said, evading a direct answer. "He needs me. I never realized how much until Christmas."

"I see."

She looked up into his black eyes with grief already building in her face.

"What's wrong?" he asked gently. "Can't you tell me?"

She forced a smile. "I'm tired. That's all, I'm just tired." She reached up and smoothed her hand slowly over his lean cheek. "I have to go inside." On an impulse, she stood on tiptoe. "Powell... would you kiss me, just once...the way you used to?" she asked huskily, her gray eyes pleading with him.

It was an odd request, but the stormy evening had robbed him of the ability to reason properly. He didn't answer. He bent, nuzzling her face, searching for her lips, and he kissed her as he had on their very first date, so long ago. His mouth was warm and searching and cautious, as if he didn't want to frighten her. She reached up to him and held him close. For a few precious seconds, there was no dreaded future, no painful past. She melted into the length of him, moaning softly when she felt the immediate response of his body to hers. He half lifted her against him, and his mouth became demanding, insistent, intimate. She gave what he asked, holding him close. For this moment, he belonged to her and she loved him so...!

An eternity later, she drew gently away without looking at him, pulling her arms from around his neck. The scent of his cologne was in her nostrils, the taste of him was in her mouth. She hoped that she could remember this moment, at the end.

She managed a smile as she stood on shaky legs. "Thanks," she said huskily. She stared up at him as if she wanted to memorize his face. In fact, she did.

He scowled. "I took you out because I wanted to talk to you," he said heavily.

"We talked," she replied, moving back. "Even if nothing got settled. There are too many scars, Powell. We can't go back. But I won't hurt Maggie, even if it means leaving the job, okay?"

"You don't have to go that far," he snapped.

She just smiled. "It will come to that," she replied. "She's got the upper hand, you see, and she knows it. It doesn't matter," she added absently as she stared at him. "In the long run, it doesn't matter at all. Maybe it's even for the best." She took a long, slow breath, drinking in the sight of him. "Goodbye, Powell. I'm glad you've been so successful. You've got everything you ever wanted. Be happy."

She turned and went into the house. She hadn't thanked him for the coffee. But, then, he probably didn't expect it. She was glad that her father was watching a television program intently, because when she called good-night, he didn't ask how it had gone. It saved her the pain of telling him. It spared her his pity when he saw the tears she couldn't stem.

* * *

Powell's step was slow and leaden as he went into his house. He was drained of emotion, tired and disheartened. Always he'd hoped that one day he and Antonia would find their way back together again, but he couldn't seem to get past the bitterness, and she'd closed doors tonight. She'd kissed him as if she were saying goodbye. Probably she had been. She didn't like Maggie, and that wouldn't change. Maggie didn't like her, either. Sally was gone, but she'd left a barrier between them in the person of one small belligerent girl. He couldn't get to Antonia because Maggie stood in the way. It was a sad thought, when he'd realized tonight how much Antonia still meant to him.

Surprisingly he found his daughter sitting on the bottom step of the staircase in her school clothes, waiting for him when he walked into his house.

"What are you doing up? Where's Mrs. Bates?" he asked.

She shrugged. "She had to go home. She said I'd be okay since you weren't supposed to be gone long." She studied his face with narrowed, resentful eyes. "Did you tell Miss Hayes that she'd better be nice to me from now on?"

He frowned. "How did you know I took Miss Hayes out?"

"Mrs. Bates said you did." She glared harder.

"She said Miss Hayes was sweet, but she's not. She's mean to me. I told her that you hated her. I told her that you wanted her to go away and never come back. You did say that, Daddy, you know you did."

He felt frozen inside. No wonder Antonia had been so hostile, so suspicious! "When did you tell Miss Hayes that?" he demanded.

"Last week." Her lower lip protruded. "I want her to go away, too. I hate her!"

"Why?" he asked.

"She's so stupid," she muttered. "She goes all gooey when Julie brings her flowers and plays up to her. She doesn't even know that Julie's just doing it so she can be teacher's pet. Julie doesn't even come over to play with me anymore, she's too busy drawing pictures for Miss Hayes!"

The resentment in his daughter's face was a revelation. He remembered Sally being that way about Antonia. When they'd first been married, she'd been scathing about Antonia going to college and getting a job as a teacher. Sally hadn't wanted to go away to school. She'd wanted to marry Powell. She'd said that Antonia had laughed about his calling off the wedding and saying that she'd marry George who was richer anyway…lies, all lies!

"I want you to do your homework from now on," Powell told the child. "And stop behaving badly in class."

"I do not behave badly! And I did my homework! I did!"

He wiped a hand over his brow. Maggie was a disagreeable child. He bought her things, but he couldn't bear to spend any time around her. She always made him feel guilty.

"Did she tell you I wasn't behaving?" she demanded.

"Oh, what does it matter what she said?" He glared at her angrily, watching the way she backed up when he looked at her. "You'll toe the line or else."

He stormed off, thoroughly disgusted. He didn't think how the impulsive outburst might hurt a sensitive child who carefully hid her sensitivity from the cold adults around her. All her belligerence was nothing more than a mask she wore to keep people from seeing how much they could hurt her. But now, the mask was down. She stared up after her father with blue eyes brimming with tears, her small fists clenched at her sides.

"Daddy," she whispered to herself, "why don't you love me? Why can't you love me? I'm not bad. I'm not bad, Daddy!"

But he didn't hear her. And when she went to bed, her head was full of wicked Miss Hayes and ways to make her sorry for the way her daddy had just treated her.

Chapter 7

The class had a test the following Monday. Maggie didn't answer a single question on it. As usual, she sat with her arms folded and smiled haughtily at Antonia. When Antonia stopped beside her desk and asked if she wasn't going to try to answer any of the questions, things came to a head.

"I don't have to," she told Antonia. "You can't make me, either."

Antonia promptly took Maggie to the principal's office and decided to let Powell carry through with his threat to get her fired. It no longer mattered very much. She was tired of the memories and the future, and she was no closer to an answer about her own dilemma. Part of her wanted to take the chance that drastic therapy might save her. Another part was scared to death of it.

"I'm sorry," she said when Mrs. Jameson came out into the waiting room, "but Maggie refuses to do the test I'm giving the class. I thought perhaps if you explained the seriousness of the situation to her…"

This was Maggie's best chance, and she took it at once. "She hates me!" Maggie cried piteously, pointing at Antonia. "She said I was just like my mommy and that she hated me!" She actually sobbed. Real tears welled in her blue eyes.

Antonia's face went red. "I said no such thing, and you know it!" she said huskily.

"Yes, you did," Maggie lied. "Mrs. Jameson, she said that she was going to fail me and there was nothing I could do about it. She hates me 'cause my daddy married my mommy instead of her!"

Antonia leaned against the door facing for support, staring at the child with eyes that were full of disbelief. The attack was so unexpected that she had no defense for it. Had Powell been merciless enough to tell the child that? Had he been that angry?

"Antonia, surely this isn't true," Mrs. Jameson began hesitantly.

"No, it's not true," Antonia said in a stilted tone. "I don't know who's been saying such things to her, but it wasn't me."

"My daddy told me," Maggie lied. Actually she'd overheard Mrs. Bates telling that to one of her friends last night on the telephone. It had given Maggie a trump card that she was playing for all it was worth.

Antonia felt the blow all the way to her heart. She'd known that Powell was angry, but she hadn't realized that he was heartless enough to tell Maggie such a painful truth, knowing that she'd use it as a weapon against her despised teacher. And it was a devastating remark to make in the school office. One of the mothers was in there to pick up a sick child, and the two secretaries were watching with wide, eager eyes. What Maggie had just said would be all over town by nightfall. Another scandal. Another humiliation.

"She's awful to me," Maggie continued, letting tears fall from her eyes. It wasn't hard to cry; all she had to do was think about how her father hated her. Choking, she pointed at Antonia. "She says she can be as mean to me as she wants to, because nobody will believe me when I tell on her! I'm scared of her! You won't let her hit me, will you, Mrs. Jameson?" she added, going close to the older woman to look up at her helplessly. "She said she was going to hit me!" she wailed.

Mrs. Jameson had been wavering. But Maggie's eyes were overflowing with tears and she wasn't a hard enough woman to ignore them. She opened her office door. "Go inside and sit down, please, dear," she said. "Don't cry, now, it will be all right. No one will hurt you."

The little girl sniffed back more tears and wiped her eyes on the back of her hand. "Yes, ma'am," she said, keeping her eyes down so that Antonia wouldn't see the triumph in them. *Now you'll have to go away,* she thought gleefully, *and Mrs. Donalds will come back.*

She closed the door behind her. Antonia just stared at Mrs. Jameson.

"Antonia, she's never been that upset," Mrs. Jameson said reluctantly. "I've never seen her cry. I think she's really afraid of you."

Hearing the indecision in the other woman's voice, Antonia knew what she was thinking. She'd heard all the old gossip, and she didn't know Antonia well. She was afraid of Powell's influence. And Maggie had cried. It didn't take a mind reader to figure the outcome. Antonia knew she was beaten. It was as if fate had taken a hand here, forcing her to go back to Arizona. Perhaps it was for the best, anyway. She couldn't have told her father the truth. It would have been too cruel, and very soon now her health was going to break. She couldn't be a burden on the man she loved most.

She met the older woman's eyes tiredly. "It's just as well," she said gently. "I wouldn't have been able to work much longer, anyway."

"I don't understand," Mrs. Jameson said, frowning.

She only smiled. She would understand one day. "I'll save you the trouble of firing me. I quit.

I hope you'll release me without proper notice, and I'll forfeit my pay in lieu of it," she said. "Maybe she was right," she said, nodding toward the office. "Maybe I could have been kinder to her. I'll clear out my desk and leave at once, if you can have someone take over my class."

She turned and walked out of the office, leaving a sad principal staring after her.

When Maggie came back to the classroom, after a long talk with Mrs. Jameson and then lunch, Miss Hayes was no longer there. Julie was crying quietly while the assistant principal put the homework assignment on the board.

Julie glared at Maggie for the rest of the day, and she even refused to speak to her until they left the building to catch the bus home.

"Miss Hayes left," Julie accused. "It was because of you, wasn't it? I heard Mr. Tarleton say they fired her!"

Maggie's face flushed. "Well, of course you liked her, teacher's pet! But she was mean to me!" Maggie snapped. "I hated her. I'm glad she's gone!"

"She was so kind," Julie sobbed. "You lied!"

Maggie went even redder. "She deserved it! She would have failed me!"

"She should have!" Julie said angrily. "You lazy, hateful girl!"

"Well, I don't like you, either," Maggie yelled

at her. "You're a kiss-up, that's all you are! Mrs. Donalds doesn't like you, she likes me, and she's coming back!"

"She's having a baby, and she isn't coming back!" Julie raged at her.

"Why did Miss Hayes have to leave?" one of the boys muttered as he and his two friends joined them at the bus queue.

"Because Maggie told lies about her and she got fired!" Julie said.

"Miss Hayes got fired? You little brat!" the boy, Jake, said to Maggie, and pushed her roughly when the bus started loading. "She was the best teacher we ever had!"

"She wasn't, either!" Maggie said defensively. She hadn't realized that people were going to know that she got Miss Hayes fired, or that the teacher had been so well liked by her class.

"You got her fired because she didn't like you," Jake persisted, holding up the line. "Well, they ought to fire the whole school, then, because nobody likes you! You're ugly and stupid and you look like a boy!"

Maggie didn't say a word. She ignored him and the others and got on the bus, but she sat alone. Nobody spoke to her. Everybody glared and whispered. She huddled in her seat, trying not to look at Jake. She was crazy about him, and he hated her, too. It was a good thing that nobody knew how she felt.

At least, Miss Hayes was gone, she thought victoriously. That was one good thing that had come out of the horrible day.

Antonia had to tell her father that she'd lost her job and she was leaving town again. It was the hardest thing she'd ever had to do.

"That brat!" he raged. He went to the telephone. "Well, she's not getting away with those lies. I'll call Powell and we'll make her tell the truth!"

Antonia put her hand over his on the receiver and held it in place. She coaxed him back into his easy chair and she sat on the very edge of the sofa with her hands clenched together.

"Powell believes her," she said firmly. "He has no reason not to. Apparently she doesn't tell lies as a rule. He won't believe you any more than he believed me. He'll side with Maggie and nothing will change. Nothing at all."

"Oh, that child," Ben Hayes said through his teeth.

She smoothed down her skirt. "I disliked her and it showed. That wasn't her fault. Anyway, Dad, it doesn't matter. I'll still come back and visit and you can come and see me. It won't be so bad. Really."

"I'd only just got you home again," he said heavily.

"And maybe I'll come back one day," she replied, smiling. She'd spared him the truth, at least. She hugged him. "I'll leave in the morning. It's best if I don't drag it out."

"What will they do about a teacher?" he demanded.

"They'll hire the next person on their list," she said simply. "It isn't as if I'm not expendable."

"You are to me."

She kissed him. "And you are to me. Now, I'd better go pack."

She phoned Barrie that night and was invited to share her apartment for the time being. She didn't tell Barrie what was wrong. That could wait.

She said goodbye to her father, climbed into her car and drove off toward Arizona. He'd wanted her to take the bus, but she wanted to be alone. She had plenty of thinking to do. She had to cope with her fears. It was time for that hard decision that she might already have put off for too long.

Back in Arizona, Barrie fed her cake and coffee and then waited patiently for the reason behind her best friend's return.

When Antonia told her about Powell's daughter's lies, she was livid.

Barrie bit her lower lip, a nervous habit that sometimes left them raw. "I could shake them both," she said curtly. "You're so thin, Annie, so worn. Maybe it's for the best that you came back here. You look worse than ever."

"I'll perk up now that I'm back. I need to see about my job, if they've got something open."

"Your replacement, Miss Garland, was offered a job in industry at three times the pay and she left without notice," Barrie told her. "I expect they'd love you to replace her. There aren't many people who'll work as hard as we do for the pay."

That made Antonia smile. "Absolutely. That's a bit of luck at last! I'll phone first thing tomorrow."

"It's good to have you back," Barrie said. "I've really missed you."

"I've missed you, too. Have you heard from Dawson... Barrie!"

Barrie had bitten right through her lip.

Antonia handed her a tissue. "You have to stop doing that," she said, glad to be talking about something less somber than her sudden departure from Bighorn.

"I do try, you know." She dabbed at the spot of blood and then stared miserably at her friend. "Dawson came to see me. We had an argument."

"About what?"

Barrie clammed up.

"All right, I won't pry. You don't mind if I stay here? Really?"

"Idiot," Barrie muttered, hugging her. "You're family. You belong here."

Antonia fought tears. "You're family, too."

She patted the other woman's back. "I know. Now let's eat something before we start wailing, and I'll tell you about the expansion plans they've just announced for the math department. I may be offered the head teaching position in the department!"

"I'm so happy for you!"

"So am I. Oh, I'm so lucky!" Her enthusiasm was catching. Antonia closed her eyes and leaned silently on Barrie's strength. She had to keep going, she told herself. There must be a reason why she was here, now, instead of happily teaching for what was left of her life in Bighorn. There had to be some purpose to the chain of events that had brought her back to Arizona. The thought of the treatments still frightened her, but not as much as they had only three weeks before. She would go back and see the doctor, and discuss those options.

Maggie was spending the weekend without any company. Julie wouldn't speak to her, and she had no other friends. Mrs. Bates, having heard all about why Miss Hayes had to leave, was avoiding the child as well. She'd moved into the house just to take care of Maggie, because she refused to stay with Julie. But it was a very tense arrangement, and Mrs. Bates muttered while she kept house.

Powell had gone to a business meeting in Denver on Thursday. He'd been out of town when the trouble started. He arrived back without knowing about Antonia's sudden departure. He'd thought about nothing except his disastrous date with Antonia and the things she'd said to him. He'd finally admitted to himself that she really was innocent of any affair with George Rutherford. Her accusations that he'd only used her for financial gain had clinched it.

Of course that wasn't true; he'd never thought of doing such a thing. But if she believed it, it would explain why she hadn't tried to defend herself. She'd never thought he cared one way or the other about her. Presumably she thought he'd been in love with Sally all along, and the fact that Maggie had been premature had helped convince her that he was sleeping with Sally during their engagement. It wasn't true. In fact, he'd only ever slept with Sally once, the night after Antonia left town. He'd been heartbroken, betrayed and so drunk he hardly knew what he was doing.

When he woke the next morning beside Sally, the horror of what he'd done had killed something inside him. He'd known that there was no going back. He'd seduced Sally, and he'd had to marry her, to prevent another scandal. He'd been trapped, especially when she missed her regular period only two weeks later and turned to him to protect her from scandal. Ironically, he had.

Antonia didn't know that. She didn't know he'd loved her, because he'd never told her so. He hadn't been able to bring himself to say the words. Only when it was too late did he realize what he'd lost. The years between had been empty and cold and he'd grown hard. Sally, knowing he didn't love her at all, knowing he hated her for breaking up his engagement to Antonia, had paid the price, along with her daughter.

Sally had turned to alcohol to numb her pain, and once she'd started, she'd become an alcoholic. Powell had sent her to one doctor after another, to treatment centers. But nothing had worked. His total rejection had devastated her, and even after she'd died he hadn't been able to mourn her.

Neither had Maggie. The child had no love for either of her parents, and she was as cold a human being as Powell had ever known. Sometimes he wondered if she was his child, because there seemed to be nothing of him in her. Sally had hinted once that Powell hadn't been her first lover. She'd even hinted that Powell wasn't Maggie's father. He'd wondered ever since, and it had colored his relationship with the gloomy child who lived in his house.

He tossed his suitcase onto the floor in the hall and looked around. The house was empty, or seemed to be. He looked up the staircase and Maggie was sitting there, by herself, in torn jeans and a stained sweatshirt. As usual, she was glowering.

"Where's Mrs. Bates?" he asked.

She shrugged. "She went to the store."

"Don't you have anything to do?"

She lowered her eyes to her legs. "No."

"Well, go watch television or something," he said irritably when she didn't look up. A thought struck him. "You didn't get in trouble at school again, did you?" he asked.

Her shoulder moved again. "Yes."

He moved to the bottom step and stared at her. "Well?"

She shifted restlessly. "Miss Hayes got fired."

He didn't feel his heart beating. His eyes didn't move, didn't blink. "Why did she get fired?" he asked in a soft, dangerous tone.

Maggie's lower lip trembled. She clenched her hands around her thin knees. "Because I lied," she said under her breath. "I wanted her...to go away, because she didn't like me. I lied. And they fired her. Everybody hates me now. Julie especially." She swallowed. "I don't care!" She looked up at him belligerently. "I don't care! She didn't like me!"

"Well, whose fault is that?" he asked harshly.

She hid the pain, as she always did. Her stubborn little chin came up. "I want to go live somewhere else," she said with a pathetic kind of pride.

He fought down guilt. "Where would you go?" he asked, thinking of Antonia. "Sally's parents live in California and they're too old to take care of you, and there isn't anybody else."

She averted her wounded eyes. He sounded as if he wanted her to leave, too. She was sick all over.

"You'll go to school with me in the morning, and you'll tell the principal the truth, do you understand?" he asked flatly. "And then you'll apologize to Miss Hayes."

She clenched her teeth. "She's not here," she said.

"What?"

"She left. She went to Arizona." She winced at the look in his dark eyes.

He took an unsteady breath. The expression in his eyes was like a whiplash to Maggie.

"You don't like her," she accused in a broken voice. "You said so! You said you wished she'd go away!"

"You had no right to cost her that job," he said coldly. "Not liking people doesn't give you the right to hurt them!"

"Mrs. Bates said I was bad like my mama," she blurted out. "She said I was a liar like my mama." Tears filled her eyes. "And she said you hate me like you hated my mama."

He didn't speak. He didn't know what to say, how to deal with this child, his daughter. He hesitated, and in that split second, she got up and ran up the stairs with a heart that broke in two, right inside her. Mrs. Bates was right. Everybody hated her! She ran into her room and closed the door and locked it.

"I'm bad," she whispered to herself, choking on the words. "I'm bad! That's why everybody hates me so."

It had to be true. Her mother had gotten drunk and told her how much she hated her for trapping her in a loveless marriage, for not looking like her father, for being a burden. Her father didn't know that. She couldn't talk to him, she couldn't tell him things. He didn't want to spend any time with her. She was unlovable and unwanted. And she had no place at all to go. Even if she ran away, everybody knew her and they'd just bring her back. Only it would make things worse, because her dad would be even madder at her if she did something like that.

She sat down on the carpeted floor and looked around at the pretty, expensive things that lined the spacious room. All those pretty things, and not one of them was purchased with love, was given with love. They were substitutes for affectionate hugs and kisses, for trips to amusement parks and zoos and carnivals. They were guilt offerings from a parent who didn't love her or want her. She stared at them with anguish in her eyes, and wondered why she'd ever been born.

* * *

Powell got into his car and drove over to Antonia's father's house. He didn't expect to be let in, but Ben opened the door wide.

"I won't come in," Powell said curtly. "Maggie told me what she did. She and I will go to Mrs. Jameson in the morning and she'll tell the truth and apologize. I'm sure they'll offer Antonia her job back."

"She won't come," Ben replied in a lackluster tone. "She said it was just as well that things worked out that way, because she didn't want to live here."

Powell took off his hat and smoothed back his black hair. "I can only say I'm sorry," he said. "I don't know why Maggie dislikes her so much."

"Yes, you do," Ben said unexpectedly. "And you know why she dislikes Maggie, too."

His chest rose and fell in a soundless breath. "Maybe I do. I've made a hell of a lot of mistakes. She said I wouldn't believe the truth because I couldn't admit that." His shoulders shifted. "I suppose she was right. I knew it wasn't true about her and George. But admitting it meant admitting that I had ruined not only her life, but mine and Sally's as well. My pride wouldn't let me do that."

"We pay a high price for some mistakes," Ben said. "Antonia's still paying. After all these years, she's never looked at another man."

His heart jumped. He searched Ben's eyes. "Is it too late?"

Ben knew what the other man was asking. "I don't know," he said honestly.

"Something's worrying her," Powell said. "Something more than Maggie, or the past. She looks ill."

"I made her go see Dr. Harris. She said he prescribed vitamins."

Powell stared at him. He recognized the suspicion in the other man's eyes, because he'd felt it himself. "You don't buy that, Ben. Neither do I." He took a long breath. "Look, why don't you call Dr. Harris and ask him what's going on?"

"It's Sunday."

"If you don't, I will," the younger man said.

Ben hesitated only for a minute. "Maybe you're right. Come in."

He phoned Dr. Harris. After a few polite words, he asked him point-blank about Antonia.

"That's confidential, Ben," the doctor said gently. "You know that."

"Well, she's gone back to Arizona," Ben said hotly. "And she looks bad. She said you told her all she needed was vitamins. I want the truth."

There was a hesitation. "She asked me not to tell anyone. Not even you."

Ben glanced at Powell. "I'm her father."

There was a longer hesitation. "She's under the care of a doctor in Tucson," Dr. Harris said after a minute. "Dr. Harry Claridge. I'll give you his number."

"Ted, tell me," Ben pleaded.

There was a heavy sigh. "Ben, she's taking too long to make up her mind about having treatment. If she doesn't hurry, it…may be too late."

Ben sat down heavily on the sofa, his face pale and drawn. "She needs treatment…for what?" he asked, while Powell stood very still, listening, waiting.

"God, I hate having to tell you this!" the doctor said heavily. "I'm violating every oath I ever took, but it's in her best interest…."

"She's dragging her feet over treatment for what?" Ben burst out, glancing at Powell, whose face was rigid with fear.

"For cancer, Ben. The blood work indicates leukemia. I'm sorry. You'd better speak with Dr. Claridge. And see if you can talk some sense into her. She could stay in remission for years, Ben, years, if she gets treatment in time! They're constantly coming up with new medicines, they're finding cures for different sorts of cancer every day! You can't let her give up now!"

Ben felt tears stinging his eyes. "Yes. Of course. Give me…that number, will you, Ted?"

The phone number of the doctor in Arizona was passed along.

"I won't forget you for this. Thank you," Ben said, and hung up.

Powell was staring at him with dawning horror. "She refused treatment. For what?"

"Leukemia," Ben said heavily. "She didn't come home to be with me. She came home to die." He looked up into Powell's white, drawn face, furiously angry. "And now she's gone, alone, to face that terror by herself!"

Chapter 8

Powell didn't say a word. He just stared at Ben while all the hurtful things he'd said to Antonia came rushing back to haunt him. He remembered how brutally he'd kissed her, the insulting things he'd said. And then, to make it worse, he remembered the way she'd kissed him, just at the last, the way she'd looked up at him, as if she were memorizing his face.

"She was saying goodbye," he said, almost choking on the words.

"What?"

Powell drew in a short breath. There was no time for grief now. He couldn't think of himself. He had to think of Antonia, of what he could do for her. Number one on the list was to get her to accept help. "I'm going to Arizona." He put his hat back on and turned.

"You hold on there a minute," Ben said harshly. "She's my daughter…!"

"And she doesn't want you to know what's wrong with her," Powell retorted, glaring over his shoulder at the man. "I'll be damned if I'm going to stand around and let her do nothing! She can go to the Mayo Clinic. I'll take care of the financial arrangements. But I'm not going to let her die without a fight!"

Ben felt a glimmer of hope even as he struggled with his own needs, torn between agreeing that it was better not to let her know that he was aware of her condition and wanting to rush to her to offer comfort. He knew that Powell would do his best to make her get treatment; probably he could do more with her than Ben could. But Powell had hurt her so badly in the past….

Powell saw the hesitation and relented. He could only imagine how Ben felt about his only child. He wasn't close enough to his own daughter to know how he might react to similar news. It was a sobering, depressing thought. "I'll take care of her. I'll phone you the minute I can tell you something," he told Ben quietly. "If she thinks you know, it will tear her up. Obviously she kept it quiet to protect you."

Ben grimaced. "I figured that out for myself. But I hate secrets."

"So do I. But keep this one for her. Give her

peace of mind. She won't care if I know," he said
with a bitter laugh. "She thinks I hate her."

Ben was realizing that whatever Powell felt, it
wasn't hate. He nodded, a curt jerk of his head.
"I'll stay here, then. But the minute you know
something…!"

"I'll be in touch."

Powell drove home with his heart in his throat.
Antonia wouldn't have told anyone. She'd have
died from her stubborn refusal to go ahead and
have treatment, alone, thinking herself unwanted.

He went upstairs and packed a suitcase with
memories haunting him. He'd have given anything to be able to take back his harsh accusations.

He was vaguely aware of eyes on his back.
He turned. Maggie was standing there, glowering again.

"What do you want?" he asked coldly.

She averted her eyes. "You going away again?"

"Yes. To Arizona."

"Oh. Why are you going there?" she asked
belligerently.

He straightened and looked at the child, unblinking. "To see Antonia. To apologize on your
behalf for costing her her job. She came back
here because she's sick," he added curtly. "She
wanted to be with her father." He averted his

eyes. The shock was wearing off. He felt real fear. He couldn't imagine a world without Antonia.

Maggie was an intelligent child. She knew from the way her father was reacting that Miss Hayes meant something to him. Her eyes flickered. "Will she die?" she asked.

He took a breath before he answered. "I don't know."

She folded her thin arms over her chest. She felt worse than ever. Miss Hayes was dying and she had to leave town because of Maggie. She lowered her eyes to the floor. "I didn't know she was sick. I'm sorry I lied."

"You should be. Furthermore, you're going to go with me to see Mrs. Jameson when I get back, and tell her the truth."

"Yes, sir," she said in a subdued tone.

He finished packing and shouldered into his coat.

Her wounded blue eyes searched over the tall man who didn't like her. She'd hoped all her young life that he'd come home just once laughing, happy to see her, that he'd catch her up in his arms and swing her around and tell her he loved her. That had never happened. Julie had that sort of father. Maggie's dad didn't want her.

"You going to bring Miss Hayes back?" she asked.

"Yes," he said flatly. "And if you don't like it, that's too bad."

She didn't answer him. He seemed to dislike her all over again now, because she'd lied. She turned and went back into her room, closing the door quietly. Miss Hayes would hate her. She'd come back, but she wouldn't forget what Maggie had done. There'd be one more person to make her life miserable, to make her feel unloved and unwanted. She sat down on her bed, too sad even to cry. Her life had never seemed so hopeless before. She wondered suddenly if this was how Miss Hayes felt, knowing she was going to die and then losing the only job she could get in town, so she had to go live in a place where she didn't have any family.

"I'm really sorry, Miss Hayes," Maggie said under her breath. The tears started and she couldn't stop them. But there was no one to comfort her in the big, elegant empty house where she lived.

Powell found Mrs. Bates and told her that he was going to Arizona, but not why. He left at once, without seeing Maggie again. He was afraid that he wouldn't be able to hide his disappointment at what she'd done to Antonia.

He made it to Tucson by late afternoon and checked into a hotel downtown. He found Antonia's number in the telephone directory and called it, but the number had been disconnected. Of course, surely she'd had to give up her apartment when she went back to Bighorn. Where could she be?

He thought about it for a minute, and knew. She'd be staying with Dawson Rutherford's stepsister. He looked up Barrie Bell in the directory. There was only one B. Bell listed. He called that number. It was Sunday evening, so he expected the women to be home.

Antonia answered the phone, her voice sounding very tired and listless.

Powell hesitated. Now that he had her on the phone, he didn't know what to say. And while he hesitated, she assumed it was a crank call and hung up on him. He put the receiver down. Perhaps talking to her over the phone was a bad idea, anyway. He noted the address of the apartment, and decided that he'd just go over there in the morning. The element of surprise couldn't be discounted. It would give him an edge, and he badly needed one. He got himself a small bottle of whiskey from the refrigerator in the room and poured it into a glass with some water. He didn't drink as a rule, but he needed this. It had occurred to him that he could lose Antonia now to something other than his own pride. He was afraid, for the first time in his life.

He figured that Antonia wouldn't be going immediately back to work, and he was right. When he rang the doorbell at midmorning the next day after a sleepless night, she came to answer it, Barrie having long since gone to work.

When she saw Powell standing there, her shock gave him the opportunity to ease her back into the apartment and close the door behind him.

"What are you doing here?" she demanded, recovering.

He looked at her, really seeing her, with eyes dark with pain and worry. She was wearing a sweatshirt and jeans and socks, and she looked pitifully thin and drawn. He hated the pain he and Maggie had caused her.

"I talked to Dr. Harris," he said shortly, bypassing her father so that she wouldn't suspect that Ben knew about her condition.

She went even paler. He knew everything. She could see it in his face. "He had no right...!"

"You have no right," he snapped back, "to sit down and die!"

She took a sharp breath. "I can do what I like with my life!" she replied.

"No."

"Go away!"

"I won't do that, either. You're going to the doctor. And you'll start whatever damn treatment he tells you to get," he said shortly. "I'm through asking. I'm telling!"

"You aren't telling me anything! You have no control over me!"

"I have the right of a fellow human being to

stop someone from committing suicide," he said quietly, searching her eyes. "I'm going to take care of you. I'll start today. Get dressed. We're going to see Dr. Claridge. I made an appointment for you before I came here."

Her mind was spinning. The shock was too sudden, too extreme. She simply stared at him.

His hands went to her shoulders and he searched her eyes slowly. "I'm going to take Maggie to see Mrs. Jameson. I know what happened. You'll get your job back. You can come home."

She pulled away from him. "I don't have a home anymore," she said, averting her face. "I can't go back. My father would find out that I have leukemia. I can't do that to him. Losing Mother almost killed him, and his sister died of cancer. It was terrible, and it took a long time for her to die." She shuddered, remembering. "I can't put him through any more. I must have been crazy to try to go back there in the first place. I don't want him to know."

He couldn't tell her that her father already knew. He shoved his hands into his pockets and stared at her straight back.

"You need to be with people who care about you," he said.

"I am. Barrie is like family."

He didn't know what else to say, how to approach her. He jingled the loose change in his pocket while he tried to find ways to convince her.

She noticed his indecision and turned back to him. "If you'd made this decision, if it was your life, you wouldn't thank anyone for interfering."

"I'd fight," he said, angry with her for giving up. "And you know it."

"Of course you would," she said heavily. "You have things to fight for—your daughter, your wealth, your businesses."

He frowned.

She saw the look and laughed bitterly. "Don't you understand? I've run out of things to fight for," she told him. "I have nothing! Nothing! My father loves me, but he's all I have. I get up in the morning, I go to work, I try to educate children who'd rather play than do homework. I come home and eat supper and read a book and go to bed. That's my life. Except for Barrie, I don't have a friend in the world." She sounded as weary as she felt. She sat down on the edge of an easy chair with her face propped in her hands. It was almost a relief that someone knew, that she could finally admit how she felt. Powell wouldn't mind talking about her condition because it didn't matter to him. "I'm tired, Powell. It's gaining on me. I've been so sick lately that I'm barely able to get around at all. I don't care anymore. The treatment scares me more than the thought of dying does. Besides, there's nothing left that I care enough about to want to live. I just want it to be over."

The terror was working its way into his heart

as he stared at her. He'd never heard anyone sound so defeated. With that attitude, all the treatment in the world wouldn't do any good. She'd given up.

He stood there, staring down at her bent head, breathing erratically while he searched for something to say that would inspire her, that would give her the will to fight. What could he do?

"Isn't there anything you want, Antonia?" he asked slowly. "Isn't there something that would give you a reason to hold on?"

She shook her head. "I'm grateful to you for coming all this way. But you could have saved yourself the trip. My mind is made up. Leave me alone, Powell."

"Leave you alone...!" He choked on the words. He wanted to rage. He wanted to throw things. She sounded so calm, so unmoved. And he was churning inside with the force of his emotions. "What else have I done for nine long, empty damn years?" he demanded.

She leaned forward, letting her long, loose blond hair drape over her face. "Don't lose your temper. I can't fight anymore. I'm too tired."

She looked it. His eyes lingered on her stooped posture. She looked beaten. It was so out of character for her that it devastated him.

He knelt in front of her, taking her by the wrists and pulling her toward him so that she had to look up.

His black eyes bit into her gray ones from point-blank range. "I've known people who had leukemia. With treatment, you could keep going for years. They could find a cure in the meantime. It's crazy to just let go, not to even take the chance of being able to live!"

She searched his black eyes quietly, with an ache deep inside her that had seemed to have been there forever. Daringly, her hand tugged free of his grasp and found his face. Such a beloved face, she thought brokenly. So dear to her. She traced over the thick hair that lay unruly against his broad forehead, down to the thick black eyebrows, down his nose to the crook where it had been broken, over one high cheekbone and down the indented space to his jutting chin. Beloved. She felt the muscles clench and saw the faint glitter in his eyes.

He was barely breathing now, watching her watch him. He caught her hand roughly and held it against his cheek. What he saw in her unguarded face tormented him.

"You still love me," he accused gruffly. "Do you think I don't know?"

She started to deny it, but there was really no reason to. Not anymore. She smiled sadly. "Oh, yes," she said miserably. Her fingers touched his chiseled, thin mouth and felt it move warmly beneath them as he reacted with faint surprise to her easy admission. "I love you. I never stopped.

I never could have." She drew her fingers away. "But everything ends, Powell. Even life."

He caught her hand, pulling it back to his face. "This doesn't have to," he said quietly. "I can get a license today. We can be married in three days."

She had to fight the temptation to say yes. Her eyes fell to his collar, where a pulse hammered relentlessly. "Thank you," she said with genuine feeling. "That means more to me than you can know, under the circumstances. But I won't marry you. I have nothing to give you."

"You have the rest of your life," he said shortly. "However long that is!"

"No." Her voice was weaker. She was fighting tears. She turned her head away and tried to get up, but he held her there.

"You can live with me. I'll take care of you," he said heavily. "Whatever you need, you'll get. The best doctors, the best treatment."

"Money still can't buy life," she told him. "Cancer is…pretty final."

"Stop saying that!" He gripped her arms, hard. "Stop being a defeatist! You can beat anything if you're willing to try!"

"Oh, that sounds familiar," she said, her eyes misting over with memory. "Remember when you were first starting to build your pedigree herd up? And they told you you'd never manage it with one young bull and five heifers. Remember what you said? You said that anything was possible." Her eyes grew warm. "I believed you'd do it. I never doubted it for a minute. You were so proud, Powell, even when you had nothing, and you fought on when so many others would have dropped by the wayside. It was one of the things I admired most about you."

He winced. His face clenched; his heart clenched. He felt as if he was being torn apart. He let her go and got to his feet, moving away with his hands tight in his pockets.

"I gave up on you, though, didn't I?" he asked with his back to her. "A little gossip, a few lies and I destroyed your life."

She studied her thin hands. It was good that they were finally discussing this, that he'd finally admitted that he knew the truth. Perhaps it would make it easier for him, and for her, to let go of the past.

"Sally loved you," she said, making excuses for her friend for the first time. "Perhaps love makes people act out of character."

His fists clenched in his pockets. "I hated her, God forgive me," he said huskily. "I hated her every day we were together, even more when she announced that she was pregnant with Maggie." He sighed wearily. "God, Annie, I resent my own child because I'm not even sure she's mine. I'll never be sure. Even if she is, every time I look at her, I remember what her mother did."

"You did very well without me," she said without malice. "You built up the ranch and made a fortune doing it. You have respect and influence...."

"And all it cost me was you." His head bowed. He laughed dully. "What a price to pay."

"Maggie is a bright child," she said uncertainly. "She can't be so bad. Julie likes her."

"Not recently. Everybody's mad at her for making you leave," he said surprisingly. "Julie won't speak to her."

"That's a shame," she said. "She's a child who needs love, so much." Antonia had been thinking of what had happened the past few weeks, and Maggie's role in it.

He turned, scowling. "What do you mean?"

She smiled. The reasons for Maggie's bad behavior were beginning to be so clear. "Can't you see it in her? She's so alone, Powell, just like you used to be. She doesn't mix with the other children. She's always apart, separate. She's belligerent because she's lonely."

His face hardened. "I'm a busy man..."

"Blame me. Blame Sally. But don't blame Maggie for the past," she pleaded. "If nothing else comes out of this, there should be something for Maggie."

"Oh, God, St. Antonia speaks!" he said sarcastically, because her defense of his daughter made him ashamed of his lack of feeling for the child. "She got you fired, and you think she deserves kindness?"

"She does," she replied simply. "I could have been kinder to her. She reminded me of Sally, too. I was holding grudges of my own. I wasn't deliberately unkind, but I made no overtures toward her at all. A child like Julie is easy to love, because she gives love so generously. A child like Maggie is secretive and distrustful. She can't give love because she doesn't know how. She has to learn."

He thought about that for a minute. "All right. If she needs it, you come home with me and teach me how to give it."

She searched over his rigid expression with eyes that held equal parts of love and grief. "I'm already going downhill," she said slowly. "I can't do that to her, or to you and my father." Her eyes skimmed over his broad shoulders lovingly. "I'll stay with Barrie until I become a liability, then I'll go into a hospice… Powell!"

He had her up in his arms, clear off the floor, his hot face buried in her throat. He didn't speak, but his arms had a fine tremor and his breathing was ragged. He held her so close that she felt vaguely bruised, and he paced the floor with her while he tried to cope with the most incredible emotional pain he'd ever felt.

"I won't let you die," he said roughly. "Do you hear me? I won't!"

She slid her arms around his neck and let him hold her. He did care, in his own way, and she was sorry for him. She'd had weeks to come to grips with her condition, but he'd only had a day or so. Denial was a very real part of it, as Dr. Claridge had already told her.

"It's because of the night you took me to the bar, isn't it?" she asked quietly. "There's no need to feel guilty about what you said. I know it hasn't been an easy nine years for you, either. I don't hold any more grudges. I don't have time for them now. I've put things into perspective in the past few weeks. Hatred, guilt, anger, revenge…they all become so insignificant when you realize your time is limited."

His arms contracted. He stopped pacing and stood holding her, cold with fear.

"If you take the treatments, you have a chance," he repeated.

"Yes. I can live, from day to day, with the fear of it coming back. I can have radiation sickness, my hair will fall out, the very quality of my life will be impaired. What there is left of it, that is."

He drew in a sharp breath, rocking her against him. His eyes, if she could have seen them, were wide and bleak in a face gone rigid with grief.

"I'll be there. I'll help you through it! Life is too precious to throw away." His mouth searched against her throat hungrily. "Marry me, Annie.

If it's only for a few weeks, we'll make enough memories to carry us both into eternity!"

His voice was husky as he spoke. It was the most beautiful thing he'd ever said to her. She clung, giving way to tears at last.

"Yes?" he whispered.

She didn't speak. It was too much of a temptation to resist. She didn't have the willpower to say no, despite her suspicion of his motives.

"I want you," he said harshly. "I want you more than I've ever wanted anything in my life, sick or well. Say yes," he repeated insistently. "Say yes!"

If it was only physical, if he didn't love her, was she doing the right thing to agree? She didn't know. But it was more than she could do to walk away from him a second time. Her arms tightened around his neck. "If you're sure…if you're really sure."

"I'm sure, all right." His cheek slid against hers. He searched her wet eyes. His mouth closed them and then slid down to cover her soft, trembling, tear-wet mouth. He kissed her tenderly, slowly, feeling her immediate response.

The kisses quickly became passionate, intense, and he drew back, because this was a time for tenderness, not desire. "If you'll have the treatments," he said carefully, "if it's even remotely possible afterward, I'll give you a child."

As bribery went, it was a master stroke. She

looked as if she thought he was going insane. Her pale eyes searched his dark ones warily.

"Don't you want a child, Antonia?" he asked curtly. "You used to. It was all you talked about while we were engaged. Surely you didn't give up those dreams."

She felt the heat rush into her cheeks. It was an intimate thing to be talking about. Her eyes escaped his, darting down to the white of his shirt.

"Don't," she said weakly.

"We'll be married," he said firmly. "It will all be legal and aboveboard."

She sighed miserably. "Your daughter won't like having me in the house, for however long I have."

"My daughter had better like it. Having you around her may be the best thing that ever happened to her. But you keep harping on my daughter—I told you before, I don't even think Maggie's mine!"

Her eyes came up sharply.

"Oh, you think you're the only one who paid the price, is that it?" he asked bluntly. "I was married to an alcoholic, who hated me because I couldn't bear to touch her. She told me that Maggie wasn't mine, that she'd been with other men."

She tried to pull away, but he wouldn't let her. He put her back on her feet, but he held her there in front of him. His eyes were relentless, like his hold on her. "I told you that I believed Sally about George, but I didn't. After that one, she told so many lies…so many…!" He let go of her abruptly and turned his back, ramming his hands into the pockets of his slacks as he went to look out the window that overlooked the city of Tucson with "A" Mountain in the distance. "I've lived in hell. Until she died, and afterward. You said you couldn't bear Maggie in your class because of the memories, and I accused you of cruelty. But it's that way with me, too."

The child's behavior made a terrible kind of sense. Her mother hadn't wanted her, and neither did her father. She was unloved, unwanted. No wonder she was a behavioral problem.

"She looks like Sally," she said.

"Oh, yes. Indeed she does. But she doesn't look like me, does she?"

She couldn't argue that point, as much as she might have liked to reassure him.

She joined him at the window. Her eyes searched his. The pain and the anguish of his life were carved into his lean face, in deep lines and an absence of happiness. He looked older than he was.

"What stupid mistakes we make, Antonia, when we're young. I didn't believe you, and that hurt you so much that you ran away. Then I spent years pretending that it wasn't a lie, because I couldn't bear to see the waste and know that I caused it. It's hard to admit guilt, fault. I fought it tooth and nail. But in the end, there was no one else to blame."

She lowered her eyes to his chest. "We were both much younger."

"I never used you to get loans on your father's name," he said bluntly. "That was the furthest thing from my mind."

She didn't answer him.

He moved closer, so that as she stared at the floor, his legs filled her line of vision. They were long legs, muscular and powerful from hours working in the saddle.

He took her cold hands in his. "I was a loner and a misfit. I grew up in poverty, with a father who'd gamble the food out of a baby's mouth and a mother who was too afraid of him to leave. It was a rough childhood. The only thing I ever wanted was to get out of the cycle of poverty, to never have to go hungry again. I wanted to make people notice me."

"You did," she said. "You have everything you ever wanted—money and power and prestige."

"There was one other thing I wanted," he said, correcting her. "I wanted you."

She couldn't meet his eyes. "That didn't last."

"Yes, it did. I still want you more than any woman I've ever known."

"In bed," she scoffed.

"Don't knock it," he replied. "Surely by now you've learned how passion can take you over."

She looked up. Her eyes were guileless, curious, totally innocent.

He caught his breath. "No?"

She lowered her gaze again. "I stopped taking risks after you. Nobody got close enough to hurt me again. In any way."

He caught her small hand in his and rubbed his thumb slowly over its delicate back. He watched the veins in it, traced their blue paths to her fingers. "I can't say the same," he replied quietly. "It would have been more than I could bear to go without a woman for years."

"I suppose it's different for men."

"For some of us," he agreed. He clasped her fingers tight. "They were all you," he added on a cold laugh. "Every one was you. They numbed the pain for a few minutes, and then it came back full force and brought guilt with it."

She reached out hesitantly and touched his dark hair. It was cool under her fingers, clean and smelling of some masculine shampoo.

"Hold me," he said quietly, sliding his arms around her waist. "I'm as frightened as you are."

The words startled her. By the time she reacted to them, he had her close, and his face was buried in her throat.

Her hands hovered above his head and then finally gave in and slid into his hair, holding his cheek against hers.

"I can't let you die, Antonia," he said in a rough whisper.

Her fingers smoothed over his hair protectively. "The treatments are scary," she confessed.

He lifted his head and searched her eyes. "If I went with you, would it be so bad?" he asked softly. "Because I will."

She was weakening. "No. It wouldn't be…so bad, then."

He smiled gently. "Leukemia isn't necessarily fatal," he continued. "Remission can last for years." He traced her mouth. "Years and years."

Tears leaked out of her eyes and down into the corners of her mouth.

"You'll get better," he said, his voice a little rough with the control he was exercising. "And we'll have a baby together."

Her lips compressed. "If I have to have radiation, I don't think I can ever have children."

He hadn't wanted to think about that. He took her hand and brought it hungrily to his mouth. "We'll talk to the doctor. We'll find out for certain."

It was like being caught in a dream. She stopped thinking and worrying altogether. Her eyes searched his and she smiled for the first time.

"All right?" he prompted.

She nodded. "All right."

* * *

Dr. Claridge was less than optimistic about pregnancy, and he said so. "You can't carry a child while you're undergoing the treatment," he explained patiently, and watched their faces fall. He hated telling them that.

"And afterward?" she asked, clinging to Powell's strong hand.

"I can't make any promises." He looked at her file, frowning. "You have a rare blood type, which makes it even more dangerous...."

"Rare blood type?" she echoed. "I thought Type O positive was garden variety."

He stared at her. "Yours is not O positive—it's much more rare."

"It is not!" she argued, surprised. "Dr. Claridge, I certainly do know my own blood type. I had an accident when I was in my teens and they had to give me blood. You remember," she told Powell. "I wrecked my bike and cut a gash in my thigh on some tin beside the house."

"I remember," he said.

She looked back at Dr. Claridge. "You can check with Dr. Harris. He'll tell you I'm Type O."

He was frowning as he read the test results again. "But, this is your file," he said to himself. "This is the report that came back from the lab. The names match." He buzzed his nurse and had her come in and verify the file.

"Have we ever done a complete blood profile

on Antonia in the past?" he asked. "There's no record of one here."

"No, we haven't," the nurse agreed.

"Well, do one now. Something is wrong here."

"Yes, sir."

The nurse went out and came back a minute later with the equipment to draw blood. She drew two vials.

"Get a rush on that. Get a local lab to do it. I want to know something by morning," he told her.

"Yes, sir."

The doctor turned back to Antonia. "Don't get your hopes up too high," he said. "It might be a misprint on the blood type and everything else could still be correct. But we'll double-check it. Meanwhile," he added, "I think it would be wise to wait until tomorrow to make any more decisions. You can call me about ten. I should know something then."

"I'll do that. Thank you."

"Remember. Don't expect too much."

She smiled. "I won't."

"But, just on the off chance, has anyone you've been in contact with had infectious mononucleosis lately?"

She blinked. "Why, yes. One of my female students had it a few weeks ago," she said. "I remember that her mother was very concerned because the girl had played spin the bottle at a party. Ten years old, can you imagine…?" She laughed nervously.

He went very still. "Did you come into contact with any of her saliva?"

She chuckled weakly. "I don't go around kissing my girls."

"Antonia!"

"We shared a soda," she recalled.

He began to smile. "Well, well. Of course, there's still the possibility that we're no better off, but mono and leukemia are very similar in the way they show up in blood work. A lab technician could have mixed them up."

"It might have been a mistake?" she asked hopefully.

"Maybe. But only maybe. We can't discount the other symptoms you've had."

"A maybe is pretty good," she said. "What are the symptoms of mononucleosis?"

"Same as leukemia," he confirmed. "Weakness, sore throat, fatigue, fever…" He glanced at Powell and cleared his throat. "And highly contagious."

Powell smiled crookedly. "I wouldn't care."

The doctor chuckled. "I know how you feel. Well, go home, Antonia. We'll know something in the morning. The labs are careful, but mistakes can happen."

"If only this is one," she said huskily. "Oh, if only!"

When they were outside, Powell held her hand tight in his, and paused to bend and kiss her very gently on her mouth.

"I can't think of anything I'd rather have than mononucleosis," he remarked.

She smiled tearfully. "Neither can I!"

"You're sure about that blood type."

"Positive."

"Well, we'll cross our fingers and pray. Right now, let's get some lunch. Then we might go for a drive."

"Okay."

He took her back to his hotel for lunch and then they drove out of town, through the Saguaro National Monument and looked at the giant cacti. The air was cold, but the sun was out and Antonia felt a little more hopeful than she had before.

They didn't talk. Powell simply held her hand tight in his and the radio played country and western music.

Barrie was home when they drove up to her apartment building. She was surprised to see Powell, but the expression on his face and on Antonia's made her smile.

"Good news, I hope?" she asked.

"I hope so," Antonia said.

Barrie frowned, and then Antonia realized that she didn't know what was going on.

"We're getting married," Powell said, covering for her.

"We are?" Antonia asked, shocked.

"You said yes, remember? What else did you think I meant when I started talking about children?" he asked haughtily. "I won't live in sin with you."

"I didn't ask you to!"

"Good. Because I won't. I'm not that kind of man," he added, and he smiled at her with a new and exciting tenderness.

Antonia caught her breath at the warmth in the look he gave her, tingling from head to toe with new hope. *Please God,* she thought, *let this be a new beginning.*

Barrie was smiling from ear to ear. "Do I say congratulations?"

"Does she?" Powell asked Antonia.

Antonia hesitated. She knew that Powell only wanted her; maybe he felt sorry for her, too. He hadn't really had time to get used to the possibility that she might die. His motives disturbed her. But she'd never stopped loving him. Would it be so bad to marry him? He might learn to love her, if there was enough time.

"I'll tell you tomorrow," she promised.

He searched her eyes quietly. "It will be all right," he promised. "I know it."

She didn't. She was afraid to hope. But she didn't argue.

"There's a nice film on television tonight, if you're staying," Barrie told Powell. "I thought I'd make popcorn."

"That's up to Antonia," he said.

Antonia smiled at him. "I'd like you to stay."

He took off his hat. "I like butter on my popcorn," he said with a grin.

Chapter 9

It was the longest night of Antonia's life. Powell went to his hotel at midnight, and she went to bed, still without having told Barrie what she had to face in the morning.

After Barrie went to work, Antonia got dressed. When Powell came for her at nine, she was more than ready to sit in the doctor's waiting room. She wasn't about to trust the telephone about anything that important. And apparently, neither was he.

They drove around until ten, when they went to Dr. Harris's office for their appointment. They sat in his waiting room and waited patiently through an emergency until he invited Antonia into his office, with Powell right behind her.

They didn't need to ask what he'd found. He was grinning from ear to ear.

"You're garden variety Type O," he told her

without preamble, smiling even wider at her delight as she hugged an equally jubilant Powell. "Furthermore, I called the lab that did the blood work before, and they'd just fired a technician who kept mixing up test results. Yours was one he did. The other assistants turned him in, apparently. They're very professional. They don't tolerate sloppy work."

"Oh, thank God!" Antonia burst out.

"I'm very sorry for the ordeal you've had because of this," he added.

"I hid my head in the sand," she said. "If I'd come right in for treatment, and you'd done more blood work, you'd have discovered it sooner."

"Well, there is some bad news," he added with a rueful smile. "You really do have mononucleosis."

Dr. Claridge explained the course of the disease, and then warned them again about how contagious mono was.

"I've seen this run through an entire school in the cafeteria in the old days," he recalled. "And sometimes people spend weeks in bed with it. But I don't believe that'll be necessary in your case. I don't think you will lose a lot of work time."

"She won't have to worry about that," Powell said. "She's marrying me. She won't have to work. And I don't think she'll mind a few days in bed, getting rid of the infection."

She looked up at his suddenly grim face and

realized that he was going through with the marriage regardless of her new diagnosis. It didn't make sense for a minute, and then it made terrible sense. He'd given his word. He wouldn't go back on it, no matter what. His pride and honor were as much a part of his makeup as his stubbornness.

"We'll talk about that later," she said evasively. "Dr. Claridge, I can't thank you enough."

"I'm just happy to be able to give a cheerful prognosis on your condition now," he said with genuine feeling. "These things happen, but they can have tragic consequences. There was such a lab work mix-up in a big eastern city many years ago…it caused a man to take his own life out of fear. Generally I encourage people to have a second blood test to make sure. Which I would have certainly done in your case, had you come back to see me sooner," he added deliberately.

She flushed. "Yes. Well, I'll try to show a little more fortitude in the future. I was scared to death and I panicked."

"That's a very human reaction," Dr. Claridge assured her. "Take care. If you have any further problems, let me know."

"We'll be going back to Bighorn," Powell said. "But Dr. Harris will be in touch if he needs to."

"Good man, Harris," Dr. Claridge said. "He was very concerned about you when he contacted me. He'll be happy with the new diagnosis."

"I'm sure he will. I'll phone him the minute I get home and tell him," Antonia added.

They left the doctor's office and Antonia paused on the sidewalk to look around her with new eyes. "I thought I'd lost everything," she said aloud, staring with unabashed delight at trees and people and the distant mountains. "I'd given up. And now, it's all new, it's all beautiful."

He caught her hand in his and held it tight. "I wish I'd known sooner," he said.

She smiled faintly. "It was my problem, not yours."

He didn't answer that. He could tell from her attitude that she was going to try to back out of their wedding. Well, he thought, she was going to find that it was more difficult than she imagined. He had her. He wasn't letting go now.

"If you're hungry, we can have something to eat. Late breakfast or early lunch, whichever you like. But first, we'll get these filled," he added, putting the prescriptions into his pocket.

They filled the prescriptions and then went straight to Powell's hotel, and up in the elevator to his luxurious suite overlooking the Sonoran Desert.

"We can eat up here, and we can talk in private," he said, "without prying eyes. But first, I want to phone your father."

"My father? Why?"

He picked up the telephone, got an outside line and dialed. "Because he knew," he said.

"How?"

He glanced at her. "I made him phone Dr. Harris. We both felt that something was wrong. He wanted to rush down here, but I didn't want you to know... Hello, Ben? There was a mix-up at the lab. She has mononucleosis, not cancer, and she'll be back on her feet in no time." He smiled at the excitement on the other end of the line. "He wants to talk to you," he said, holding out the receiver.

"Hi, Dad," Antonia said softly, glaring at Powell. "I didn't know you knew."

"Powell wouldn't rest until he had the truth. It is the truth, this time?" Ben asked sharply. "It really was a mistake?"

"It really was, thank God," she said with genuine relief. "I was scared to death."

"You weren't the only one. This is wonderful news, girl. Really wonderful news! When are you coming back? Powell tell you Maggie was going to tell the truth? You can get your old job back."

She glanced at Powell warily. He was listening, watching, intently. "Nothing's definite yet. I'll phone you in a day or two and let you know what I decide to do. Okay?"

"Okay. Thank God you're all right," he said heavily. "It's been a hell of a couple of days, Antonia."

"For me, too. I'll talk to you soon. Love you, Dad."

"Love you."

She hung up, turning to glare at Powell. "You had to interfere!"

"Yes, I did," he agreed. "I agree with your father—I don't like secrets, either."

He took off his hat, holding her gaze the whole time. He looked incredibly grim. He slipped off his jacket and his tie, and loosened the top buttons of his shirt, exposing a dark, muscular chest thick with black hair.

The sight of him like that brought back long-buried needs and hungers.

"What are you doing?" she asked when his belt followed the rest and he'd dropped into a chair to shed his boots.

"Undressing," he said. He got back up again and moved toward her.

She started to sidestep, but she was seconds too late. He picked her up and carried her into the bedroom. He threw her onto the bed, following her down with a minimum of exertion.

With his arms on either side of her supporting his weight, she was trapped.

"Powell…"

His black eyes were faintly apologetic. "I'm sorry," he murmured as his mouth eased down against hers.

In the old days, their lovemaking had been

passionate, but he'd always been the one to draw back. His reserve was what had convinced her later that he hadn't loved her.

Now, there was no reserve at all, and he was kissing her in a way he never had. His lips didn't cherish, they aroused, and aroused violently. He made her tremble with longings she'd never felt, even with him. His hands were as reckless as his mouth, touching, invading, probing against her naked skin while the only sounds in the room were his quick, sharp breaths and the thunder of his heart beating against her bare breasts.

She didn't even realize he'd half undressed her. She was too involved in the pleasure he was giving her to care about anything except that she wanted him to have access to her soft, warm skin. She needed the feel of his mouth on her, ached for it, hurt to have it. She arched up against him, moaning when the pleasure became more than she could bear.

Vaguely she was aware that a lot of skin was touching other skin. She felt the warm strength of his body against hers and there didn't seem to be any fabric separating them anymore. The hair on his long legs brushed her bare ones as he separated them and moved so that he was lying completely against her in an intimacy they'd never shared.

She panicked then, freezing when she felt his aroused body in intimate contact with her own.

His mouth softened on hers, gentled, so tender that she couldn't resist him. His hands smoothed up and down her body, and he smiled against her lips.

"Easy," he whispered, lifting his head so that he could see her wet, dazed eyes. His hips moved and she stiffened. "Does that hurt?" he asked softly.

She bit her lower lip. Her hands clenched against his hard arms. "It...yes."

"You're embarrassed. Shocked, too." He brushed his lips against hers as he moved again, tenderly, but even so, the pain was there again and she flinched. His eyes searched hers and the look on his face became strained, passionate, almost grim. "I guess it has to hurt this time," he said unsteadily, "but it won't for long."

She swallowed. "It's...wrong."

He shook his head. "We're going to be married. This is my insurance."

"In...surance?" She gasped, because he was filling her...

"Yes." He moved again, and this time she gasped because it was so sweet, and her hips lifted to prolong it. "I'm giving you a baby, Antonia," he breathed reverently, and even as the words entered her ear, his mouth crushed down over hers and his body moved urgently, and the whole world dissolved in a sweet, hot fire that lifted her like a bird in his arms and slung her headlong up into the sky…

He didn't look guilty. That was her first thought when his face came into vivid focus above her. He was smiling, and the expression in his black eyes made her want to hit him. She flushed to the very roots of her hair, as much from the intimacy of their position as from her memories of the past few hectic, unbelievably passionate minutes.

"That settles all the arguments you might have against marriage, I trust?" he asked outrageously. He drew a strand of damp blond hair over her nose playfully. "If we'd done this nine years ago, nothing could have come between us. It was sweeter than I dreamed it would be, and believe me, I dreamed a lot in nine years."

She sighed heavily, searching his black eyes. They were warm and soft now and she waited for the shame and guilt to come, but it didn't. It was very natural to lie naked in his arms and let him look at her and draw his fingers against her in lazy, intimate caresses.

"No arguments at all?" he asked at her lips, and kissed her gently. "You look worried."

"I am," she said honestly. Her wide eyes met his. "I'm midway between periods."

He smiled slowly. "The best time," he mused.

"But a baby so soon…!"

His fingers covered her lips and stopped the words. "So late," he replied. "You're already twenty-seven."

"I know, but there's Maggie," she said miserably. "She doesn't like me. She won't want me there at all…and a baby, Powell! It will be so hard on her."

"We'll cross bridges when we come to them," he said. His eyes slid down her body and back up and desire kindled in their black depths again. His face began to tauten, his caresses became arousing. When she shivered and a soft moan passed between her parted lips, he bent to kiss them with renewed hunger.

"Can you take me again?" he whispered provocatively. "Will it hurt?"

She slid closer to him, feeling the instant response of his body, feeling him shiver as she positioned her body to accept his. She looked into his eyes and caught her breath when he moved down.

He stilled, watching her, his heartbeat shaking them both. He lifted and pushed, watched. Her eyes dilated and he eased down again, harder this time, into complete possession.

She gasped. But her hands were pulling at him, not pushing. He smiled slowly and bent to cover her mouth with his. There had never been a time in his life when he felt more masculine than now, with her soft cries in his ear and her body begging for his. He closed his eyes and gave in to the glory of loving her.

Eventually they had lunch and went to Barrie's apartment when she was due home. One look at them told the story, and she hugged Antonia warmly.

"Congratulations. I told you it would work out one day."

"It worked out, all right," Antonia said, and then told her friend the real reason why she'd come back to Arizona.

Barrie had to sit down. Her green eyes were wide, her face drawn as she realized the agony her friend had suffered.

"Why didn't you tell me?" she burst out.

"For the same reason she didn't tell me," Powell murmured dryly, holding Antonia's hand tight in his. "She didn't want to worry anyone."

"You idiot!" Barrie muttered. "I'd have made you go back to the doctor."

"That's why I didn't tell you," Antonia said. "I would have told you eventually, though."

"Thanks a lot!"

"You'd have done exactly the same thing, maybe worse," Antonia said, unperturbed, as she grinned at Barrie. "You have to come to the wedding."

"When is it?"

"Ten in the morning, day after tomorrow, at the county courthouse here," Powell said with a chuckle. "I have the license, Dr. Claridge did the blood work this morning and we're going back to Bighorn wearing our rings."

"I have a spare room," Barrie offered.

Powell shook his head. "Thanks, but she's mine now," he said possessively, searching Antonia's face with quick, hungry eyes. "I'm not letting her out of my sight."

"I can understand that," Barrie agreed. "Well, do you have plans for the evening, or do you want to take in a movie with me? That new period piece is on at the shopping center."

"That might be fun," Antonia said, looking up at Powell.

"I like costume dramas," he seconded. "Suits me."

Besides, he told Antonia later, when they were briefly alone, she wasn't going to be in any shape for what he really wanted for another day or so. That being the case, a movie was as good as anything to pass the time. As long as they were together, he added quietly. If she felt like it. He worried about not keeping her still. She ignored that. She could rest when they got back to Bighorn, she informed him.

Antonia clung to his hand during the movie, and that night, she slept in his arms. It was as if the past nine years had never happened. He still hadn't said anything about love, but she knew that he wanted her. Perhaps in time, love would

come. Her real concern was how they were going
to cope with Maggie's resentment, especially if
their passion for each other bore fruit. It was too
soon for a baby, but Powell's ardor had been too
headlong to allow for precautions, and his hunger for a child with her was all too obvious. He
wasn't thinking about Maggie. He was thinking
about all those wasted years and how quickly he
could make up for them. But Antonia worried.

The wedding service was very small and
sedate and dignified. Antonia wore a cream-
colored wool suit to be married in, and a hat with
a small veil that covered her face until the justice of the peace pronounced them man and wife.
Powell lifted the veil and looked at her face for
a long moment before he bent and kissed her. It
was like no kiss he'd ever given her before. She
looked into his eyes and felt her legs melt under
her. She'd never loved him so much.

Barrie had been one of their witnesses and a
sheriff's deputy who was prevailed upon by the
justice of the peace was the other. The paperwork
was completed, the marriage license handed back
with the date and time of the wedding on it. They
were married.

The next day they were on the way to Bighorn
in Powell's Mercedes-Benz. He was more tense

than he'd been for three days and she knew it was probably because her body was still reeling from its introduction to intimacy. She was better, but any intimacy, even the smallest, brought discomfort. She hated that. Powell had assured her that it was perfectly natural, and that time would take care of the problem, but his hunger for her was in his eyes every time he looked at her. At this stage of their new relationship, she hated denying him what he craved. After all, it was the only thing they did have right now.

"Stop looking so morose," he taunted when they neared the Wyoming border hours later. "The world won't end because we can't enjoy each other in bed again just yet."

"I was thinking of you, not me," she said absently.

He didn't reply. His eyes were straight ahead. "I thought you enjoyed it."

She glanced at him and realized that she'd unintentionally hurt his ego. "Of course I did," she said. "But I think it must be more of a need for a man. I mean…"

"Never mind," he mused, glancing at her. "You remembered what I said, didn't you—that I can't go for a long time without a woman? I was talking about years, Antonia, not days."

"Oh."

He chuckled softly. "You little green girl. You're just as you were at eighteen."

"Not anymore."

"Well, not quite." He reached out his hand and she put hers into it, feeling its comforting strength. "We're on our way, honey," he said gently, and it was the first time that he'd used an endearment to address her. "It will be all right. Don't worry."

"What about Maggie?" she asked.

His face hardened. "Let me worry about Maggie."

Antonia didn't say anything else. But she had a bad feeling that they were going to have trouble in that quarter.

They stopped by her father's house first, for a tearful reunion. Then they dropped the bombshell.

"Married?" Ben burst out. "Without even telling me, or asking if I wanted to be there?"

"It was my idea," Powell confessed, drawing Antonia close to his side. "I didn't give her much choice."

Ben glared at him, but only for a minute. He couldn't forget that Powell had been more than willing to take on responsibility for Antonia when he thought she was dying. That took courage, and something more.

"Well, you're both old enough to know what you're doing," he said grudgingly, and he smiled at his daughter, who was looking insecure. "And if I get grandkids out of this, I'll shut up."

"You'll have grandchildren," she promised shyly. "Including a ready-made one to start with."

Powell frowned slightly. She meant Maggie.

Antonia looked up at him with a quiet smile. "Speaking of whom, we'd better go, hadn't we?"

He nodded. He shook hands with Ben. "I'll take care of her," he promised.

Ben didn't say anything for a minute. But then he smiled. "Yes. I know you will."

Powell drove them to his home, palatial and elegant, sitting on a rise overlooking the distant mountains. There were several trees around the house and long, rolling hills beyond where pure-bred cattle grazed. In the old days, the house had been a little shack with a leaking roof and a porch that sagged.

"What a long way you've come, Powell," she said.

He didn't look at her as he swung the car around to the side of the house and pressed the button that opened the garage.

The door went up. He drove in and closed the door behind them. Even the garage was spacious and clean.

He helped Antonia out. "I'll come back for your bags in a few minutes. You remember Ida Bates, don't you? She keeps house for me."

"Ida?" She smiled. "She was one of my mother's friends. They sang together in the choir at church."

"Ida still does."

They went in through the kitchen. Ida Bates, heavyset and harassed, turned to stare at Antonia with a question in her eyes.

"We were married in Tucson," Powell announced. "Meet the new lady of the house."

Ida dropped the spoon in the peas she was stirring and rushed to embrace Antonia with genuine affection. "I can't tell you how happy I am for you! What a surprise!"

"It was to us, too," Antonia murmured with a shy glance at her new husband, who smiled back warmly.

Ida let her go and cast a worried look at Powell. "She's up in her room," she said slowly. "Hasn't come out all day. Won't eat a bite."

Antonia felt somehow responsible for the child's torment. Powell noticed that, and his jaw tautened. He took Antonia's hand.

"We'll go up and give her the news."

"Don't expect much," Ida muttered.

The door to Maggie's room was closed. Powell didn't even knock. He opened it and drew Antonia in with him.

Maggie was sitting on the floor looking at a book. Her hair was dirty and straggly and the clothes she was wearing looked as if they'd been slept in.

She looked at Antonia with real fear and scrambled to her feet, backing until she could hold on to the bedpost.

"What's the matter with you?" Powell demanded coldly.

"Is she…real?" she asked, wide-eyed.

"Of course I'm real," Antonia said quietly.

"Oh." Maggie relaxed her grip on the bedpost. "Are you…real sick?"

"She doesn't have what we thought," Powell said without preamble. "It was a mistake. She has something else, but she's going to be all right."

Maggie relaxed a little, but not much.

"We're married," Powell added bluntly.

Maggie didn't react at all. Her blue eyes lifted to Antonia and she didn't smile.

"Antonia is going to live with us," Powell continued. "I'll expect you to make her feel welcome here."

Maggie knew that. Antonia would certainly be welcome, as Maggie never had been. She looked at her father with an expression that made Antonia want to cry. Powell never even noticed the anguish in it.

Pick her up, she wanted to tell him. Hold her. Tell her you still love her, that it won't make any difference that you've remarried. But he didn't do that. He stared at the child with an austerity that made terrible sense of what he'd said to Antonia. He didn't know if Maggie was his, and he resented her. The child certainly knew it. His attitude all but shouted it.

"I'll have to stay in bed for a while, Maggie," Antonia said. "It would be nice if you'd read to me sometimes," she added, nodding toward the book on the floor.

"You going to be my teacher, too?" Maggie asked.

"No," Powell said firmly, looking straight at Antonia. "She's going to have enough to do getting well."

Antonia smiled ruefully. It looked as if she was going to have a war on her hands if she tried to take that teaching job back.

"But you and I are still going to see Mrs. Jameson," he told his daughter. "Don't think you're going to slide out of that."

Maggie lifted her chin and looked at him. "I already done it."

"What?" he demanded.

"I told Mrs. Jameson," she said, glaring up at him. "I told her I lied about Miss Hayes. I told her I was sorry."

Powell was impressed. "You went to see her all by yourself?" he asked.

She nodded, a curt little jerk of her head. "I'm sorry," she said gruffly to Antonia.

"It was a brave thing to do," Antonia remarked. "Were you scared?"

Maggie didn't answer. She just shrugged.

"Don't leave that book lying there," Powell instructed, nodding toward it on the carpet. "And take a bath and change those clothes."

"Yes, Daddy," she said dully.

Antonia watched her put the book away, and wished that she could do something, say something, interfere enough that she could wipe that look from Maggie's little face.

Powell tugged her out of the room before she could say anything else. She went, but she was determined that she was going to do something about this situation.

Antonia and Maggie had not started out on the right foot, because of what had happened in the past. But now Antonia wanted to try with this child. Now that she saw the truth in Powell's early words—that Maggie had paid a high price. That price had been love.

Maggie might not like her, but the child needed a champion in this household, and Antonia was going to be her champion.

Chapter 10

When they were in the master bedroom where Powell slept, Antonia went close to him.

"Don't you ever hug her?" she asked softly. "Or kiss her, and tell her you're glad to see her?"

He stiffened. "Maggie isn't the sort of child who wants affection from adults."

His attitude shocked Antonia. "Powell, you don't really believe that, do you?" she asked, aghast.

The way she was looking at him made him uncomfortable. "I don't know if she's mine." He bit off the words defensively.

"Would it matter so much?" she persisted. "Powell, she's lived in your house since she was born. You've been responsible for her. You've watched her grow. Surely you feel something for her!"

He caught her by the waist and pulled her to him. "I want a child with you," he said quietly. "I promise you, it will be loved and wanted. It will never lack for affection."

She touched his lean cheek. "I know that. I'll love it, too. But Maggie needs us as well. You can't turn your back on her."

His eyebrows went up. "I've always fulfilled my responsibilities as far as Maggie is concerned. I've never wanted to see her hurt. But we've never had a good relationship. And she isn't going to accept you. She's probably already plotting ways to get rid of you."

"Maybe I know her better than you think," she replied. She smiled. "I'm going to love you until you're sick of it," she whispered, going close to him. "Love will spill out of every nook and cranny, it will fill you up. You'll love Maggie because I'll make you love her." She drew his head down and nibbled at his firm mouth until it parted, until he groaned and dragged her into his arms, to kiss her hungrily, like a man demented.

She returned his kisses until sheer exhaustion drained her of strength and she lay against his chest, holding on for support.

"You're still very weak," he remarked. He lifted her gently and carried her to the bed. "I'll have Ida bring lunch up here. Dr. Claridge said you'd need time in bed and you're going to get it now that we're home."

"Bully," she teased softly.

He chuckled, bending over her. "Only when I need to be." He kissed her softly.

Maggie, passing the door, heard him laugh, saw the happiness he was sharing with Antonia, and felt more alone than she ever had in her young life. She walked on, going down the stairs and into the kitchen.

"Mind you don't track mud in here," Ida Bates muttered. "I just mopped."

Maggie didn't speak. She walked out the door and closed it behind her.

Antonia had her lunch on a tray with Powell. It was so different now, being with him, loving him openly, watching the coldness leave him. He was like a different man.

But she worried about Maggie. That evening when Ida brought another tray, this time a single one because Powell had to go out, she asked about Maggie.

"I don't know where she is," Ida said, surprised. "She went out before lunch and never came back."

"But aren't you concerned?" Antonia asked sharply. "She's only nine!"

"Little monkey goes where she pleases, always has. She's probably out in the barn. New calf out there. She likes little things. She won't go far. She's got no place to go."

That sounded so heartless. She winced.

"You eat all that up, now. Do you good to have some hot food inside you." Ida smiled and went out, leaving the door open. "Call if you need me!"

Antonia couldn't enjoy her meal. She was worried, even if nobody else was.

She got up and searched in her suitcases for a pair of jeans, socks, sneakers and a sweatshirt. She put them on and eased down the stairs, through the living room and out the front door. The barn was to the side of the house, a good little walk down a dirt road. She didn't think about how tired she was. She was worried about Maggie. It was late afternoon, and growing dark. The child had been out all day.

The barn door was ajar. She eased inside it and looked around the spacious, shadowy confines until her eyes became accustomed to the dimness. The aisle was wide and covered in wheat straw. She walked past one stall and another until she found a calf and a small child together in the very last one.

"You didn't have anything to eat," she said.

Maggie was shocked. She stared up at the woman she'd caused so much trouble for and felt sick to her stomach. Nobody else cared if she starved. It was ironic that her worst enemy was concerned about her.

Her big blue eyes stared helplessly up at Antonia.

"Aren't you hungry?" Antonia persisted.

Maggie shrugged. "I had a candy bar," she said, avoiding those soft gray eyes.

Antonia came into the stall and settled down beside the calf in the soft, clean hay. She touched the calf's soft nose and smiled. "Their noses are so soft, aren't they?" she asked. "When I was a little girl, I used to wish I had a pet, but my mother was allergic to fur, so we couldn't have a dog or cat."

Maggie fidgeted. "We don't have dogs and cats. Mrs. Bates says animals are dirty."

"Not if they're groomed."

Maggie shrugged again.

Antonia smoothed the calf's forehead. "Do you like cattle?"

Maggie watched her warily. Then she nodded. "I know all about Herefords and black Angus. That's what my daddy raises. I know about birth weights and weight gain ratios and stuff."

Antonia's eyebrows arched. "Really? Does he know?"

Maggie's eyes fell. "It wouldn't matter. He hates me on account of I'm like my mother."

Antonia was surprised that the child was that perceptive. "But your mother did have wonderful qualities," Antonia said. "When we were in school, she was my best friend."

Maggie stared at her. "She married my daddy instead of you."

Antonia's hand stilled on the calf. "Yes. She told a lie, Maggie," she explained. "Because she loved your daddy very much."

"She didn't like me," Maggie said dully. "She used to hit me when he wasn't home and say it was my fault that she was unhappy."

"Maggie, it wasn't your fault," Antonia said firmly.

Maggie's blue eyes met hers. "Nobody wants me here," she said stiffly. "Now that you're here, Daddy will make me go away!"

"Over my dead body," Antonia said shortly.

The child sat there like a little statue, as if she didn't believe what she'd heard. "You don't like me."

"You're Powell's little girl," she replied. "I love him very much. How could I possibly hate someone who's part of him?"

For the first time, the fear in the child's eyes was visible. "You don't want to make me go away?"

"Certainly not," Antonia said.

She nibbled on her lower lip. "They don't want me here," she muttered, nodding her head curtly toward the house. "Daddy goes off and leaves me all the time, and she," she added in a wounded tone, "hates having to stay with me. It was better when I could stay with Julie, but she hates me, too, on account of I got you fired."

Antonia's heart went out to the child. She wondered if in all her life any adult had taken the time to sit down and really talk to her. Perhaps Mrs. Donalds had, and that was why Maggie missed her so much.

"You're very young to try to understand this," she told Maggie slowly. "But inadvertently it was because I lost my job that I went back to the doctor and discovered that I didn't have cancer. Your dad made me go to the doctor," she added with a reflective smile. "He came after me when I left. If he hadn't, I don't know what might have happened to me. Things seem fated sometimes, to me," she added thoughtfully. "You know, as if they're meant to happen. We blame people for playing their part in the scheme of things, and we shouldn't. Life is a test, Maggie. We have obstacles to overcome, to make us stronger." She hesitated. "Is any of this making sense to you?"

"You mean God tests us," the child said softly.

Antonia smiled. "Yes. Does your dad take you to church?"

She shrugged and looked away. "He doesn't take me anywhere."

And it hurt, Antonia thought, because she was beginning to understand just how much this child was enduring. "I like going to church," she said. "My grandparents helped build the Methodist

Church where I went when I was little. Would you…" She hesitated, not wanting to lose ground by rushing the child.

Maggie turned her head and looked at her. "Would I…?" she prompted softly.

"Would you like to go to church with me sometimes?"

The change the question made in that sullen face was remarkable. It softened, brightened, with interest. "Just you and me?" she asked.

"At first. Your dad might come with us, eventually."

She hesitated, toying with a piece of wheat straw. "You aren't mad at me anymore?" she asked.

Antonia shook her head.

"He won't mind?"

She smiled. "No."

"Well…" She shifted and then she frowned, glancing up at the woman with sad eyes. "Well, I would like to," she said. "But I can't."

"Can't? Why not?"

Maggie's shoulders hunched forward. "I don't got a dress."

Tears stung Antonia's gray eyes. Hadn't Powell noticed? Hadn't anybody noticed?

"Oh, my dear," she said huskily, grimacing.

The note in her voice got the child's attention. She saw the glitter of tears in the woman's eyes and felt terrible.

"Antonia!"

The deep voice echoed through the barn. Powell saw them together and strode forward.

"What the hell are you doing out of bed?" he demanded, lifting her to her feet with firm hands. He saw the tears and his face hardened as he turned to the child on her knees by the calf. "She's crying. What did you say to her?" he demanded.

"Powell, no!" She put her hand across his lips. "No! She didn't make me cry!"

"You're defending her!"

"Maggie," Antonia said gently, "you tell your dad what you just told me. Don't be afraid," she added firmly. "Tell him."

Maggie gave him a belligerent glare. "I don't got a dress," she said accusingly.

"Don't have a dress," Antonia corrected her belatedly.

"I don't have a dress," Maggie said obligingly.

"So?" he asked.

"I want to take her to church with me. She doesn't have anything to wear," Antonia told him.

He looked down at his daughter with dawning realization. "You haven't got a dress?"

"No, I don't!" Maggie returned.

He let out a heavy breath. "My God."

"Tomorrow after school you and I are going shopping," Antonia told the child.

"You and me?" Maggie asked.

"Yes."

Powell stared from one of them to the other with open curiosity. Maggie got to her feet and brushed herself off. She looked up at Antonia warily. "I read this fairy tale about a woman who married a man with two little kids and she took them off and lost them in the forest."

Antonia chuckled. "I couldn't lose you, Maggie," she told the child. "Julie told me that you could track like a hunter."

"She did?"

"Who taught you how to track?" Powell demanded.

Maggie glared at him. "Nobody. I read it in a Boy Scout manual. Jake loaned me his."

"Why didn't you ask your dad to buy you one of your own?" she asked the child.

Maggie glared at him again. "He wouldn't," she said. "He brings me dolls."

Antonia's eyebrows lifted. She looked at Powell curiously. "Dolls?"

"She's a girl, isn't she?" he demanded belligerently.

"I hate dolls," Maggie muttered. "I like books."

"Yes, I noticed," Antonia said.

Powell felt like an idiot. "You never said," he muttered at his daughter.

She moved a little closer to Antonia. "You never asked," she replied. She brushed at the filthy sweatshirt where wheat straw was sticking to it.

"You look like a rag doll," Powell said. "You need a bath and a change of clothes."

"I don't got no more clothes," she said miserably. "Mrs. Bates said she wouldn't wash them because I got them too dirty to get clean."

"What?"

"She threw away my last pair of blue jeans," Maggie continued, "and this is the only sweatshirt I got left."

"Oh, Maggie," Antonia said heavily. "Maggie, why didn't you tell her you didn't have any other clothes?"

"Because she won't listen," the child said. "Nobody listens!" She looked at her father with his own scowl. "When I grow up, I'm going to leave home and never come back! And when I have little kids, I'm going to love them!"

Powell was at a complete loss for words. He couldn't even manage to speak.

"Go and have a bath," Antonia told the child gently. "Have you a gown and robe?"

"I got pajamas. I hid them or she'd have throwed them away, too," she added mutinously.

"Then put them on. I'll bring up your supper."

Powell started to speak, but she put her hand over his mouth again.

"Go ahead, Maggie," she urged the child.

Maggie nodded and with another majestic glare at her father, she stalked off down the aisle.

"Oh, she's yours, all right," Antonia mused when she'd gone out of the barn and they were alone. "Same scowl, same impatient attitude, same temper, same glare..."

He felt uncomfortable. "I didn't know she didn't have any damned clothes," he said.

"Now you do. I'm going to take her shopping to buy new ones."

"You aren't in any shape to go shopping or to carry trays of food," he muttered. "I'll do it."

"You'll take her shopping?" she asked with mischief twinkling in her gray eyes.

"I can take a kid to a dress shop," he said belligerently.

"I'm sure you can," she agreed. "It's just the shock of having you volunteer to do it, that's all."

"I'm not volunteering," he said. "I'm protecting you."

She brightened. "Was that why? You sweet man, you."

She reached up and kissed him softly, lingeringly, on his hard mouth. He only resisted for a split second. Then he lifted her clear off the ground, and kissed her with muted hunger, careful not to make any more demands on her than she was ready for. He turned and carried her down the aisle, smiling at her warmly between kisses.

* * *

Mrs. Bates was standing in the middle of the floor looking perplexed when they walked in, although she smiled at the sight of the boss with his wife in his arms.

"Carrying her over the threshold?" she teased Powell.

"Sparing her tired legs," he corrected. "Did Maggie go through here?"

"Indeed she did," Mrs. Bates said with a rueful smile. "I'm a wicked witch because I threw away the only clothes she had and now she has to go shopping for more."

"That's about the size of it," he agreed, smiling at Antonia.

"I didn't know," Mrs. Bates said.

"Neither did I," replied Powell.

They both looked at Antonia.

"I'm a schoolteacher," she reminded them. "I'm used to children."

"I guess I don't know anything," Powell said with a heavy sigh.

"You'll learn."

"How about taking a tray up to Maggie?" Powell asked Mrs. Bates.

"It's the least I can do," the older woman said sheepishly. "I'll never live that down. But you can't imagine the shape those jeans were in. And the sweatshirts!"

"I'm taking her shopping tomorrow after

school," Powell said. "We'll get some new stuff for her to wear out."

Mrs. Bates was fascinated. In all the years she'd worked here, Powell Long hadn't taken his daughter anywhere if she wasn't in trouble.

"I know," he said, reading the look accurately. "But there has to be a first step."

Mrs. Bates nodded. "I guess so. For both of us."

Antonia just smiled. Progress at last!

Powell felt out of place in the children's boutique. The saleslady was very helpful, but Maggie didn't know what to get and neither did he.

They looked at each other helplessly.

"Well, what do you want to buy?" he demanded.

She glared at him. "I don't know!"

"If I could suggest some things," the saleslady intervened diplomatically.

Powell left her to it. He couldn't imagine that clothes were going to do much for his sullen child, but Antonia had insisted that it would make a difference if he went with her. So far, he didn't see any difference.

But when the child went into the dressing room with the saleslady and reappeared five minutes later, he stared at her as if he didn't recognize her.

She was wearing a ruffled pink dress with lace at the throat, a short-skirted little thing with white leggings and patent leather shoes. Her hair was neatly brushed and a frilly ribbon sat at a jaunty angle in it beside her ear.

"Maggie?" he asked, just to be sure.

The look on her dad's face was like a miracle. He seemed surprised by the way she looked. In fact, he smiled. She smiled back. And the change the expression made in her little face was staggering.

For the first time, he saw himself in the child. The eyes were the wrong color, but they were the same shape as his own. Her nose was going to be straight like his—well, like his used to be before he got it broken in a fight. Her mouth was thin and wide like his, her cheekbones high.

Sally had lied about this, too, about Maggie not being his. He'd never been so certain of anything.

He lifted an ironic eyebrow. "Well, well, from ugly duckling to swan," he mused. "You look pretty."

Maggie's heart swelled. Her blue eyes sparkled. Her lips drew up and all at once she laughed, a gurgle of sound that hit Powell right in the heart. He had never heard her laugh. The impact of it went right through him and he seemed to see down the years with eyes full of sorrow and regret. This child had never had a chance at happiness. He'd subconsciously blamed her for Sally's betrayal, for the loss of Antonia. He'd never been a proper father to her in all her life. He wondered if it was going to be too late to start now.

The laughter had changed Maggie's whole appearance. He laughed at the difference.

"Hell," he said under his breath. "How about something blue, to match her eyes?" he asked the saleslady. "And some colorful jeans, not those old dark blue things she's been wearing."

"Yes, sir," the saleslady said enthusiastically.

Maggie pirouetted in front of the full-length mirror, surprised to see that she didn't look the way she usually did. The dress made her almost pretty. She wondered if Jake would ever get to see her in it, and her eyes brightened even more. Now that Antonia was back, maybe everyone would stop hating her.

But Antonia was sick, and she wouldn't be teaching. And that was still Maggie's fault.

"What's the matter?" Powell asked gently. He went down on one knee in front of the child, frowning. "What's wrong?"

Maggie was surprised that he was concerned, that he'd even noticed her sudden sadness. He didn't, usually.

She lifted her eyes to his. "Miss Hayes won't be teaching. It's still my fault."

"Antonia." He corrected her. "She isn't Miss Hayes anymore."

A thought occurred to her. "Is she...my mom, now?"

"Your stepmother," he said tersely.

She moved closer. Hesitantly she reached out and put her hand on his shoulder. It barely touched and then rested, like a butterfly looking for a place to light. "Now that she's back, you don't...hate me anymore, do you?" she asked softly.

His face contorted. With a rough sound, deep in his throat, he swept her close and held her, standing with her in his arms. He hugged her and rocked her, and she clung to him with a sound like a muffled sob.

"Please don't...hate me...anymore!" She wept. "I love you, Daddy!"

"Oh, dear God," Powell whispered huskily, his eyes closed as he weighed his sins. His arms contracted. "I don't hate you," he said curtly. "God knows, I never hated you, Maggie!"

She laid her head on his shoulder and closed her own eyes, savoring the newness of a father's arms, a father's comfort. This was something she'd never known. It was so nice, being hugged. She smiled through her tears.

"Say," he said after a minute, "this is nice."

She gurgled.

He put her down and looked into her uplifted face. Tears were streaming down it, but she was smiling.

He dug in his pocket and cursed under his

breath. "Hell. I never carry handkerchiefs," he said apologetically.

She wiped her eyes on the back of her hands. "Me, neither," she said.

The saleslady came back with an armload of dresses. "I found a blue suit," she said gaily, "and another skirt and top in blue."

"They're very pretty!" Maggie said enthusiastically.

"Indeed they are. Why don't you try them on?" he said invitingly.

"Okay!"

She danced off with the saleslady and he watched, astonished. That was his child. He had a very pretty daughter, and she loved him in spite of all the mistakes he'd made. He smiled reflectively. Well, well, and they said miracles didn't happen. He felt in the middle of one right now. And somehow, it all went back to Antonia, a cycle that had begun and ended with her in his life. He smiled as he thought about the process that had brought them, finally, together and made such a vital change in the way things had been. He glanced at himself in the mirror and wondered where the bitter, hard man he'd been only weeks before, had gone.

Chapter 11

Maggie ran into Antonia's bedroom ahead of her father, wearing the blue dress and leggings and new shoes.

She came to a sudden stop at the side of the bed and seemed to become suddenly shy as she looked at the pink-clad woman in the bed. Antonia's blond hair was around her shoulders and she was wearing a pink lacy gown with an equally lacy bed jacket. She looked fragile, but she also looked welcoming, because she smiled.

"Oh, how nice," Antonia said at once, wondering at the change in the child. "How very nice! You look like a different girl, Maggie!"

Maggie felt breathless. "Daddy got me five new outfits and jeans and shirts and sweatshirts and shoes," she sputtered. "And he hugged me!"

Antonia's face lit up. "He did?"

Maggie smiled shyly. "Yeah, he did!" She laughed. "I think he likes me!"

"I think he does, too," Antonia said in a loud whisper.

Maggie had something in her hand. She hesitated, glancing warily at Antonia. "Me and Daddy got you something," she said shyly.

"You did?" she asked, too surprised to correct the child's grammar.

Maggie moved forward and put it into Antonia's hands. "It plays a song."

It was a small box. Antonia unwrapped it and opened it. Inside was a music box, a fragile, porcelain-topped miniature brass piano that, when wound and opened, played "Clair de Lune."

"Oh," she exclaimed. "I've never had anything so lovely!"

Maggie smiled crookedly.

"Did your dad pick it out?" she asked, entranced by the music.

Maggie's face fell.

Antonia saw the expression and could have hit herself for what she'd asked. "You picked it out, didn't you?" she asked immediately, and watched the child's face brighten again. She would have to be careful not to do any more damage to that fragile self-esteem. "What wonderful taste you have, Maggie. Thank you!"

Maggie smiled. "You're welcome."

Powell came in the door, grinning when he

saw Antonia with the music box. "Like it?" he asked.

"I love it," she replied. "I'll treasure it, always," she added with a warm glance at Maggie.

Maggie actually blushed.

"You'd better put your clothes away," Powell said.

Maggie winced at the authority in his tone, but when she looked up at him, he wasn't angry or impatient. He was smiling.

Her eyes widened. She smiled back. "Okay, Dad!"

She glanced again at Antonia and darted out the door.

"I hear we're handing out hugs today," Antonia murmured dryly.

He chuckled. "Yes, we are. I could get to like that."

"She could, too."

"How about you?" he asked with a speculative glance.

She held out her arms. "Why don't you come down here and find out?"

He laughed softly as he tossed his hat into the chair and eased down on the bed beside her, his arms on either side of her to balance him. She reached up to draw him down, smiling under the warm, slow crush of his mouth.

He kissed her hungrily, but with a tenderness she remembered from their early days together.

She loved the warmth of his kisses, the feel of his body against her. She writhed under his weight suggestively and felt him tense.

"No," he whispered, easing to one side.

She sighed wistfully. "Heartless man."

"It's for your own good," he said, teasing her lips with his forefinger. "I want you to get well."

"I'm trying."

He smiled and bent to nuzzle her nose against his. "Maggie looks pretty in blue," he murmured.

"Yes, she does." She searched his black eyes. "You noticed, didn't you?"

"Noticed what?"

"How much she favors you. I saw it when she smiled. She has the same wrinkles in her face that you have in yours when you smile. Of course, she has your nasty temper, too."

"Curses with the blessings." He chuckled. His eyes searched hers and he drew in a heavy breath. "I never dreamed when I went off to Arizona to find you that it would end up like this."

"Is that a complaint?"

"What do you think?" he murmured and kissed her again.

He carried her down to the table, and for the first time, he and Antonia and Maggie had a meal together. Maggie was nervous, fidgeting with the utensils because she didn't know which one to use.

"There's plenty of time to learn that," Powell said when he saw her unease. "You aren't under the microscope, you know. I thought it might be nice to have a meal together for a change."

Maggie looked from one adult to the other. "You aren't going to send me away, are you?" she asked her father.

"Idiot," he muttered, glaring at her.

She glared right back. "Well, you didn't like me," she reminded him.

"I didn't know you," he replied. "I still don't. That's my fault, but it's going to change. You and I need to spend more time together. So suppose instead of riding the bus, I take you to and from school all the time?"

She was elated and then disappointed. Jake rode the bus. If she didn't, she wouldn't get to see him.

Powell didn't know about Jake. He scowled even more at her hesitation.

"I'd like to," Maggie said. She blushed. "But…"

Antonia remembered what Julie had told her. "Is there someone who rides the bus that you don't want to miss seeing?" she asked gently, and the blush went nuclear.

Powell pursed his lips. "So that's it," he said, and chuckled. "Do I know this lucky young man who's caught my daughter's eye?"

"Oh, Daddy!" Maggie groaned.

"Never mind. You can go on riding the bus,"

he said, with a wicked glance at Antonia. "But you might like to come out with me some Saturdays when I'm checking up on my cattle operation."

"I'd like to do that," Maggie said. "I want to know about your weight gain ratios and heritability factors."

Powell's fork fell from his fingers and made a clanging noise against his plate. To hear those terms coming from a nine-year-old floored him.

Maggie saw that, and grinned. "I like to read about cattle, too. He's got these herd books," she explained to Antonia, "and they have all the statistics on proper genetic breeding. Do you breed genetically, Daddy?"

"Good God," he said on a heavy breath. "She's a cattleman."

"Yes, she is," Antonia agreed. "Surprise, surprise. Speaking of genetics, I wonder who she inherited that from?"

He looked sheepish, but he grinned from ear to ear. "Yes, I do breed genetically," he told his daughter. "If you're that interested, I'll take you around the operation and show you the traits I'm breeding for."

"Like easy calving and low birth weight?" Maggie asked.

Powell let out another breath, staring at his daughter with pure admiration. "And here I was worried that I wouldn't have anyone to leave the ranch to."

Antonia burst out laughing. "It looks as if you're going to leave it in the right hands," she agreed, glancing warmly at Maggie.

Maggie blushed and beamed, all at once. She was still in shell shock from the sudden change of her life. She owed that to Antonia. It was like coming out of the darkness into the sunshine.

Antonia felt the same when she looked at her ready-made family.

"That reminds me," she said. "Your granddad would like to take you with him on an antique-buying binge next weekend. He's going to drive over to an auction in Sheridan."

"But I don't got a granddad," Maggie said, perplexed.

"Don't have," Antonia corrected her. She smiled. "And yes, you do have one. My father."

"A real granddaddy of my own?" Maggie asked, putting down her fork. "Does he know me?"

"You went to see him with your dad. Don't you remember?"

"He lived in a big white house. Oh, yes." Her face brightened, and then it fell. "I was scared and I didn't speak to him. He won't like me."

"He likes you very much," Antonia said. "And he'll enjoy teaching you about antiques, if you'd like to learn. It's his hobby."

"That would be fun!"

"I can see that you're going to be much in demand from now on, Maggie," Antonia said, smiling. "Will you mind?"

Maggie shook her head. She smiled a little unsteadily. "Oh, no, I won't mind at all!"

Antonia was half asleep when Powell slid into bed beside her with a long sigh and stretched.

"She beat me," he said.

Antonia rolled over, pillowing her head on his bare, hair-roughened chest. "At what?" she murmured drowsily.

"Checkers. I still don't see how she set me up." He yawned. "God, I'm sleepy!"

"So am I." She curved closer. "Good night."

"Good night."

She smiled as she slipped back into oblivion, thinking as she did how lucky they were to have each other. Powell had changed so much. He might not love her as she loved him, but he seemed very content. And Maggie was friendly enough. It would take time, but she felt very much at home here already. Things looked bright.

The next morning, she was afraid she'd spoken too soon. Maggie went off to school, and Powell went to a cattle sale, leaving Antonia at home by herself on what was Mrs. Bates's day off. The persistent ringing of the doorbell got her out of bed, and she went downstairs in a long white robe, still half asleep, to answer it.

The woman standing on the other side of the door came as a total shock.

If Antonia was taken aback, so was the gorgeous redhead gaping at her with dark green eyes.

"Who are you?" she demanded haughtily.

Antonia looked her over. Elegant gray suit, pink camisole a little too low-cut, short skirt and long legs. Nice legs. Nice figure. But a little ripe, she thought wickedly. The woman was at least five years older than she was; perhaps more.

"I'm Mrs. Powell Long," Antonia replied with equal hauteur. "What can I do for you?"

The woman just stared at her. "You're joking!"

"I'm not joking." Antonia straightened. "What do you want?"

"I came to see Powell. On a private matter," she added with a cold smile.

"My husband and I don't have secrets," Antonia said daringly.

"Really? Then you know that he's been at my house every night working out the details of a merger, don't you?"

Antonia didn't know how to answer that. Powell had been working late each night, but she'd never thought it was anything other than business. Now, she didn't know. She was insecure, despite Powell's hunger for her. Desire wasn't love, and this woman was more beautiful than any that Antonia had ever seen.

"Powell won't be home until late," Antonia said evasively.

"Well, in that case, I won't wait," the redhead murmured.

"Can I take a message?"

"Yes. Tell him Leslie Holton called to see him," she replied. "I'll, uh, be in touch, if he asks. And I'm sure he will." Her cold eyes traveled down Antonia's thin body and back up again with faint contempt. "There's really no understanding the male mind, is there?" she mused aloud and with a nod, turned and walked back to her late-model Cadillac.

Antonia watched her get in it and drive away. The woman even drove with an attitude, haughty and efficient. She wished and wished that the car would run over four big nails and have all four tires go flat at once. But to her disappointment, the car glided out of sight without a single wobble.

So that was the widow Holton, who was trying to get her claws into Dawson Rutherford and Powell. Had she succeeded with Powell? She seemed very confident. And she was certainly lovely. Obviously he hadn't been serious about marrying the widow, but had there been something between them?

Antonia found herself feeling uncertain and

insecure. She didn't have the beauty or sophistication to compete with a woman like that. Powell did want her, certainly, but that woman would know all the tricks of seduction. What if she and Powell had been lovers? What if they still were? Antonia hadn't been up to bouts of lovemaking, since that one long night she'd spent with Powell. Was abstinence making him desperate? He'd teased her about not being able to go without a woman for long periods of time, and he'd said years, not weeks. But was he telling the truth or just sparing Antonia's feelings? She had to find out.

Late that afternoon, another complication presented itself. Julie Ames came home with Maggie and proceeded to make herself useful, tidying up Antonia's bedroom and fluffing up her pillows. She'd come in with a bouquet of flowers, too, and she'd rushed up to hug Antonia at once, all loving concern and friendliness.

Maggie reacted to this as she always had, by withdrawing, and Antonia wanted so badly to tell her that Julie didn't mean to hurt her.

"I'll go get a vase," Maggie said miserably, turning.

"I'll bet Julie wouldn't mind doing that," Antonia said, surprising both girls. "Would you?" she asked Julie. "You could ask Mrs. Bates to find you one and put water in it."

"I'd be happy to, Mrs. Long!" Julie said enthusiastically, and rushed out to do as she was asked.

Antonia smiled at Maggie, who was still staring at her in a puzzled way.

"Whose idea was it to pick the flowers?" she asked knowingly.

Maggie flushed. "Well, it was mine, sort of."

"Yes, I thought so. And Julie got the credit, and it hurt."

Maggie was surprised. "Yes," she admitted absently.

"I'm not as dim as you think I am," she told Maggie. "Just try to remember one thing, will you? You're my daughter. You belong here."

Maggie's heart leaped. She smiled hesitantly.

"Or I'm your stepmother, if you'd rather..."

She moved closer to the bed. "I'd rather call you Mom," she said slowly. "If...you don't mind."

Antonia smiled gently. "No, Maggie. I don't mind. I'd be very, very flattered."

Maggie sighed. "My mother didn't want me," she said in a world-weary way. "I thought it was my fault, that there was something wrong with me."

"There's nothing wrong with you, darling," Antonia said gently. "You're fine just the way you are."

Maggie fought back tears. "Thanks."

"Something's still wrong, isn't it?" she asked softly. "Can you tell me?"

Maggie looked at her feet. "Julie hugged you."

"I like being hugged."

She looked up. "You do?"

She smiled, nodding.

Maggie hesitated, but Antonia opened her arms, and the child went into them like a homing pigeon. It was incredible, this warm feeling she got from being close to people. First her own dad had hugged her, and now Antonia had. She couldn't remember a time when anyone had wanted to hug her.

She smiled against Antonia's warm shoulder and sighed.

Antonia's arms contracted. "I do like being hugged."

Maggie chortled. "So do I."

Antonia let her go with a smile. "Well, we'll both have to put in some practice, and your dad will, too. You're very pretty when you smile," she observed.

"Here's the vase!" Julie said, smiling as she came in with it. She glanced at Maggie, who was beaming. "Gosh, you look different lately."

"I got new clothes," Maggie said pointedly.

"No. You smile a lot." Julie chuckled. "Jake said you looked like that actress on his favorite TV show, and he was sort of shocked. Didn't you see him staring at you in class today?"

"He never!" Maggie exclaimed, embarrassed. "Did he?" she added hopefully.

"He sure did! The other boys teased him. He didn't even get mad. He just sort of grinned."

Maggie's heart leaped. She looked at Antonia with eyes brimming with joy and discovery.

Antonia felt that same wonder. She couldn't ever regret marrying Powell, regardless of how it all ended up. She thought of the widow Holton and grew cold inside. But she didn't let the girls see it. She only smiled, listening to their friendly discussion with half an ear, while she wondered what Powell was going to say when she told him about their early-morning visitor.

He said nothing at all, as it turned out. And that made it worse. He only watched her through narrowed black eyes when she mentioned it, oh, so carelessly, as they prepared for bed that night.

"She didn't tell me what she wanted to discuss with you. She said that it was personal. I told her I'd give you the message. She did say that she'd be in touch." She peered up at him.

His hard face didn't soften. He searched her eyes, looking for signs of jealousy, but none were there. She'd given him the bare bones of Leslie's visit with no emotion at all. Surely if he meant anything to her, it would have mattered that he was carrying on private, personal discussions with another woman. And Leslie's name had been linked with his in past years. She must have known that, too.

"Was that all?" he asked.

She shrugged. "All that I remember." She smiled. "She's a knockout, isn't she?" she added generously. "Her hair is long and thick and wavy. I've never seen a human being with hair like that...it's almost alive. Does she model?"

"She was a motion picture actress until the death of her husband. She was tired of the pace so when she inherited his fortune, she gave it up."

"Isn't it boring for her here, in such a small community?"

"She spends a lot of time chasing Dawson Rutherford."

That was discouraging, for Barrie, anyway. Antonia wondered if Barrie knew about her stepbrother's contact with the woman. Then she remembered what her father had said about Dawson.

"Does he like her?" she asked curiously.

"He likes her land," he replied. "We're both trying to get her to sell a tract that separates his border from mine. Her property has a river running right through it. If he gets his hands on it, I'll have an ongoing court battle over water rights, and vice versa."

"So it really is business," she blurted out.

He cocked an eyebrow. "I didn't say that was all it was," he replied softly, mockingly. "Rutherford is a cold fish with women, and Leslie is, how can I put it, overstimulated."

Her breath caught in her throat. "How over-stimulated is she?" she demanded suddenly. "And by whom?"

He pursed his lips and toyed with his sleeve. "My past is none of your concern."

She glared at him and sat upright in the bed. "Are you sleeping with her?"

His eyebrows jumped up. "What?"

"You heard me!" she snapped. "I asked if you were so determined to get that land that you'd forsake your marriage vows to accomplish it!"

"Is that what you think?" he asked, and he looked vaguely threatening.

"Why else would she come here to the house to see you?" she asked. "And at a time when she knew you were usually home and Maggie was in school?"

"You're really unsettled about this, aren't you? What did she say to you?"

"She said you'd been at her house every evening when you were supposedly working late," she muttered sharply. "And she acted as if I were the interloper, not her."

"She wanted to marry me," he remarked, digging the knife in deeper.

"Well, you married me," she said angrily. "And I'm not going to be cuckolded!"

"Antonia! What a word!"

"You know what I mean!"

"I hope I do," he said quietly, searching her furious eyes. "Why don't you explain it to me?"

"I wish I had a bottle, I'd explain it," she raged at him, "right over your hard head!"

His dark eyes widened with humor. "You're so jealous you can't see straight," he said, chuckling.

"Of that skinny redheaded cat?" she retorted.

He moved closer to the bed, still grinning. "Meow."

She glared at him, her fists clenched on the covers. "I'm twice the woman she is!"

He cocked one eyebrow. "Are you up to proving it?" he challenged softly.

Her breath came in sharp little whispers. "You go lock that door. I'll show you a few things."

He laughed with sheer delight. He locked the door and turned out the top light, turning back toward the bed.

She was standing beside it by then, and while he watched, she slid her negligee and gown down her arms to the floor.

"Well?" she asked huskily. "I may be a little thinner than I like, but I…"

He was against her before she could finish, his arms encircling her, his mouth hungry and insistent on her lips. She yielded at once, no argument, no protest.

He laid her down and quickly divested himself of everything he was wearing.

"Wait a minute," she protested weakly, "I'm supposed to be…proving something."

"Go ahead," he said invitingly as his mouth opened on her soft breast and his hands found new territory to explore.

She tried to speak, but it ended on a wild little cry. She arched up to him and her nails bit into his lean hips. By the time his mouth shifted back to hers and she felt the hungry pressure of his body over her, she couldn't even manage a sound.

Later, storm-tossed and damp all over from the exertion, she lay panting and trembling in his arms, so drained by pleasure that she couldn't even coordinate her body.

"You were too weak," he accused lazily, tracing her mouth with a lazy finger as he arched over her. "I shouldn't have done that."

"Yes, you should," she whispered huskily, drawing his mouth down over hers. "It was beautiful."

"Indeed it was." He smiled against her lips. "I hope you were serious about wanting children. I meant to stop by the drugstore, but I forgot."

She laughed. "I love children, and we've only got one so far."

He lifted his head and searched her eyes. "You've changed her."

"She's changed me. And you." Her arms tightened around his neck. "We're a family. I've never been so happy. And from now on, it will only get better."

He nodded. "She's very forgiving," he replied. "I've got to earn back the trust I lost along the way. I'm ashamed for what I've put her through."

"Life is all lessons," she said. "She's got you now. She'll have sisters and brothers to spoil, too." Her eyes warmed him. "I love you."

He traced the soft line of her cheek. "I've loved you for most of my life," he said simply, shocking her, because he'd never said the words before. "I couldn't manage to tell you. Funny, isn't it? I didn't realize what I had until I lost it." His eyes darkened. "I wouldn't have wanted to live, if you hadn't."

"Powell," she whispered brokenly.

He kissed away the tears. "And you thought I wanted the widow Holton!"

"Well, she's skinny, but she is pretty."

"Only on the outside. You're beautiful clean through, especially when you're being Maggie's mom."

She smiled. "That's because I love Maggie's dad so much," she whispered.

"And he loves you," he whispered back, bending. "Outrageously."

"Is that so?" she teased. "Prove it."

He groaned. "The spirit is willing, but you've worn out the flesh. Besides," he added softly, "you aren't up to long sessions just yet. I prom-

ise when you're completely well, I'll take you to
the Bahamas and we'll see if we can make the
world record book."

"Fair enough," she said. She held him close
and closed her eyes, aglow with the glory of loving and being loved.

Chapter 12

The new teacher for Maggie's class found a
cooperative, happy little girl as ready to help as
Julie Ames was. And Maggie came home each
day with a new outlook and joy in being with her
parents. There were long evenings with new mov-
ies in front of the fire, and books to look at, and
parties, because Antonia arranged them and invited all the kids Maggie liked—especially Jake.

Powell had done some slowing down, although
he was still an arch rival of Dawson Rutherford's
over that strip of land the widow Holton was dan-
gling between them.

"She's courting him," Powell muttered one evening. "That's the joke of the century. The man's ice
clean through. He avoids women like the plague,
but she's angling for a weekend with him."

"Yes, I know. I spoke to Barrie last week. She

said he's tried to get her to come home and chaperone him, but they had a terrible fight over it and now they're not speaking at all. Barrie's jealous of her, I think."

"Poor kid," he replied, drawing Antonia closer. "There's nothing to be jealous of. Rutherford doesn't like women."

"He doesn't like men, either."

He chuckled. "Me, especially. I know. What I meant was that he's not interested in sexual escapades, even with lovely widows. He just wants land and cattle."

"Women are much more fun," she teased, snuggling close.

"Barrie might try showing him that."

"She'd never have the nerve."

"Barrie? Are we talking about the same woman who entertained three admirers at once at dinner?"

"Dawson is different," she replied. "He matters."

"I begin to see the light."

She closed her eyes with a sigh. "He's a nice man," she said. "You don't like him because of his father, but he's not as ruthless as George was."

He stiffened. "Let's not talk about George."

She lifted away and looked at him. "You don't still believe…!"

"Of course not," he said immediately. "I meant that the Rutherfords have been a thorn in my side

for years, in a business sense. Dawson and I will
never be friends."

"Never is a long time. Barrie is my friend."

"And a good one," he agreed.

"Yes, well, I think she might end up with Dawson one day."

"They're related," he said shortly.

"They are not. His father married her mother."

"He hates her, and vice versa."

"I wonder," Antonia said quietly. "That sort of
dislike is suspicious, isn't it? I mean, you avoid
people you really dislike. He's always making
some excuse to see Barrie and give her hell."

"She gives it right back," he reminded her.

"She has to. A man like that will run right over
a woman unless she stands up to him." She curled
her fingers into his. "You're like that, too," she
added, searching his black eyes quietly. "A gentle
woman could never cope with you."

"As Sally found out," he agreed. His fingers
contracted. "There's something about our marriage that I never told you. I think it's time I did.
Maggie was born two months premature. I didn't
sleep with Sally until after I broke our engagement. And I was so drunk that I thought you'd
come back to me," he added quietly. "You can't
imagine how sick I felt when I woke up with her
the next morning and realized what I'd done. And
it was too late to put it right."

She didn't say anything. She swallowed down the pain. "I see."

"I was cruel, Antonia," he said heavily. "Cruel and thoughtless. But I paid for it. Sadly, Sally and Maggie paid with me, and so did you." He searched her eyes. "From now on, baby, if you tell me green is orange, I'll believe it. I wanted to tell you that from the day you came back to your father's house and I saw you there."

"You made cutting remarks instead."

He smiled ruefully. "It hurts to see what you've lost," he replied. "I loved you to the soles of your feet, and I couldn't tell you. I thought you hated me."

"Part of me did."

"And then I found out why you'd really come here to teach," he said. "I wanted to die."

She went into his arms and nuzzled closer to him. "You mustn't look back," she said. "It's over now. I'm safe, and so are you, and so is Maggie."

"My Maggie," he sighed, smiling. "She's a hell of a cattlewoman already."

"She's your daughter."

"Mmm. Yes, she is. I'm glad I finally realized that Sally had lied about that. There are too many similarities."

"Far too many." She smiled against his chest. "It's been six weeks since that night I offered to prove I was more of a woman than the widow Holton," she reminded him.

"So it has."

She drew away a little, her eyes searching his while a secret smile touched her lips. But he wasn't waiting for surprises. His lean hand pressed softly against her flat stomach and he smiled back, all of heaven in his dark eyes.

"You know?" she whispered softly.

"I sleep with you every night," he replied. "And I make love to you most every one. I'm not numb. And," he added, "you've lost your breakfast for the past week."

"I wanted to surprise you."

"Go ahead," he suggested.

She glared at him. "I'm pregnant," she said.

He jumped up, clasped his hands over his heart and gave her such a look of wonder that she burst out laughing.

"Are you, truly?" he exclaimed. "My God!"

She was all but rolling on the floor from his exaggerated glee. Mrs. Bates stuck her head in the door to see what the commotion was all about.

"She's pregnant!" he told her.

"Well!" Mrs. Bates exclaimed. "Really?"

"The home test I took says I am," she replied. "I still have to go to the doctor to have it confirmed."

"Yes," Powell said. "And the results from this test won't be frightening."

She agreed wholeheartedly.

* * *

They told Maggie that afternoon. She was apprehensive when they called her into the living room. Things had been so wonderful lately. Perhaps they'd changed their minds about her, and she was going to be sent off to school...

"Antonia is pregnant," Powell said softly.

Maggie's eyes lit up. "Oh, is that it!" she said, relieved. "I thought it was going to be something awful. You mean we're going to have a real baby of our own?" She hugged Antonia warmly and snuggled close to her on the sofa. "Julie will be just green, just green with envy!" she said, laughing. "Can I hold him when he's born, and help you take care of him? I can get books about babies...."

Antonia was laughing with pure delight. "Yes, you can help," she said. "I thought it might be too soon, that you'd be unhappy about it."

"Silly old Mom," Maggie said with a frown. "I'd love a baby brother. It's going to be a boy, isn't it?"

Powell chuckled. "I like girls, too," he said.

Maggie grinned at him. "You only like me on account of I know one end of a cow from another," she said pointedly.

"Well, you're pretty, too," he added.

She beamed. "Now, I'll have something really important to share at show and tell." She looked up. "I miss you at school. So does everybody else. Miss Tyler is nice, but you were special."

"I'll go back to teaching one day," Antonia promised. "It's like riding a bike. You never forget how."

"Shall we go over and tell your granddad?" Powell asked.

"Yes," Maggie said enthusiastically. "Right now!"

Ben was overwhelmed by the news. He sat down heavily in his easy chair and just stared at the three of them sitting smugly on his couch.

"A baby," he exclaimed. His face began to light up. "Well!"

"It's going to be a boy, Granddad," Maggie assured him. "Then you'll have somebody who'll appreciate those old electric trains you collect. I'm sorry I don't, but I like cattle."

Ben chuckled. "That's okay, imp," he told her. "Maybe some day you can help teach the baby about Queen Anne furniture."

"He likes that a lot," Maggie told the other adults. "We spend ever so much time looking at furniture."

"Well, it's fun," Ben said.

"Yes, it is," Maggie agreed, "but cattle are so much more interesting, Granddad, and it's scientific, too, isn't it, Dad?"

Powell had to agree. "She's my kid. You can tell."

"Oh, yes." Ben nodded. He smiled at the girl warmly. Since she'd come into his life, whole new worlds had opened up for him. She came over sometimes just to help him organize his books. He had plenty, and it was another love they shared. "That reminds me. Found you something at that last sale."

He got up and produced a very rare nineteenth-century breed book. He handed it to Maggie with great care. "You look after that," he told her. "It's valuable."

"Oh, Granddad!" She went into raptures of enthusiasm.

Powell whistled through his teeth. "That's expensive, Ben."

"Maggie knows that. She'll take care of it, too," he added. "Never saw anyone take the care with books that she does. Never slams them around or leaves them lying about. She puts every one right back in its place. I'd even lend her my first editions. She's a little jewel."

Maggie heard that last remark and looked up at her grandfather with an affectionate smile. "He's teaching me how to take care of books properly," she announced.

"And she's an excellent pupil." He looked at Antonia with pure love in his eyes. "I wish your mother was here," he told her. "She'd be so happy and proud."

"I know she would. But, I think she knows, Dad," Antonia said gently. And she smiled.

That night, Antonia phoned Barrie to tell her the news. Her best friend was overjoyed.

"You have to let me know when he's born, so that I can fly up and see him."

"Him?"

"Boys are nice. You should have at least one. Then you'll have a matched set. Maggie and a boy."

"Well, I'll do my best." There was a pause. "Heard from Dawson?"

There was a cold silence. "No."

"I met the widow Holton not so long ago," Antonia remarked.

Barrie cleared her throat. "Is she old?"

"About six years older than I am," Antonia said. "Slender, redheaded, green-eyed and very glamorous."

"Dawson should be ecstatic to have her visiting every weekend."

"Barrie, Dawson really could use a little support where that woman is concerned," she said slowly. "She's hard and cold and very devious, from what I hear. You never know what she might do."

"He invited her up there," Barrie muttered.

"And then had the audacity to try and get me to come play chaperone, so that people wouldn't think there was anything going on between them. As if I want to watch her paw him and fawn all over him and help him pretend it's all innocent!"

"Maybe it is innocent. Dawson doesn't like women, Barrie," she added. "They say he's, well, sexually cold."

"Dawson?"

"Dawson."

Barrie hesitated. She couldn't very well say what she was thinking, or what she was remembering.

"Are you still there?" Antonia asked.

"Yes." Barrie sighed. "It's his own fault, he wants that land so badly that he'll do anything to get it."

"I don't think he'd go this far. I think he just invited Mrs. Holton up there to talk to her, and now she thinks he had amorous intentions instead of business ones and he can't get rid of her. She strikes me as the sort who'd be hard to dissuade. She's a very pushy woman, and Dawson's very rich. It may be that she's chasing him, instead of the reverse."

"He never said that."

"Did you give him a chance to say anything?" Antonia asked.

"It's safer if I don't," Barrie muttered. "I don't

know if I want to risk giving Dawson a whole weekend to spend giving me hell."

"You could try. He might have had a change of heart."

"Not likely." There was a harsh laugh. "Well, I'll call him, and if he asks me again, I'll go, but only if there are plenty of people around, not just the widow."

"Call him up and tell him that."

"I don't know…"

"He's not an ogre. He's just a man."

"Sure." She sounded unconvinced.

"Barrie, you're not a coward. Save him."

"Imagine, the iceman needing saving." She hesitated. "Who told you they called him that?"

"Just about everybody I know. He doesn't date. The widow is the first woman he's been seen with in years." Antonia's voice softened. "Curious, isn't it?"

It was, but Barrie didn't dare mention why. She had some ideas about it, and she wondered if she had enough courage to go to Sheridan and find out the truth.

"Maybe I'll go," Barrie said.

"Maybe you should," Antonia agreed, and shortly afterward, she hung up, giving Barrie plenty to think about.

Powell came to find her after she'd gotten off the phone, smiling at her warmly. "You look pretty in pink," he remarked.

She smiled back. "Thanks."

He sat down beside her on the sofa and pulled her close. "What's wrong?"

"The widow Holton is giving Dawson a hard time."

"Good," Powell said.

She glared at him. "You might have the decency to feel sorry for the poor man. You were her target once, I believe."

"Until you stepped in and saved me, you sweet woman," he replied, and bent to kiss her warmly.

"There isn't anybody to save Dawson unless Barrie will."

"He can fight his own dragons. Or should I say dragonettes?" he mused thoughtfully.

"Aren't you still after that strip of land, too?"

"Oh, I gave up on it when we got married," he said easily. "I had an idea that she wanted more than money for it, and you were jealous enough of her already."

"I like that!" she muttered.

"You never had anything to worry about," he said. "She wasn't my type. But, I had an idea she'd make mischief if I kept trying to get those few acres, so I let the idea go. And I'll tell you something else," he added with a chuckle. "I don't think Dawson Rutherford's going to get that strip, either. She may string him along to see if she can get him interested in a more permanent arrangement, but unless he wants to propose…"

"Maybe he does," she said.

He shook his head. "I don't like him," he said, "but he's not a fool. She isn't his type of woman. She likes to give orders, not take them. He's too strong willed to suit her for long. More than likely, it's because she can't get him that she wants him."

"I hope so," she replied. "I'd hate to see him trapped into marriage. I think Barrie cares a lot more for him than she'll admit."

He drew her close. "They'll work out their own problems. Do you realize how this household has changed since you married me?"

She smiled. "Yes. Maggie is a whole new person."

"So am I. So are you. So is your father and Mrs. Bates," he added. "And now we've got a baby on the way as well, and Maggie's actually looking forward to it. I tell you, we've got the world."

She nestled close to him and closed her eyes. "The whole world," she agreed huskily.

Seven months later, Nelson Charles Long was born in the Bighorn community hospital. It had been a quick, easy birth, and Powell had been with Antonia every step of the way. Maggie was allowed in with her dad to see the baby while Antonia fed him.

"He looks like you, Dad," Maggie said.

"He looks like Antonia," he protested. "You look like me," he added.

Maggie beamed. There was a whole new relationship between Maggie and her father. She wasn't threatened by the baby at all, not when she was so well loved by both parents. The cold, empty past was truly behind her now, just as it had finally been laid to rest by her parents.

Antonia had asked Powell finally what Sally had written in the letter she'd sent back, so many years ago. Sally had told him very little about it, he recalled, except he recalled one line she'd quoted from some author he couldn't quite remember: Take what you want, says God, and pay for it. The letter was to the effect that Sally had discovered the painful truth of that old proverb, and she was sorry.

Too late, of course. Much too late.

Sally had been forgiven, and the joy Antonia felt with Powell and Maggie grew by the day. She, too, had learned a hard lesson from the experience, that one had to stand and fight sometimes. She would teach that lesson to Maggie, she thought as she looked adoringly up at her proud husband, and to the child she held in her arms.

* * * * *

CATTLEMAN'S CHOICE

DIANA PALMER

For Alicia
And for Arizona's Stephanie, Ellen,
Trish and Nita.

Chapter 1

At first, Mandelyn thought the pounding was just in her head; she'd gone to bed with a nagging headache. But when it got louder, she sat up in bed with a frown and stared at the clock. The glowing face told her that it was one o'clock in the morning, and she couldn't imagine that any of the ranch hands would want to wake her at that hour without cause.

She jumped up, running a hand through the glorious blond tangle of her long hair, and pulled on a long white robe over her nightgown. Her soft gray eyes were troubled as she wound through the long ranch-style house to the front door that overlooked the Chiricahua Mountains of southeastern Arizona.

"Who is it?" she asked in the soft, cultured tones of her Charleston upbringing.

"Jake Wells, ma'am," came the answer.

That was Carson Wayne's foreman. And without a single word of explanation, she knew what was wrong, and why she'd been awakened.

She opened the door and fixed the tall, blond man with a rueful smile. "Where is he?" she asked.

He took off his hat with a sigh. "In town," he replied. "At the Rodeo bar."

"Is he drunk?" she asked warily.

The foreman hesitated. One corner of his mouth went up. "Yes, ma'am," he said finally.

"That's the second time in the last two months," she said with flashing gray eyes.

Jake shrugged, turning his hat around in his hands. "Maybe money's getting tight," he guessed.

"It's been tight before. And it isn't as if he doesn't have options, either," she grumbled, turning. "I've had a buyer for that forty-acre tract of his for months. He won't even discuss it."

"Miss Bush, you know how he feels about those condominium complexes," he reminded her. "That land's been in his family since the Civil War."

"He's got thousands of acres!" she burst out. "He wouldn't miss forty!"

"Well, that particular forty is where the old fort stands."

"Nobody's likely to use it these days," she said with venom.

He only shrugged, and she went off to change her clothes. Minutes later, dressed in a yellow sweater and designer jeans, she drew on her suede jacket and went out to climb in beside Jake in the black pickup truck with the Circle Bar W logo of Carson Wayne's cattle company emblazoned in red on the door.

"Why doesn't anybody else ever get called to go save people from him?" she asked curtly.

Jake glanced at her with a faint smile. "Because you're the only person in the valley who isn't scared of him."

"You and the boys could bring him home," she suggested.

"We tried once. Doctor bills got too expensive." He grinned. "He won't hit you."

That was true enough. Carson indulged her. He was fiery and rough and lived like a hermit in that faded frame building he called a house. He hated neighbors and he was as savage a man as she'd ever known. But from the first, he'd warmed to her. People said it was because she was from Charleston, South Carolina and a lady and he felt protective of her. That was true, up to a point. But Mandelyn also knew that he liked her because she had the same wild spirit he possessed, because she stood up to him fearlessly. It had been that way from the very beginning.

They wound along the dusty ranch road out to the highway. There was just enough light to see the giant saguaro cacti lifting their arms to the sky, and the dark mountains silhouetted against the horizon. Arizona was beautiful enough to take Mandelyn's breath away, even after eight years as a resident. She'd come from South Carolina at the age of eighteen, devastated by personal tragedy, expecting to find the barren land a perfect expression of her own emotional desolation. But her first sight of the Chiricahua Mountains had changed her mind. Since then, she'd learned to look upon the drastically different vegetation with loving, familiar eyes, and in time the lush green coastline of South Carolina had slowly faded from memory, replaced by the glory of creosote bushes in the rain and the stately stoicism of the saguaro. Her cultured upbringing was still evident in her proud carriage and her soft, delicately accented voice, but she was as much an Arizonian now as a Zane Grey character.

"Why does he do this?" she asked as they wound into the small town of Sweetwater.

"Not my business to guess," came the reply. "But he's a lonely man, and feeling his years."

"He's only thirty-eight," she said. "Hardly a candidate for Medicare."

Jake looked at her speculatively. "He's alone, Miss Bush," he said. "Problems don't get so big when you can share them."

She sighed. How well she knew that. Since her uncle's death four years before, she'd had her share of loneliness. If it hadn't been for her real estate agency, and her involvement in half a dozen organizations, she might have left Sweetwater for good just out of desperation.

Jake parked in front of the Rodeo bar and got out. Mandelyn was on the ground before he could come around the hood. She started toward the door.

The bartender was waiting in the doorway, wringing his apron, his bald head shining in the streetlight.

"Thank God," he said uneasily, glancing behind him. "Mandelyn, he's got a cowboy treed out back."

She stopped, blinking. "He's what?"

"One of the Lazy X's hands said something that set him off. God knows what. He was just sitting quiet at the table, going through a bottle of whiskey, not bothering anybody, and the stupid cowboy..." He stopped on an impatient sigh. "He busted my mirror, again. He broke half a dozen bottles of whiskey. The cowboy had to go to the hospital to get his jaw wired back together...."

"Wait a minute," she said, holding up a hand. "You said he had the cowboy treed..."

"The cowboy whose jaw he broke had friends," the bartender sighed. "Three of them. One is out cold on the floor. Another one is hanging from his jacket on a hook where Carson put him. The third one, the last one, is up in a tree out back of here and Carson is sitting there, grinning, waiting for him to come down again."

Carson never grinned. Not unless he was mad as hell and ready for blood. "Oh, my," Mandelyn sighed. "How about the sheriff?"

"Like most sane men, he gave the job of bringing Carson in to his deputy."

Mandelyn lifted her delicate eyebrows. "And?"

"The deputy," the bartender told her, "is in the hall closet, asking very loudly to be let out."

"Why don't you let him out?" she persisted.

"Carson," the bartender replied, "has the key."

"Oh."

Jake pulled his hat low over his eyes. "I'm going to sit in the truck," he said.

"Better go get the bail bondsman out of bed first, Jake," the bartender said darkly.

"Why bother?" Jake asked. "Sheriff Wilson isn't going to get out of bed to arrest the boss, and since Danny's locked in the closet, I'd say it's all over but the crying."

"And the paying," the bartender added.

"He'll pay you. He always does."

The bartender made a harsh sound in his throat. "That doesn't make up for the inconvenience. Having to order mirrors...clean up broken glass...it used to be once every few months, about time his taxes came due. Now it's every month. What's eating him?"

"I wish I knew," Mandelyn sighed. "Well, I'd better go get him."

"Lots of luck," the bartender said curtly. "Watch out. He may have a gun."

"He may need it," she told him with a cold smile.

She walked through the bar, out the back door, just in time to catch the tail end of a long and ardent string of curses. They were delivered by a tall man in a sheepskin coat who was glaring up at a shivering, skinny man in the top of an oak tree.

"Miss Bush," the Lazy X cowboy wailed down at her. "Help!"

The tall, whipcord-lean man turned, pale blue eyes lancing at her from under thick black eyebrows. He was wearing a dark ranch hat pulled low on his forehead, and his lean, tough face needed a shave as much as his thick, ragged hair needed cutting. He had a pistol in one hand and just the look of him would have been enough to frighten most men.

"Go ahead, shoot," she dared him, "and I'll haunt you, you bad-tempered Arizona sidewinder!"

He stood slightly crouched, breathing slowly, watching her.

"If you're not going to use that gun, may I have it?" she asked, nodding toward the weapon.

He didn't move for a long, taut minute. Then

he silently flipped the gun, straightening as he
held the butt toward her.

She moved forward, taking it gently, carefully.
Carson was unpredictable in these moods, but
she'd been dealing with him for a long time, now.
Long enough to know how to handle him. She
emptied the pistol carefully and stuck it in one
coat pocket, putting the bullets in the other.

"Why is that man in the tree?" she asked Carson.

"Ask him," Carson said in a deep drawl.

She looked up at the thin cowboy, who was
young and battered-looking. She recognized him
belatedly as one she'd seen often in the grocery
store. "Bobby, what did you do?"

The young cowboy sighed. "Well, Miss Bush,
I hit him over the back with a chair. He was choking Andy, and I was afraid he was going to do
some damage."

"If he apologizes," she said to Carson, who
was slightly unsteady on his feet, "can he come
down?"

He thought about that for a minute. "I guess."

"Bobby, apologize!" she called up.

"I'm sorry, Mr. Wayne!" came the prompt reply.

Carson glared up toward the limb. "All right,
you…"

Mandelyn had to grit her teeth as Carson went
through a round of unprintable words before he
let the shivering cowboy come down.

"Thanks!" Bobby said quickly, and ran for it, before Carson had time to change his mind.

Mandelyn sighed, staring up at Carson's hard face. It was a long way up. He was tall and broad shouldered, with a physique that would have caught any woman's eye. But he was rough and coarse and only half civilized, and she couldn't imagine any woman being able to live with him.

"Jake with you?" he bit off.

"Yes. As usual." She moved closer and slowly reached out to catch his big hand in hers. It was callused and warm and it made her tingle to touch it. It was an odd reaction, but she didn't stop to question it. "Let's go home, Carson."

He let her lead him around the building, as docile as a lamb, and not for the first time she wondered at that docility. He would have attacked any man who tried to stop him. But for some reason he tolerated Mandelyn's interference. She was the only person his men would call to get him.

"Shame on you," she mumbled.

"Button up," he said curtly. "When I want a sermon, I'll call a preacher."

"Any preacher you called would faint dead away," she shot back. "And don't give me orders, I don't like it."

He stopped suddenly. She was still holding his hand and the action jerked her backward.

"Wildcat," he said huskily, and his eyes glittered in the dim light. "For all your culture and polish, you're as hard as a back-country woman."

"Sure I am," she replied. "I have to be, to deal with a savage like you!"

Something darkened his eyes, hardened his jaw. All at once, he turned her, whipped her around, and bent to jerk her completely off the ground and into his hard arms.

"Put me down, Carson!" she said curtly, pushing at his broad shoulders.

He ignored her struggles. One of his arms, the one that was under her shoulders, shifted, so that his hand could catch her long blond hair and pull her head back.

"I'm tired of letting you lead me around like a cowed dog," he said in a gruff undertone. "I'm tired of being called a savage. If that's what you think I am, maybe it's time I lived down to my reputation."

His grip on her hair was painful, and she only half heard the harsh words. Then, with shocking precision, he brought his hard mouth down on her parted lips and took possession.

It was the first time he'd touched her, ever. She went rigid all over at the unfamiliar intimacy of his whiskey-scented mouth, the rasp of whiskers that raked her soft skin. Her eyes, wide open and full of astonished fear, looked up at his drawn eyebrows, at the thick black lashes that lay against his hard, dark-skinned cheek. He made an odd sound, deep in his throat, and increased the pressure of his mouth until it became bruisingly painful.

She protested, a wild sound that penetrated the mists of intoxication and made his head slowly lift.

His chiseled lips were parted, his eyes as shocked as her own, his face harder than ever as he looked down at her. His hard gaze went to her lips. In that ardent fury his teeth had cut the lower one.

All at once, he seemed to sober. He put her gently down onto her shaky legs and hesitantly took her by the shoulders.

"I'm sorry," he said slowly.

She touched her trembling lips, all the fight gone out of her. "You cut my mouth," she whispered.

He reached out an unsteady finger and touched it while his chest lifted unsteadily.

She drew back from that tingling contact, her eyes wide and uncertain.

He let his hand fall. "I don't know why I did that," he said.

She'd never wondered before about his love life, about his women. But the feel of his mouth had fostered an unexpected intimacy between them, and suddenly she was curious about him in ways that unsettled her.

"We'd better go," she said. "Jake will be worried."

She turned, leaving him to follow. She couldn't have borne having to touch him again until some of the rawness subsided.

Jake opened the door, frowning when he saw her face. "You okay?" he asked quickly.

"Just battle-scarred," she replied with a trace of humor. She climbed in, drawing her knees together as a subdued Carson climbed in beside her and slammed the door shut.

"Get going," he told Jake without looking at him.

It was a horrible ride back home for Mandelyn. She felt betrayed. In all their turbulent relationship, she'd never once thought of him in any physical way. He was much too coarse to be an object of desire, too uncivilized and antisocial. She'd vowed that she'd never love a man again, that she'd live on the memory of the love she'd lost so many years ago. And now Carson had shocked her out of her apathy with one brutal kiss. He'd robbed her of her peace of mind. Tonight, he'd changed the rules, without any warning, and she felt empty and raw and a little afraid.

When Jake pulled up at her door, she waited nervously for Carson to get out of the truck.

"Thanks," Jake whispered.

She glanced at him. "Next time, I won't come," she said curtly.

Leaving him to absorb that, she jumped down from the cab and walked stiffly toward the front door without a word to Carson. As she closed the door, she heard the pickup truck roar away. And then she cried.

Chapter 2

When dawn burst over the valley in deep, fiery lights, Mandelyn was still awake. The night before might have been only a dream except for the swollen discomfort of her lower lip, where Carson's teeth had cut it.

She sat idly on the front porch, still dressed, staring vacantly at the mountains. It was spring, and the wildflowers were blooming among the sparse vegetation, but she wasn't even aware of the sparkling early morning beauty.

Her mind had gone back to the first day she'd ever seen Carson, when she was eighteen and had just moved to Sweetwater with her Uncle Dan. She'd gone into the local fast-food restaurant for a soda and Carson had been sitting on a nearby stool.

She remembered her first glimpse of him, how

her heart had quickened, because he was the only cowboy she'd seen so far. He was lean and rangy looking, his hair as unruly then as it was now, his face unshaven, his pale eyes insolent and intimate as he lounged back against the counter and stared at her with a blatant lack of good manners.

She'd managed to ignore him at first, but when he'd called to her and asked how she'd like to go out on the town with him, her Scotch-Irish temper had burst through the restraints of her proper upbringing.

Even now, she could remember his astonished look when she'd turned on the stool, coldly ladylike in her neat white suit. She had glared at him from cold gray eyes.

"My name," she'd informed him icily, "is Miss Bush, not, 'hey, honey.' I am not looking for some fun, and if I were, it would not be with a barbarian like you."

His eyebrows had shot up and he'd actually laughed. "Well, well, if it isn't a Southern belle. Where are you from, honey?'

"I'm from Charleston," she said coldly. "That's a city. In South Carolina."

"I made good grades in geography," he replied.

She'd given a mock gasp. "You can read?"

That had set him off. The language that had followed had made her flush wildly, but it hadn't backed her down.

She'd stood up, ignoring the stares of the astonished bystanders, walked straight over to him, and coolly slapped him with all the strength of her slender body behind her small hand. And then she'd walked out the door, leaving him staring at her.

It was days later that she learned they were neighbors. He'd come to talk to Uncle Dan about a horse, and that was when she'd found out who Carson Wayne was. He'd smiled at her, and confessed to her uncle what had happened in town, as if it amused him. It had taken her weeks to get used to Carson's rowdy humor and his unpolished behavior. He would slurp his coffee and ignore his napkin, and use language that embarrassed her. But since he was always around, she had to get used to him. So she did.

Later that first year, she'd gone to the rodeo, and Carson had been beating the stuffing out of another cowboy as she was coming out of the stands. Obviously intoxicated, he was throwing off the men who tried to stop him. Without a thought of defeat, she'd walked over to Carson and touched him lightly on the arm. He'd stopped hitting the other man immediately, looking down at her with dark, quiet eyes. She'd taken his hand, and he'd let her lead him around the corral, to where Jake was waiting nervously. After that, Jake went looking for her whenever his boss went on a spree. And she always went to the rescue. But after last night, she'd never go again.

With a long sigh, she walked back into the house and put on a pot of coffee. She fixed a piece of toast and ate it with her coffee, checking the time. She had a meeting at nine with Patty Hopper, a local woman who'd just come back home fresh out of veterinary school and needed an office. Then, after lunch, she had to talk to the developer who was interested in Carson's forty-acre tract. It was going to be another long day. The man had insisted on seeing Carson personally, but after last night, it was going to be heavy going. Mandelyn didn't particularly relish the thought.

Patty met her at the vacant house Mandelyn wanted to show her. The small, dark-eyed woman had light brown hair and a broad, sweet face. She and Mandelyn had been on the verge of friendship when Patty went away to college, and they still met occasionally when the younger woman was home on vacation.

"Well, what do you think?" Mandelyn answered her. "Isn't it a great location, just off the town square? And I can help you get a great interest rate if you want to finance it over a twenty-year period."

"I'm speechless." Patty grinned warmly. "It's exactly what I wanted. I've got space for an operating room here, and enough acreage out back to put in fences for runs. This gigantic living room will make a perfect waiting room. Yes, I like it. I like the price, too."

"I just happen to have all the paperwork right here," Mandelyn laughed, producing an envelope from her large purse. "Then you can meet with James over at the bank and convince him you need the loan."

"James and I went to school together," Patty told her. "That won't be any problem at all. I've saved up a hefty down payment, and I'm a good credit risk. Just ask all my classmates who loaned me money!"

"I believe you." Mandelyn smiled as she watched Patty sign the preliminary agreement. "This is a sunny office. I can see you making your fortune right here."

"I hope you're right." Patty stood up, folding her arms over the tan sweater she was wearing with casual jeans. "Wow! All mine."

"Yours and the bank's, at least," came the dry reply.

"You're a jewel, Mandy," Patty told her. She glanced curiously at Mandelyn's lip. "I heard you were riding around with Jake in the early morning hours."

"Small towns," Mandelyn said gruffly. "Yes, I was. Carson had the local bar in an uproar again."

Patty laughed. "Just like old times," she said, and looked oddly relieved. "Carson's a bearcat, isn't he? I'm on my way out there next, on a large animal call. He's got a sick bull."

"Don't get too close, he might make a grab for you," Mandelyn teased.

"Me? Not Carson, he's too polite."

"That's rich!" Mandelyn laughed bitterly. "He's a savage. Something right out of ancient history."

"He's always been polite to me," Patty said. "Strange, isn't it, that he's never married?"

Mandelyn felt her blood boil. "It doesn't seem strange to me. He's too uncivilized to get a woman. He'd have to kidnap one and point a gun at her to get a wife!"

"I thought he was your friend," Patty said.

"He was," Mandelyn said coldly. She turned. "Well, I've got a developer coming round in about an hour. I'd better go and have my lunch. I'm glad you liked the office."

"Me too," Patty said, laughing. "Say, do you really think Carson would be all that bad in bed?" she added curiously. "He's awfully sexy."

Mandelyn couldn't meet her friend's eyes. "If you say so. I'll give you a call later about the details of the agreement, okay?" she said with a forced smile.

"Sure," Patty said. "Thanks again."

"My pleasure."

Mandelyn had a salad at the local cafe, but she didn't enjoy it. Her thoughts kept returning to Carson and to Patty's disturbing remarks about him. Afterward, she went back to her office where the developer was pacing back and forth, waiting for her. She made a sly wink at Angie, her new secretary.

"Hello, Mr. Denton," she said pleasantly, extending her hand. "Sorry I'm late. I was finalizing another deal."

"Perfectly all right," he returned, a tall, dignified man in a gray suit. "I'd like to go out to the ranch, if you're ready?"

She hesitated. "I'd better check with Mr. Wayne first," she said.

"I had your secretary do that," he said curtly. "He's waiting for us. I'll drive my car."

She didn't like his high-handedness, but she couldn't afford to antagonize a potential client, so she ground her teeth together in a false smile and followed him out the door.

"Sorry," Angie mouthed at her.

Mandelyn gave her a shrug, and winked again.

All the way to the ranch, Mandelyn felt as if her stomach was tied in knots. She glanced out across the grassy valley rather than ahead to the ramshackle house nestled in the cottonwood trees with the mountains behind it. She didn't want to see Carson. Why was fate tormenting her this way?

His black Thunderbird was sitting near the house, covered with dust and looking unused. The pickup truck Jake had driven the night before was parked by the barn. The corral was deserted. The front door was standing open, but she couldn't see through the screen.

"This is where he lives?" Mr. Denton asked in astonishment as he pulled his green Lincoln up in front of the rough wood house.

"He's rather eccentric," she faltered.

"Crazy," he muttered. He got out of the car, looking neat and alien in his city clothing, and Mandelyn fell reluctantly into step beside him. She was wearing a blue knit suit, with her hair in a bun. She looked elegant and cool, and felt neither. She'd tried to disguise her swollen lip with lipstick, but it was raw where her tongue touched it.

As they started up the steps, Carson walked out onto the porch with quick strides. He looked even taller in his work boots. He was wearing faded denim jeans and a blue chambray shirt half unbuttoned over his broad, hair-roughened chest. He looked tired and hung over, but his blue eyes were alert and at least he seemed approachable.

"Mr. Wayne?" the developer said, putting on his best smile. "Nice place you have here. Rustic."

Carson bent his head to light a cigarette, pointedly ignoring the developer's outstretched hand.

"You won't take no for an answer, will you?" Carson asked him with a cold blue glare.

Denton looked a little ruffled but he withdrew his hand and forced the smile back onto his thin lips. "I got rich that way," he replied. "Look, I'll up my previous offer by two thousand an acre. It's a perfect tract for my retirement village. Lots of water, flat land, beautiful view…"

"It's the best grazing land I've got," Carson replied. "And there's a fort on the place that dates back to the earliest settlement."

"The fort could be moved. I'd be willing…"

"My great-grandfather built it," came the cold reply.

"Mr. Wayne," the developer began.

"Look," Carson said curtly, "I don't like being pushed. This is my place, and I don't want to sell it. I told you that. I told her that," he added, glancing toward Mandelyn. "I'm tired of talking. Come out here again and I'll load my gun."

"You can't threaten me, you backwoods…!" the developer began.

"Oh, no," Mandelyn ground out, covering her face with her hands. She knew even as Carson began cursing what was going to happen. She flinched at the first thud, the shocked cry, the heavy sound of a body landing on hard ground. She peeked between her fingers. The developer was trying to sit up, holding his jaw. Carson was standing over him with calm contempt, smoking his cigarette. He didn't even look rumpled.

"Get off my land, you…" He tacked on a few rough words and bent to lift the other man by the collar. He frog-marched him to the Lincoln, tossed him inside, and slammed the door. "Va-moose!" he growled.

Mandelyn stood there, frozen, while the Lincoln jerked out of the yard. She stared for a long minute and then, with a sigh, started after it.

"Where the hell do you think you're going?" Carson asked.

"Back to town."

"Not yet. I want to talk to you."

She whirled and glared at him. "I don't want to talk to you."

He took her arm and half led, half dragged her up the steps and into the house. "Did I ask?"

"No, you never do!" she shot back. "You just move in and take over! He made you a very generous offer. You've cost me a fortune...!"

"I told you not to bring him out here."

"You told my secretary he could come!" she floundered.

"Like hell I did. I told her to tell him he could come if he felt lucky."

And poor little Angie hadn't realized what that meant.

"Angie's new," she muttered, standing still in the dim living room. He didn't even have electricity. He had kerosene lanterns and furniture that she didn't want to sit on. It looked as if it were made with leftover gunnysacks.

"Sit," he said curtly, dropping into a ragged armchair.

She shifted uncomfortably on her feet. She'd only been in this house once or twice, with her uncle. Since his death, she'd found excuses to stay on the porch or in the yard when she stopped by to talk business with Carson.

His face hardened when he saw the look she was giving the sparse furniture. He got up, furiously angry, and walked into the kitchen.

"In here," he said icily. "Maybe the kitchen chairs will suit you better."

She felt cruel. She hadn't meant to be rude. With a sigh, she walked past him and sat down in one of the cane-bottomed chairs around the table with its red-checked oilcloth cover. "I'm sorry," she said. "I wasn't trying to be rude."

"You didn't want to soil your designer clothes on my filthy furniture," he laughed through narrowed eyes. He sat down roughly and leaned back in the chair, glaring at her. "Why pussyfoot around?"

She stared at him unblinkingly. "What do you want?"

"There's a question," he replied softly. His blue eyes wandered slowly over her face, down to her lips, and hardened visibly. "Hell," he breathed at the swollen evidence of his brutality. He pulled an ashtray toward him with a sigh and crushed out his half-finished cigarette. "I didn't realize how rough I'd been."

"I'll put it down to experience," she said curtly.

"Do you have much?" he asked, holding her gaze. "Did you fight because you were afraid?"

"You were hurting me!" she said, red with embarrassment and bad temper.

His nostrils flared as he breathed. He paused a moment, and his next words took her completely by surprise. "You told Patty I was too savage to get a woman."

Her mouth flew open. She just sat and stared, hardly able to believe Patty's betrayal.

"I... I never dreamed..."

"That she'd tell me?" he asked coolly. He pulled another cigarette from his pocket and lit it with an impatient snap of his lighter. "She was kidding around, she didn't mean anything. I guess you didn't either." He stared at the cigarette. "I've been thinking about it a lot lately, about getting older, being alone." He looked up. "When Patty said that this morning, it made me mad as hell. Then I realized that you were right, that I don't even know how to behave in polite society. That I'm not...civilized."

"Carson..." she began, at a loss for words.

He shook his head. "Don't apologize. Not for telling the truth." He sighed, stretching, and the hard, heavy muscles of his chest were evident beneath his shirt. Her eyes were drawn to the mat of dark hair visible in the opening, and she felt a sensation that shocked her. "I didn't sleep," he said after a minute, watching her. "I'm sorry I cut your lip, that I manhandled you. I guess you knew I was drinking."

"You tasted of whiskey," she said without thinking, and then flushed when she remembered exactly how he'd tasted.

"Did I?" His eyes dropped to her swollen lip. "I don't know what came over me. And you fought me...that only made it worse. You should have known better, little debutante."

"I've been fighting you for years," she reminded him.

"Verbally," he agreed. "Not physically."

She glared at him. "What was I supposed to do, lie back and enjoy it?" she challenged.

His eyes darkened. His chest rose and fell roughly. "All right, I'm sorry," he growled. "For God's sake, what do you expect? I never knew my mother, never had a sister. My whole life revolved around a man who beat the hell out of me when I disobeyed...."

She stood quietly, forcing away her bad temper, hearing him without thinking until the words began to penetrate. She turned slowly and stared up at him. "Beat you?"

He drew in a slow breath, then glanced down at her bare arm where his strong, tanned fingers held it firmly. His thumb moved on the soft skin experimentally. "My father was a cattleman," he said. "My mother couldn't live with him. She ran away when I was four. He took me in hand, and his idea of discipline was to hit me when I did something he didn't like. I had a struggle just to get through school—he didn't believe in education. But by then, I outweighed him by fifty pounds," he added with glittering eyes, "and I could fight back."

It explained a lot of things. He never talked about his childhood, although she'd heard Jake make veiled references to how rough it had been.

Her eyes searched his hard face curiously.

He lifted his hand to her face and touched her lip gently. "I'm sorry I kissed you like that."

She went flaming red. She felt as if his eyes could see right through her.

"I've never been gentle," he said, "because I never knew what it was to be treated gently. And now, I'm thirty-eight years old, and I'm lonely. And I don't know how to court a woman. Because I'm a savage. This," he sighed bitterly, tracing her swollen lip, "is proof of it."

She stared up at him, searching his eyes quietly as his hand dropped. "Didn't you have any other relatives?" she asked.

"Not one," he said. He turned away and went to stand by the window. "I ran away from home once or twice. He always came after me. Eventually I learned to fight back, and the beatings stopped. But I was fourteen by then. The damage had already been done."

She studied his long back in silence, and then

shifted, looking around the messy kitchen until her eyes found a facsimile of a coffeepot. She got to her feet. "Mind if I make some coffee?" she asked. "I'm sort of thirsty."

"Help yourself." He watched her with a familiar, unblinking scrutiny. "You look odd, doing that," he remarked.

"Why?" she asked with a laugh. "I'm very domestic. I cook, too, or don't you remember those dinners Uncle used to invite you to?"

"It's been years since I've eaten at your table."

She stared down at the pot she was filling. How could she possibly confess that she was too uneasy with him to enjoy his company? He disturbed her, unsettled her and she didn't understand why. Which only made it worse.

"I've been too busy for guests," she said. Her eyes went up to the tattered curtains at the window. "You could use some new curtains."

"I could use a lot of things," he said curtly. "This house is falling apart."

"You're letting it," she reminded him. She put the pot on to boil, grimacing at the grease that had congealed and blackened on top of the once-white range.

"There hasn't been any reason to fix it up before," he said. "Just me, living alone, not much company. But I've hired a construction firm to do some renovations."

That was startling. She turned to face him, her

gray eyes wide and curious. "Why?" she asked without thinking.

"It has something to do with the reason I brought you in here," he admitted. He finished the cigarette and crushed it out. "I need some help."

"You!" she burst out.

He glared at her. "Don't make jokes."

"Okay," she sighed. "What do you want me to do?"

He hesitated uncharacteristically. His face hardened. "Hell, look at me," he growled finally, ramming his hands into the pockets of his worn, faded jeans. "You told Patty I was too savage to get a woman, and you were right. I don't know how to behave in civilized company. I don't even know which fork to use in a fancy restaurant." He shifted restlessly, looking arrogant and proud and self-conscious all at once. "I want you to teach me some manners."

"Me?" Mandelyn exclaimed in shock.

"Of course you," he shot back. "Who else do I know with a cultured background? I need educating."

She blinked away her confusion. "After all these years, why now?"

"Females," he said angrily. "You always have to know it all, don't you? Every single damned thing...all right," he sighed roughly, running a hand through his thick hair. "There's a woman."

She didn't know whether to laugh or cry. She stood there like an elegant statue, staring at him. Patty! she thought. It had to be Patty! It was the only possibility that made sense. His unreasonable anger about what Mandelyn had said to Patty, his sudden decision to renovate the house coinciding with Patty's return to Sweetwater. So that was it. The invulnerable man was in love, and he thought Patty had become too citified to like him the way he was. So he was making the supreme sacrifice and having himself turned into a gentleman. Pygmalion in reverse.

"Well?" he persisted, glaring at her. "Yes or no?"

She lifted her shoulders. "Surely there's someone else."

"Not someone like you," he returned. His eyes wandered over her, full of appreciation and something much darker that she missed. "You're quality. A real, honest-to-God lady. No, there's no one else who could teach me as well as you could."

She dropped her eyes to the coffeepot and watched it bubble away.

"Look on it as a challenge," he coaxed. "Something to fill your spare hours. Don't you ever get lonely?"

Her face lifted and she studied him. "Yes," she said. "Especially since Uncle died."

"You don't date?" he said.

She shifted uncomfortably. There was a reason for that, but she didn't want to discuss it with him, not now. "I like my own company."

"It isn't good for a woman to live alone. Haven't you ever thought about getting married?"

"I've thought about a lot of things. What do you want in your coffee?"

She poured it out and braved the refrigerator for cream. Inside there was a basket of eggs, some unsliced bacon, some moldy lumps and what appeared to have been butter at one time.

"I don't have any milk, if that's what you're looking for," he muttered.

She gaped at him. "You have hundreds of cows on this ranch, and you don't have any milk?"

"It isn't a dairy farm," he said.

"A cow is a cow!"

"If you want the damned milk, go milk one of them, then!"

She put her hands on her hips and glared at him. He scowled back. Eventually, she gave in with a sigh and put the cups on the table.

"That's what I like most about you," he said as she sat down gingerly in one of the rickety old chairs.

Her eyes came up. "What?"

He smiled slowly, and his blue eyes darkened, glittered. "You fight me."

Her skin tingled at the way he said it. Before she thought, she said, "You didn't like it last night."

His smile faded. He sighed and lifted the cracked mug to his lips. "I was drunk last night."

"Why?"

He shrugged. "Things got on top of me. I started thinking about how alone I was...." His eyes shot up, pinning hers. "I didn't expect to see you today. I thought you'd never speak to me again."

She fidgeted uncomfortably. "We all get depressed sometimes, even me. It's all right, no harm done." She touched her lower lip with her tongue. "Well, no permanent harm, anyway," she added dryly.

"What you told Patty was true," he said.

"I didn't really mean that, or what I called you last night," she said, watching him. "You're not an unattractive man, Carson."

"Pull the other one," he said curtly and put his cup down to light another cigarette. "I've finally got a little money, and I'm working on some investments that will pay a good dividend. But there's nothing about me that would attract a woman, physically or intellectually, and you know it."

She caught her breath. Did he really believe that? Her eyes wandered slowly over the lean, tough length of him, the powerful muscles of his arms and chest, the narrow flat stomach and long legs. He was devastating physically. Even his craggy face was appealing, if it were shaved and his hair trimmed. She remembered suddenly what Patty had said about how he'd be in bed, and she turned crimson.

He looked up in time to catch that blush and he frowned. "What brought that on?"

She wondered what he'd say if she admitted that she and Patty had been wondering how he was in bed. "Nothing," she said, "just a stray thought."

"Twenty-six, and you still blush like a virgin," he murmured, watching her. "Are you one?" he asked, smiling faintly.

"Carson Joseph Wayne!" she exclaimed.

His blue eyes searched her gray ones. "I didn't realize you knew my middle name."

She toyed with her coffee cup. "It was on the deed, when I sold you that ten-acre parcel that used to be part of Uncle's land."

"Was it?" He sipped some more of his coffee. "You still haven't answered me. Will you teach me?"

She went hot all over at the way he said it. "Carson, any woman who wanted you wouldn't mind the way you are…" she began diplomatically.

"This one would," he said harshly.

She was suddenly jealous and didn't know why. How ridiculous! She touched her temple with a long finger. "Well…"

"I'm not stupid," he said shortly. "I can learn."

"Oh, all right," she said with equal curtness.

He seemed to relax a little. "Great. Where do we start?"

Her eyes wandered over him. God help her, it would take a miracle. "You'll need some new clothes," she said. "A haircut, a shave…"

"What kind of clothes?"

"Shirts and slacks and jeans, and a suit or two."

"What kind? What color?"

She grimaced. "Well, I don't know!"

"You'll have to come with me to Phoenix," he said. "There are some big department stores there."

"Why not Carter's Men's Shop in Sweetwater?" she protested.

His jaw tightened. "No way am I going in there with you, while old man Carter laughs in his whiskers watching us."

She almost laughed at the fierce way he said it. "Okay. Phoenix it is."

"Tomorrow," he added firmly. "It's Saturday," he reminded her when she started to protest. "You can't have any business that won't wait until Monday."

"That sounds as if I'd better not," she laughed.

"You work too hard as it is," he said. "Tomorrow you'll have a holiday. I'll even buy you lunch. You can teach me some table manners at the same time."

It looked like this was going to be a fulltime

job, but suddenly she didn't mind. The project might be fun at that. After all, Carson did have distinct possibilities. His physique was superb. Why hadn't she ever noticed that? She lifted her cup and sipped her coffee while Carson slurped his.

"That's the first thing," she said, indicating the cup. "Sip, don't slurp."

And when he tried it, unoffended, and succeeded, she grinned at him. He grinned back and a wild flare of sensation tingled up her spine. She'd have to be careful, she told herself. After all, she was revamping him for another woman, not herself. And then she wondered why that was such a depressing thought.

Chapter 3

If it had sounded like a simple thing, helping Carson buy clothes, Mandelyn soon lost her illusions.

"You can't be serious," he told her, glaring as she tried to convince him that a pale blue pin-striped shirt with a white collar was very trendy and chic. "The boys would laugh me out of the yard."

She sighed. "Carson, it's a whole new world. Nobody has to go around in white shirts anymore unless they want to."

"What kind of tie would I wear with that... thing," he asked shortly, while the small salesman hovered nearby chewing on his lower lip.

"A solid one, or something with a small print."

"God save us," Carson burst out.

"And with a solid colored shirt—say, pink—you'd wear a striped tie."

"I'm not wearing pink shirts," he retorted. "I'm a man!"

"A caveman," she agreed. "If you don't want my advice, I'll go buy a tube of lipstick."

"Hold it," he called as she started to walk away. He stared down at the packaged shirt. "All right, I'll get it."

She didn't smile, but it took an effort. Her eyes went over him. He was wearing a beige corduroy jacket and a worn white turtleneck shirt and tan polyester slacks. He'd had a haircut and a shave, though, and already he looked different. In the right clothes, he'd be an absolute knockout, she realized.

After a few minutes, she convinced him that striped shirts weren't at all effeminate, and he bought several more in different colors and ties to match. Then she coaxed him toward the suits.

The salesman took him to the changing rooms, and when he came back minutes later in a vested blue pinstriped suit wearing a blue shirt and burgundy tie, she almost fell off her chair. He didn't look like Carson anymore, except for the rigid features and glittering blue eyes.

"Oh, my," she said softly, staring at him.

His expression softened just a little. "Will I do?" he asked.

"Yes, you'll do," she agreed, smiling. "Women, look out!"

He smiled reluctantly. "Okay, what else do I need?"

"How about something tan?" she asked. "One of those Western-cut suits."

He tried one on, with similar results. He had just the physique to look good in a suit, and the Western cut showed it off to perfection. She let the salesman point him toward some sports coats and slacks, and then after he had paid for his purchases, she talked him into two pairs of new boots and a gray Stetson and a brown one to top it all off.

Just before they left the store she remembered some items they hadn't shopped for. She turned, but she lost her tongue immediately when she tried to say what was on her mind.

His eyebrows arched. "Something wrong?"

"Something we forgot," she said hesitantly.

A corner of his mouth pulled up. "I don't wear pajamas."

"How about things to go under them?" she said finally, averting her eyes.

"My God, you're shy," he laughed, astonished.

"So what?" she returned, her whole stance belligerent. "I've never gone shopping with a man before. And do you have socks?"

"I guess I'd better go back, hadn't I?" He put

the parcels in the car. Then he opened the passenger door and helped Mandelyn inside.

"Will you be all right here until I get back?" he asked.

"Sure," she said.

"Won't be a minute."

She watched him walk away, and smiled. Transforming him was getting to be fun, even if it did have its difficult moments.

Her eyes went over the interior of the car. It was spotless, and she guessed that he'd had the boys give it a cleaning for him, because it had never looked so clean. Her hand reached out to touch the silver arrowhead he had suspended from the rear-view mirror and she frowned slightly as she realized what it was attached to. It was a blue velvet ribbon, one she remembered having lost. She'd worn it around her hair in a ponytail one day years ago when Carson had come to see Uncle Dan. She remembered Carson tugging the ponytail, but she hadn't looked back, and later she'd missed the ribbon. It was odd, that a man as unsentimental as Carson would keep such a thing. Perhaps he liked the color, she thought, and turned her eyes back toward the store. It was hot, and there was no shade nearby. She fanned herself with her hand.

Minutes later, he came back, tossed his parcels into the trunk and climbed in beside her.

"I'm sorry, honey," he said suddenly, studying

her flushed, perspiring skin. "I didn't expect to be so long. There was a crowd."

She smiled. "I'm okay."

He studied her eyes for a long moment, and his face seemed to go rigid. "Oh, God, you're something," he said under his breath.

The passion in his soft words stirred something deep inside her. She stared back at him and couldn't drag her eyes away. It was a moment out of time. Her eyes dropped involuntarily to his hard mouth.

"Don't," he laughed roughly, turning back to twist the ignition key savagely. "Keep those curious glances to yourself, unless you want me to kiss you again."

He'd shocked her, and her face showed it. She wondered if he wanted her. Then she remembered Patty and went cold. Her eyes gazed out the window. If he had any emotion in him at all, it would naturally be for Patty. Wasn't the object of this whole crusade to make him into a man Patty would want? She crossed her long legs with a sigh and stared out over the city.

"Hungry?" he asked after a minute.

"I could eat a salad," she agreed.

"Rabbit food," he shot back. "You can get that any day."

Her eyebrows arched. "That sounds like you're taking me someplace special," she said, glancing at him with a grin. "Are you?"

"Do you like crepes?" he asked.

Her eyes lit up. "Oh, yes!"

He smiled faintly. "A cattleman I know told me about a place. We'll give it a try."

It turned out to be a hotel restaurant, a very classy one. Mandelyn had definite misgivings about how this was going to turn out, but she'd never be able to teach Carson any manners without going into places like this. So she crossed her fingers and followed him in.

"Do you have a reservation, monsieur?" the maître d' asked with casual politeness, his shrewd eyes going over Carson's worn jacket and polyester trousers. "We are very crowded today."

There were empty tables, Mandelyn could see them, and she knew what was going on. She touched Carson's arm and whispered, "Give him a tip."

"A tip?" Carson growled, glaring down at the shorter man with eyes that threatened to fry him to a crisp. "A tip, hell! I want a table. And I'd better get one fast, sonny, or you and your phony French accent are going right out that front door together." He grinned as he said it, and Mandelyn hid her face in her hands.

"A table for two, monsieur?" the maître d' said with a shaky smile and a quick wave of his hand. "*Mais oui!* Just follow me, *s'il vous plait!*"

"Tip him, hell," Carson scoffed. "You just have to know the right words to say."

She didn't answer. All around the exclusive dining room, people were staring at them. She tried to follow some distance behind him; maybe she could look as if she were alone.

"Don't hang back there, for God's sake, I'll lose you," Carson said, gripping her arm to half drag her to the table the maître d' was indicating. "Here. Sit down."

He plopped her into a chair and jerked out one for himself, "How about a menu?"

The maître d' turned pink. "Of course. At once."

He signaled a waiter with almost comical haste. "Henri will take care of you, monsieur, mademoiselle," he said, and bowing, beat a hasty retreat.

Henri moved to the table and presented the menus with a flourish. "Would monsieur and mademoiselle like a moment to peruse the menus?" he asked politely.

"Hell, no, we want these crepes," Carson said, pointing at the entry on the menu. "I'll have about five. Get her two, she needs fattening up. And bring us some coffee."

Mandelyn looked under the table, wondering if she might fit beneath it if she tried hard enough.

Henri swallowed. "*Oui,* monsieur. Would you care for a wine list?"

"Hell, what would I do with that?" Carson asked, glaring belligerently at the waiter. "I don't give a damn what kind of wine you've got. Want me to give you a list of my herefords, lot numbers and all? I've got several hundred...."

"I will bring the coffee, monsieur!" the waiter said quickly, and exited.

"This is easy," Carson said, smiling at Mandelyn. "And they say it's hard to get service in fancy restaurants."

She covered her face with her hands again, trying to get her mind settled so that she could explain it to him. But meanwhile, he'd spotted a fellow cattleman across the room.

"Hi, Ben!" he yelled in that deep, slow drawl that carried so well out on the range—and even in this crowded restaurant. "How's that new bull working out? Think your cows will throw some good crossbreeds next spring?"

"Sure hope so, Carson!" the cattleman called back, lifting his wineglass in a salute.

Carson didn't have anything to salute back with, so he raised a hand. "So that's what the wine's for," he told Mandelyn. "To make toasts with. Maybe I better order us a bottle."

"No!" she squeaked, grabbing his hand as he started looking around for Henri.

He stared pointedly at her long, slender hand, which was wrapped around half of his enormous, callused one. "Want to hold hands, do you?" he murmured drily. His fingers caught hers, and all at once the rowdy humor went out of him. He searched her gray eyes. His fingers smoothed over her skin, feeling its texture, and her heart went wild.

"Soft," he murmured. "Soft, like your mouth." He stared at her lower lip for a long moment. "I'd like to kiss you when I was sober," he said under his breath, "just to see how it would feel."

Her fingers trembled, and he felt it. His hand contracted and brought hers to his mouth. "You smell of perfume," he breathed huskily. "And you go to my head like whiskey when you look at me that way."

She tried to draw her hand back, but he wouldn't let go of it.

"You said you'd teach me," he reminded her with a slow smile. "I'm just getting in some practice."

"I said I'd teach you manners," she replied in a high-pitched tone. "You don't threaten maître d's and waiters and yell across classy restaurants, Carson."

"Okay," he said, smoothing the backs of her fingers against his hard cheek. "What else shouldn't I do?"

"What you're doing right now," she whispered.

"I'm only holding your hand," he said reasonably.

But it didn't feel that way. It felt as if he were reaching over the table and taking possession of her, total and absolute possession of her mind and her heart and even her body.

"Mandelyn," he whispered, as if he were savoring the very sound of her name, and she realized with a start that he'd hardly ever said it. It was usually some casual endearment when he spoke to her. He made her name sound new and sweet.

She watched his dark head bend over her hand with wonder, watched his chiseled lips touch it, brush it with a tenderness she hadn't imagined him capable of. Her breath caught in her throat and tremors like the harbingers of an earthquake began deep in her body.

"Carson?" she whispered back.

His eyes lifted, as if he'd heard something in her voice that he wasn't expecting.

But before he could say anything, the waiter was back with the coffee.

"Where are my crepes?" Carson asked curtly.

"It will be only a minute, monsieur, just a minute," Henri promised with a worried smile and a fervent glance toward the kitchen.

Carson stared after him. "It had better be," he said.

Henri retreated, and Mandelyn had to smother a grin. "You do come on strong, don't you?" she managed with a straight face.

"I learned early that it was the only way to

come out on top," he returned. "I don't like being put down. Never did."

"They aren't trying to put you down," she began.

"Like hell," he said, smiling coldly.

She moved restlessly in her chair. "Lifestyles among the well-to-do are different."

"You and I are pretty far apart, aren't we?" he asked quietly.

"Oh, I don't know," she murmured. "I used to think I'd enjoy going fishing once in a while, in a pair of old dungarees and a worn-out shirt."

"Did you? I could take you fishing sometime, if you like."

She looked up, half amused, and it dawned on her that she hadn't ever seen him smile as much as he had this one day. "Could you?"

He let his eyes run slowly over her. "I could loan you some old jeans and a shirt, too." He leaned back and lit a cigarette. "After all, you ought to get something out of this deal. You teach me what I need to know. And then I'll teach you a few things." He was looking straight at her when he said it, and she tingled all over.

Henri came back with the crepes seconds later, and Mandelyn was able to damp down her suddenly intense awareness of Carson while she instructed him in the use of flatware.

"Why don't they just give you a fork and let it go at that?" he grumbled when she'd explained the formal arrangement of knife, forks and spoons.

"Because it's etiquette," she told him. "Besides, you can't very well eat soup without a soup spoon, or sweeten tea without a teaspoon, or..."

"I get the idea," he sighed. "I suppose you'd never forgive me for eating peas on my knife.'

She laughed softly. "I think you might make a record book or two for managing that."

"It's easy," he returned. "All you have to do is get mashed potatoes on the knife and dip it in the peas."

She burst out laughing at the mischief in his eyes. "I give up."

"Not yet, you don't. Eat your crepes. You could use a few extra pounds. You're too thin."

Her eyebrows arched. "I never would have expected you to notice something like that."

He didn't smile. "I notice a hell of a lot about you, Mandelyn."

Once again, the way he said her name made her head swim, and she actually blushed. Her gaze fell back to her plate while Carson slowly cut his crepes.

Minutes later, after a companionable silence and a second cup of coffee, they sampled the restaurant's strawberry crepes.

Mandelyn licked whipped cream from her upper lip and Carson watched the action with an expression she didn't understand. She lifted her eyes to his and felt tremors along her spine.

"It's sexy, don't you know?" he said under his breath as he read the question in her eyes.

"Eating whipped cream?" she laughed nervously, deliberately misunderstanding him.

"Don't play dumb. You know exactly what I mean."

She ignored him and her quickened heartbeat, and finished her crepe.

"How about a movie before we go back to Sweetwater?" he asked.

"Sorry," she laughed. "I have some paperwork to do before I go to bed."

He didn't like that. His eyes glittered across the table at her. "Do you work all the time?"

"Don't you?" she returned. "I can't remember a time in the past few years when you actually took a vacation."

"Vacations are for rich men," he said, dropping his eyes to his coffee cup. He toyed with it idly. "Maybe everyone's right. Maybe I'm not cut out to be a rancher."

"What else could you be?" she teased.

"What do you mean, that I'm too crude and stupid to be anything but a cattleman?" he asked coldly. His voice carried so that people at the other tables immediately looked to see if he fit his own description of himself.

"That's not what I meant at all, and will you please lower your voice?" she asked in a squeaky tone.

"Why should I?" he asked curtly. He threw his

napkin down on the table and stood up, glaring around him. "And what are you people staring at?" he asked haughtily. "Who wrote the rules and said that you have to keep your eyes down and speak in whispers and never do anything out of the ordinary in a snobby restaurant? Do you think the waiters here drive Lincolns—is that why you're so afraid of them? Do you think that head waiter has a villa on the Riviera and owns stock in AT&T?" He laughed coldly while Mandelyn seriously considered hiding under the tablecloth. "These people that wait on you are no better or worse than any of you, and you're paying to be here just like I am, so why are you all letting these stuck-up dudes push you around?"

The cattleman a few tables over who was a friend of Carson's burst out laughing.

"Hell, yes, why are we?" he burst out, grinning. "You tell 'em, Carson!"

A lady closer to their table glared at Carson. "It's amazing the kind of people they allow in these restaurants," she said with hauteur.

Carson glared back at her. "Yes, isn't it?" he agreed with a speaking glance. "And it's amazing how many people think they're better than other people because of what they've got, right, lady?"

The lady in question turned red, got up and left.

"Please sit down," Mandelyn pleaded with Carson.

"You sit. I'm leaving. If you're coming with

me, come on. And where the hell is the check?"
he demanded of a trembling Henri. "I want it
now, not when you get around to it."

Henri was writing it as he came, his hand
shaking. "Here, monsieur!"

Carson took it and stormed out toward the ca-
shier, leaving Mandelyn to fend for herself. She
got up quietly and walked slowly out of the dining room, her poised serenity drawing reluctant
admiration. She was Miss Bush of Charleston
from her head to her toes.

But serene was the last thing she felt when she
caught up with Carson in the parking lot.

"You hot-tempered, ill-mannered, overbearing
son of Satan," she began, her small fists clenched
at her sides, her eyes throwing off silvery sparks,
her hair glinting with blond fire in the sunlight.

"Flattery won't work with me," he assured her,
grinning at her display of temper. "Get in, firecracker, and I'll take you home."

"I've never been so embarrassed…!" she began.

"Why?"

"Why!"

He stared at her as she stood rigidly beside
the car, not opening her door. "Well, get in," he
repeated.

"When you open the door for me," she said
icily. "Women's lib or not, it is good manners."

With a resigned sigh, he went around and made

an elaborate production of opening the door, helping her inside the car and closing it again.

"I'll never go anywhere with you again as long
as I live," she fumed when he'd climbed in beside
her and turned the key in the ignition.

"You started it," he reminded her as he pulled
out onto the highway. "Making that crack about
my ignorance…"

"I did no such thing," she shot back. "I simply
asked what else you'd do. You love cattle, you always have. You'd be miserable in any other job
and you know it.'

"You meant that I wasn't capable of doing anything else," he returned, his eyes growing fiery
again.

"I can't talk to you!" she ground out. "You're
always on the defensive with me, you take everything I say the wrong way!"

"I'm a savage, remember?" he asked mockingly. "What else do you expect?"

"God knows," she said. She turned her eyes out
the window to the long, arid stretch of land that
stretched toward the horizon. "None of this was
my idea," she reminded him. "I don't care if you
eat peas off your knife for the rest of your life."

There was a long, pregnant silence. He lit a
cigarette and smoked it quietly as the miles went
by. Eventually, she glanced at him. His face was
rigid, his eyes staring straight ahead. He looked
unhappy. And she felt guilty about that, guilty

about losing her temper. He wanted Patty, and without some polishing, he'd never get her. He must know that and the knowledge was eating him alive.

"How far did you get in school?" she asked suddenly.

He took a deep, slow breath, and wouldn't look at her. "I have a bachelor's degree in business administration, with a minor in economics."

She felt shocked, and it showed.

"I got my education while I was in military service, in the Marines," he told her bluntly. "But that was a long time ago. I've lived hard and I've worked hard and I haven't had time for socializing. I hate pretense. I hate people lying to each other and cutting at each other and pretending to be things they aren't. Most of all," he added hotly, "I hate places that put you down on the basis of your bank account. God, how I hate it!"

He must have spent a good part of his youth being looked down on, humiliated. Her heart thawed. She reached out and touched his sleeve very gently, and he tensed even at that light touch.

"I'm sorry," she said. "Sorry that I lost my temper, that I yelled at you."

"I have scars," he said quietly. "They don't show, and I try to forget them. But they're pretty deep."

She dropped her eyes to his stubborn, square chin. "Still want to take me fishing?"

"I reckon."

"How about Monday?"

He hesitated, and her eyes came up.

"You work on Monday," he reminded her, and there was a strangely puzzled look about him, as if he hadn't expected her to take him seriously.

"So I'll play hookey." She grinned.

He laughed softly. "All right. So will I."

She settled her head back against the seat with a sigh. "If you'll put the worm on the hook," she added. "I'm not committing homicide on any helpless worms."

Later, she thought about that sudden decision to take a day off—something she never did—and go fishing with Carson, of all people. How odd that he'd never mentioned that business degree he held, almost as if he was ashamed of it. She felt vaguely sorry for him. Carson wasn't a bad man. He had wonderful qualities. He'd stayed two nights with old Ben Hamm and his wife on their ranch when the couple had the flu. He'd fed them and taken care of them, and then paid their utility bills for the month because Ben had been unable to work for a week and had gotten behind. Then there was the poor family that he'd "adopted" for Christmas. He'd bought toys for the kids and had a huge turkey with all the trimmings delivered to their home. Yes, Carson was a caring man. He just had an extremely hard shell, and Mandelyn decided that he probably had plenty of reasons for it. What would it be like to know the man beneath the shell? She fell asleep on the thought.

Chapter 4

Bright and early Monday morning she called Angie at home and told her she wasn't coming in to the office.

"I'm going fishing. I'll call in later to see if there are any messages," she told the younger woman.

"Fishing?" Angie burst out.

"Why not?' she replied.

"Excuse me, Miss Bush." Angie cleared her throat. "It's just that I never thought you'd like fishing."

"Well, we'll both find out after this morning. Have a good day."

"You, too."

Mandelyn didn't own a pair of old jeans. She wore a slightly worn pair of designer jeans with a colorful striped pullover shirt and sneakers, and left her hair long. She looked a little less proper than usual, she decided finally.

Carson wasn't outside when she drove up, and she hesitated at the front door when he called for her to come inside. It was a little unnerving to be totally alone with him, but she chided herself for her continuing feeling of uneasiness with him and went inside anyway.

"Just be a minute," he called from the back of the house. The bedrooms must be located there, but she'd never seen them.

"Take your time," she replied. She sighed over the worn furniture and bare walls. With a little paint and love, this house had great possibilities. It wasn't all that old, and it was built sturdily. She pursed her lips, studying it. The room was big, but it could be comfortable, and there was a huge rock fireplace that would be a showpiece with a little cleaning up. The windows were long and elegant, and the floor would have a beauty all its own if it were varnished.

"You won't find any sidewinders under the rug, if that's what you're looking for," Carson taunted from the doorway.

She turned and had to force herself to look away again. He'd obviously just come from a shower. He was fully dressed except for the shirt he was shrugging into, a blue printed one that matched his eyes. She got a wildly exciting glimpse of broad, tanned muscles and a thick pelt of hair running down past the buckled belt around his lean hips, and her heart started beating unexpectedly hard. She'd seen Carson without a shirt before, for God's sake, she told herself, why was it affecting her this way all of a sudden?

"You look elegant even in jeans," he murmured drily. "Couldn't you find anything worn?"

"This is worn." She pouted, turning to find him closer than she'd expected. She took a slow breath and inhaled the scent of a men's cologne that was one of her particular favorites. "You smell good," she blurted out.

"Do I?" He laughed softly.

His hands had stilled on the top buttons of the shirt and he looked down at her in a way that threatened and excited all at the same time. His chiseled mouth was smiling in a faint, sexy way and his blue eyes narrowed as they studied her.

"Why are you so nervous?" he asked with his head lifted, so that he was looking down his crooked nose at her. "You've been alone with me before."

"You were always dressed before," she said without meaning to.

"Is that it?" He watched her face and deliberately flicked open the buttons he'd fastened. "Does this bother you?" he asked in a deep, lazy tone, moving the shirt aside to let the hair-roughened expanse of his chest show.

Her breath caught and she didn't understand why. Her lips went dry, but she barely noticed.

He lifted her hands with slow, easy movements, and brought her fingers to his cool skin, letting her feel the hard muscles.

"No flab," she laughed unsteadily, trying to keep things light between them, but her legs felt shaky.

"Not a bit," he agreed. "I work too hard for that." He pressed her fingers hard against him and moved them in a slow, sensuous pattern down the center of his chest and back up again. "I don't suppose you brought a fishing pole?"

"I don't...own one," she replied. Incredible, that they were conducting an impersonal conversation while what they were doing was growing quickly more intimate.

His chest rose and fell unevenly. He pressed her palms flat against his hardened nipples and she could hear his heartbeat, actually hear it. He moved, so that he was closer than ever, and his breath stirred the hair at her temples.

She couldn't look up, because she wanted his mouth desperately, and she knew he'd see it. She didn't understand her own wild hungers or his unexpected reaction to her nearness and her touch. She didn't understand anything.

The room seemed dark and private. There was no sound in it, except for his breathing and the loud tick of the mantel clock.

He drew his open mouth tenderly across her forehead, his breath hot, his chest shuddering with the harshness of his breathing. Impatiently, he took her hands in his and guided them down the hard muscles of his chest and around to his lean hips. She protested, a stiff little gesture.

"Don't fight me," he whispered unsteadily, moving her hands down the sides of his legs and back up to his hips. "There's nothing to be afraid of."

But there was! Her own reaction to him was terrifying. She felt his legs touch hers and she made an odd sound in her throat, one that he heard.

His head moved nearer. Her eyes closed and she felt his warm breath at her forehead, her nose, the open softness of her mouth. Unaware of her response, she opened her mouth to invite his, tilted her head back to give him full access. And waited, breathing in his scent as his mouth came closer. Would it be gentle this time, she wondered, or would he hurt…?

"Mr. Wayne!" The loud call was like a gunshot. Carson's head jerked up. He looked dazed, and his eyes were a dark blue, haunted, hungry as they met hers for just an instant before he moved away.

"What is it, Jake?" he asked curtly, buttoning his shirt as he went out onto the porch.

Mandelyn heard the voices with a sense of unreality. She was still trembling, and her mouth was hungry for the kiss she hadn't gotten. Her misty eyes searched for Carson and found him standing outside the door. She looked at him with open wonder, letting her rapt eyes wander down the superb masculinity of his back and hips and legs. She remembered the feel of his skin, the smell of him. Her breasts ached and as she crossed her arms, she felt the nipples' hardness.

She licked her dry lips and ground her teeth together as she tried to get her rebellious body back under control. It wanted him. God, it wanted him, all of him, skin against skin, mouth against hungry mouth. She almost moaned aloud at the force of that wanting, at the urgency she'd never felt before. Her sweet memories of the man in her past had faded completely away during that passionate onslaught, had been replaced with a different emotion. With a wildness that she'd never known, a violent need.

How in the world could she face Carson now, after giving herself away so completely? He was still a man, he wouldn't hesitate to take anything that was offered, despite their long friendship. If she acted like a temptress, what could she expect? He was human.

She cleared her throat as he came back into the room. If only she could find an excuse to go home.

"I'll find you a pole," he said good-humoredly, grinning at her. "Got a hat?"

"No."

"Here." He reached into the closet and tossed her a straw one that just fit. "It belonged to me, years back. Well, let's go."

He herded her out the door before she had a chance to protest, and minutes later they went bumping over his pasture in the pickup truck toward the stream where the swimming and fishing hole spread out invitingly past some cottonwood trees.

"We used to swim here," he told her as they sat on upside-down minnow buckets in the cool shade. "Some of the boys still do, but it's a good fishing spot, nevertheless. Here."

He handed her the bait can and she stared at it distastefully.

"Please?" she asked softly, looking up at him.

His eyes remained on hers for a minute before he turned them back to the bait can. "I'll show you how."

"But, Carson..."

"Just watch."

He threaded worms onto the hook while she grimaced. "Soft-hearted little thing," he chided. "I'll never take you rabbit hunting, that's for sure."

She stuck out her tongue at him. "Well, I wouldn't go, so don't ask me."

"Patty's having a party next Friday night," he said as he threw her line into the stream. The red cork bobbed gaily against the murky water. He glanced at her.

"Is she?" she asked in a breathless tone.

He threaded worms onto his own hook. "Kind of a social gathering, I think, so folks can get acquainted with her and tour her new office."

"She's really proud of it," she murmured.

He threw his own line in and leaned his elbows on his knees, holding the pole between them. Nearby birds were calling, and crickets made pleasant sounds in the underbrush.

She glanced at him. "Are you going?"

He laughed shortly. "You know I don't socialize."

She looked down at the ground. "I could... teach you."

His eyes glanced sideways. "Could you?"

"You've got the clothes now," she reminded him. "All you need to know is some of the new dance steps and how to talk to people."

He stared at her for a long moment. "Yes."

She shifted on the bucket. "Well, do you want to?"

"Want to what?" he asked huskily.

She looked up into his eyes and felt herself going hot all over. She dragged her gaze back to the water. "Uh, do you want me to teach you?"

"I think you may be the one who needs teaching," he said.

Her face flamed, because she knew exactly what he was talking about. She felt like a girl on her first date, tongue-tied and expectant.

"I know how to dance," she said.

"Deliberately misunderstanding me again?" he said with a soft laugh.

"I thought we came here to fish?"

"I am."

"Do you want to learn to dance or not?" she asked impatiently.

"I guess so."

"You can come over tomorrow night, if you want to," she said. "I'll make supper."

He studied her for a long moment. "All right."

She tingled from head to toe in a new, exciting way. She smiled, and he watched the movement of her lips with an expression that it was just as well she didn't see. It would have frightened her.

She studied the bobbing red cork with drowsy, contented eyes, hardly aware when it went straight under. When she felt the tug on the line and realized what was happening, she jerked too soon. The hook came flying up on the bank, straight into her shirt and caught there.

"My God, were you trying to send the fish to the moon?" Carson drawled. "You caught something at least."

She glared at him. "My favorite shirt," she moaned, letting her eyes fall to the hook sticking through the soft fabric just above the peak of her tiptilted breast.

"Hold still and I'll get it out for you," he said. He put down his pole and knelt beside her.

She hadn't realized how intimate it was going

to be. In order to extricate the barbed hook, he had to slide one lean, work-roughened hand into the V-neck of the shirt. And Mandelyn wasn't wearing a bra. That discovery made Carson start violently.

His eyes met hers. She could see the dark blue circles around his lighter blue irises, and the black thickness of his lashes. But what she was feeling was the touch of his knuckles on her bare breast, and her body was reacting noticeably to it.

"Carson, I can get it out," she said too quickly.

"Let me," he whispered. But he was holding her eyes when he said it, and his fingers were moving very delicately on bare skin. She trembled.

He smelled of wind and fir trees and desert. And his skin was rough against her softness, but it was a natural roughness, like sand against silk, or bark against water.

Even the crickets seemed to have gone mute. There was silence all around them in the little glade. Nothing existed except Mandelyn's awed face and Carson's hard one, and the sound of his breathing as he closed his eyes and tenderly cradled Mandelyn's head in one big hand.

She jerked a little in reaction, but he shook his head slowly and lowered his face toward her.

"Sit still, Mandy," he whispered as his lips stroked her mouth. "I just want to see how you taste when I'm sober."

"Carson, your hand..." she whispered half-heartedly, and her slender fingers touched his hairy wrist in token protest.

"Shh," he breathed. His mouth was like a teasing breeze, brushing at her lips. His fingers stroked over the soft curve of her breast, edging toward the hard tip with every movement, teasing her body as he teased her mouth.

She stiffened, moved. Her eyes opened, her breath quickened. His face was so close that all she could see was his mouth. He'd shaved. That registered. And he tasted of smoke and coffee and mint. But his hand...!

She caught it just as his thumb and forefinger found the hard tip, and her nails bit into him helplessly and she moaned. It took every ounce of will power she had to move his hand away. She was afraid of the new sensations she was feeling. She was afraid of Carson.

"All right," he said softly, not offended at all. Her flushed face and wide, frightened eyes told him everything he needed to know. His hand brushed the long strands of hair away from her cheeks, and he looked at her with such reverence that she couldn't seem to move.

"The hook," she reminded him.

"Yes," he murmured, smiling faintly. "Later. I want that kiss, honey."

Her heart was beating so wildly that she could barely breathe at all. His head bent and she waited for his mouth, no protest left in her, only a sense of anticipation.

His lips were warm and hard and exquisitely tender. She closed her eyes with a soft sigh and let him do what he wanted. He eased between her trembling lips, letting her feel the texture of his own. Her hands dug into the hard muscles of his shoulders in an agony of wanting.

But still he teased her, rubbing his closed lips between her open ones, nibbling at her soft mouth. And then he stopped. She moaned aloud as he got to his feet and reached down to bring her body into the hard curve of his.

"It's all right," he murmured, wrapping her securely in his arms. "I only want to feel you while we kiss."

She reached up, hesitant, and touched his hard face.

"Carson," she whispered.

His chest rose and fell roughly. "I've waited years for you to say my name that way," he murmured unsteadily as he bent again. "Years, centuries…"

"Hard," she pleaded, trembling. "Hard, please…!"

A tremor ran through him, probably of shock, she thought dizzily as he took her open mouth. She'd shocked herself with the whispered demand. She tasted him, experienced him with every sense she had as he gently crushed her breasts into his hard chest and his mouth merged roughly, intimately with her own. His tongue stabbed between her teeth, into the dark warmth of her mouth, tangling with her tongue in a wild, exquisite exploration.

He groaned against her mouth. A faint tremor shook his arms, and she arched into his body. She wanted him. Her body told her that, it screamed at her to end this sweet torment. She wanted to feel his skin against hers, she wanted the driving power of his body to overwhelm her, possess her. She wanted his open mouth on her soft breasts....

When he lifted his head abruptly, it was like being thrown to the ground. She shivered.

His darkened blue eyes searched hers quickly, intensely, and although he'd loosened his grip, he still held her by the arms. He started to draw back and her shirt came with him.

"Oh, hell," he muttered, looking down. The hook that had gone through her blouse had caught in the thick pocket of his shirt.

She started laughing as reaction set in. Her twinkling eyes sought his. "I've hooked you," she teased.

He stared at her for a long moment. "I haven't seen you laugh before. Not like this."

"I haven't felt like this before," she blurted out. "I mean, being relaxed and going fishing and... and being myself."

"Stand still while I get us untangled," he said, and reached down, frowning as he tried to extract the barbed end of the hook from his pocket. "Damn, I'll have to cut it," he muttered. He dove into his pocket and dragged out an old pocket knife, expertly extracting the blade and slicing deftly through the fabric. His eyes glanced at her apologetically. "Sorry, honey, but this is the only way. I'll buy you another blouse."

"You don't have to do that. It was my fault, after all," she said breathlessly.

"Stand still, so I don't nick you," he said softly and slid his hand under the fabric again, against her bare skin.

She felt wildly female at the feel and sight of that dark-skinned, tough hand inside her blouse. Her lips parted and she studied the face so close to hers with wide, fascinated eyes.

He felt the stare and looked down into her eyes. His hands paused in their task and he watched her for a long moment. "Why didn't you want me to touch you?" he whispered.

Her lower lip trembled a little. "I…haven't been touched…that way since I was eighteen, Carson," she said unsteadily.

"If I'd persisted a minute longer, you'd have let me, though, wouldn't you?" he asked.

She licked her dry lips and her wide gray eyes searched his blue ones with uncertainty. "I didn't expect that," she whispered.

"Why not? I'm human, Mandy. I may be rough

and half-civilized, but I'm capable of wanting a woman."

"Oh, I didn't mean it like that," she said, touching his hard mouth with her fingers. She searched his eyes curiously. "Carson...you...you've had women, haven't you?"

Time seemed to hang suspended between them. "Yes," he said quietly.

Her breath shuddered out of her throat. Her fingers traced his lips unsteadily, with helpless pleasure. "I've never been to bed with a man," she breathed.

His nostrils flared. His chest rose and fell raggedly. "You're twenty-six."

She smiled nervously. Having him this close was affecting her wildly. "Yes, I know. Do you think I might get in the record books?"

"Not," he sighed heavily, "if you keep touching me that way."

"Oh!" Belatedly she realized just how intimate her fingers had grown on his face. She moved them back down to his arm. "Sorry."

"You excite me," he admitted, turning his attention back to the hook. He sliced the fabric gently, not unaware of her hot blush or the increasing pressure of her fingers. "So watch out."

That wasn't going to be easy, she realized, feeling his warm fingers being slowly removed from her blouse. "Thank you," she said as he removed the hook as well.

"My pleasure," he murmured drily.

"Carson, I didn't mean to…" she began, losing her train of thought when he looked down into her eyes. "I didn't know… I wasn't…"

"Hush." He handed her the fishing pole with a warm, knowing look. "I haven't been with a woman in a long time," he said slowly. "It was a moment out of time, that's all. Nothing to be afraid of."

"Of course." She managed to get a worm on the hook and began talking real estate, out of nervousness. She'd reacted to Carson's love-making like a shy young girl, and she knew now that while he might need lessons in deportment, he'd never need them as a lover. He knew exactly what to do with a woman. And now she was more afraid of him than ever. In all the years she'd known him, she'd never thought of him as a lover. Now it was impossible to think of him any other way.

He followed her lead in conversation, and they talked about general things for a long time while the day moved lazily by. After they had caught a good number of fish, they packed up their gear and went back to the house.

"I've enjoyed today. Thank you," she said. She was reluctant to leave him, and that was odd. In the past she'd always been glad to get out of his sight.

"So have I," he replied. He studied her for a

long moment. "Want to stay for supper? We can cook the fish together."

She should have said no. But she didn't. Her face lit up and she smiled. "Sure!"

He chuckled. "Want to clean them for me?"

She frowned. "Carson, I hate to be a drag, but I don't think I know how. Uncle didn't fish, you know."

"Yes, and cleaning fish isn't something you learn in finishing school, is it, little lady?"

He didn't say it in an insulting way. She searched his hard face. "Does it bother you, my background?"

"No," he said firmly. "If you want to know, I think a lot of you. Until you came along, I'd never met a real lady."

"You wouldn't think I was one at times, though," she murmured, smiling at him as she followed him into the kitchen.

"You're a firecracker sometimes, all right," he agreed. He caught her by the waist after he'd put down the string of fish, and jerked her against his body. "But I like you that way, Mandy. A woman with a temper," he murmured, bending, "is usually pretty passionate...."

His mouth crushed down against hers and she moaned, the sound unusually loud in the confines of the room as she savored his strength, the urgency of his hard kiss.

He lifted his head, his eyes glittering with

some new emotion. "Why did you moan?" he asked roughly. "Fear or pleasure?"

Her lips trembled and, embarrassed, she pulled away. "I'll get started on the fish."

He watched her for a minute speculatively and then he smiled. "I'll get some potatoes to fry."

It was a quiet supper. She enjoyed her crisp fish, but Carson seemed preoccupied.

"Want to call it off?" she asked.

His head came up. "What?"

"Tomorrow night."

He shook his head. "No. I want to learn to dance." His eyes dropped to her soft mouth. "With you," he added softly.

Her chest felt tight. He was doing it again, using that wicked charm that she hadn't known he possessed.

"I have to practice on somebody, don't I?" he asked when he saw her hesitation. "I thought teaching me how to make love went part and parcel with teaching me to court a woman," he added with a wicked smile.

She flushed. "You don't need teaching in that department, and well you know it," she said.

His eyebrows arched. "I don't?"

She looked up. Her wide eyes pleaded with him. "Don't take advantage, will you?" she asked softly. "I'm afraid of you, a little."

"Yes, I know you are," he replied, his voice deep and quiet in the stillness of the room. He reached across the table and took her small hand in his, rubbing his thumb over the silky skin. "Haven't you ever wanted a man, or was it that exclusive upbringing that kept you innocent?"

"That exclusive upbringing is the downfall of a lot of girls," she murmured drily. "Most of the others were quite experienced."

"Didn't you date?"

That brought back painful memories, and she didn't want to face them. She shrugged. "I was terribly shy in those days. It was hard for me to talk to men at all."

"Not when you got out here," he chuckled. "I'll never forget the first time I saw you."

"I slapped you," she recalled with a wicked smile. "I didn't know at the time how dangerous that was."

"I would never hit you back," he said. "I'd cut off my arm first."

"That's what Jake knows, that's why I always get rousted out of bed to come and save the world from you," she laughed.

He studied her hand. "Jake isn't as blind as you are, I guess."

"Blind?"

"It doesn't matter." He let go of her fingers and lit a cigarette. His eyes searched hers. "Getting dark. You'd better go home, before somebody makes a remark about your being here alone with me after dark."

"Would that bother you?"

"Yes," he said simply. "I don't want any blemish on your reputation. I'd fire any one of my men who suggested that anything improper went on here."

"It did this afternoon," she blurted out and then flushed.

He searched her eyes slowly. "I wanted to see if I could make you want me," he explained quietly.

She got up from the table in such a rush that she almost knocked over her chair. "I'd better go," she faltered.

He got up, too, and walked along behind her at a slow, steady, confident pace.

"Was that too crude a remark for a gentleman to make?" he murmured drily. "Sorry, Mandy, I don't always think before I say things to you. Look on it as getting some sexual experience. You seem to be pretty backward yourself in that department."

She turned at the front porch and met his stare levelly. "Are you sorry? Would you rather I was experienced?"

He reached out and put his knuckles against her lips. "I'd like, very much, to let you get that kind of experience with me," he said quietly. "Because the way I'd take you, even the first time would be good. I'd make sure of it."

She could hardly walk, her knees felt so weak.

She headed for her car in a daze, wondering at the explosive quality of their changing relationship.

"Hey," he called as she opened her car door.

"What?" she asked.

"What time tomorrow night?"

She swallowed and looked back. He was standing on the porch, leaning against a post. The soft light of the kerosene lanterns outlined his superb physique. He looked devastating, and she wondered what he'd do if she walked back up on that porch and kissed him.

"Oh…about six," she faltered.

"Do I dress?"

"You'd better," she said, "if we're going to do the thing properly."

"By all means," he murmured drily. "'Night, honey."

"Good night, Carson."

She drove off, jerking the car as she never had before. Carson was getting to her! She must be off her rocker to let him get under her skin that way. She was the teacher, not Carson. At least, it had started out that way. She had to be careful. Her memories of love were too sweet to let reality interfere with them. She'd learned the hard way that loving was the first step to agony. She didn't want to go through it again. She couldn't! From now on, she'd just keep Carson at arm's length. It was safer that way.

Chapter 5

Mandelyn went home and paced the floor until bedtime. And then she tossed and turned for hours, remembering vividly the touch of Carson's lean fingers on her breast, the fierce hunger of his mouth on her own. She felt on fire for him, and part of her hated the reaction.

It had been years. Years, since she'd felt passion. She hadn't wanted to give herself over to it again, and yet Carson had kindled an emotion in her that overwhelmed her tenderest memories of the past. She'd never felt so violent, so hungry. She rolled over onto her back and stared at the ceiling. Perhaps it was her age. Perhaps she'd reached the brink of spinsterhood and was feeling alone, as Carson felt alone.

She could picture him, blue eyes devouring her face, dark-skinned hands so gentle on her body....

Of course, it could just be infatuation. He was her creation, after all, she was teaching him. Yes, that could be it. She could be like Svengali, overcome by pride. But if that was it, why did she tingle when she thought about Carson? She closed her eyes and thought about birds.

Patty came by the office the next day at lunchtime with some documents from the bank. "Here are the loan papers," she said with a grin. "What time do we meet with that attorney?"

"Today at five," Mandelyn said. "Happy?"

"Just ecstatic," came the reply. "I've got to run out to Carson's and see about that bull. Want to come along, and we'll swing by the barbecue place and have lunch on the way back?"

"Yes, I'd like that," Mandelyn said. "Angie, just close up at noon when you get your own lunch, okay?"

Angie nodded. "Have fun."

Fun! Mandelyn's heart was racing wildly as she climbed into the red pickup truck beside Patty. She didn't really want to see Carson, but he was coming to her house for dinner that night so she couldn't very well avoid him.

Carson wasn't at the house when they drove up. The door was closed and locked.

"I wonder where he could be?" Patty asked, nibbling on her lip. "Surely to goodness he knew I was coming?"

"Maybe he's in the barn," Mandelyn suggested.

Patty sighed. "Boy, am I sharp, not to have thought of that. Maybe I should try another profession...yep, look, there's the ranch pickup."

They walked down to the barn. Mandelyn wished she hadn't worn the spiked high heels that went so well with her jaunty little two-piece blue and white suit. But when she entered the barn and saw the frank appreciation on Carson's face, she decided it was worth a little discomfort. He was half kneeling beside his bull, with Jake at his side, and he couldn't seem to take his eyes off her.

Both men got to their feet, and Mandelyn couldn't help noticing how animated Patty suddenly became. She was wearing jeans and a T-shirt, and had her hair pulled back in a bun, but she still looked feminine and cute, and Carson gave her a big grin and hugged her.

"There's my best girl," he said, and Mandelyn felt suddenly murderous.

"How's my patient?" Patty asked, hugging him back while Jake looked at them with an expression Mandelyn couldn't quite describe.

"Well, he's about the same," Carson sighed, staring down at the bull. He still had an arm around Patty, and Mandelyn found she resented it.

Patty got down beside the big animal, a Hereford, and checked him over with professional thoroughness. "We'll try another dose of the same, and see if that won't do it. He's improved some, Carson, I think we can save him."

"If you don't, I may never speak to you again," Carson assured her. "And I'll guarantee at least five of my cows will die of broken hearts, judging by the way they've behaved since he's been out of action."

Mandelyn flushed, but Patty only laughed. "We'll restore him to his former vigor. Let me get my bag. Mandy, you aren't in a rush to get back, are you?"

"No," came the quiet reply. "I don't have anything pressing."

"Here, I'll help with that bag," Jake said curtly, and walked out of the barn behind Patty with a determined stride. Mandelyn had never actually seen the easygoing foreman move so quickly.

Carson studied Mandelyn with narrow, thoughtful eyes, hands on his hips, powerful legs apart. "You're quiet. And you won't look at me. Why?"

Her eyes glanced off his and back down to the bull. "What's the matter with the bull?" she asked nervously.

He moved closer, ignoring the question. So close that she could smell him, feel him, touch him if she chose. His shirt was half unbuttoned, and she wanted to reach out and rip it open....

His fingers tilted her oval face up to his eyes, and he looked at her for a long time. "Shy, Mandy?" he asked softly.

She flushed and tried to look away, but he wouldn't let her. Her lips parted on a rush of breath.

"Tonight," he whispered, making a promise of it as he searched her wide eyes.

Her lips trembled and he started to bend toward them, his eyes intent, his lean hand moving to the back of her head to position her face where he wanted it. And just as his open mouth started to touch hers, the truck door slammed.

He laughed. "I seem to spend my life trying to kiss you without interruptions, don't I, honey?"

She managed a nervous laugh, too, but her eyes were wary. She didn't miss the speculative look he sent toward Patty and Jake, or the way he moved quickly back to his bull. Was he trying to make the other girl jealous?

She didn't say another word until Patty was ready to go, and then she all but ran for the truck. Carson made her nervous, he intimidated her. She sat there listening as Patty told him what else to do for the sick bull. And all the while Mandelyn never actually looked at him. She was frightened of what her eyes might tell him.

"You sure were quiet today," Patty remarked as they ate a hamburger at a local restaurant known for its barbecue. "You and Carson have a fight or something?"

"Oh, nothing like that," Mandelyn said. "We, uh, I just couldn't think of anything to say, that's all. I don't know a lot about animals."

"I love them," Patty sighed. "I always did. There was never anything I wanted to be more than a vet." She glanced suspiciously at Mandelyn. "What was going on in the barn when Jake and I walked in, by the way? You were hot and bothered like I've never seen you. Carson make a pass?"

"You know I don't feel that way about Carson," Mandelyn said nervously, making a jerking motion with her hand that knocked over her cup of soda.

Patty ran for more napkins, and Mandelyn sat there in the ruin of her suit wondering if it would be undignified to scream.

The rest of the day was no better. She didn't make a single sale, although she did show one undecided young couple six houses only to learn that at least one major thing was wrong with each. She stopped by the attorney's office for the closing on Patty's new building, and then locked up her own office with a weary sigh. She still had to think of something to fix for supper. And Carson was coming!

She jumped in her car and made a wild rush home to see what she had to cook. Thank goodness there was some chicken she could fry and some vegetables. She took off her suit, put on jeans and a loose shirt, and got to it. She didn't even think about what lay ahead; it made her too nervous. Things were getting entirely out of hand with him, and she didn't know what to do anymore. What had begun as a simple etiquette course now promised to be a full-fledged affair if she didn't watch her step. It occurred to her that he wanted her, physically. But she knew that he could feel that way and still be in love with Patty. It wasn't the same with men as it was with women. Which made her even more nervous about her own survival instincts. They didn't seem to work with Carson.

Just before six, she tried on five outfits before deciding on a demure little yellow sundress. She left her hair down and brushed it to silky perfection, and then stared at herself in the mirror and hoped she didn't look too eager or too dressed up. She hadn't been so excited in years, and over Carson, of all people!

He got there five minutes early, just as she'd finished dishing up the chicken and vegetables. She ran to the door to let him in, and smiled in helpless appreciation at the way he looked.

He was wearing one of the new outfits they'd bought him—tan slacks with a patterned shirt and a casual white and tan plaid blazer. He was freshly shaven and his hair, under his Stetson, was well-groomed. He smelled of fine cologne and he looked good enough to eat.

"Well?" he asked impatiently.

She stood aside to let him in, sensitive to the sweeping glance he gave her. "You look very nice," she murmured.

"So do you. Good enough to be the main course, in fact."

She grinned. "I'd give you a rash."

"Think so?" He tossed his hat onto the chair and there was a sudden sharp gleam in his eyes.

She knew what he was thinking, and it frightened her. She went hurriedly ahead of him into the dining room, where the table was already laid, including iced tea in tall glasses.

"I'd just finished," she explained. "Shall we start?"

He sighed. "I guess so," he said with a wistful glance in her direction.

She stood by her chair while he sat down and shook out his napkin.

"Ahem!" she cleared her throat.

He glanced up. "Something wrong with your throat?"

"I'm waiting for you to seat me."

"Oh." He got to his feet, frowning. The gleam came back into his blue, blue eyes. He pulled out her chair and bent and lifted her in his hard arms. "Like this?" he asked softly, putting her down in the chair with his mouth hovering just above her own.

"N-not exactly," she whispered back. Her eyes fell to his mouth, and she wanted it. Wanted it...!

He seemed to know that, because he straightened with a purely masculine smile on his face and went back to his own chair.

"This looks good," he murmured while she tried to get her heart to settle down, her lungs to work again.

"I hope it tastes that way," she said tautly. "It was a rush job. I had a long afternoon."

"So did I."

"How's your bull?" she asked, handing him the platter of chicken.

"He'll make it. He was better after that second shot. Poor old critter, I felt sorry for him."

"I thought it was the cows you felt sorry for," she murmured demurely.

He studied her downbent head for a long moment before he dished out some mashed potatoes onto his plate. "You ought to come over when I turn him back out into the pasture," he said drily. "You'd learn a few things."

She all but overturned her tea glass, and he threw back his black head and laughed uproariously.

"All right, I give up, you're out of my league," she burst out. "You terrible man!"

"You need to spend some time around Patty,"

he remarked. "She'd put you on the right track soon enough. A girl after my own heart."

Which was probably true, she thought miserably. Patty would suit him to a tee. He might want Mandelyn, but Patty appealed to his mind and heart. How terrible, to be wanted only for her body.

"You put out salad forks," he remarked. "Why? You didn't make a salad."

"I meant to," she said.

"Etiquette," he scoffed. "I'll be damned if I understand any of it. A bunch of rules and regulations for snobs, if you ask me. Why dress up a table like this when all you do is eat, anyway? Who the hell cares which fork you eat what with?"

"Ladies and gentlemen do," she said, biting down hard on a roll.

"I'm not much of a gentleman, am I?" he sighed. "I don't suppose if I worked at it all my life, I'd improve a hell of a lot."

"Yes, you will," she said softly. She studied his craggy face, liking its hardness, its strength. Her eyes fell to his slender hand and she remembered how tender it had been on her bare skin. She dropped her fork noisily against her plate and scrambled to pick it up.

"Do I make you nervous, Mandelyn?" he murmured wryly. "That's a first."

She shifted in her seat. "I'm not used to entertaining men here," she admitted.

"Yes, I know that."

He was watching her, the way he always did, and that made her more nervous than ever. They finished the meal in silence, and he helped her carry the dishes into the kitchen. Not only that— he insisted on helping as she washed them. He dried them, smiling at her confusion.

"I'm handy in the kitchen," he reminded her. "I have to be or I'd have starved to death years ago. I don't have women over to cook my dinner."

She lifted her eyes to his hard face and searched it curiously.

He looked down at the curious expression on her flushed face. "Yes, once in a while they come over for other purposes," he said softly. "I'm a man, not a plaster saint, and I have all the usual needs."

Her face colored slowly and he grinned. She tore her eyes away, but her hands trembled and she hated that giveaway sign.

"You're such a little greenhorn," he murmured. "You don't know anything about men and women, do you?"

"I'm not ignorant," she muttered.

"I didn't say you were. Just innocent." He finished drying the last dish and put it to one side. "I like that. Your being innocent, I mean. I like it a lot."

She couldn't meet his eyes. He made her feel shy and young and all thumbs.

"Why hasn't there been a man?" he asked quietly.

"Let's start your dancing lessons, shall we?" she began nervously. She started past him, but he caught her.

"Why, Mandelyn?" he persisted.

"Carson..."

His big hands caught her waist and crushed her body against his. "Why, damn it?" he burst out, his patience at an end.

Her vulnerability to his nearness shocked her. She panicked and suddenly tore away from him as if she couldn't bear for him to touch her. She stood with her back to him, shivering.

She knew he hadn't liked her withdrawal, not one bit. But she couldn't help it, he terrified her. She was getting in over her head, and she didn't know how to stop him, how to handle him. Carson was more man pound for pound than she'd ever seen.

She swallowed down a rush of shyness and turned back to face him. He was preoccupied, as if he was thinking deep thoughts. He came close again, his gaze intent.

"Suppose you show me how to dance," he said at last. "Then next week comes culture. I've bought tickets for a ballet in Phoenix. I thought you might come along and explain it all to me."

She laughed. "You, at a ballet?"

He glared at her. "Stop that!"

"Yes, Carson," she said demurely.

"Turn on that damned stereo, will you?"

A moment later the music flowed sweetly into the silence. Mandelyn went easily into his arms and showed him how to hold her, not too tightly, not too loosely. Then she taught him what to do with his feet. He was a little clumsy at first, but an apt enough student.

"Why do I have to hold you so far away?" he asked. "I've seen couples practically making love on the dance floor."

"Not in polite company," she said huskily, staring at her feet.

"Yes, in polite company," he murmured. His hands brought her gently closer, until she was standing right up against him, so close that she could feel his heartbeat against her breasts. "Like this. Here." He brought one of her hands up to his neck and slid his arm further around her, resting his chin on her head. "Mmm," he murmured, "much better."

That depended on one's point of view, she thought nervously. She felt stiff, because her body was reacting to his like wildfire.

"Don't panic," he said softly. "We'll just dance."

But she was all too close to him, and something had happened to his body that she'd never experienced before. She tried to edge a little away from him, but he held her fast.

"Carson," she protested weakly.

"Mandelyn, I know you're a virgin," he said quietly. "I'm not going to make a wild grab for you."

"Yes, I know, but…but…"

"But you can feel me wanting you and you're frightened, isn't that it?" He lifted his head and searched her eyes. "I'm not embarrassed. Why should you be? It's a man's very natural reaction to a lovely woman."

She'd never heard it put like that. She studied his hard face.

"I've spent my life working with animals," he said, his voice quiet, deep. "I don't find anything distasteful about reproduction, about sex. You shouldn't either. It's God's way of perpetuating the species, and it's beautiful."

She flushed, but she didn't look away. "You make it sound that way," she said softly.

His eyes searched hers intimately. "I don't like the idea of one-night stands and affairs, or people living together without marriage. I'm old-fashioned enough to want a woman with principles when I marry, and not a woman who'll proposition me just because she feels liberated."

Her eyebrows arched. "Has that ever happened to you?" she asked.

He laughed softly. "As a matter of fact, yes,

at a cattle convention, of all places. She was a little rodeo rider and as pretty as a picture. She came up to me, touched me in a way I won't even tell you about and invited me to spend the night with her."

She hesitated. "Did you?" she asked in a tiny voice, all eyes.

He studied her mouth for a long moment. "Shame on you. A well brought up young woman like you, asking a man that kind of question...."

"Did you sleep with her?" she persisted.

"No, as a matter of fact, I didn't," he chuckled. "I like to do the chasing."

"Yes, I imagine you would," she replied, but she felt relieved all the same.

His hand slid down her back to the bottom of her spine and pushed her just a little closer, and she caught her breath and froze.

"Too intimate?" he murmured. "Okay, I get the message. The kind of girls I'm used to don't mind being held like that. But I guess I've got a lot to learn about civilized behavior."

She nuzzled her face against his chest with a sigh. "I've got a lot to learn about the reverse," she said with a smile. "No one's ever held me this way."

His hands contracted on her waist, and she gasped. "Hey, not so tight," she laughed. "That hurts!"

"Why don't you go out with anyone?"

That was a good question, but it wasn't the time for confessions. "I like my own company," she said after a minute.

"You'll need a man one day."

"No," she protested. "I don't want anyone."

His hand caught suddenly in the thick length of her hair and tugged sharply. She gasped at the twinge of pain and stared at him as if he were a stranger.

"You can't live alone forever," he said harshly, his eyes glittering down into hers. "You need more than your work."

"What do I need, since you're such an expert on the subject?" she challenged hotly.

He pulled her hair, more gently now, forcing her head down onto his shoulder while the music played on, forgotten. "You need to be dragged into a man's bed and loved all night long. That's what you need."

"Not with you," she protested, pushing against his hard chest. "You've got a woman already!"

He wouldn't let go. "I have?"

"Of course," she grumbled, pushing harder. "The one we're remodeling you for, remember? The one who's too stuck up to like you the way… you are…will you let go of me, damn it!" She stood still, hating the slow, sweet stirrings of her own body as he held her and she felt his heartbeat merging with her own.

His chest rose and fell with gathering speed,

and the hand holding her long hair released it and began a caressing motion.

It dawned on her that the music was still playing, a sultry tune that only made more dangerous an already flammable situation.

"Dance, don't fight," he whispered deeply. "Don't fight me."

Her legs were trembling as he drew her into a rhythm that was more like making love to music than dancing. His hard thighs brushed her own and never in her life had she felt weaker or more vulnerable.

"I'm afraid." She didn't know that she'd said it out loud, or that Carson's pale blue eyes glittered like diamonds when he heard her.

"Yes, I know," he breathed into her hair. His fingers slid between hers caressingly. "I won't hurt you."

Her nails pressed unconsciously against his chest and he stiffened. She frowned, drawing back so that she could see his face. What she found there disturbed her.

His nostrils flared, his jaw clenched. "No, you aren't the only one who's vulnerable," he said curtly.

Her fascinated eyes searched his. Her rebellious hands liked his visible reaction to them. They opened the top button of his shirt, and his breath caught, but he didn't make a move to stop her.

Her lower lip trembled. "I... Carson?" she whispered questioningly.

"Go ahead," he breathed. "Do it."

"But..."

His open mouth touched her forehead. "Do it."

He was trembling already. By the time she fumbled open the shirt and eased the edges aside, his quickened breathing was visible as well. Fascinated, she put her hands flat on the hair-roughened flesh and began to caress him with slow, tentative movements. He seemed to like what she was doing, if the intent hardness of his expression was any indication.

She slid her hands around to his muscular back and laid her hot cheek against his bare skin and closed her eyes. He smelled clean and sexy, and she drew her cheek, then her lips, against his body with dreamy motions.

His fingers tangled in her hair and turned her face, so that her mouth was against him.

"Kiss me," he whispered. "No, honey, not like that. Open your mouth and do it. Yes," he groaned unsteadily, and his hands grew rough. "Yes."

She drew her mouth over every hard inch of his chest, up to his shoulders, his throat, his chin. But even on tiptoe, she couldn't reach his mouth.

"Carson," she moaned protestingly, tugging at his thick hair.

"Do you want my mouth?" he whispered.

"Oh, yes," she whispered back. She moved her

body against his slowly. "Oh, yes, I want it very, very much!"

He bent and touched her lips with his, savoring them for a few taut seconds until her mouth opened. His arms drew her close, his hand held the back of her head still, and the kiss became explosive and hot. He groaned as he felt her quick, fervent response to it. His hands moved down to her hips and pushed them against his, and this time she didn't protest.

Her hands worshipped him, running hungrily up his spine, to his shoulder blades, around to his hard ribs and, daringly, to the muscular stomach above his belt.

He shuddered and lifted his head. She stared up at him with dazed, misty eyes and a swollen mouth.

"Shouldn't I touch you like that?" she whispered.

"I like letting you touch me like that," he replied huskily. "Unfasten it."

She flushed. "No, I couldn't!"

He held her hands against him, tenderly. "It's my body, isn't it?" he whispered. "If I don't mind, why should you? Aren't you curious?"

She was. She'd never wanted to touch a man that way, not even Ben when she was eighteen, and the realization shook her to her very shoes.

"Mandy," he said quietly, "I wouldn't seduce

you. You'd have to want it, too, before I'd go that far."

"But…"

"But what, honey?" He bent and brushed his lips across her eyebrows, her closed eyes.

"Why…are you making love to me?"

His mouth smiled. "Because it feels good. Because I've never made love to a virgin."

She drew back and studied him curiously. "Never?" she whispered.

He shook his head, smiling. "You're my first."

She felt young and shy and a little embarrassed. Her eyes fell to his bare chest and she tingled just looking at it. "You're…my first," she confessed. "I never let anyone…"

"Never let anyone what, baby?" he whispered.

"Touch me…the way you did yesterday," she said finally.

"Here?" he asked softly, and brushed his knuckles over her soft breast.

"Y…yes," she faltered. She pressed close to him, shivering a little. He made her feel the wildest hungers.

His hands smoothed down her back and around to her hips. He moved her body lazily against his and caught his breath at the rush of sensation.

"Don't faint," he teased when she stiffened. "Think of it as private tutoring, Mandy. You're teaching me to be a gentleman. Let me teach you how to be a woman."

"I'm afraid!"

"I won't force you, precious," he whispered. "I won't ever force you. Let me show you what magic two people can make. Let me show you how sweet it can be."

He lifted her gently in his arms and looked down into her hungry gray eyes while his own blazed with pale blue flames. "I've got to have more of you than this," he whispered. "I want to feel you under me, just once, just for a few seconds."

"Carson...!" she moaned against his suddenly devouring mouth.

"Sweet," he whispered unsteadily, biting at her open, pleading lips. "God, you're so sweet...."

She felt him moving, but his mouth was seducing hers, and she clung to him and closed her eyes. She knew he was taking her to the bedroom. She knew, too, that once he had her down on the mattress and could feel her body yielding under the hard pressure of his own that no power on earth was going to stop him from taking her. Despite all the promises, he was on fire for her. And she was on fire for him. It was going to happen, and she wasn't even sorry. She sensed something in him that calmed her, that made her relax and return his tender caresses.

He carried her into the dark bedroom and laid her down on the soft coverlet. His hand traveled down from her shoulder, tracing her breasts, her waist, her stomach, the long line of her legs.

"I won't make you pregnant," he promised tautly, "and I won't hurt you. Okay?"

She trembled a little as she realized what he was saying, how explosive the passion between them had become. She felt his hands easing her dress down to her waist, over her hips. There was nothing under it but her briefs, and very gently he removed those, too, so that she was nude.

"You're trembling," he whispered as one big, warm hand rested on her belly. "You've never been nude with a man, either, have you?"

"No," she managed weakly.

"Your body feels like cream, Mandelyn," he said softly. He ran his hands over her, letting her feel their rough tenderness as he learned the soft contours of her body. "Slender, and beautiful, and soft to touch. Honey and spice and cotton candy…"

He bent and his mouth touched her stomach. She cried out, shocked by the intimacy of his lips there and by her own violent reaction to it.

"Hush, baby," he whispered in the darkness. "Hush now, there's nothing to be afraid of. I know what I'm doing."

"Yes, I know," she laughed shakily, "that's why I'm frightened. You…you said you wouldn't…"

"I want you," he whispered. "I've wanted you for so long, Mandy. I look at you and ache.

Couldn't you pity me enough to give me one night?"

She wanted that night, too, but pity wasn't what was motivating her. She saw his head bend, his face a pale blur in the darkness and a piercing sweetness washed over her. Carson. He was Carson, and as familiar as her own face in the mirror, and no part of him was repulsive to her. She wanted him, too.

"Yes," she breathed. "Oh yes."

He seemed to freeze for a moment, and then he crushed her to him. "Let me turn on the light," he whispered hoarsely. "Let me watch you when it happens."

His hand went out before she could respond. He turned on the bedside lamp, flooding the room with light. She shrunk from him slightly in embarrassment. But he wasn't looking at her. His eyes were on the large color photograph in the ornate silver frame on the bedside table. His face paled. He reached out a hand and picked it up and stared down at the boyish face through the glass and his hand shook.

"Who?" he asked, his voice sounding dazed.

Her eyes barely focused. "It's Ben. Ben Hammack. He...was my fiancé."

Chapter 6

"Your fiancé?" He spoke as if he wasn't sure he'd heard her in the first place, and his eyes were riveted to the photograph.

The lovely, sultry sweetness between them had been dissipated by the stark light, and she fumbled with the coverlet, drawing it quickly over her body.

"You were engaged?" he persisted. "When?"

"Before I came out here," she faltered.

He stood up, replacing the photograph. His hand ran roughly through his disheveled hair, and she stared up at him helplessly. His shirt was still open and his mouth was faintly swollen from the pressure of the kisses they'd given each other. His eyes still bore traces of frustrated passion when they burned down into hers.

"Why didn't you tell me about him before?" he

demanded. "When I asked if you'd ever wanted a man before...."

She shivered at the accusation in his tone.

"It was when I was eighteen, Carson," she said, tugging the coverlet closer.

"Stop that," he growled. "I know every inch of you now, so stop behaving like a little prude. Was that a lie, too, are you really a virgin?"

"I haven't lied to you!"

"By omission!" he returned. "You never said anything about a fiancé! So where is he now? Did he throw you over? Are you still hung up on him, is that it?"

"Will you calm down?"

"Calm down, hell!" he ground out, glaring at her as he fumbled to light a cigarette. "I hurt all over. How could you let me make love to you with the image of another man sitting right here beside the bed...!"

She dropped her eyes, clutching the coverlet, embarrassed. "I was out of my head," she said miserably.

"So was I. I've never in my life wanted a woman so much. And if I hadn't turned on that damned light, we wouldn't be talking now. I'd be loving you."

The way he said it caused shimmers of sensation all over her bare body. "Yes, I know," she whispered.

"You'd have hated me for it," he added curtly.

"Would I?" she murmured.

His face hardened and he turned away from her to smoke the cigarette. "Where is he, this ex-fiancé?"

She sighed and stared down at her hands, unconsciously letting the coverlet slide a little. "He's dead."

That seemed to startle him. He turned around and came back to her, sitting down on the bed beside her. "Dead?"

She drew in a slow breath. "He was killed in a plane crash, on his way to a banker's convention in Washington, D.C. It was a small plane and it crashed into a hillside. You see, they...picked him up in pieces...."

He caught her hand reluctantly, and held it firmly in his. "I'm sorry. That would have made it worse."

She nodded. Her hand clung to his. "He was twenty-three, and I loved him with all my heart." Her eyes went past him to the photograph, and Ben looked very young to her now, with his blond hair tousled and his green eyes wicked and mischievous. "He came from a very old Charleston family. We had the same background and our families were friendly. He was brilliant, cultured and he could have gone to the moon. I could hardly believe it when he asked me to marry him. I wasn't his usual kind of girl at all. I was shy and quiet and he was so outgoing...." She shrugged and the coverlet, unnoticed, slipped again. Carson's eyes dropped as she spoke, his face going rigid as he stared at the soft, exposed curves. "After he died, I very nearly went crazy. Uncle had inherited the real estate office here and the ranch, and he'd planned to resell it. But when he saw what was happening to me, he moved us out here instead. I think it probably saved my sanity. I couldn't stop thinking about the way Ben died. It was killing me."

He forced his eyes back up to hers. "That's why you didn't date," he said suddenly.

"Of course." She stared at the photograph. "I loved him so much. I was afraid to try again, to risk losing anybody else. I went out with one or two clients over the years, in a strictly platonic way. But most men won't be satisfied with just companionship, and when I realized that, I just gave up on it completely."

"Now it makes sense," he murmured.

She looked up. "What does?"

"The way you've been with me," he said quietly. "As if you were starving to death for a little love."

Her mouth trembled. "I'm not!"

"Aren't you?" He reached out, and slowly peeled the coverlet back, letting it drop to her waist. And he looked down at her creamy, hard-tipped breasts with an expression that pleased her almost beyond bearing. "You see?" he said. "You like it when I look at you."

She did. Her hands trembled as she jerked the coverlet back in place, her face red, her eyes wild. "I don't!"

"Deny it until hell freezes over, but you would have given in before I turned on the light," he said hotly. "You wanted me, damn you!"

Her eyes closed and her hands trembled, clutching the fabric. She couldn't answer him, because he was right and they both knew it.

He got up abruptly and turned away. "God, this is rich," he said, a note of despair in his voice. He paced, smoking like a furnace. "I thought it was because you were a virgin, that being made love to was new and you were learning things about me that you liked. And all the time, I was substituting for a ghost."

That shocked her. "No," she began, because she couldn't let him believe that. It just wasn't true.

"A dead man. A shrine." He seemed to get angrier as he went along. His eyes burned when he whirled suddenly to glare down at her. "Why did you let me bring you in here?" he burst out.

She shivered a little at his tone. "I don't know."

He lifted the cigarette to his lips jerkily and his eyes went involuntarily to the photograph. "You were still mourning him when we met, weren't you?" he asked. "That's why you got so mad at me when I made a pass."

"I couldn't bear the thought of another relationship," she hedged, staring down at the coverlet.

"Hell! You mean, you couldn't bear the thought of some ruffian wanting you. I didn't measure up, did I? I wasn't fit to wear his shoes!"

"Carson, no!" she said fiercely. "No, it isn't like that!"

"I'm rough and hard and I've got no manners," he ground out. "I don't come from a socially prominent family and I didn't go to Harvard. So I'm not even in the running. I never was. You've built him into a little tin god and you keep his picture by your bed to remind you that you've climbed into the grave with him, isn't that it!"

She got up, dragging the cover with her, and went to stand in front of him, her eyes wide, her heart aching. He was hurting, and she'd done that to him. All because of a past she couldn't let go of.

"Carson," she said softly, reaching out to touch his hard arm.

The muscles contracted. "Don't do it, honey," he cautioned in a dangerously soft voice. "I'm feeling pretty raw right now."

"Well, so am I," she burst out. "I didn't want you to start pushing your way into my life, to back me into a corner! I didn't start kissing *you...!*"

"As if you ever would have," he said quietly. His eyes were bleak, his face pale and hard. "I guess I've been dreaming. You're as far out of my league as I am out of yours. It's just as well that you aren't civilizing me for yourself, isn't it?"

Her smooth shoulders lifted and fell. "I guess so." She stared down at his boots.

"We'd better forget the dancing lessons," he said coldly. "And before you start getting the wrong idea about what happened tonight, I told you once that I've been without a woman for a while. You went to my head, that's all."

That hurt. She had to fight down a flood of tears. Her eyes lifted proudly to his. "Same here," she said curtly.

"Yes, I know that," he said with a mocking smile. He nodded toward the photograph. "Why don't you take that to bed with you, and see if it makes you burn the way I did."

She lifted her hand, but he caught her wrist and held it easily, letting her feel his strength.

It brought her to her senses like a cold shower of rain. "You can let go," she said defeatedly. "I won't try to hit you."

He dropped her wrist as if it had scorched him. "Hadn't you better put your clothes on? You might catch cold—if ice can."

Her eyes flashed at him. "I wasn't cold with you," she said fiercely.

The hasty words seemed to kindle something in him. His eyes narrowed and glittered. He reached out and caught the back of her head and before she could turn her mouth, his lips crushed down on it. He twisted her mouth under his, hurting her for an instant, before he lifted it again and glared into her eyes.

"Firecracker," he said heavily, "if you weren't worshipping a damned ghost, I'd throw you down on that bed and make you beg for my body. But as things stand, I'd say we both had a lucky escape."

He let her go and strode out of the room. Seconds later, the door slammed, and she heard his car start and roar away. The house was so still that she could hear the clock in the living room, like a bomb. Tick. Tick. Tick.

She hardly slept at all that night. Her eyes had been well and truly opened by Carson's cutting remarks. She hadn't realized just how much she'd been living in the past until he'd accused her of making a shrine for Ben. Of trying to climb into the grave with him.

With a cup of coffee in her hand the next morning, she sat on the edge of her bed and stared at the photograph. Ben looked impossibly young. And as she gazed at his picture, she remembered how things had been all those years ago. It hadn't been a great love affair. He'd been a handsome, eligible bachelor with a magnetic personality, and she'd been young and shy and flattered by his attention. But over the years, she had built his image into something unrealistic. It had taken Carson's feverish lovemaking to teach her that.

She flushed remembering how it had been between them the night before. He'd been so tender, so achingly tender and patient. And if he hadn't seen that photograph…

She got to her feet, frowning, and paced the floor. Her eyes went involuntarily to the bed and her mind traced, torturously, every wild second she'd spent on it the night before. Carson, kissing her with such sweet hunger, Carson touching her in ways no one else ever had. Carson, looking at her with eyes that ate her. Loving her.

Her eyes closed. It had been loving, of a kind. He'd wanted her quite desperately, and not for the first time last night. He'd wanted her for a long time; perhaps from the very beginning. But he hadn't let her know it. Not until he asked her for those "lessons." And now she had to wonder if that had been only a means to an end. If he'd decided it was past time to do something about his violent hunger.

Did he care, though? That was the thing that tortured her. Was it just a physical hunger that he was trying to satisfy, or did he feel something for her? And did it matter to her?

She put her cup back in the kitchen and got dressed to go to work. It probably was a moot point now, she thought miserably. If the way he'd looked and talked last night was any indication, he'd never want to see her again.

* * *

Angie had several messages from prospective clients which Mandelyn took to her office and stared at blankly. It was an hour before she could get into the mood to work, and even then she did it halfheartedly. She spent the day staring at the phone, hoping that Carson would call. But by five o'clock, he hadn't, and she realized that he probably wouldn't want to. She went home in a daze and spent the evening staring at the walls.

Friday came dragging around, finally, and Patty stuck her head in the door of the real estate office to remind Mandelyn about coming to her party that night.

"The party?" Mandelyn felt sick all over. Carson had been going to take her. "I… I don't know, Patty."

"You've got to come," she prodded. "Carson said he was bringing you."

Mandelyn's heart jumped. "Recently?" she asked hesitantly.

"This morning, when I went out to give his bull the all-clear." Patty grinned. "He was in a foul mood until I mentioned that the Gibson boys were coming to play for me. He used to sit in with them years ago. He's a heck of a good guitarist, you know."

"No, I didn't," Mandelyn said slowly. There were a lot of things she didn't know about Carson, it seemed.

"Anyway, they'll probably jam for a while. It's going to be lots of fun. See you about six!"

"Okay," she replied with a wan smile.

"I wish I could come," Angie sighed when Patty was gone. "I've got to babysit my sister's kids. Three of them. All preschoolers. Patty was going to introduce me to a guy who'll be there. Now I'll have to load a gun and look for my own. All on account of my sister's bridge game."

Mandelyn almost laughed at the younger woman's miserable look. "I'd offer to stand in for you, if I could," she said, and really would have considered it. She wasn't looking forward to spending an evening around Carson, whom she was certain hated her.

"I'd almost let you," Angie replied. "But don't worry, I'll survive. I was a girl scout."

"I guess that would help.

"Survival training usually does, with preschoolers," Angie murmured, and reached for the phone, which was ringing off the hook. She pressed the "hold" button. "It's for you. Mr. Wayne."

Mandelyn's heart tried to reach into her throat. She was tempted to have Angie tell him she couldn't come to the phone. Amazing, how he brought out these cowardly instincts of hers.

"Okay," she said, and wandered slowly back into her office. She picked up the phone with trembling hands. "Hello," she said professionally.

"Can you be ready by five-thirty?" Carson asked coldly, and without any preliminaries.

The sound of his voice made her ache. She closed her eyes and wrapped the cord around her fingers. "Yes," she said.

"Patty's idea," he reminded her. "I'd as soon have gone alone."

"Well, if you'd rather...!" she began, feeling hurt and hating him.

"Hell, yes, I would, but I won't give this whole town something to gossip about by refusing to go with you. And neither will you. Be ready." And he slammed the phone down.

Mandelyn slammed her own receiver down, gave a furious groan and heaved a telephone directory at the door.

Angie, shocked, rushed to the doorway. "Are you okay?" she asked, her eyes wide and fascinated. She'd never seen the very proper Miss Bush throw things.

"No," Mandelyn said with blazing eyes. "No, I'm not. I'll kill him one day. I'll shoot him through the heart. I'll feed him cactus branches. I'll..."

"Mr. Wayne?" Angie gasped. "But you're friends."

"Me? Friends with that animal?"

Angie stood quietly, fishing for the right words.

"I'm going home," Mandelyn said. She

grabbed up her purse and stormed out the door. "Close up, will you?"

"Sure. But…"

"I'll put alum in his punch," Mandelyn was muttering. "I'll put burrs under his saddle…."

Angie just shook her head. "It must be love," she murmured drily, and then laughed at the thought. Miss Bush and Carson Wayne would be the mismatch of the century. Miss Bush was cool and proper and Carson was a wild man. She couldn't picture the two of them in love. Not in a million years. She went back to her desk and started clearing it.

Mandelyn sped home at such a rate that she attracted the attention of Sheriff's deputy Danny Burton. Considering that Danny hardly ever noticed speeders, that was quite a feat.

She pulled over when she heard the siren, and sat there fuming until the short, dark-headed deputy came around to her window.

"Let's see your license, Miss Bush, and your registration," Danny said drily. "Might as well do the thing properly. Where's the fire—that's the other part of my speech."

"The fire is going to be under Carson Wayne, just as soon as I can find some wood and matches," she said venomously.

He stared at her. "You're his pal," he reminded her.

"That rattlesnake?" she burst out.

He cleared his throat and took the license and registration from her shaking hands. "He must have done something pretty bad to rile you. Poor old feller."

"Poor old feller? He locked you in a closet, have you forgotten already?"

He grinned. "He's been locking me in closets for six years. I've got used to it. Besides, when he sobers up, he always buys me lunch at Rosie's. He ain't a bad guy." He handed back the license and finished writing up the ticket. "Why were you in such a rush?" he asked.

"Patty's party's tonight," she murmured.

"Oh, yeah. I'm going, too. Looks like it's going to be a real hummer, especially since the Gibsons and Carson will be together again. Damn, that Carson can make a guitar sing!"

Why did everybody know that except her? It made her even madder. She took the ticket with a sigh.

"Now slow down," he cautioned. "If you wreck the car, you can't very well go dancing tonight, can you, Miss Bush?"

She sighed. "I guess not. Sorry, Danny. I'll slow down."

"Good girl. See you later."

"Yes. See you later."

She drove home under a black cloud. Even after she'd dressed in a full red printed skirt and a white peasant blouse, with low-heeled shoes, she still hadn't cooled down. She felt wild. Furious at Carson, furious at the circumstances that forced her to be near him. She only wanted to close him out of her life and forget that he even existed. He was haunting her!

When he drove up, her heart began to race wildly. She didn't want to see him, she didn't want him near her! Her body tingled as she opened the door and looked at him. He was wearing jeans and a red print Western shirt with a red bandana. His brown boots were the new ones they'd bought together in Phoenix. They were highly polished, and matched the tan hat he'd bought to go with them. And he looked so handsome and virile that she ached.

His own eyes were busy, sweeping over her body in the unfamiliar casual clothing. Her hair was loose around her shoulders, and she seemed smaller and much more feminine than before. His teeth ground together and his face grew harder.

"Ready?" he asked curtly.

"When I get my purse and shawl, yes," she returned icily. She jerked them up from the sofa and locked the door behind her.

He opened the door of the Thunderbird for her, but she hardly noticed. She was still angry at his curtness.

He got in and started the car, then sped out onto the highway.

"Keep that up and you'll get one, too," she said, staring straight ahead.

"Get one, what?" he asked.

"Speeding ticket."

His eyebrows jerked up. "The way you drive, you got a ticket? Sheriff Wilson hire a new man or something?"

She continued to stare out the window. "Danny gave it to me."

"Pull the other one. Danny never stops anybody."

"I was doing ninety-five at the time.'

The car went all over the road before he righted it. "Ninety-five, on these roads?"

"Go ahead, make some nasty remark," she challenged, her eyes glittering up at him. "Go on, I dare you!"

His eyes studied hers for an instant before they went back to the road. "In a temper?"

"You ought to know. Yours isn't so sweet today, either."

"I think I'm entitled to a bad temper, considering how I got it."

She flushed and wouldn't look at him. She wouldn't talk to him, either. He didn't seem to mind. He drove all the way to Patty's house without saying a word.

Chapter 7

"Carson! Mandy! It's about time you got here!" Patty laughed, rushing forward to grab Carson by the arm. She looked nervous and flustered, and nearby, Jake was talking to a group of cowboys.

Mandelyn had never in her life felt such a violent urge to hit another woman. Patty, blissfully unaware of her friend's reaction, clung closer to Carson's sleeve and grinned.

"The Gibsons have been waiting for you," she teased. "Jack said he wouldn't even play if you didn't come."

Carson laughed, and Mandelyn could have cried, because it seemed that the day was long gone when he would laugh with her that way.

"In that case, I'd better get over there, I reckon. You look sweet," he added in a soft drawl, glancing down at Patty's blue polka-dotted dress and white shoes.

"Thank you," Patty said, and curtsied. Her eyes flirted with him. "It's nice to have my efforts appreciated."

Her hair was loose tonight, too, and she'd never looked less tomboyish. Jake glanced at her out of the corner of one eye and scowled. Mandelyn was the only one who caught that look, and she wondered for an instant if Jake might be jealous. What an odd idea. Carson's foreman never looked at women.

"Excuse us, Mandy," Patty said politely and dragged Carson away. He went like a lamb, without a backward glance.

Mandelyn felt out of place. She was in no humor to enjoy partying this evening. But Jake seemed to sense that, and excused himself from the other cowboys to join her.

"You look as out of place as I feel, Miss Bush," he said wryly. "I'm not much of a partygoer."

"And I'm not in much of a party mood," she sighed, clasping her hands tightly in front of her. She was watching Carson. He shook hands with the four brothers at the bandstand and accepted a big guitar from one of them. Tossing his hat to Patty, he sat down with them.

"Quite a treat, to hear the boss play," Jake murmured. "He doesn't do that very often these days."

"I've never heard him play," she mentioned.

He glanced down at her. "I'm not much surprised. He probably thinks you'd prefer something classical."

"Everybody seems to know me better than I know myself," she sighed. Actually, she liked Country-Western music very much.

They were tuning up and Carson said something and they all laughed. He seemed so different here, with people he knew. He was relaxed and cheerful and outgoing...a stranger. He seemed to sense her watching him and glanced up, but his eyes weren't smiling. She dropped her own to avoid the accusation and frank dislike in his gaze.

"You two have a falling-out?" Jake asked quietly. "He's been pure hell the past few days."

"I noticed," she said shortly.

Jake shrugged and leaned back against the doorway to listen. The Gibson brother who led the band gave them the beat and they swung into a fast, furious rendition of "San Antonio Rose." The others muted their own instruments, two guitars, a bass and a fiddle, and Carson's lean fingers flew across the steel strings of his guitar with beautiful precision. Mandelyn gaped at him. She'd expected that he'd be passable, but what he was doing with the instrument made her knees weak. He was expert.

"Good, ain't he?" Jake grinned. "I used to fuss because he wouldn't go professional, but he said running all over the country with a band wasn't his idea of fun. He liked cattle better."

She watched Carson with sad, quiet eyes. "He's marvelous," she said softly, and her tone hinted that she didn't mean only as a musician.

Jake glanced at her curiously, puzzled by her rapt expression, by the odd look in her gray eyes. So that was it. He looked back at his boss and smiled slowly.

Patty was standing near him, clapping and laughing. He glanced up at her and grinned as he finished the piece. The band gave the last chord and cheered.

"How about 'Choices'?" Jake yelled.

Carson looked up and frowned when he saw Jake standing beside Mandelyn.

"Yes, how about it?" Patty seconded. "Come on, Carson, do it!"

"He wrote that one," Jake told Mandelyn. "We made him copyright it, but he never would let anyone record it."

She studied the man in the red checkered shirt and couldn't fathom him. He gave in to the prodding finally. What he did to the guitar then was so sweet and heady that Mandelyn felt a rush of emotion. It was a love song, pure and simple. All about two different worlds with no bridge between them. And he sang it in a deep, sultry voice that would have made a dedicated spinster's heart whirl. He had the sexiest voice Mandelyn had ever heard, and she watched, spellbound, while he sang. His eyes lifted once, glanced off hers, and went to Patty. He smiled. And Mandelyn closed her eyes on a wave of pain.

When he finished, there was a moment's pause, and then uproarious applause.

"And he's raising cattle, can you believe it?" Patty burst out. She laughed and bent over to kiss Carson firmly on the mouth. "You're great!"

Mandelyn felt sick. Jake said something rough under his breath. He looked down, noticed her sudden paleness and took her arm.

"Are you okay, ma'am?" he asked gently.

"Just a little wobbly," she laughed nervously. "I've been working hard lately.

"You're not alone. So has boss man."

The band had started to play some dance music now. Jake glanced at his boss, who was glaring in his direction. He glared back.

"Would you dance with me, Miss Bush?" he asked.

"Well…"

"He dared me," he said curtly, glancing past her to Carson. "Two can play that game."

"I don't understand."

He led her onto the dance floor. "Never mind," he grumbled. He shuffled around, much the way Carson had the night she'd taught him to dance.

Patty was looking at the two of them curiously.

Jake gave her a cold smile and whirled Mandelyn around.

Mandelyn looked up, and saw murderous fury
in his face. So that was it, she realized, Jake and
Carson were competing for Patty!

Her eyes fell to Jake's collar. She sighed miserably. It seemed that she wasn't the only one suffering. So Jake wanted Patty, too. He wouldn't
win. She knew instinctively that Carson would
beat the younger man in any kind of competition,
especially when it came to loving.

"Are you sure you feel okay?" Jake asked quietly.

"Not really," she admitted. "But I'll make it."

He smiled at her. "Yes, ma'am, I imagine you
will."

The evening wore on, and Carson never left
the brothers Gibson for a minute. He played and
Patty stayed by him. Mandelyn sat down after the
first dance, leaving Jake to circulate among the
other women. There was a large crowd, larger,
she suspected, than Patty had anticipated. But everyone seemed to be having a great time.

Patty brought Carson a beer and held it to his
firm lips while he played. Mandelyn got more and
more morose, until finally she was praying that it
would all be over and she could go home. She'd
never been more miserable in her life. Watching
Patty and Carson ogle each other was more than
she could bear.

Eventually, Jake joined her again, squatting down beside her chair to watch with narrowed angry eyes as Carson and Patty talked while the band was preparing to play their closing song.

"Patty looks nice," she said quietly.

He shrugged. His eyes went to a piece of string that he was twisting into a hangman's noose in his hands. "Yeah, I guess so."

She felt a sudden kinship with Jake and impulsively murmured, "You, too, huh?"

He looked up, flushed, and looked down again. "Maybe it's contagious."

"Maybe it's curable."

He laughed reluctantly. "Reckon? If you find an antidote, share it with me."

"Same here."

He glared toward Carson and Patty. "It's disgusting. She's too young for him."

Her eyes widened as she gaped at him. "You're almost Carson's age. She's a little young for you, too, isn't she?"

"What's that got to do with anything?" he grumbled.

She only smiled. He probably felt as miserable as she did. She laid a gentle hand on his broad shoulder. "Don't let it get you down. Take up the guitar and practice."

"I can't even carry a tune," he sighed. He looked up. "You might study veterinary medicine."

"I faint at the sight of blood," she confessed.

He smiled warmly. "I guess we're both out of the running."

"I guess." She smiled back.

It was too bad they didn't look across the room at that moment. If they had, they'd have seen two furious pairs of eyes glaring at them from the bandstand.

Carson hadn't danced one single dance all evening. But as the band launched into the "Tennessee Waltz" he led Patty to the floor and held her close during that last dreamy tune.

He shook hands with the Gibson boys, bent down to brush his lips over Patty's cheek and thanked her for the evening. And then he turned to Mandelyn with such evident reluctance that she wanted to scream and throw things.

"Thanks, Patty," she said with forced politeness. "I had a lovely time."

"Good. I'm glad," Patty said with equally forced politeness. "See you."

Mandelyn shot out the door past Carson and climbed into the Thunderbird with ill-concealed impatience. He sauntered along, taking his time, cocking his hat at a jaunty angle.

"You're in a flaming rush," he remarked as he climbed in beside her and started the car.

"I'm tired," she said. Her gaze went out the window to the ghostly shapes of the saguaro cactus against the sky.

"From what?" he asked. "You only danced once. With Jake."

"Jake dances very well."

"He stepped all over you."

She stared ahead as the headlights penetrated the darkness. She almost said, "So did you the other night." But she wasn't going to fall into that trap. She kept her silence.

"Patty looked good, didn't she?" he remarked. "I haven't seen her let her hair down and wear a dress in years."

"She looked lovely," she said through her teeth.

He glanced at her and away again. "Want to declare a truce? At least until the ballet? It would be a shame to waste those tickets."

"I'm not going to any damned ballet with you," she said vehemently. "And, no, I don't want to declare a truce. I hate you!"

He whistled through his teeth. "Temper, temper."

"I've seen so much of yours lately that it's affected my mind," she said sweetly.

"I thought it was your loving memory of your late fiancé that had done that," he said.

She turned, eyes glittering. "Stop this car and let me out, right now!" she demanded.

Amazingly, he did just that. He stopped the car abruptly. "Okay! If you want to walk, go ahead. It's seven more miles."

"Fine. I love long walks!" She got out, slammed

the door violently, and started down the road. He took off, leaving skid marks behind him.

She couldn't believe he'd really done that. She stood gaping at his disappearing tail-lights and tears welled up in her soft gray eyes. She felt lost and frightened, and she really did hate him then. Leaving her alone in the darkness on a deserted highway.

She looked around nervously. She could hardly see her feet at all, and she just knew there were rattlesnakes all around her. Diamondbacks! She began to move gingerly, wishing she had a flashlight, wishing she could have kept her stupid mouth shut. She'd set him off again, just when his temper seemed to be improving.

Her lips trembled. She was really afraid now, and there wasn't a soul in sight. There were no houses, no cars, no nothing. She rounded a curve, shaking, and there was the Thunderbird. Carson was leaning against it, smoking a cigarette.

"Damn you!" she bit off, but she was crying and the words hardly registered.

He said something rough and threw the cigarette to the ground. The next minute, she was in his arms.

He held her much too close, rocking her, his arms warm and hard and protective. And she cried, because of the miserable night she'd had, because of the way things were between them.

"I'm sorry," he said at her ear. "I'm sorry."

She trembled at the deep softness in his voice. "I was afraid," she admitted unsteadily.

His arms tightened slowly. She felt the length of him and something kindled in her own body. Her eyes closed. She clung to him, her hands flat against the rippling muscles of his back, her breasts crushing softly into his chest, her legs brushing the powerful muscles of his. Out on the desert, a coyote howled and the wind blew. And Mandelyn had never felt so safe, or so happy.

"We'd better get home," he said after a minute. "Come on."

He held her hand, led her to the car, and put her in on the driver's side. She slid reluctantly across, wondering what would have happened if she'd stayed close to him. Probably, she thought miserably, he'd have pushed her away.

Driving, it was only a short way from there to her house. He stopped outside the door, but he didn't switch off the engine.

"I...would you like some coffee?" she offered.

"No, thanks. I've got to get some sleep. We're moving cattle in the morning."

"Oh. Thanks for the ride."

"Sure. Any time."

She opened her door and hesitated. "About the ballet..."

"Since I've already got the tickets, it would be a shame to waste them. I can't take anyone but you with me." He laughed shortly. "Patty would laugh her head off."

Her teeth ground together. "No doubt. What night?"

"Wednesday. We'll need to leave here by five, to get there in time."

"I'll close up early." She got out, hating him more than ever, and slammed the door.

"Mandelyn."

She paused. He'd rolled down the passenger window and was leaning across. "Yes?"

"This will be the last time," he said curtly. "I think when we get through with the ballet, I'll have learned enough to cope."

"Good. It was getting a bit boring, wasn't it?" she asked coldly.

"I'll tell you something, honey," he said quietly. "I've about decided that I like my world better than I like yours. Mine has the advantage of real people and honest emotions. Yours is an old house with elegant furniture and the warmth of a tomb. Speaking of which, there's yours. Why don't you go and moon over your lost love?"

Her fists clenched by her sides. "If I had a gun, I'd blow you in half," she spat.

"Hell. If you had a gun, you'd shoot yourself in the foot. Good night."

He rolled up the window while she was stomping onto the porch. She jammed the key into the lock and broke it in half as he roared away.

Her eyes widened. The back door had an old lock and she didn't have its key. The windows were down and locked. Now what was she going to do?

With a heavy sigh, she went out and got a big rock. She took it to the side of the house and flung it through the window. The sound of shattering glass made her feel a little better, even though she knew she was going to have an interesting story to tell the repairman in the morning.

Unfortunately, the handyman she had to call was out working on the renovations at Carson's place. He was too busy to come. She managed to talk his wife into giving her the number of a man who put in windows in his spare time. She contacted him and got a promise that he'd do the window first thing Monday morning. Meanwhile she got a locksmith to come out and fix the door. She hadn't asked the handyman's wife how things were going over at Carson's, although she was curious about how the house would look when they got through. Carson's preparations were none of her business. Probably Patty knew, though, she thought miserably.

She went up to Phoenix and spent the rest of the weekend there just to get away. How drastically things had changed in just a few short weeks, she thought. She and Carson had been on the verge of friendship, but those few days together had changed everything. Actually, she decided, that long, hard kiss he'd given her behind the bar had done it. She'd been curious about him after that, and when he'd made a pass, she hadn't had the strength to put him off. She'd wanted to know how he would be as a lover. And now she knew, and the knowledge was eating her up like acid. She'd never known that a man could be so tender, so protective and possessive. She could have had all that, if not for Carson's obsession with changing to suit Patty.

Patty. She went out to the balcony of her hotel room and glared over the city's lights. The wind tore through her hair and she drank in the sounds and smells of the night. He'd kissed Patty at her party. Why had he done that? She closed her eyes and she could almost hear Carson's deep, slow voice as he sang. She leaned her head against the wall and wondered how it would be to sit with him on his porch late on a summer evening while he sang to her. And if there were children, they could sit on her lap....

The thought was intensely painful. She remembered how it had been that night, the night she'd wanted him so much. If only he hadn't turned on the light and seen Ben's photograph.

Dear Ben. Her bastion against emotional involvement. Her wall that kept love out of her life. And now she was twenty-six and alone and she'd lost the only man in the world she wanted to live with.

Of course, she hadn't a chance against Patty. She'd always known that. Carson was too fond of the woman. She turned back into her room. How odd that he wanted to learn cultural things for Patty, though. Especially when Patty seemed to like country things and country people. How very odd.

She went back to Sweetwater late Sunday night, feeling drained and no more refreshed than before. It was going to be another long week.

It didn't help that Patty came into her office early Monday morning with a complaint about the property.

"The roof leaks," she grumbled. "It poured rain here, and you told me that roof was sound. I had ten half-drowned cats before I thought to check."

"I'm sorry, Mandelyn said formally. "The previous owner assured me he'd had a new roof put on recently. You know I'd never purposely misrepresent a property," she added. "You're going to have trouble finding a roofer. Carson seems to have every workman in town out at his place."

"It's coming along nicely, too," Patty remarked. "He's had new furniture put in the house and carpeting...it's a showplace already. Once they get the new roof on, and the painting finished, it will make most houses in the valley look like outbuildings."

"You'll like that, I'm sure," Mandelyn murmured under her breath.

"I'll call Carson and see if he can loan me his roofer," Patty said suddenly. "Why didn't I think of that myself?"

"Good idea," Mandelyn said with a wan smile.

Patty started out the door and paused. "Uh, Jake spent a lot of time with you at the party," she murmured. "Seen him since?"

"I've been out of town," Mandelyn said noncommittally. "I haven't seen anybody."

"Jake's been out of town, too," Patty said, her smile disappearing. She opened the door and went out, slamming it behind her.

Angie glanced up from her typewriter with a curious stare. "You and Jake...?"

"Oh, shut up," Mandelyn said. "I haven't been anywhere with Jake. She's just mad because Carson isn't running after her fast enough, I suppose. He isn't good enough for her...."

She went into her office and slammed the door, too. Angie shrugged and went back to work.

Mandelyn didn't hear from Carson at all. Wednesday, she went ahead and dressed to go to the ballet, feeling not at all happy about it. She'd rather have stayed home and bawled. It was how she felt. She wasn't even sure that Carson would show up at all. He was getting to be wildly unpredictable.

She chose a floor-length blue velvet gown with

white accessories and put her hair up with a blue velvet ribbon. She kept remembering that blue velvet ribbon in Carson's car, and wished she could get it out of her mind. He must not have gotten it from her, after all.

At five-thirty, he still hadn't shown up, and she was on her way back to her bedroom to change her clothes when she heard a car pull up.

She felt as nervous as a girl on her first date. She was probably overdressed, but she'd wanted to look pretty for him. That was idiotic. But she couldn't help herself.

She opened the door, and found him in a tuxedo. That was one item they hadn't bought together, and she couldn't help but stare. He was so striking that she couldn't drag her eyes away. He had the perfect physique for a tuxedo, and the whiteness of the silk shirt he was wearing made his complexion darker, his hair blacker. His blue eyes were dark, too, as they looked down at her.

"You...look very nice," she faltered.

"So do you," he said, but his eyes were cold. Like his face. "We'd better go."

She followed him outside, forgetting her wrap in the excitement. They were halfway to Phoenix before she remembered.

"My stole," she exclaimed.

"You aren't likely to freeze to death," he said curtly.

"I didn't say I was, Carson," she replied.

He tugged at his tie. "I'll be glad when this is over," he grumbled.

"It was your idea," she said sweetly.

"I've had some pretty bad ideas lately."

"Yes, I know."

His eyes drifted slowly over her. "Was it necessary to wear a dress that was cut to the navel?" he asked harshly.

She wouldn't let him rattle her. "It was the only dressy thing I had."

"Left over from the days when you dated the eligible banker and were in the thick of Charleston society, no doubt," he said mockingly.

She closed her eyes and wouldn't answer him.

"No retort?" he chided.

"I won't argue with you, Carson," she said. "I'm through fighting. I've got no stomach for it anymore."

She felt that way, too, as if all the life had been drained out of her.

"You, through fighting?" he laughed coldly.

"People change."

"Not enough. They never change enough to suit other people. I'm dressed up in this damned monkey suit going to a form of entertainment I don't understand or even like. And it isn't going to change what I am. I'm no fancy dude. I never will be. I've accepted that."

"Will your fancy woman accept it?" she

laughed unpleasantly. "Will she want you the way you are?"

"Maybe not," he replied. "But that's how she'll take me."

"So masterful!" she taunted. "How exciting for her!"

He turned his head slowly and the look in his eyes was hot and dangerous. "You'll push me too far one day."

She turned her gaze toward the city lights of Phoenix.

He pulled up near the auditorium and parked. There was a crowd, and she kept close to Carson, feeling a little nervous around all the strangers.

He glanced down at her, frowning. "Aren't you afraid to get that close to me?" he taunted.

"I'm less afraid of you than I am of them," she confessed. "I don't like crowds."

He stopped dead and looked down at her with narrow, searching eyes. "But you like culture, don't you, honey?"

The sarcasm in his voice was cutting. She looked back at him quietly. "I like men with deep voices singing love songs, too," she said.

He seemed disconcerted for a minute. He turned away, guiding her into the throng with a puzzled frown.

Everything seemed to go wrong. Their tickets were for another night, and Carson was told so, politely but firmly.

"Wrong night, hell," he told the small man at the door. Then he grinned and that meant trouble. "Listen, sonny, they were supposed to be for tonight. I'm here. And I'm staying.'

"Sir, please lower your voice," the little man pleaded, looking nervously around him.

"Lower it? I plan on raising it quite a bit," Carson returned. "You want trouble, you can have it. In spades."

Mandelyn closed her eyes. This was getting to be a pattern. Why did she let herself in for this kind of embarrassment?

"Please go in, sir. I'm sure the mixup is our fault," the small man said loudly and with a forced smile.

Carson nodded at him and smiled coldly. "I'm sure it is. Come on, Mandy."

He guided her into the auditorium and seated her on the aisle beside him. He stuck out his long legs and stared down at the program. He scowled.

"Swan Lake?" he asked, staring at the photos in the printed program. He glanced at Mandelyn. "You mean we came all this way to watch some woman dressed up like a damned bird parading across the stage?"

Oh, God, she prayed, give him laryngitis!

Around them were sharp, angry murmurs. Mandelyn touched his hand. "Carson, ballet is an art form. It's dancing. You know that."

"Dancing, okay. But parading around in a bird suit, and her a grown woman?"

She tapped him on the arm with her program.

"Swatting flies?" he asked.

She hid her face behind her program, slid down in the seat, and prayed for a power failure. There were too many lights. Everyone could see that the loud man was with her.

He continued to make loud comments until the lights went down. Mandelyn almost sagged with relief in the darkness. But she should have known better. The minute the orchestra began to play and the lead ballerina finally appeared, he sat up straight and leaned forward.

"When does the ballet start?" he demanded.

"It just did!" she hissed.

"All she's doing is running around the stage!" he protested.

"Shut up, could you!" the man behind Carson said curtly.

Carson turned around and glared through the darkness. "I paid for my ticket, just like you did. So shut up yourself. Or step outside."

The man was twice Carson's age, and rather chubby. He cleared his throat, trying to look belligerent. But he held his peace.

Carson glanced down at Mandelyn. "Something in your shoe?" he asked. "Why are you hiding?"

"I'm not hiding," she choked, red-faced as she sat back up.

He was staring at the stage. Out came a muscular male dancer, and Carson gaped and caught his breath and burst out laughing.

"Oh, do be quiet," she squeaked.

"Hell, look at that," he roared. "He looks like he's wearing long johns. And what the hell is that between his legs…?"

"Oh, God," she moaned, burying her hands in her face.

"Better not bother Him, lady," the man behind her suggested. "If He hears what that man's saying, He'll strike him dead."

Mandelyn was only hoping for hoarseness, but it didn't happen. Carson kept laughing, and she couldn't stand it another minute. Everyone near them was talking; they had disrupted the entire performance. She climbed over Carson and ran for the front door. She made her way through the lobby and into the women's rest room. She stayed there for a long time, crimson to the roots of her hair. How could he? He knew better than to behave like that. He'd done it deliberately, and she knew it. He'd been trying to embarrass her, to humiliate her in front of what he thought was her own set. And that hurt most of all. That he'd done it to wound her.

Carson was waiting for her, his head down,

glaring at his dress shoes when she came back out of the rest room. He heard her step and looked up.

His eyes were dark blue. Quiet. Searching. He took his hands out of his pockets and moved toward her.

"You've had your fun," she said with dignity. "Or revenge. Or whatever you like to call it. Now that you've ruined my evening, please take me home.'

His jaw tightened. "Miss Bush of Charleston, to the back teeth," he said mockingly. "Dignity first."

"I have very little dignity left, thank you," she replied. "And I'm through trying to civilize you. I know a hopeless case when I see one."

His eyes flashed. "Giving up?"

"Oh, yes," she said with a cool smile. "And I wish your woman joy of you, Carson. Maybe if she can put a bridle on you, she can tell people you're a horse and don't know any better manners."

The expression that crossed his face was indescribable. He turned on his heel and led the way out the door. She followed him stiffly, standing aside to let him unlock her side of the car.

It was a long, harrowing ride home. He turned on the radio and let it play to fill the silence. When they pulled up in front of her house, she was too drained to even notice what was playing.

He'd told her in actions just how much contempt he felt for her.

"Mandelyn," he said.

She didn't even look at him. "Goodbye, Carson."

"I'd like to talk to you," he said through his teeth. "Explain something."

"What could you possibly say that would be of interest to me? You and I have absolutely nothing in common," she said with cool hauteur and a look that spoke volumes. "Do invite me to the wedding. I'll see if I can find something homespun to wear. And I'll even send you a wedding gift. How would you like a set of matching knives for your table? After all, you have to have something to eat your peas with, don't you? Just the thing for a savage like you!"

She got out of the car, slammed the door and marched up the steps. It took her the rest of the night to try to forget the look on Carson's face when she'd said that to him. And she cried herself to sleep for her own cruelty. She hadn't meant it. She'd only wanted to hurt him as much as he'd hurt her. He'd as much as told her that her world was shoddy and superficial. It had been the killing blow. Because she understood all at once why it hurt so much. She was in love with Carson. And she'd just lost him forever.

Chapter 8

Mandelyn couldn't even go to work the next day, she was so sick about what had happened the night before. She shouldn't have behaved so badly, even though Carson had provoked her. She shouldn't have hurt him like that.

"I've got a migraine," she told Angie. She knew she sounded unwell from crying all night. "If anyone needs me, tell them I'll be back tomorrow, okay?"

Angie hesitated. "Uh, Patty came by as soon as I opened up."

"Oh?"

"Yes. She asked if I knew that Carson was in jail."

Mandelyn gripped the receiver hard.

"What?"

"She said he went on a bender last night and

dared Jake to call you. Danny had to lock him up. They said he set new records for broken glass, and to top it all off, he ran his Thunderbird into Jim Handel's new swimming pool."

Her eyes closed and tears welled up behind her swollen eyelids. Because of her, she knew. Because of the way she'd hurt him.

"Is he still there?" she asked after a minute.

"No, ma'am. Patty bailed him out. She took him over to her place to look after him. He's pretty bruised and battered, but she says he'll be okay. She, uh, thought you might want to know."

"Well I don't," she said quietly. "I don't want to hear about Carson Wayne again as long as I live. See you tomorrow, Angie," she added on a sob and hung up.

He was at Patty's. He was hurt, and he was at Patty's. And she was nursing him and taking care of him and loving him....

Mandelyn burst into tears. Somehow, she was going to have to stop crying. Her heart was breaking.

She didn't eat breakfast or lunch. Around midafternoon she heard the sound of a car coming up the driveway.

She looked out the window and was shocked to see Patty's truck pulling up at the front door. Her eyes flashed. She wouldn't answer the doorbell. She wouldn't even talk to the other woman! Patty had Carson now, what else did she want?

Patty rang the bell and Mandelyn ignored her.

"Mandy!" Patty called. "Mandy, I know you're in there!"

"Go away!" Mandelyn called back, her voice wobbling. "I've got an awful headache. I can't talk to you!"

"Well, you're going to," Patty said stubbornly. "Shall I break a window?"

Mandelyn decided that another broken window would be too much trouble. Reluctantly, she opened the door.

Patty paused, shocked by the other woman's pale features.

"What do you want?" Mandelyn asked. Her voice sounded hoarse.

"I came to see about you," Patty said, surprised. "Angie said you had a migraine, and I thought you might want me to go to the pharmacy for you."

"You've already got one patient, just take care of him and leave me alone."

Patty moved closer, eyeing her friend closely. "Mandy, what's wrong?" she asked softly.

That was the straw that broke the camel's back. Mandelyn started crying again, and couldn't stop. Her body shook with broken sobs.

"Oh, Mandy, don't, I can't stand to see you like this," Patty pleaded, helping her to sit down in the living room. "What's wrong? Please, tell me!"

Mandelyn shook her head. "Nothing."

"Nothing." Patty looked toward the ceiling. "Carson takes his car into the swimming pool with him and you play hookey from work with a nonexistent headache, and nothing's wrong."

"You've got him now, what do you care what happens to me?" Mandelyn ground out, glaring at her.

"I've got him? Him, who? Carson?" Her eyes widened. "You think I'm after Carson?"

Mandelyn dabbed at her eyes. "Aren't you? He did it all for you, you know. Learning all about culture, and going to ballets and making fun of ballerinas and fixing up his house. You ought to be proud of yourself! He didn't think he was good enough for you the way he was, so he got me to give him lessons in etiquette!"

Patty's mouth opened. "Carson isn't in love with me!"

"Of course he is," Mandelyn said with trembling lips. "And I wish you every happiness!"

"Me? What about you?" Patty shot back. "You went away for the weekend with Jake!"

It was Mandelyn's turn to look shocked. "I went to Phoenix...alone."

Patty flushed. "Oh." She glared. "But you were all over him at my party."

"We were consoling each other," Mandelyn said wearily. "I suggested maybe he could learn to play a guitar and sing like Carson, and he said maybe I could go to veterinarian's school...."

"Jake was jealous?" Patty asked. "Of me?"

"Boy, are you dense," Mandelyn grumbled. "Of course he was jealous. Mad at Carson, mad at you. He asked me to dance so he wouldn't have to watch the two of you together. And when you kissed Carson, I thought he was going to go wild."

Patty's eyes misted. "Oh, my," she whispered.

A dawning realization made Mandelyn's tears dry up. "Patty...it's Jake, isn't it?"

"It's always been Jake," Patty confessed. She stared down at her jeans. "Since I was a teenager. But he wouldn't give me the time of day. I thought after I went away, maybe he'd miss me, but he didn't even write or call me. And when I came back here, I found all sorts of excuses to go out to the ranch, but he didn't notice. At the party I'd just about given up. I was hurting so much I couldn't stand it, and Carson knew and he played up to me to try to make Jake jealous. But I thought it backfired, because Jake wouldn't come near me. Last night, when I got Carson out of jail and took him home with me, Jake came to the front door and raised hell. I yelled back at him, and I thought it was all over. But now..."

"Jake loves you," Mandelyn whispered.

"Yes, I think he might," Patty faltered tearfully. "But why won't he admit it?"

"He's Carson's foreman. He isn't an educated

man. And you've a degree. Maybe he doesn't feel worthy."

"I'll soon rid him of that silly notion, wait and see." Patty grinned. "I'll seduce him."

Mandelyn blushed wildly and Patty laughed.

"You might try that yourself," she suggested gently. "The way Carson lets you lead him around, I don't think he'd be able to stop you."

"I don't feel that way about Carson. I just feel guilty." The flush got worse. Mandelyn stared down at her shoes. "He hates me."

"Oh, sure he does."

"But he does!" Mandelyn wailed. She blurted out the whole painful story through a mist of tears. "I could just die! I hurt him and he could have been killed. I'd never have forgiven myself."

"Carson's tough," Patty said. "At least, he's tough with everyone but you."

"He's nice to you," Mandelyn reminded her.

"Oh, Carson and I go back a long way. We grew up together. I love him like a brother, and he knows it. But he's never been with anyone the way he is with you, honey. You must be the only person in Sweetwater who doesn't know that Carson's in love with you."

Mandelyn stared at her friend as if she'd lost her senses. Her eyes widened and her heart began to race.

"Didn't you ever wonder why he'd let you save

people from him when he was drinking?" Patty asked, her eyes soft.

"Because I wasn't afraid of him," she replied.

Patty shook her head. "Because he would have done anything for you. We all knew it. And he'd sit and stare at you and have the damndest lost look on his face...."

"But...but he said there was a woman." Mandelyn hesitated. "He said she wouldn't have him the way he was, that he wanted to change and get cultured so that he could have a chance with her."

"He was talking about you," Patty said. "You, with your genteel background and your exquisite manners. It was like wishing for a star, and he must have known all along how impossible it was. But I guess he had to try."

Mandelyn felt as if someone had hit her over the head with a mallet. Carson loved her?

"Don't feel so bad," Patty said. "He'll get over it. He's almost back to normal this morning. Once he's realized what a silly idea it was, he'll come around, and you two will be friends again. Carson doesn't hold grudges. He'll thank you for having brought him to his senses." She stood up, grinning. "Imagine, you and Carson. That would be something, wouldn't it? The debutante and the outlaw. Wow!" She stretched. "Well, I'll never be able to tell you how grateful I am to know how Jake really feels. And don't you torment yourself about Carson. You only helped him see the light. He'll be okay. He's mostly just hung over."

"Would you...tell him I said I'm sorry?" she asked.

Patty studied her. "Wouldn't you like to come with me and tell him yourself?"

"No!" Mandelyn took a steadying breath. "No, I don't think so. It's too soon yet."

"Well, I'll relay the message. Feel better now? He isn't hurt. He's just dented."

Mandelyn nodded. "Thanks for coming by. I'm sorry I was ratty."

"No problem. I know what guilt can do to people. Say, you weren't getting sweet on Carson, were you?"

"Who me?" Mandelyn laughed nervously. "As you said, that would be something, wouldn't it?"

"A pretty wild match. What interesting kids you'd have. Okay, I'm going!" she laughed when Mandelyn started to look homicidal. "See you!"

Mandelyn sat by the window for a long time, thinking over what Patty had said. Bits and pieces of conversation came back to her, and she began to realize that it might have been true. Carson might have been falling in love with her. But whatever he'd felt before, he hated her now. He hated her for trying to live in the past with Ben, and for what she'd said to him at the ballet. He hated her for making him feel worthless and savage.

She fixed herself a light supper, trying to decide what to do. Her life was so empty now that she didn't know how she was going to survive. Perhaps she could go back to Charleston.

That thought appealed for only a few minutes. No, she couldn't leave Sweetwater. She couldn't leave Carson. Even if she only caught glimpses of him for the rest of her life, she couldn't bear being half a country away from him.

Several times, she went to the telephone and stared at it, wanting to call him, wanting to apologize. Or just to hear his voice. Finally, after dark, she dialed Patty's number.

"Hello," Patty said cheerfully.

"It's Mandelyn. Is…is Carson still there?"

"No, honey, he went home to nurse his bruises alone," Patty said. "He's feeling pretty low, though. You might try him there."

"Okay. Thanks."

"My pleasure," Patty murmured, and a male voice laughed softly in the background.

Mandelyn hung up, smiling faintly. It had sounded like Jake's voice, and she was glad that for Patty, at least, the long wait was over.

She dialed Carson's number and waited and waited until finally he picked it up.

"Hello," he said deeply, in a defeated kind of voice.

She was afraid he'd hang up on her. So she only said, very softly, "I'm sorry."

There was a long pause. "Why apologize for telling the truth?" he asked coldly.

At least he was talking to her. She sat down and leaned back against the sofa with her eyes closed. "How are you?"

"I'll live," he said curtly.

She couldn't think of anything to say. Except, maybe, "I love you." Because she did, so desperately. Patty had said that he loved her, but those days were gone for good. She knew she'd killed the delicate feelings he had for her.

"Do…do you need anything?" she asked hesitantly.

"Not from you, Mandelyn."

She knew that, but hearing it hurt. She swallowed down the tears. "I just wanted to see how you were. Good night."

She started to hang up, but he said her name in a way that made her toes curl up.

"Yes?" she whispered.

There was a long pause and she held her breath, hoping against hope for some crumb, some tiny clue that he still cared.

"Thanks for the lessons," he said after a minute. "I'll put them to good use."

"You're welcome," she replied, and hung up. Maybe Patty was wrong, she thought desperately. Maybe there was a woman neither of them knew about, a woman in Phoenix or some other town. And that thought tortured her long into the night.

Chapter 9

The next few days were agonizing ones for Mandelyn. She lost her appetite for food, for living itself. For the first time, work wasn't enough to sustain her. And her memories of Ben, which had kept her going for years, had become nothing more than pleasant episodes from the past. She missed Carson. It was like having half of her body cut away and trying to live on what was left.

Once, she accidentally ran into him in the local fast-food restaurant. She'd stopped to get a cold drink as she walked back to her office after an appointment, and he was just coming out.

Her heart leapt up into her throat and she dropped her eyes. She couldn't even look at him. She turned around and went back the way she'd come without bothering about the cold drink. The look in his eyes had been chilling enough.

The second week, Patty stopped by the house to invite Mandelyn to go with her to the Sweetwater Rodeo.

"Come on," Patty coaxed. "You've been moping around for days. You need some diversion."

"Well…"

"You can go with Jake and me," she coaxed, grinning. "Things are going very well indeed in that department, by the way. I've almost got him hooked."

Mandelyn smiled. "I'm happy for you. I really am." But she couldn't bear the thought of driving in the pickup with Jake and hearing him talk about Carson. "I've got something to do earlier in town, though, so I'll just drive in and meet you there. Okay?"

"Okay."

She imagined Carson would be there, and she almost backed out at the last minute. But he'd be a competitor, as he usually was, and she wouldn't get close to him. She'd be able to see him, though. And the temptation was just too much for her hungry heart. Just to see him would be heaven.

She left her house fifteen minutes before the rodeo started and had a devil of a time finding a parking space at the fairgrounds. She managed to wedge her car in beside a big pickup and left it there, hoping she could get out before the owner of the pickup wanted to leave.

Patty waved to her from the front of the bleachers, where she was sitting beside Jake, his arm around her.

"Just in the nick of time," Patty said. "Better late than never, though."

"I couldn't find a parking spot. Hi, Jake," Mandelyn said as she sat down next to Patty. It was as if they had changed roles for the day—Patty was in a green print sundress and Mandelyn in jeans and boots and a blue tank top with her hair loose and sunglasses perched atop her head.

"Hi, Miss Bush," Jake said with a wicked smile. "I didn't know you liked rodeos."

"I like a lot of strange things these days," she returned. "Looks like you didn't need to learn the guitar after all."

Jake laughed and hugged Patty close. "Good thing, since I've got ten thumbs." He glanced toward her curiously. "Boss is riding today."

Her heartbeat faltered. "Is he?"

"In the steer wrestling and bronc riding. He's been practicing. We got two steers with permanently wrenched necks and one poor old bronc with a slipped disk."

"Nasty old Carson," Mandelyn said.

"I expect he'll take top money."

Mandelyn glanced around the ring, looking for a city woman somewhere. "Doesn't he have a cheering section with him?" she asked with barely concealed curiosity.

Jake and Patty exchanged amused glances. "Sure. Right here. We're it."

Mandelyn glared toward the dirt ring. "Amazing. I would have thought the object of his affections would be around somewhere. How's the house looking?"

"Just great," Jake returned. "He's kind of lost interest, though. Says it's no use anymore."

"There isn't any woman," Patty murmured under her breath. "I've told you already, it was you."

Mandelyn's face went hot and red. "Not now."

"Do you stop loving people just because you get angry with them?" Patty asked.

No, Mandelyn thought miserably. She'd never stop loving Carson. But what good would that do her? She'd just die of unrequited love, that was all.

The bronc riding competition was exciting. Most of the cowboys who participated drew good mounts, and the scores were high. But when Carson exploded into the arena on a horse named "TNT," groans were heard all around.

He rode magnificently, Mandelyn thought dreamily, watching his lean figure. His bat-wing chaps flew, his body whipped elegantly, gracefully, as it absorbed the shock of the bronc's wild motions. And by the time the horn blew, everybody knew that top money was going to Carson that day.

"Damn, isn't he good?" Jake laughed.

"I thought you'd be riding this time," Mandelyn remarked.

Jake looked down at Patty with a dreamy expression. "No. I've got more important things on my mind."

Patty blushed and snuggled closer and Mandelyn felt empty and cold and alone.

The sun beat down as rider after rider competed in bulldogging and calf roping. And then came steer wrestling. Carson was the last competitor, and there was a wild cheer as he came down off the horse squarely in front of the long horns of the animal. He dug in his heels, gave a quick, hard twist with his powerful arms, and the steer toppled onto the ground. Applause filled the bleachers, but Mandelyn was holding her breath as Carson got to his feet. The bull headed straight for him.

"No!" she screamed, leaping to her feet. "Carson!"

But it was all unnecessary. Lithe as a cat, he was onto the fence rail even as the animal charged. The rodeo clown made a great production of heading the steer off, finally leaping into a barrel and letting the animal work its frustration off by rolling him around.

Mandelyn managed to sit back down, but her face was white. Patty put an arm around her.

"Hey," she said gently. "He's been doing this a long time. He's okay."

"Yes, of course he is," Mandelyn said, swallowing down her fear. She clasped her hands tight in her lap and sat stiffly until the end of the competitions.

Later, she was about to head for her car when Patty caught her arm and tugged her along the aisle behind the pens. Carson was just loading his horse into the trailer behind the ranch pickup, and Jake went forward to shake his hand.

"Hey, boss, you done good." Jake grinned. "Congratulations."

"And you kept saying you were too old," Patty added, hugging him. "I was proud of you."

He hugged her back, smiling down at her in a way that twisted Mandelyn's heart. At least he and Patty were still friends. She hadn't wanted to come this close; she hadn't wanted to have to talk to him.

He looked up and saw her and his face froze. His expression went from sunshine to thunderstorm in seconds.

"We're going to see Billy for a minute," Patty called. "Be right back!"

She dragged Jake away, looking smug and triumphant. Mandelyn twisted a knot in the necklace she was wearing while Carson glared at her.

"You...did very well," she said, hating the long silence.

Around them, animals snorted and whinnied, and there was a loud buzz of conversation among the milling cowboys.

"I didn't expect to find you at a rodeo," he

said, lighting a cigarette. "It isn't exactly your thing, is it?"

"I like rodeos, actually," she returned. Her eyes went down to his opened shirt, and there was a red welt across his chest, visible through the mat of black curling hair. "Carson, you're hurt!" she burst out, moving close to him with wide, frightened eyes. "The bull got you…!" She reached out her fingers to touch it, and even as they made brief, electric contact with his skin, he'd caught her wrist bruisingly hard and pushed her away.

His eyes blazed like blue lightning. "Don't touch me, damn you!" he whispered furiously.

Her face went white. She could feel every single drop of blood draining out of it as she stared at him, horrified. So it was that bad. She was so repulsive to him that he couldn't even stand to have her hands on him now. She wanted to crawl off and die. Tears burst from her eyes and a sob tore out of her throat.

She whirled and ran sightlessly through the crowd, crying so hard that she didn't hear Carson's wild exclamation or his furious footsteps behind her. She pushed people aside, jumped over saddles and trailer hitches and ran until her lungs felt like bursting. She wanted to go home. She wanted to get away. It was the only thought in her tortured mind.

She rounded the corner of the fence and squeezed by the pickup and into the front seat of her car. She was so blinded by tears that she could hardly see how to get the key into the ignition, but she managed it. She'd just started the car and was fumbling it into reverse when the door was jerked open and a lean, angry hand flashed past her to turn off the ignition and pull out the key.

"You little fool, you'll kill yourself trying to drive in that condition!" Carson said harshly. He was breathing hard as he stared down at her furiously.

The tears grew more profuse. "What the hell does it matter?" she asked brokenly. "I don't care if I die!"

"Oh, God," he ground out. He eased himself into the front seat beside her, facing her. His hands framed her face and he brought her mouth under his, tasting tears and mint and trembling lips. And the sob that rose from her throat went into his hard mouth, mingled with his rough breath.

He eased her head back against the seat with the pressure of his lips. His tongue caressed her, probed into the soft sweet darkness of her mouth. His sweaty chest pressed against her soft breasts and she could feel the hardness of muscle and the warmth of flesh and the wild thunder of his heart.

It was so sweet. So sweet, after all the long days and nights of wanting and needing and loving and pain. She slid her hands over his shoulders, up into the thick dampness of his hair and sighed shakily as her mouth opened and answered the tender pressure of his own.

His lips lifted, then came down again, kissing away the tears and the pain while she sobbed softly and tried to stop crying.

"Carson," she whispered achingly.

"It's all right," he whispered back. His hands trembled on her face. He kissed her again, so tenderly that it hurt, and she moaned.

"I'm so hungry...for you," she moaned. "So hungry...for your mouth, your...hands."

"Baby..." he protested.

She crushed her mouth against his, drowning in sensual pleasure as he answered the hard kiss. His arms slid under her, pulling, crushing, and she thought if she died now, it would be all right. Life would never offer anything more beautiful than this, than Carson wanting her.

A long time later, she felt his mouth lift, and the breeze cooled her moistened lips. Her eyes opened, dark gray, still hungry, worshipping his face.

His nostrils flared. His own eyes were fierce and hot with unsatisfied passion.

"I want...to have you," she whispered softly, searching his eyes.

His eyes closed. His teeth clenched. "It's no good! It won't change anything!"

"It will give you peace," she said, smoothing his hard face gently.

His eyes opened again, searching hers, and there was pain and hunger and loneliness in them.

She managed a tremulous smile. "Patty said once that I should seduce you. That you'd probably let me."

His fingers traced her mouth, unsteady and gentle. "That would be one for the books, wouldn't it? A shy little virgin seducing an outlaw like me?"

"Would you like it?" she whispered, wide-eyed.

He trembled before he could get his body under control, and she touched his hair, his face, with hands that loved the feel of him.

"I'd be…very careful with you," she said unsteadily, on a nervous laugh. "I wouldn't even let you get pregnant, I promise."

He burst out laughing, but his eyes were solemn and quiet. "Mandy…"

"Please," she whispered, beyond pride.

His eyes closed and he mutterd a harsh word. "Look, it's no use," he said after a minute. "You and I are too different. Desire…it fades. So I want you. And you want me. But if we had each other, it wouldn't solve the problem. It would only make things unbearable." He sighed roughly and put her away from him. "No, honey. You go your own way. Someday you'll find some cultured dude with fancy manners and you'll live happily ever after. I was a fool to think anything would change. Goodbye, Mandelyn."

He got out of the car and left her sitting there,

staring after him. She thought about what he'd said and a slow, easy smile came to her lips. That one tremor had given him away. She dried her tears and drove back to the house. She had things to do.

About midnight, she had a nice warm bath and doused herself in a faint, subtle perfume. She powdered her smooth, pink body and pulled on a button-up yellow dress, and nothing else. She brushed her hair until it shone. Then she slid into her sandals and got in her car and drove to Carson's house.

The lights were all off. She ran up onto the front porch, sure that the boys were all gone because it was Saturday night. She smiled wickedly as she thought about what she was going to do. Drastic situations called for drastic measures, and nobody had ever been this desperate, she decided. She knocked hard on the door, noticing that the woodwork was freshly painted. The porch looked nice. Very white and different, and there was a white porch swing and rocking chairs, too. She approved of the renovation.

There were muffled curses and thuds as she knocked again. The door flew open and Carson stood there, in the lighted room, without a stitch of clothing on his powerfully muscled, hair-roughened body.

Chapter 10

Carson blinked, staring at her as if he thought he was having a dream. "Mandy?" he asked softly.

She was just adjusting to the sight of him. It had been a wild shock, although he was as perfect as a man could possibly be, and her eyes were only just able to drag themselves back up to his shocked face.

He stood aside, running a hand through his disheveled dark hair, just staring at her. She opened the screen door, her heart pounding, and walked into the living room. It was as much a shock as Carson. The sparse, worn furniture was gone, replaced by heavy oak pieces with brocade fabric in cream and chocolate. The brown carpet was thick; the curtains were of the same fabric as the upholstery on the chairs. And the beautiful fireplace had been renovated and was the showpiece she'd once thought it could be.

"The house is lovely," she remarked breathlessly, forcing her eyes to stay on his face.

"What are you doing here at this time of night?" he burst out.

Her eyes glanced down and up again and she flushed. "Getting anatomy lessons."

He glanced down, too, and smiled ruefully. "Well, you should have called first."

"I guess so."

"Want me to put my pants on, or is the shock wearing off?"

She searched his blue eyes, hesitating. It had seemed so easy when she was thinking about it. And now it was becoming more impossible by the minute. The longer she waited, the weaker her nerve became. He needed a shave, but he looked vital and exquisitely masculine and she wanted to touch him all over that bronzed skin.

She moved closer to him, watching the way his eyes narrowed warily.

"I...want you...to come to bed with me," she faltered.

He glared at her. "I told you this afternoon how I felt about that," he said curtly.

"Yes, I know." She reached out and touched his chest, watching the way he stiffened. His hands caught her, but she trailed her fingers slowly down his body and his hold weakened. His body trembled and jerked.

"Don't," he whispered huskily.

It was so easy. Easier than she'd dreamed. Heady with success, she pressed her body against his and reached up to coax his head down.

"Help me," she whispered. She eased her mouth onto his and kissed him tenderly. She loved his immediate response to her. He tasted of whiskey. It was a little disturbing at first, but the warm hardness of his mouth got through to her and she became accustomed to the strong taste.

His hands caught her shoulders. "Mandy, we can't," he breathed roughly. "You're a virgin, for God's sake!"

"Yes, you'll be my first man," she whispered. "The very first."

That made his hands tremble and she stood on tiptoe, brushing her body softly against his so that something predictable and awesome happened to him. She sighed and moaned.

"It's going to be so beautiful," she said at his lips. "The most beautiful night…"

She left him long enough to close and lock the door. Then she went back to him, where he stood frozen and waiting, and reached up her arms.

"Would you carry me?" she whispered.

He bent like a man in a trance and lifted her tenderly in his hard arms. She nestled her face into his throat, feeling the thunderous beat of his pulse there, feeling his taut body absorb the shock of his footsteps as he carried her into the darkened bedroom and laid her down on his rumpled bed.

"Honey..." he began in a strangled voice.

"Here," she said, drawing his hands to the buttons of her dress.

He muttered something, and his fingers trembled as he fumbled them open. She sat up, sliding the dress off her body. She lay back, her body pale in the patch of moonlight coming through the window. She held out her arms.

"Come here, darling," she whispered. She wasn't even afraid. She wanted him. She wanted a child with him. And tonight she was going to make sure she had that, if nothing else. If he sent her away, she wanted at least the hope, the tiny hope, of having a part of him.

"Mandy," he groaned. He lay down on the bed with her like a lamb going to slaughter.

"It's all right," she whispered. She trembled a little when his hands moved down her thighs and back up over her flat stomach and her soft breasts.

"You're afraid," he whispered.

"It's very mysterious right now," she explained quietly. "I... I know the mechanics, but I don't know how it's going to feel, you see. Will... Carson, will it hurt me very much?" she whispered.

"We don't have to do it," he said.

"I have to," she breathed. "I have to!"

"Why?" he asked.

His hands were fascinated with her body, and she stretched like a cat being stroked, loving their rough tenderness. "I want a baby," she whispered. "I want your baby."

He shuddered wildly. His breath caught and he buried his face against her body, groaning helplessly.

Yes, she thought, drawing him closer, yes, that had done it. Now he wouldn't be able to stop, or stop her. It would happen now, because she'd stirred him in an unbearable way.

His mouth found hers hungrily, and his hands began to touch her in new, shocking ways. She trembled and twisted and moaned, and still his hands tormented her. His mouth went on a trembling journey of exploration that left not one inch of her untouched, that made her cry out and whisper things to him that would have shocked her speechless in daylight.

When she felt his weight on her, she stiffened a little, and his hands brushed back her damp hair, calming her.

"I won't take you in a rush," he promised tenderly. "Mandy, close your eyes for a minute. I'm going to turn on the light."

"No…!"

"Yes," he whispered, brushing his mouth over her eyes as he reached out to turn on the light at the head of the bed.

Her eyes opened, shocked, frightened and although she knew he was too committed to draw away, she was afraid the starkness of the light might make him stop.

His hands smoothed her hair, touched her hot cheeks. His eyes adored her, glazed with desire, bright with passion and hunger.

"I asked you this once before. Let me watch," he whispered shakily. "You came in here a virgin, and we're about to do something extraordinary together. Let me...watch it happen to you... please."

Her body trembled, but she didn't say a word. Her hands touched his broad, perspiring shoulders, his chest, his face. She felt him move and her eyes dilated. She stiffened, but his fingers touched her hair again, soothing, comforting as his hips eased down.

"No," he whispered when she tried to move away. His voice shook, but his smile was steady, his eyes were...loving her.

"Oh," she whispered sharply, staring straight into his eyes as his body locked with hers.

"Yes," he said, shuddering, his face clenching. "Oh, God, yes, yes...yes!

Something incredible was happening. She couldn't believe the intimacy of it. Her nails were biting into him and she didn't even realize it. Her body forgot that it had a brain and began to entice him, incite him. It arched and forced a deeper intimacy that began as pain and suddenly became easy and sweet and achingly tender.

"Now," she whispered mindlessly. "Now, I... belong...to you...!"

"Baby...was there a time...when you didn't?" he bit off. His mouth burned into hers, hot and wet and hungry, and his body began to find a new rhythm with hers. She felt his hands, holding her hips, showing her how. She closed her eyes and let her body teach her what to do, her hands touching, her mouth whispering into his. Storms. Sunlight. Wild breeze and sweet peace. Open fields and running feet. A surge. A scream. Hers. And all too soon she felt conscious again. Carson lay shuddering helplessly on her trembling body, his voice shaking as if he were in unholy torment, whispering her name like a litany.

She reached up to cradle him, to comfort him. Her eyes opened and there was the ceiling, the light fixture. She moved and felt his body move, and realized that they were still part of each other. She caught her breath at the beauty of it.

It took him a long time to calm down. She stroked him and soothed him, and wondered at the force of his passion.

"It had been a long time, hadn't it?" she whispered softly.

He levered himself over her and searched her misty eyes with regret and pain in his own. "I took you," he said jerkily.

"Not exactly," she murmured with a warm smile.

"For God's sake…!"

She arched up and kissed his mouth softly, tenderly, smiling against it.

"Don't,…"

Her hips twisted sensuously under his and something that should have been impossible, suddenly wasn't. Deliciously surprised, she closed her eyes and kissed him harder.

"Oh, God," he ground out. And then he stopped talking. She locked her arms behind his neck and held the kiss until the world exploded around them again. Finally, exhausted, they slept in each other's arms.

She awoke before he did, slipping back into her dress while she studied his long, elegant body on the bed. He was beautiful, she decided. Not cultured and citified and well-mannered. But beautiful and sensitive and he'd make the most marvelous father.…

Her face burned as she recalled the long night. Well, it was too late for regrets now. He'd marry her. He'd have to. Because if he didn't, she fully intended to move in with him anyway.

She went into the clean, neat new kitchen and found an equally new refrigerator that had been recently filled. She cooked eggs and bacon and thick, fluffy biscuits and made a pot of coffee.

When she'd set the table, she went back into the bedroom.

He was sprawled on his back, still sound asleep. She sat down beside him and bent to brush her mouth slowly over his.

"Baby…" he whispered hungrily, and reached up to kiss her lips. Then he stiffened. His eyes opened. He looked up at Mandelyn and his face went white. "Oh, my God. It happened."

"You might sound a little less horrified," she murmured drily. "You seemed to enjoy it enough last night."

His hands went to his eyes and he rubbed them. "I had a bottle of whiskey and then I went to bed. And…" His eyes opened. "You seduced me!"

She sighed. "That's what they all say," she said with mock weariness.

He sat up in bed and stared straight into her eyes. "You seduced me!" he repeated roughly.

"Well, you needn't make such heavy weather of it, Carson, I'm surely not the first woman who ever did," she reminded him reasonably.

"You were a virgin!"

She grinned. "Not anymore."

"Oh, God!"

She got up with a sigh. "I can see that you're just not in the mood to discuss this right now. So why don't you come and have breakfast?"

He threw his legs over the side of the bed and stared at her departing figure. "Why?"

She turned at the doorway, her eyes soft and possessive. "Don't you know?" And she walked out.

He made his way into the room minutes later. He was dressed now, in jeans and a brown patterned shirt and boots. But he looked half out of humor and bitterly regretful. He glared at her as he sat down.

"What a horrible expression," she remarked, handing him the platter of scrambled eggs.

"Aren't you even upset?" he burst out.

"Should I be? I mean, you did drag me into bed with you and…"

"I did not!" he growled. "You did it, you crazy little fool!"

"That's no way to talk to the mother of your children," she said calmly and poured coffee into the thick mug beside his plate.

"Children…" He put his face into his hands. "You knocked me so off balance I couldn't even hold back. What if I got you pregnant?"

"I like children." She smiled softly. "Just think, Carson, if we have a little girl, I can teach her how to be a lady. And if he's a boy, you can teach him the guitar."

He looked up with bloodshot eyes, staring as if he didn't believe what he was hearing. "Mandy?"

Her fingers reached out and brushed over

the back of his with an adoring pressure. She searched his eyes and all the amusement went out of hers. "I love you," she whispered. "I love you more than anything else in the world, Carson. And if you'll just let me live with you, I won't even ask you for anything. I'll cook and clean and have babies and you won't know I'm around, I'll be so quiet…!"

"Come here," he said in a voice that shook with emotion. "Oh, God, come here!"

She went around the table, to be dragged down into his arms and kissed to within an inch of her life.

"Love…you," he groaned against her mouth. "So much, for so…long. I was dying…."

"Darling, darling!" she whispered, clinging, loving, worshipping him with her hands, her mouth.

He couldn't seem to get enough of her soft, eager mouth. He tasted it and touched it and kissed it until it was tender from the rough pressure. His mouth slid down her body, against her breasts.

"It was me," she guessed, closing her eyes as she remembered the pain she'd caused him. "It was me you were being tutored for, because…because you thought I wouldn't want you."

His arms tightened. "Eight years, Mandelyn," he said unsteadily. "Eight years, I worshipped you. And it got to where I couldn't eat or sleep or live for loving you. I wanted to fit into your world, so that I'd have a chance with you."

"And as it turns out, yours suits me very well," she said humbly. "You were right, Carson. Your world is real and honest and the people don't put on airs. I like it better than mine." She clung to him. "Let me live with you."

"Always," he promised. "All my life. All yours. But first," he said curtly, lifting his head, "we get married. Pronto."

Her eyebrows arched. "Why the rush?"

"As if you didn't know, you little witch," he said. His big hand pressed against her stomach and he kissed her roughly. "Whispering that to me last night, when I was doing my damnest to keep my head, to stop myself. Whispering that you wanted my baby. And I went crazy in your arms. You were damned lucky I didn't hurt you."

"I wouldn't have cared," she murmured contentedly. "It was so sweet, so heavenly. Oh, Carson, I loved you and I knew, I thought, I hoped you loved me. And you were so tender, and I wanted to make it perfect for you."

"It was perfect all right. Both times," he added drily. "After we've been married a few years, remind me to tell you that what happened was impossible, will you?"

She grinned. "You said yourself you'd been a long time without a woman."

"That wasn't why," he said. His eyes held hers. "It was wanting you. Obsessively."

She kissed his closed eyelids. "I felt the same way. I could have died the night we went to the ballet. Those things I said...and when I heard about your driving the car into the pool, I got sick all over. I wanted to go down on my knees and apologize. I missed you and I loved you and I knew I'd die without you."

"I felt the same way," he confessed. He drew her close and held her securely on his lap. "Then yesterday, at the rodeo, you touched me and I wanted you so badly that..." He sighed. "I got the shock of my life when you started crying after I pushed you away. I was terrified that you were going to get in the car and have a wreck. I trampled two people getting to you. And then I knew just how bad I had it—that I was going to waste away without you. I knew you wanted me, then. But I didn't think you loved me." His eyes searched hers. "I thought you came to me last night out of pity."

She shook her head. "It was love."

"I should have realized that you'd never give yourself without it." He sighed. "You're much too fastidious for love affairs. Even with wild men you desire."

"You're not wild," she murmured. "You're just a maverick. I love you the way you are, Carson. I wouldn't change one single thing about you. Of course, I'll never go with you to another ballet…oh!"

He pinched her and laughed uproariously. "Yes, you will," he murmured. "We'll take the kids. I want them to be polished. Not like their father."

"They'll have a lovely father," she sighed, kissing him again. "When are we going to get married?"

"Today."

She sat up, and he pulled her back down. "We'll drive down to Mexico," he said gently. His eyes searched hers. "It has to be done right. Making love to you without my ring on your finger doesn't sit well. Does it?"

She lowered her eyes to his broad chest. "No," she confessed.

He tilted up her chin. "But I don't have one single regret about last night. That was the consummation. That was the wedding vows. Now we make it right."

Her fingers touched his mouth. "I adore you," she whispered passionately. Her gray eyes searched his blue ones. "I want you so much."

His hand touched her stomach, flattened, caressed it. "Tonight," he whispered. "After we're married. It will be better this time. Slower. Sweeter."

She trembled and leaned toward him, but he

shook his head with a tender smile. "First you marry me. Then you sleep with me," he said.

"We got it backwards."

"We'll get it right this time," he promised, smiling. "Up you go. I want to call Patty and see if she and Jake will stand up with us."

"They way things are going with them, it might be a double wedding," she laughed.

He looked down at her. "I was jealous of Jake."

"I was jealous of Patty. When she kissed you that night, I wanted to mop the floor with her."

He searched her eyes and smiled wickedly. "Yes. I saw that. It was the only glimmer of hope I had."

Her mouth fell open. She started to speak, but he bent and put his lips on hers. And since it felt so good, she gave up protesting and wound her arms around his neck. He might not be the world's most polished man, but he was the only one she would ever love.

They drove down to Mexico, and Mandelyn and Carson said their vows in muted, solemn voices while Jake and Patty looked on.

Mandelyn looked into his eyes while she spoke the words, and he couldn't seem to look away, even when it was time to slide the ring on her finger. He did it blindly, with amazing accuracy. And then he bent to kiss his wife.

It was a beautiful day, and Mandelyn felt like a fairy princess. She clung to Carson's lean hand, hardly believing all that had happened. When he suggested that the four of them stop by a bar on the other side of the border for a drink, she was too happy to protest.

"Isn't this nice?" Patty sighed as Carson and Jake went to get drinks. "I loved your wedding. Jake must have enjoyed it, too," she added with a grin, "because he proposed under his breath while you two were sealing the ceremony with that absurdly long kiss."

Mandelyn blushed. "I hope you'll be as happy as we are," she laughed.

"I hope so, too. Didn't it all work out…"

"What the hell do you mean, 'move over, Pop'?" Carson's deep, angry voice came across the room like a cutting whip and Mandelyn opened her mouth to say, "Oh, Carson, don't," when the sound of a hard fist hitting an even harder jaw echoed in the sudden silence.

Mandelyn gritted her teeth. "No," she groaned, watching Carson going at it with a man just his size. "Not on my wedding day. Not just before my wedding night!"

"Carson's tough," Patty promised her. "Quit worrying. It will be all right."

Just as she said that, a man who'd been standing beside Carson's opponent picked up a chair. Mandelyn's mouth flew open. Her temper flared like wildfire. That was her husband that ruffian was about to hit!

"Mandy, no!" Patty called.

But Mandelyn was already bounding over chairs. She picked up a vase from one of the tables and threw water, flowers and all into the face of the man holding the chair.

He sputtered, wiped himself off and glared at her. "Women's libber, huh?" he said curtly. "Okay, honey, put up your dukes."

"Whatever happened to chivalry?" Mandelyn wondered out loud. She brought her high heel down on the man's instep and when he bent over, she brought up her knee. The blow was apparently very painful, because he went sideways onto the floor.

She grinned, heady with success. "Hey, Carson…" she began.

Just about that time, the man who'd been trading blows with Carson took one too many hard rights and careened backwards into Mandelyn. He rammed against her and she fell headfirst into a huge planter full of ferns.

Wet, covered with dirt, she heard the sounds of the brawl escalating all around her as she struggled to get up again. As she raised her head, Carson came flying backwards from an uppercut and landed against her, and in she went again.

Somewhere there was a siren. And minutes later, she was extricated from the planter by a heavyset, blue-uniformed man who looked as if he had absolutely no sense of humor at all.

"We can explain all this," Mandelyn assured him in her most cultured voice.

"I'm sure you can, lady, but I assure you, I've heard it all before. Come along."

"But we just got married," she wailed, watching Carson being led out between two burly deputies.

"Congratulations," the uniformed man said blandly. "I'll show you both to the honeymoon suite."

As they waited to be booked Mandelyn leaned against the wall staring daggers at her new husband. Her hair was thick with dirt and traces of green leaves; her dress was ruined.

Carson cleared his throat and sighed. "Well, honey," he said with a grin, "you have to admit, I've given you a wedding day you'll never forget."

She didn't say anything but her eyes spoke volumes.

He moved closer, oblivious to the noise and confusion around them. "Mad at me?" he murmured.

"Furious, thanks," she replied.

"My Charleston lady," he whispered, smiling with such love that her poise fell apart.

"You horrible, horrible man," she murmured, "I love you so much!"

He laughed delightedly. "My poised little lady, right at home in a barroom brawl. My God, you laid that cowboy flat! I've never been so proud of you...." He lifted his head and looked stern. "But never again, honey. I don't want you fighting, even to save me. Especially not now," he added. His gaze went to her waist. "We don't know yet, remember," he whispered tenderly.

She flushed and looked up into his eyes. She knew exactly what he meant.

He bent and kissed her very gently. She managed a watery smile.

"Oh, I hope I am," she breathed fervently.

His chest rose and fell heavily. "We can make sure, if you want," he replied in a voice hoarse with passion.

"Is it too soon?" she asked.

He shook his head. "Not at our ages. We'll just be spreading love around, that's all." He grinned.

She laughed. "You can sing lullabies," she said. "And I'll sit and listen."

"Remember that song I wrote—

Choices?" he asked, searching her eyes. She nodded. "I wrote it for us. That's right," he added when she looked stunned. "I thought someday, if you ever started noticing me, I could sing it to you, and it might tell you something."

She sighed miserably. "And I was too busy being jealous of Patty to listen to the words," she mumbled.

"I'll sing it to you tonight, while we make love," he whispered.

"And here we are in jail," she moaned.

"Patty and Jake will be here any minute to bail us out," he promised. He grinned. "Don't you worry, honey. Everything's going to be fine. Next time, I won't hit, I'll just cuss. Okay?"

She burst out laughing, loving him with all her heart. "Okay. But don't change, will you?" she added seriously, searching his pale, glittering blue eyes. "Darling, I love you just the way you are."

He looked at her for a long time before he spoke. "I'm no gentleman."

"I'm no lady. Remember last night?" she whispered.

He trembled and kissed her quickly again.

Nearby, two slightly intoxicated men were staring at them. Mandelyn thought she recognized them from the brawl.

"Ain't that the blonde who threw the vase at me?" one asked the other, who squinted toward her.

"Yep. Looks like her."

"And kicked me on the foot and knocked me out with her knee?"

"The very same one."

The burly man grinned. "Lucky son of a gun," he slurred.

Carson glanced at him with a slow grin. "You don't know the half of it, pal," he murmured and bent his head again.

Mandelyn smiled, feeling as if she had champagne flowing through her body. "Darling, about that brawl…"

"What about it?" he murmured absently.

She grinned. "Could we do it again some-time?"

And that was the last thing she got to say until Jake and Patty came along to bail them out. Not that she minded. She was already making plans for the night and whispering them to a glowing new husband.

* * * * *

Give a 12 month subscription to a friend today!

Call Customer Services
0844 844 1358*

or visit
millsandboon.co.uk/subscription

* This call will cost you 7 pence per minute plus your phone company's price per minute access charge.

MILLS & BOON®

Why shop at millsandboon.co.uk?

Each year, thousands of romance readers find their perfect read at millsandboon.co.uk. That's because we're passionate about bringing you the very best romantic fiction. Here are some of the advantages of shopping at www.millsandboon.co.uk:

* **Get new books first**—you'll be able to buy your favourite books one month before they hit the shops

* **Get exclusive discounts**—you'll also be able to buy our specially created monthly collections, with up to 50% off the RRP

* **Find your favourite authors**—latest news, interviews and new releases for all your favourite authors and series on our website, plus ideas for what to try next

* **Join in**—once you've bought your favourite books, don't forget to register with us to rate, review and join in the discussions

Visit **www.millsandboon.co.uk**
for all this and more today!

MILLS_WEB

The World of
MILLS & BOON®

With eight paperback series to choose from, there's a Mills & Boon series perfect for you. So whether you're looking for glamorous seduction, Regency rakes or homespun heroes, we'll give you plenty of inspiration for your next read.

Cherish™

Experience the ultimate rush of falling in love.
12 new stories every month

Romantic Suspense
INTRIGUE

A seductive combination of danger and desire
8 new stories every month

Desire™

Passionate and dramatic love stories
6 new stories every month

n o c t u r n e™

An exhilarating underworld of dark desires
2 new stories every month

For exclusive member offers go to
millsandboon.co.uk/subscribe

WORLD_ M&B2a

The World of
MILLS & BOON®

HISTORICAL

*Awaken the romance
of the past*
6 new stories every month

*The ultimate in romantic
medical drama*
6 new stories every month

MODERN™

*Power, passion and
irresistible temptation*
8 new stories every month

By Request

*Relive the romance with the
best of the best*
12 stories every month

Have you tried eBooks?

With eBook exclusive series and titles from just **£1.99**,
there's even more reason to try our eBooks today

Visit www.millsandboon.co.uk/eBooks
for more details

WORLD_ M&B2b